The Book of Screamin' Joe BLADE

www.nefariousnotions.com

Dedicated to the godlings of Modnar, and the forgotten heroes
of North Eastworld and the lands beyond, particularly,
my brother Vance, Alex M., Erik M., David B., Pat M., Kent M.,
Gary C., James P., Terry V., Roy B., Cory B., Pam T., Aaron E.,
George C., Jeff W., Kelly M. and her Birchwood hooligans,
and to my parents for letting these worlds,
and many of the folks above, occupy their home for years.

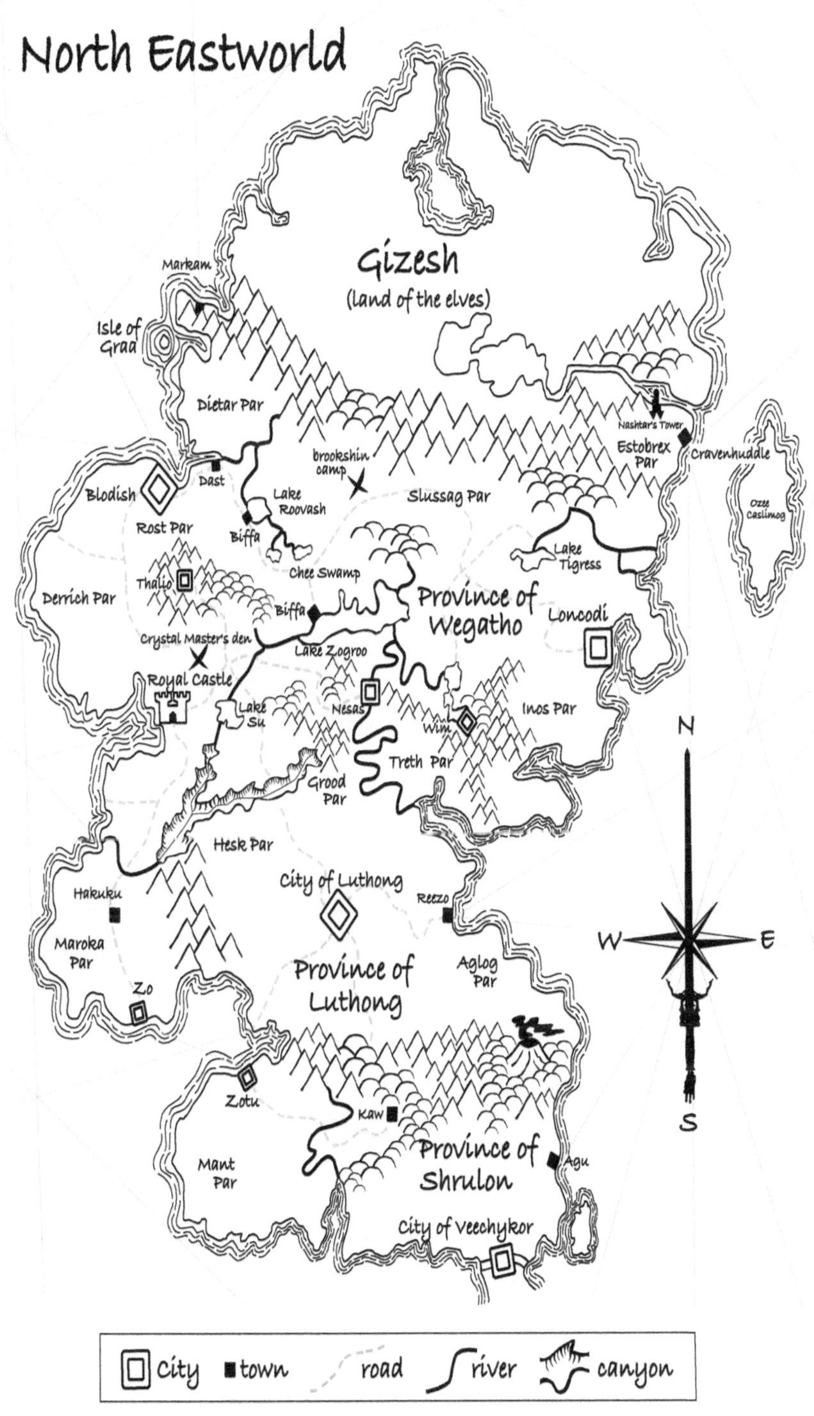

North Eastworld
Gizesh
(land of the elves)
Markam
Isle of Graa
Dietar Par
Nashtar's Tower
Estobrex Par
Cravenhuddle
brookshin camp
Slussag Par
Blodish
Dast
Lake Roovash
Ozee Caslimog
Rost Par
Biffa
Chee Swamp
Lake Tigress
Derrich Par
Thalio
Province of Wegatho
Loncodi
Biffa
Crystal Master's den
Lake Zogroo
Inos Par
Royal Castle
Lake Su
Nesas
Wim
Treth Par
Grood Par
Hesk Par
Hakuku
City of Luthong
Reezo
Maroka Par
Aglog Par
Zo
Province of Luthong
Zotu
Kaw
Mant Par
Province of Shrulon
Agu
City of Veechykor
N
W   E
S
City   town   road   river   canyon

The Book of
Screamin' Joe Blade

by Linton Valdock

Chapter 1

The smell of fish was not as much of an annoyance as the sharp prickling sensation of his left leg falling asleep, which was only mildly less irritating than the throbbing pain of a wine-induced headache that had woken him from his equally wine-induced coma. Joe was also becoming aware of the sensation of what might be several wooden splinters in his right cheek and, no, wait, yes, his upper lip. This was directly related to the unflattering way the right side of his face was pressed against the rough wooden surface of his extremely cramped surroundings. Just how small of a space he was in became frighteningly evident when he went to wipe the drool from his chin and instead found that his right hand was restricted to a tiny bit of movement somewhere around his left ass cheek. He could feel something else there. A foot? His left foot. The biting prickles that rippled through his left leg confirmed this as he squeezed what he assumed was his otherwise completely numb left heel. It was about then that some concern began to fester in his mind; it couldn't be called panic exactly, but the situation had his attention and quickly swept away the fog of his hangover.

He was unable to move at all. His left arm was wedged between his legs, while his right knee was keeping his head firmly pinned against the wall of whatever he had been so rudely crammed into. After a few moments of futile, mindless struggling and shouting for help, his concern gave way to despairing exhaustion, allowing him to assess his situation more fully.

He became aware of movement. He, or whatever he was in, was moving, or rather, going somewhere, up and down slightly too for sure and perhaps spinning a little. There was light as well, faint, but there, coming from above him. Straining his eyes as far to the left as possible, he could make out the curved edge of his prison silhouetted against the dull, luminous orange crystals that drifted by in the ceiling far above. Good, he thought, he was still in the water hills. In a barrel? Yes, definitely a barrel and drifting in the water as well, thankfully upright. Judging by the fish stench, it had to be one of the weighted bait barrels the locals tow behind their fishing skiffs. Was he being towed? No, he wasn't moving fast enough. The movement was too smooth, too subtle; adrift more likely. But how did he end up —

Chunks of memory from the night before started to tumble out of some dark vault of his mind. He had been at a tavern in one of the small fishing villages in the water hills of Beedo. There had been a girl — but wasn't there always — a serving wench? No, she was another patron, one of the pleasure hosts from the big island. Was she a blonde? No, a redhead, of course, a redhead; always so vibrant and full of fire, just as their hair suggests. He had been boasting about, no, recounting the tale of his recent tangle with the mander, a race of aquatic reptilians. Few ever saw a mander and lived to tell about it, but Joe's claim was even more challenging to swallow, though it was completely factual. He had been to the very heart of their hidden city, deep in the dark and misty swamps of the water hills. The woman had seemed to be enjoying his story but he could tell she didn't believe a word of it.

Then, there had been a couple of fishermen. That's right. A big fella, missing an eye, his clothes smeared with fish guts, and his friend, they seemed like friends anyway, a tall skinny guy, bald on top with a salt and pepper ponytail. Then there was shouting and punching; someone went through a window; no, he had gone through the window; no glass, fortunately, but throbs from the bruises on his back from going through the wooden shutters and crashing onto the wooden boardwalk were now assisting his memory. And then… then he was here, painfully, irreversibly wedged into this round waterborne fish coffin.

Joe, known in most circles as Screamin' Joe Blade, and those circles were few, was becoming aware then of an increase in the speed of the bait barrel and something else. He realized then that the sound he was hearing now had actually been there since he woke, though earlier it had been fainter and drowned out, for the most part, by his own struggles and shouts. The distinctive roar of a waterfall was growing increasingly louder. He didn't need to see out of the barrel to know where he was headed. There was only one waterfall in Beedo that loud, the Mouth of Kodin. The sound was nearly overwhelming, bouncing off the walls and the dully glowing, five-hundred-foot ceiling. Concern began to step aside to something much more like panic, and with it came more frantic attempts to wriggle free. This time, in his struggle, he had managed to wedge himself in even tighter, though now, at least, he was looking straight out the top of the barrel.

Just as a frustrated, exhausted calm was once again beginning to wash over him, the barrel lurched forward. The stone weight tied to the bottom of the barrel had caught a rock or some other debris at the edge of the falls, causing the barrel to lean nearly horizontal as the fast-flowing water rushed all around it. Every few moments, the bottom edge of the barrel opening would dip below the water surface as it bobbed in a constant struggle between its buoyancy and the buffeting stream engulfing it. Bit by bit, the barrel was filling with water.

The view was all at once terrifying and staggeringly beautiful. The crystals in the ceiling here were much like those in the major communities in the rest of Midgorn, bathing the falls in a brilliant white light. The waterfall was an enormous circle, nearly one thousand feet across, dropping well over a thousand feet. However, judging its true height was impossible, the bottom being entirely obscured by mist. At the center of the circle was a single stone column, which, although looking comparatively small to the enormity of the falls, was large enough to accommodate an entire community of monks. Their tall stone buildings, with moss-covered, flat-topped roofs, were bunched tightly together on top of the pillar while other buildings clung to the edges. The architectural arrangement made the top of the pillar look like a partially melted stonework candle, dripping down the outside of the pillar. Other ornately built openings and ledges jutted out in seemingly random locations, indicating that the community descended several hundred feet deep inside the pillar.

Joe found himself wondering how, exactly, the monks got to and from the pillar, but his barrel suddenly heaving forward snapped him back to the matter of his situation. The stone weight had worked itself free of whatever it had caught on earlier but quickly stuck on something new. The barrel was now suspended over the edge, pointing nearly straight down, giving him only a view of falling water and mist. The water that had gathered in the barrel spilled over his head and out. He felt his whole body slide toward the opening of the barrel. Though he desperately wanted out of the barrel, his body instinctively pushed against the walls with whatever parts would move, preventing him from falling out. Apparently, his body had decided it was better off hopelessly crammed into the barrel than plummeting the unknown depth of the waterfall.

The barrel had other ideas. Again the weight freed itself from whatever it had caught itself on, or perhaps the rope tying it to the base of the barrel had snapped. It didn't much matter but Joe found his mind contemplating it just the same. He found it interesting just how many thoughts one's mind could ponder in an instance such as this; things like, did he piss himself, or was that sensation from the water that had got in the barrel a moment ago, or what was the red head's name again, something like Pearly or Penny, no, something weirder like Pernesophy; and strangely, though Joe knew there must have been at least one moment, he couldn't think of a time when he had been in a worse situation. His mind quickly flashed through the nearly countless list of ridiculously bad situations he had been in before. All these things and a few thoughts about what he would eat for dinner — he was craving fish — and several exclamatory profanities crossed his mind in a single explosion of thought. Then Joe and his fish coffin tumbled down into the mist.

He was well past panic at this point, but his mind had now become completely flooded with both the wonder and terror of this new experience. He almost felt weightless, nearly like he was flying, and that was exhilarating, but he knew this was a lie. He was falling, and the landing, watery though it might be, would soon prove how weighted he was. Wonder or terror, both reactions had every muscle in his body tensed for the impending impact.

Somewhere beneath the roar of the water falling all around, there was a sharp thud and cracking sound, which coincided with the all-too-familiar sensation of some sort of arrowhead slicing into his right butt cheek. For a second, if it had been that long, he had stopped falling, or rather, the barrel had. Before Joe could even register what was happening, there was the all-too-familiar sensation of some sort of arrow being ripped from his right butt cheek, and he slipped out of the barrel as though he had never been stuck. He wasn't sure if it was the pain in his right ass cheek, the pain of sensation returning as blood flooded into his previously numb left leg, or the renewed horror of falling without the fallacious protection of the barrel, but he let out a startled scream. He flipped over uncontrollably, catching a glimpse of the barrel dangling by a thick rope before he slipped deeper into the mist. Had someone tried to save him?

Upon shooting from the barrel, Joe was instantly soaked. His scream quickly lost steam, partly due to choking on the water particles flying into his open mouth and partly from not hitting the bottom before needing to take another breath. He began wondering if the Mouth of Kodin was bottomless. The fall was long enough that he managed to figure out how to steady his fall. Although he planned to later claim that it was due to his cat-like instincts, it had really just been a matter of having the time to notice, by way of his random flails of terror, that the extension of his arms and legs was affecting the way he fell. With his arms and legs extended but bent slightly, the steadiness of his descent gave him the calm to ponder how he would prepare to hit the water. It occurred to him, though, that it would, most probably, not matter. He was likely going to die no matter how much diving skill he managed to fake, but he at least wanted to hit the water with some style, not just some random belly flop.

He had just decided upon knifing into the water, befitting his name, feet first, when a bright green glob of goo shot out from the waterfall, enveloping the entire left half of his body. Just as quickly as it had shot out, the green goo retracted, pulling Screamin' Joe Blade like a rag doll into the waterfall with it.

Chapter 2

The klopam was feeling very satisfied. It had been quite some time since it had managed to catch such a large morsel. On a good day, it might manage to snag a sizeable bottom-feeding glackfish that had swum too close to the waterfall's edge, or maybe even a bloated, dead rock toad, but this was at least twice the size of either of those and fresh; alive, even. A catch of this size could sustain it for a month, maybe more.

The klopam could feel that the digestive sac was nearly fully formed; soon, it would be ready to expel, and it could continue its nonstop scan for food, although now with far less pressure. It could even afford to be a little picky.

The nine black, egg-like ovals that made up its array of eyes scanned the falling water penetrating it with their broad spectrum vision. A few large fish and a lake jelly fell past. Although it would have appeared to any onlookers as a grimace, it was, in fact, the largest, happiest klopam smile that its broad, body-wide, toothless mouth now displayed. The klopam took this moment of unusual leisure to adjust the grip of one of its four feet that clung to the walls of its lair, a grip that had not been adjusted for several months, and the movement now felt something equivalent to the freedom one might experience running through an open field on a sunny day. The klopam gave a deep chortling grunt of satisfaction.

Each of its appendages had the girth of a large oak tree and was stretched taut to either side as well as above and below, forming a cross with its enormous, thick, grey, rough-skinned ball of a body at its center. Its feet, if they could be called such, consisted of a large pad covered in tiny suction cups. The pads were ringed along the outside edge by many little spiked claws that dug into any crevice or bump in the rock they could find. The klopam delighted in each new little hold that its spikes dug into.

A spotted purple lobster fell into view. The klopam's over-clocked brain watched it tumble by in slow motion. Such a tiny little thing, it thought, letting it fall past, chortling with satisfaction, causing its massive suspended body to bounce slightly. It began to dream of one day catching a whole hippotawg. Again its body rocked with its own form of laughter, surprised at its own folly to dream so, but today it could take a moment or two for dreams; such a very good day it was, such a full belly it had.

****

It was dark, wet, and cramped, though not as cramped as he had been in the barrel. There was something else too, a wriggling movement all around him. The walls of whatever he was in were moving, or rather, squeezing, and he had a strong impression that he was slowly sliding. At first, his neck had been hurting, though whether from the cramped conditions he had been finding himself in lately or from being snapped sideways so suddenly, he couldn't tell. That sensation, however, along with every other sense of feeling, was diminishing. Breathing was becoming very difficult; there was almost no air here, and he could feel a glimmer of panic trying to set into his increasingly fogging mind. Was this going to be the way Screamin' Joe Blade died? He wasn't even sure what this was. That didn't seem right. He should at least know what was finishing the days of Midgorn's greatest adventurer. At once, the squeezing increased around his whole body but was completely released about his feet, and he was, suddenly, and unfortunately, thoroughly familiar with his situation. He was being excreted from the anus of some massive beast.

It may have been the blood being squeezed down to his feet, the lack of oxygen, or even, and more likely, the paralytic juices he was covered in, but he was starting to lose consciousness. At least his thoughts had managed to stay calm, if not entirely clear. He had a thing; a pointy, slicey thing in a — why weren't his grabby bits moving?

Joe popped out the back end of the klopam, shooting out a few feet, landing softly in a pile of sludge made of half-digested bloody filth and unidentifiable slime. It spattered in thick, dripping clumps onto the walls, which were covered in some sort of rampant, deep purple, mossy growth. Joe was encapsulated in a thin membrane. A thick, veiny cord ran from the clinging sac surrounding him to the expelling orifice of the klopam. Two other cords coming from the orifice were connected to sacs on either side of Joe. Both of the other sacs were about a third of his size. One looked like it might have been full of decaying fish, the other, simply full of some miscellaneous blood and black marble-colored goo. A third shriveled, blackened cord dangled from the klopam, a testament to a meal long since finished.

Somehow, despite his senses diminishing with each passing second, Joe managed to fumble a hand up to his bandolier and unholster one of the six throwing knives. The sharp surface of the blade barely touched the membrane, which almost seemed to split of its own accord, its own tautness ripping the tiny cut to a giant tear. Joe gasped for air, his arms and legs flailing in a slow, uncoordinated, drugged, instinctive celebration of their reestablished freedom. The paralytic poisons that he had been subjected to inside the sac were still settling in as Joe rolled over and began to scramble blindly away in the dimly illuminated alcove. His increasingly dulled senses prevented him from noticing the angry grunts of the klopam or the barbed tentacle-like tail that it lashed out with, trying to reclaim its meal. The tail narrowly missed turning him into a grim shish kebab. He fumbled about for a short few moments before finding the hole in the floor that had been bored out by years of acid juices, refuse, decay, and water. He began quickly sliding down its steeply sloped, slimy surface, his consciousness then leaving him entirely as he fell.

Chapter 3

The first man's black marhorse shuffled, kicking up clumps of sand with its wide clawed hooves, its head bobbing up and down as the spines of its fin-like mane splayed and flattened. It was anxious to return to running along the beach as it had been a moment ago. The second man and his marhorse trotted up alongside the first, his dark grey marhorse far more relaxed. Both men were clad in polished black armor, red silk wrapped around their heads, completely obscuring their faces. The black fin of a metal helmet poked out of the top of each of their wrappings. The first man partially undid the fabric of his red silk head wrap, allowing him to speak clearly and remove his polarized crystal eye visor. Now, he could take a better look at the thing that had washed up on the beach. The second man began doing the same, but he was visibly uncomfortable with the exposure, looking in all directions for some unknown threat as he pulled his visor off.

"What do you make of it?" asked the second man gruffly.

"It? I think it looks like a man," said the first man; his nasal voice was full of a misguided arrogance fueled by an equally misguided sense of superior intelligence. He was trying to stroke out the crease his visor had left on the bridge of his long, pointed nose.

"I meant the situation, fool. Where do you think he came from?" The second man was of a much larger frame; thick body, thick jaw, thick mustache, a stubby, thick nose, and thick black eyebrows that sat on a forehead that jutted out just a little more than it ought to. His tone of frustration was tinged with the weariness of overuse.

"It appears quite obvious that he came from the sea." The thinner man began to explain as the thicker man rolled his eyes. "You roll your eyes, friend, but it's a simple matter of deduction. First, the man is completely soaked. Second, one must take into consideration his proximity to the water. Look, his feet are still in the water." He arched one thin eyebrow in a disapproving, quizzical manner as he motioned with one hand at the body that his thick friend did not, somehow, fully comprehend.

"Are you an idiot?" The second man retorted. "Clearly, he came from the sea, but what was he doing out there? There's nothing out there but monsters and fish."

"Obviously then, he was either hungry or a fisherman, perhaps both. His boat was likely ravaged by some monstrosity of the depths, and he, in his attempt to swim to shore, simply tired and drowned. I've seen just such an occurrence countless times." The thin man settled back into his saddle, folding his red-gloved hands in his lap as though that was indeed the last word on the matter.

"Countless? Countless times?" The thick man slapped his own forehead in newfound frustration, dragging his hand down his face as he tried to recompose himself. "So, this must have been during your first four years of life before you and I met in the enlistment camp, because in all of the years that you and I have been partners, in all the years we've spent riding back and forth patrolling this beach I don't recall another body washing up." He was leaning over in his saddle as if getting closer to his thin companion might facilitate the sense of his words reaching his partner's mind.

The thin man's calm demeanor remained unwavering. "You seem to be forgetting Lady Ethdab."

"She was conscious and paddling a raft!" the thick man was shouting now and leaning over so much that he was in danger of falling out of his saddle.

"Well, her companions had all drowned, and I imagine she would be quite disturbed to learn you've taken such a light stance on the value of their lives."

"They didn't drown! She clearly said that they had been eaten by a creature of unimaginable size!"

"Well, still, you said it yourself now, large creature, boat wreck, many dead; surely this is what befell this poor fel—" The thin man had begun to again motion towards the body between their marhorses, but it was no longer there.

In fact, the body seemed quite alive and was running down the beach, in an odd bow-legged manner, toward an area where the tall grasses of the surrounding plains mingled with some boulders and jutting rocks at the sea's edge.

* * * * * * * * * * * * * * * * * * *

As Joe ran down the beach, his wet, black leather pants chafing quite uncomfortably, he tried to piece together how he had got to wherever this was. He could recall slipping into a hole in the floor of the creature's lair and an uncontrollable slide down a long twisting tunnel, then nothing; no, wait, he remembered waking, sputtering in the water, half drowning, no sign of the waterfall, just seemingly endless ocean, a spot of land, and something else. What was it? Something big, something blue, something — and then it struck him. It was right in front of him, all around him, in fact, and above as well, endlessly above.

He wheeled around, trying to take the spectacle in, and stumbled over his feet, laying him flat on his back. He continued to stare into the vast empty blueness, his mind reeling, overwhelmed. There was the sound of galloping then, and something small and sharp struck him on the side of his neck. Again, blackness began to overtake his vision. Joe tried to stay awake, tried to hang on, tried to hold on to the fantastic blue vision before him, trying to comprehend the beautiful white fluffy things that drifted about in it, but it was more than he could manage.

"Where is the torvug?" Joe mumbled as the blackness overtook him once again.

Chapter 4

"Wake up, wake up, deary-boy." the words barely filtered through Joe's roughly conscious-again mind. "That's it. That's a good lad. Here now, sit up."

Joe's eyes fluttered open, and he was shocked instantly into alertness by the spectacle of a wrinkled, pointed-toothed — and she only had three teeth — one-eyed face of a hag looming inches above his own. The image of her face was made all the grimmer by the deep moving shadows cast by the flickering lamp set nearby on the ground. He scrambled back along the floor a bit, giving him some space before sitting up against a slimy, black stonework wall. His hands fumbled at his chest for one of the six knives he carried with him at all times, but his bandolier was missing.

"Staggered by my beauty, I see." the hag pawed at the twelve or so limp, white strands of hair on her head as if maintaining some fabulous hairstyle. "Boys will be boys, they say, but try to contain yourself, sweet one. I'm just here to give you a speck o' food." She rattled a large wooden bowl off to the side on the floor. It was nearly full to the brim with some unidentifiable pink and brown mush. "Guess theys don't wantcha dyin' of starvation before theys chop that pretty head o' yours off tomorrah morning." She cackled at this to the point of being breathless.

"Where am I? Wait, chop my head?" Joe tried leaping to his feet, but an unexpected weakness combined with the slipperiness of the wall that he was trying to push off of resulted in him just sort of flailing and flopping like a beached fish.

"Calm yerself, deary. Calm." She cooed, placing a wrinkled, clawed hand on his chest, and Joe settled back. Seeing that he was going to be a proper audience then, the old crone stood up with remarkable ease and vigor for one of her apparent extreme age. She brushed and patted her ragged, filthy clothes a little, stirring up puffs of dust that couldn't possibly have accumulated in the short time she was in the room or on the floor. Clearing her throat as if about to recite a rehearsed speech, she continued. "You, my sweet young man, are ins the dungeon of Lord Goms Ethdab, conqueror an' king of alls upper Senuvia."

"Senuvia?" Joe interrupted.

"Oh, you must be froms Westerlan then; somewhere in Marka by yours clothing. Quite a journey yous must'a had. Your people calls this land North Eastworld." She examined him, hoping to see some understanding.

"Um…ya…no." Joe had no idea what she was talking about. In all of his travels through Midgorn, and he had, to his knowledge, been everywhere, he had never come upon any areas known as Upper Senuvia, North Eastworld, Westerlan or Marka. He must be deep down indeed, he thought, maybe even deeper than the trall mines. Perhaps this was the fabled land of Agartha or Shambhala, homes to the immortals. That would explain the impossibly high torvug, the word for the illuminated ceilings in each major community in Midgorn. As described in the stories told to children in Midgorn, Agartha and Shambhala had torvugs so high that they could not be seen, obscured by light and mist, and just like the tales, there had even been a blinding spot of fire hanging high in the air, so intense that he had felt its heat on his skin. Even the sand seemed to be warmed from its radiance.

"No." the hag interrupted his thoughts as if she had read his mind because she had. "No, my confused sweet thing, this is not Agartha, though we's have our tales of that land as well, and until this moment, I hads never known of lands called Midgorn or Shambhala. How curious that yous never seen the sun and sky before. How delightful that must be. Like a wee babe you are." She cackled at this thought. "Shame theys going to kill you. Best eat up." With that, she turned and began walking to the windowless, wooden jail door.

Ignoring the confusion rumbling through his mind, Joe fell into the usual blind swagger that had always guided him out of bad situations such as this, though arguably, this same approach invariably got him into just such bad situations. "Listen, lady, I don't know who you are, but you seem nice enough. I mean, you brought me whatever this is." He nudged the bowl of pink and brown mush. "So why don't you be a doll and tell your boss, this Ethdab fella, that there's been some sort of misunderstanding. Your people obviously have some sort of grudge against these Westerlan folk. Maybe somebody's great, great, great grandpa crapped in someone's great, great uncle-daddy's porridge; I don't know, but I'm not about to become a martyr over a bad bowl of mush for a bunch of well-dressed muck munchers." Shakily, he began to stand himself up. "And like Screamin' Joe Blade always says, 'No one's worth dying for 'less she can balance two gold crits on her nipples while riding a wild vrox.'"

"Who is this shouting Joe fellow?" she reached down and picked up the lamp.

"Me, I'm Screamin' Joe Blade." he slapped his chest indicating himself. He was a little annoyed at the lack of recognition, or at least understanding.

"Well, yous don't seem to be screaming at all. You're actually surprisingly civil."

"Surprisingly civil? You were expecting me to be –"

"More troublesome; at least, that's the way he described yous."

"The way who described me?" Joe took a couple shaky steps towards her.

"Why the Crystal Master, o' course. Said he owed you one." She took a couple of steps back, reaching the cell door. "And now I've really said mores than I oughts to have." She thumped with her fist on the door three times, shouting for the guard as she did.

"Wait, who are you? How does the Crystal Master know me? I don't know him. I think I'd remember somebody owing me something." Joe was finding the whole situation more and more perplexing.

"Oh, you'll knows him soon enough. I be Vella." She lowered her voice as the heavy footfalls of a guard approaching could be heard beyond the cell door. "Tell him hello from me and that my's debt too, is paid."

"What?" Joe was not processing any of it.

The door swung open then. Yellow light spilled in around the massive silhouette of the guard who motioned for the woman to pass.

"Eat your porridge, deary-boy," she said with a sly smile over her shoulder at Joe as she stepped out of the cell. The door slammed shut, leaving Joe entirely in the dark in more than one way, maybe even more than two.

Joe staggered back and slid down the wall, sitting himself back on the floor. He was lost. He had escaped from many dungeons and prison cells in the past, but in most of those cases, being jailed had been somewhat intentional or, at the very least, expected, and he had always had a plan. This was different. For one thing, he had no idea where he was being kept. By the lack of windows, it was likely a dungeon, but the cell could just as easily be in a tower. It would do him no good to waste time and energy digging or knocking a hole in the wall if he didn't know which was the right course to take. His situation, with a looming execution, was, after all, somewhat time-sensitive.

His captors had been rather clever in leaving him no furnishings, so there would be no hope of fashioning some sort of weapon. Once, jailed over a period of weeks, he had managed to construct a short spear out of splinters of wood from a window frame, his own hair, and various body fluids. It had only been effective against one of the guards, breaking apart after causing a fatal wound. Still, it caused enough confusion between the other two guards that he had managed to make his escape.

That was another thing; he had no idea how many guards stood outside or where he was going to go once beyond the area of the prison cell. For that matter, he had no idea where he was going to go in this land of Senuvia. He couldn't gamble on charity from oppressed locals. For all he knew, this Goms fellow treated his people well. There is nothing worse for a man on the run than content citizens. In Midgorn, it was for this very reason that he tried to avoid any sort of trouble in the city of Advan; far too happy, those people. Other than trying to make a break for it when they came to execute him, he was not sure what he would do, which was perplexing because it directly contradicted item number one in his ten-point guide to life.

Screamin' Joe Blade's Ten-Point Guide to Life:
Point #1: Always remember that Joe has a plan.

Sometimes, Joe's plans were not immediately obvious even to himself, and in just such situations, he found it better to sit back and let the plan reveal itself. His best plans often worked that way, so this plan was clearly going to be amazing.

He noticed something then, his ass didn't hurt. He distinctly remembered something that felt like an arrow piercing it when he was going over the falls in the barrel, but there was no pain now. A quick feel confirmed that there was, in fact, a hole in his pants but no corresponding wound on his butt cheek. Nor did his face, he noted then, seem to be afflicted with the splinters he had acquired while in the barrel. Curious, all of it, but he couldn't waste too much thought on it. It would distract him from the plan.

The plan, of course, the plan, it was so clear! How could he have overlooked it? It was the bowl of porridge. The woman, what was her name, Velma, said that the Crystal Master had sent her, or something like that. While he didn't know the man personally, the Crystal Master was a name he recognized. Adventurers in Midgorn looking to make a quick fortune often sought out the halls of the Crystal Master, which were said to hold a vast treasure. The trick was that his realm was also packed with monsters, some of which were said to be the Crystal Master's own creations. Joe had never sought adventure or fortune in the Crystal Master's halls. Peril seemed to do a fair enough job of finding Joe on a regular basis without him having to go looking for it. So how did this Crystal Master know him? As nasty a piece of work as the man was said to be, why would he be under the impression that he owed Joe a favor? Joe couldn't worry about that now; the important thing was that he had, at some point, obviously, put things in motion to deal with just this sort of situation. He could figure out the details later. What was important was, as usual, he probably, maybe, had a plan.

He was extremely hungry, so eating the slop seemed like the sensible first move of the plan. The empty bowl was likely going to be of some use. He would ponder that as he ate, he decided. His eyes had adjusted to the sliver of soft light that seeped through the minuscule gap between the door and the floor. He could just barely make out the shadowy shape of the bowl just past his right foot, and he reached for it.

The sludgy food was cold and had a chalky grit to it, but it actually tasted a little like strawberries. Using three fingers as a makeshift spoon, he slapped globs of it into his mouth. Despite the clumpy, gritty bits that made him instinctively want to chew, it was a much more pleasant experience if he simply swallowed it. By his fifth mouthful, he had nearly emptied the bowl and was in the process of gulping it down when something solid suddenly stuck in his throat. Choking, he desperately tried to make himself cough. Whatever it was, it was large and wasn't moving. He felt as if his head was going to explode, and he was starting to go a little dizzy when, finally, it flew free. He gasped for air as the object and a thick pile of the strawberry goo shot from his mouth. He heard the object hit the stone floor with a slight tinkling clatter. A green light appeared in the darkness then. It was the object that had been hidden in the porridge; a crystal, roughly cylindrical in shape but with eight flat sides, the ends coming to narrow, blunt points. Though it felt like a boulder in his throat, it was actually smaller than his pinky finger. The light was growing increasingly intense, the color cycling to blue, then a sort of pinkish purple.

He picked the crystal up. It was warm. Great, he thought, now he had some light and could properly contemplate how the bowl fit into his plan, and with his other hand, scooped up the last little mouthful of goo out of the bowl. Strangely tasty for prison food, he mused to himself, and immediately, he felt fully invigorated, tingling a little even, as though overloaded with energy. The crystal continued to grow brighter and warmer in his hand. It had turned red in color and was shifting slightly towards orange when its temperature abruptly spiked to being painfully hot.

He swore as it seared his hand, causing him to instinctively toss it across the room. It was a bright yellow now, growing whiter and brighter every second. Soon, the room was fully illuminated, and the light was so bright that he had to shield his eyes. At its brightest, Joe could feel the heat coming off of it from where it lay across the room between the door and the far wall. It was then that it began to emit a high-pitched whining sound that lasted for no more than three seconds. Then it exploded.

* * * * * * * * * * * * * * * * * *

Joe had been slammed up against the wall just two feet behind him and knocked senseless; how long he had been out this time, he couldn't say, but he assumed it could only have been for a moment or two. It took him a few more moments to gather his senses and recall what had just happened.

In the rubble that had once been part of the wall of his prison cell and its door, he saw a guard who had fared far worse than Joe in the explosion. The guard was missing his right arm nearly at the shoulder and was bleeding profusely, too dazed and in shock to accomplish much more than flail feebly with his remaining arm and legs like some sort of steel-shelled turtle flipped on its back.

Joe's senses returned quickly as he realized this was his opportunity to escape. He quickly scrambled over the rubble of the wall, but as he made his way past the maimed guard, the man reached out with his remaining hand, grabbing Joe with a surprising strength and wheezing through gritted teeth, simply, "No."

Joe kicked at the guard with his free foot, but the guard held on. After the first three kicks, the guard started pulling on Joe's leg, forcing him to use his free leg to stay upright, though he nearly stumbled on the man's former right arm, still encased in plate armor. It gave Joe an instinctive shiver, and he could feel himself getting a little frantic. He knew the explosion would be attracting others soon, and there was a strong possibility of the ceiling collapsing from the damage at any moment. He needed to be away from here fast. Looking around, as the guard's grip only seemed to tighten, there were no weapons in reach. The guard's sword lay several feet away. Any portions of the wall here were either too big to pick up or too small to be anything but insulting for the lack of attention-getting injury they would inflict on a man who was presently bleeding out from his shredded shoulder stump. He grabbed the only thing he could, the man's amputated arm, and started beating the guard with it.

At that moment, another guard came running down the hallway leading to Joe's former cell. He was a young man, thin, too thin, and too young to be a member of the guard, but his uncle was a friend of King Goms, and dungeon detail rarely involved any sort of real danger. Arriving on the scene of Joe bludgeoning the other guard with the man's own severed limb, blood spattering everywhere with each swing, was more than the young guard was ready for. He let out a primal scream like some sort of crazed, frightened monkey and bolted back down the hall, crying for help.

A moment later, the guard's grip on Joe's leg relented; he was dead from loss of blood more than from the beating he had taken from his own appendage. Joe immediately ran free, scooping up the dead guard's large, curved, one-handed sword as he went. The sword was heavier than Joe anticipated, and it caused him to trip over his own feet slightly, but he quickly regained his balance without losing a step. He had to catch and stop the other guard now.

Ahead, Joe could hear the young guard's armor clatter on the stone floor as he stumbled in his panic to get away, and though the guard continued trying to call for help, it was coming out in choked, incoherent grunts now. Screamin' Joe rounded the corner in the long torch-lit hall and could see the young man just picking himself up. Living up to his name, Joe screamed down the hall as he ran. It was a well-practiced guttural, bone-shaking battle cry that had rattled the nerves of many previous opponents. To be precise, it was actually a long, drawn-out version of the trall word for a long, flat, purple-colored pasta, but his cry was so long and distorted that even a trall wouldn't be likely to identify it as such.

The young guard fell to the floor again, trying to look over his shoulder as he tried to simultaneously propel himself to his feet and down the hall but failed at both. Joe was quickly on top of him, kicking the terrorized fellow swiftly in the head. Knocked out or dead, Joe wasn't sure, but he wasn't about to linger long enough to make the assessment. It was enough that the man was down. He continued to charge down the hall. There was another turn ahead. He halted short of the corner and listened. It seemed quiet. Quickly but carefully, poking his head around the corner, he saw only another empty torch-lit corridor, but this was much shorter and ended in a simple wooden door. A small wooden table, solidly built, with two equally heavy-looking chairs, was by the door. Clearly, this had been the guard post. On the wall above the table a single large jail key, painted bright yellow, hung on a spike. A lamp looking very much like the one the woman had used in the cell was on the table, along with one of Screamin' Joe's knives. Across the back of one of the chairs was his bandolier with the other five knives.

He rushed forward, quickly putting his blades back on. He felt infinitely less vulnerable, but the way beyond the door might be a little more hands-on than he had hoped.

"One key?" Joe whispered to himself as he pondered how that might affect his escape. There had been no other prison cell doors, halls, or exits, and now this single key suggested that he wouldn't be finding any other prison cells. This King Goms was obviously not in the habit of keeping more than one prisoner at a time or at least didn't waste space on individual cells for his prisoners. Joe would not have the advantage of making his escape amongst the chaos of rioting, newly freed fellow inmates.

With nothing else to be gained here, he quietly eased open the door. A staircase leading upward lay beyond.

"Here we go," he muttered to himself, knowing all too well from past experience what was to follow.

He began to creep up the stairs cautiously; he could hear voices ahead. The stairs wound upwards in a tight spiral, ending in an open archway, intersecting a hallway. He crouched low on the stairs, trying to stay in shadow as the voices drew near. A man and a woman, servants perhaps by their dress, passed by, locked in a conversation about the slight earth tremor they had just felt and whether a larger quake was to come. Their voices quickly faded and were followed by the distant sound of a door slamming shut.

Time to go. Sword ready in his left hand, he charged up the last few steps. Turning in the direction the man and woman had come from. There were many doors on either side of the hall, staggered from side to side nearly every ten feet with small gargoyle wall sconces between them. Oil-fed fires burned from the monsters' sharp-toothed maws.

No time for doors now, Joe thought. He would run until he found an obvious exit. A window would do fine, in fact, it was the sort of exit he was used to, preferred, truly, in a situation such as this. There was always less oncoming traffic. The corridor was winding gently to the right. That's good, he thought; that means the way out is probably to the left. He heard a door open behind him as he ran and then a shocked gasp from a woman. Somewhere further back was the clamor of many feet and armor. Someone realized the explosion wasn't an earthquake. He didn't have time to worry about them or the gasping woman and didn't even look back. A moment later, he came upon another set of ascending stairs intersecting the hallway from the left. Up he went.

These stairs ended in a large, heavy wood and metalwork door. Not a good sign, he thought. He would have to hope that it wasn't locked. He couldn't risk trying it first. A novice at this point would have tried to open the door stealthily, but Joe had been through this drill enough times to know that approach, at this point, usually landed you back in the prison cell. They wouldn't be putting him back in his cell, he mused to himself, but since they seemed bent on executing him, he'd best play this smart just the same.

Fortunately, the door was unlocked. Unlatching the door quickly, Joe jumped back and kicked it open as hard as he could. Bright light spilled down the stairs, nearly blinding Joe. From the left, he heard the door slam into something hard, followed by a man cursing loudly about his hand. From the right, a large figure stepped into the doorway. It was an armored guard. Joe slashed at the man's head with the sword before the guard could react. The sword rattled off of the man's helmet, but it was enough to knock him off balance. Joe grabbed the guard by the collar of his plated armor and yanked him forward, throwing him down the stairs. The second guard appeared then, seeming to have trouble drawing his sword. Joe tackled the man to the floor and jumped off him, running. A woman screamed somewhere nearby.

He was in some sort of large walled-in courtyard. A stone walkway led about one hundred feet to the only other visible exit; an enormous set of wooden double doors with heavy iron facets. Statues of various scantily clad men and women in thought-filled or heroic poses lined the walk. Brightly colored birds with varying elaborate displays of plumage quickly strutted between the statues or had just abandoned their perches upon them in reaction to Joe's sudden arrival. Two artificial streams fed by two man-made waterfalls poured from the walls at each end of the courtyard, the streams bisecting the grass and gardens on either side of the path, ending in a large pool at either end, with a stone lip meant for sitting. A moment ago, in fact, there had been a significant number of men and women and a few minstrels doing precisely that before Screamin' Joe Blade disrupted their serene fountain-side afternoon. Now, they were all running for the large double doors at the far end of the courtyard.

Men were shouting, and women were screaming. One man, dressed entirely in yellow silks with equally golden, shoulder-length hair and a well-groomed mustache that curled upwards on both ends, stood firmly in the center of the stone walkway as the others fled from their seats at the pools. The man's face was nearly as pale as the white marble statues that lined the path. His eyes were a dazzling turquoise color. As Joe ran towards him, the man drew a long, straight, narrow-bladed sword. Joe's right hand was a blur of movement, taking one of the knives from his chest and hurtling it at the man blocking his way. The man in yellow, otherwise motionless, not even blinking, gave the slightest flick of his wrist, knocking Joe's flying blade harmlessly to the side with his sword. The knife clattered on the stone path behind the man in yellow. Joe continued to charge. Again, his right hand blurred, and another knife was airborne, and just as quickly, it too was knocked to the side. Having closed the gap between them, Joe had no more options; he was within striking distance of the man's sword then.

With a sudden flourish of skilled movement, the man in yellow brandished his weapon in a series of deadly arcs. Joe's body, filled with a lifetime of brawling experience, instinctively reacted to the assault. In one fluid movement, Joe spun around, back arching to avoid the blade, stepped on the man in yellow's leading foot, pushed the man's sword arm aside with his free right hand, and struck him squarely in the nose with the hilt of the large curved sword that Joe held in his left hand. The man in yellow staggered back, his nose gushing blood. One of the birds from the yard, a large scarlet bird with a long tail, came flying from somewhere over Joe's left shoulder, flying directly at the man in yellow, squawking as it came. Already off balance from Joe's assault, the bird flapping in his face caused him to trip over the pool's edge to the right, tossing his sword into the air as he failingly tried to catch his balance. The bird flew off, landing on a nearby statue of a provocatively contemplative love goddess. It chortled in a way that almost sounded like laughter.

Joe caught the sword in his right hand and, after briefly comparing the two swords he now held, decided he liked the man in yellow's sword better—much better. It was more streamlined and lighter, better suited for running. The gemstones and two naked female figures worked into the sword's design didn't hurt either.

"Screamin' Joe Blade thanks you for your generosity." Joe bowed as he tossed the guard's sword into the water beside the man in yellow, who was floundering and shouting in the foot-deep pool as though he were drowning. Joe then turned and gave a deep bow to the scarlet bird, which was now too concerned with preening itself to notice.

Four guards, armed with halberds, ran into the courtyard then from the large double doors through which the garden crowd had fled. Undaunted and without another clear exit other than the way he came, Joe continued running up the path toward them. Again, his right hand blurred, and four knives were briefly airborne before burying themselves in the throats of two of the men, the eye of the third and the opening in the armor between the left shoulder and chest of the fourth. The first three men were no longer a problem, two frantically clutching their throats as they joined the third, who had already fallen dead. The fourth still needed to be dealt with, but he was having trouble using both hands to wield his long weapon due to the knife in his shoulder.

Joe scooped up the two knives he had thrown at the man in yellow as he continued his charge at the remaining guard, and then he was on him. The guard swung his halberd weakly, grunting out in pain as he did so. Joe ducked and wheeled, flashing out with his newly acquired nimble sword. The weapon caught the guard in another unprotected spot, the back of his knee, slicing through the tendons there. So incredibly sharp was Joe's newly acquired toy that it encountered nearly no resistance as it sliced through cloth, flesh, muscle, and bone. Joe hadn't noticed it, but he had almost taken the guard's leg off. The man let out a horrid cry and dropped to the ground then, his leg flopping to the side at a horrid angle. Joe quickly went to work gathering up his four remaining knives. As he wrenched the last knife from the head of the third guard, he noticed a minstrel hiding behind a nearby hedge. The man gave out an audible yelp of shock, seeing that he had been noticed.

"For future reference, I was wrongfully imprisoned; probably," Joe shouted to the terrified musician who had already fled in a random direction. "Wrongfully imprisoned!" he emphasized again to the remaining guard whose leg was bleeding profusely. Joe kicked the man's halberd out of reach, just to be safe, and noticed then that the minstrel had forgotten his instrument in his haste.

"Hey, you left your harp-thing!" Joe shouted, but the man was already out of view, having found another shrubbery to hide behind in another part of the courtyard.

"No one takes pride in their craft anymore." He said, turning to the moaning guard, but the guard only swore, spitting at Joe as he did. "I can respect that," Joe replied. "It's clear that you're having just as bad a day as I am, possibly worse." Again, the man swore before passing out. Joe looked around, trying to assess what he could of his situation. He had to keep moving. Distantly, he could hear the commotion of more security being rallied.

He didn't like the idea of going back inside, but going through the double doors into what looked like the keep of this castle looked like his best bet for finding a way out. The walls of the courtyard were too high to vault over and too smooth to climb.

Inside the doors, Joe found himself in a grand hall with great, smooth marble pillars that lined either side of a walkway equal in width to the stone path in the courtyard. A rich, deep, green woven carpet that ran its length defined the walkway. Massive banners of an identical green color hung from the ceiling, each adorned with the coat of arms of the house of Ethdab, a large white tree insignia, the trunk of the tree being a sword. At the far end of the hall opposite Joe, where the green carpet came to an end, was a three-tiered rectangular dais upon which sat an enormous throne. It looked to be entirely made of gold and was shaped as though formed from the twisting trunks, roots, and branches of three trees joined as one. The top of the throne was a canopy of very natural-looking leaves of gold. Joe was tempted to make a detour to pocket a few leaves, but there was no time. He could hear multiple voices coming from one of the two archways to either side of the dais. He had to keep moving.

There were doors behind the pillars on either side of the great hall, but he didn't have the time to risk any of them being locked and had no idea where any of them led. At this point, he did not want to end up any deeper inside the castle. Midway, however, on the left was an enormous archway through which light was spilling. It might not lead out of the castle, but it definitely led outside. He bolted for it.

Joe was just ten feet from the archway when guards began pouring into the hall, not from just the one door by the dais, but both. He ran a little harder. There was no way he would be able to face down the twenty or more guards rushing to intercept him. Reaching the ornate archway, which opened to a large stone balcony, his way was blocked by the ominous silhouette of an enormous man nearly eight feet tall. He was immensely broad too, muscular, almost to the point of absurdity. He was covered head to toe in a close-fitting scale-style armor, but the scales were styled as gold leaves, not unlike the canopy of the throne. In contrast to the gold armor, he wore boots of plain brown leather and an equally plain, brown leather belt held in place a thin tunic that he wore over the armor. It was the same green as the banners and bore the sword-tree insignia. The man's face looked as though it had been chiseled in a permanent scowl from hard white marble, and his eyes were so black in color that there was no determining where iris ended and pupil began. Upon his head was a gold crown, fashioned like seven talons sprouting from a tangle of thorns. There was no mistaking this man for anyone other than the King, Goms Ethdab.

"I believe Baron Solvar will be wanting his sword back." Goms's voice was a subtle, deep, rumbling thunder. Even at this civil tone, it was enough to shake a person to the bone. It made Joe pause for a moment. Forty or more armored guards now assembled behind Joe but stood well back as King Ethdab calmly raised one of his massive, pale, stony hands, indicating that they should do exactly that.

"I really don't have time to chat, and that Solvar fella is just going to have to cry it off," Joe replied shrugging and with that, he darted to the right leaping over the edge of the balcony.

He managed to grab hold of one of the massive Ethdab coat of arms tapestries that draped down the length of the walls of the keep on either side of the balcony, sliding down the thirty feet to the ground, his callused hands mildly warmed from the friction. He was in the entranceway and stable yard of the castle.

"Stop him!" boomed Goms. "And get that gate closed!"

Joe was already running, fast as he could, for the exit. On the wall, two guards, just as far from the gate as Joe, scrambled to get to the set of large wooden levers above the gate, one of which would drop the portcullis. Six other guards came barreling out of a large door at the base of the keep just below the balcony, only a second or two behind Screamin' Joe. There were shouts from the balcony, shouts from the wall, and Joe's purple pasta battle cry muddying up all of it. The disarray was just what Joe had hoped for. The guards here were more accustomed to keeping people out than trying to hold them in. Still, doing this alone was a lot of pressure. He would have preferred a prison riot.

A few servants, taken by surprise by the sudden chaos in the yard, abandoned their chores to find somewhere to hide as Joe raced down the center. From one of the towers behind Joe, a crossbow bolt zinged over his left shoulder, disappearing into a nearby, enormous barrel; wine spouted from the fresh hole like a red fountain.

Two of the chasing guards lost their footing on the wine-slick stones and fell, while a third, not anticipating their fall, stumbled over them, crashing head first to the stony ground knocking himself senseless. The other three leaped over or swerved around their companions continuing the pursuit but their armor was putting them at a definite disadvantage in the chase. Joe was slowly putting distance between him and them.

A young redheaded servant girl, no more than eighteen, crossing the yard carrying a bucket of milk and lost in her daily daydream of being swept away by some random, handsome, adventurous knight suddenly became aware of the approaching commotion. She stood there stunned, her mind trying to catch up to the onrushing reality of the moment, and then Joe was on her. Sweeping her in tight with his sword arm, he spun her around, taking the bucket of milk in his free hand as he bent her back, kissing her deeply. She immediately swooned, her mind a complete blur, simply giving into the situation that seemed to be something of a realization of her daydream. Just as suddenly as the passionate moment had taken her, it was over, and she was thrown gently aside, still spinning.

"Thank you, Miss!" Joe shouted, a wide, bright smile on his face and more than a glint of mischief in his eyes as he spun around, tossing the bucket of milk at his pursuers. "Always a redhead," he muttered contemplatively to himself.

The bucket hit the first of these men, full in the chest, busting apart into clattering chunks of wood and metal. Milk was everywhere. It was all enough to trip up and slow two of the remaining men chasing him down, but the third, having learned from the plight of the first three guards still wallowing in wine, simply bounded around them, leaving these two wallowing in milk.

Joe was nearly at the gate, but the guard was already upon him, shooting a hand out to grab Joe's shoulder. Precisely at that moment, another crossbow bolt seemed to bloom from the back of the man's hand. It had nearly gone all the way through and had even nicked the leather on Joe's shoulder. The guard screamed out in pain, halting and looking back at the bowman in the tower that was already being cussed out by one of his fellow tower men.

Joe was oblivious to all of it. He could see the guards above the gate nearly at the leavers.

"FOOLS!" boomed Goms's voice like thunder across the yard. Joe couldn't help but glance over his shoulder ever so briefly. He saw the king leaping from the balcony but didn't have the time to watch him fall. Poor guy, he thought, killing himself like that. I must be the first guy that ever escaped. He's really taking it way too hard.

He heard two loud clacks then as levers above the gate were activated. He dove, narrowly being missed by the free-falling portcullis, and rolled right back onto his feet, back into a run. The sound of gears and chains winding now echoed loudly in the gatehouse, and he could see that the castle had a massive drawbridge of wood, stone, and steel that was rising very slowly. Instinctively, he dove again as he reached the outer arch. There was another loud clack sound above him, and the heavy iron outer gate, with its spiked bottom edge, crashed down like the teeth of a hungry monster. Joe rolled out along the inclining drawbridge. He stumbled a little, trying to right himself on the ever-increasing angle of the bridge, but managed to keep his momentum just the same. There was more shouting from the wall as Joe jumped down the few feet to the footbridge that the drawbridge had raised from. The sounds of metal banging and chain rattling followed as the drawbridge came to a halt. Not looking back, Joe bolted through the barbican, which had fortunately been unmanned. He half stumbled, half ran, down the steep, clear-cut hill, zigging and zagging erratically as crossbow bolts whizzed past. Ironically, the barbican had actually provided him a fair amount of cover from crossbow assault.

Soon, he was in the surrounding woods, an old forest made up of massive pines, with trunks large enough to carve a small house into and grand oaks nearly as large as the pines, whose gnarled and tangled roots made them look as though each was protected by a horde of giant serpents.

The undergrowth was lush as well, but it was mostly small, soft growth; mushrooms, ferns, moss, grasses, and the occasional sapling, many of these sprouting from old fallen trees. It was easy enough to walk through and easy enough to disappear in. It reminded Joe quite a bit of the forest surrounding the Midgorn city of Dreema. After about an hour of walking, sometimes running, Joe felt he was significantly lost enough not to have to worry about being recaptured by any of Goms's men.

He came upon a large log that looked to be a suitable spot to take a break. The bright orange mushrooms growing from its side caught his eye, and it brought a disturbing thought to mind. He had no idea what he could or couldn't eat in this land. Hopefully, he'd find some small animal to eat. They were usually a safer bet than the potentially poisonous nature of berries, mushrooms, or greenery. Catching some small creature would simply raise another issue. He had no means of generating a fire either, aside from damaging the fine sword he had recently acquired, sparking it off of some rock. It just didn't seem like a good idea. He was at a bit of a loss as to what he should do next, and so he sat there staring at the finely crafted sword, hoping some brilliant idea would come to his frustratingly blank mind.

Behind him, something snapped. He leaped up onto the log and drew one of his knives, pointing the sword in one direction while pointing the dagger in the other, quickly looking in either direction. He then spun around, scanning the forest in all directions, but there was nothing to be seen. It became clear to Joe that he was far too on edge, and he sat back down with more resolve than before to simply relax. He holstered his knife, giving a couple wary looks over his shoulders before letting himself fully unwind. Convinced that all was quiet then, he started to take a closer look at his newly acquired prize, and quite a prize it was.

The pommel of the sword had been fashioned to look like a skeletal hand. It gripped a large, rough-shaped, black gemstone. The dark stone had the subtlest translucence to it, with an undefinable depth that seemed to swallow light. The handle was wrapped in a series of black leather strips woven around each other. There was just a slight hint of red in the leather's color here in the sunlight.

The truly striking feature of the sword, however, was the elaborate cross guard.

Two naked women, nearly identical, had their backs to the sword blade. Each gripped the sword with their hands, just behind their heads, just below the small, oblong, bejeweled hand guard. Their backs arched past small triangular barbs pointing out from either side of the blade base. The buttocks of each figure were set firmly against the blade, just where it began to taper on either side into sharp edges, the blade edges being nestled between the figures' buttock cheeks. The women's legs appeared to be set in something of a dramatic running pose. The extended leading leg of each woman formed the sword's crossguard and rested on the foot of the opposite figure's trailing leg, each of which wrapped around opposite sides of the blade.

Holding the sword blade up, as Joe was, the figures were upside down. Their pose reminded Joe of the rod and pillar dancers of Beedo back in Midgorn. He let out a dirty little chuckle, despite himself, as his memory began to wander back to his most recent visit to the island community. He was brought back from his memory safari as he noticed a small detail on one of the figures. Their wavy hair, passing just past the shoulders on each figure, looked identical at first glance, but Joe noticed that the hair was displaced enough on one of the figures to clearly reveal a pointed ear. The only people he knew to have pointed ears in Midgorn were the reclusive Danuwan.

The Danuwan were wielders of strange magic and seldom came down from their lofty caves to mingle with the people of Midgorn. Joe had seen a danuwan woman only once, just a few months ago. She had been a competitor in a dangerous annual event called the Grand Fain. It was always held in the same location, the community of Manri. Mercenaries of every sort, chacklers, wizards, soldiers, memory seekers, even farmers, and other common folk from all of Midgorn and beyond, came to compete in the tournament, often leading to many of their deaths. The goal of the competition is to determine who is the most skilled and resourceful, but ultimately, as the winner, who could ask the highest price for their services. Aside from being clever and agile, the danuwan woman had been astonishingly beautiful, even from the nosebleed seats from where Joe had watched the competition. Such beauty was said, however, to be a natural trait of the Danuwan.

It occurred to Joe then that the man in yellow was quite possibly a danuwan himself. He had been rather unsettlingly handsome. Continuing to examine the sword, this was almost a certainty, for up the entire length of the blade, if held at just the right angle to the light, words written in fayrseen, the language of the danuwan, would appear. The words seemed to float at an impossible depth in the steel of the sword, shimmering in every color imaginable.

"Death Seed, the kiss of oblivion, purveyor of darkness." A male voice in Joe's left ear startled him so much that he nearly dropped the sword, but in a flash, he was on his feet, standing on the log and brandishing one of his knives.

"That's what it says on the sword." continued the hooded figure, covered in a ragged, blackened cloak that looked like it had once been blue in color. Before Joe had jumped up, the figure had to have been sitting right next to Joe, but inexplicably, Joe had not even noticed him approach. With all the twigs and dead leaves about, there should have been at least some alerting sound. As Joe stood there, both weapons pointed at the man, trying to assess the situation, the mysterious man just kept talking. "Well, the direct elvish translation is quite a bit bawdier, but that's elves for you."

"Shut up! Who are you? Wh-where did you - how did you…" Joe's composure was shaken far more than he would ever admit. "Well, which is it? Do you want me to shut up, or do you want to make introductions?" The figure on the log sat motionlessly, his face still shrouded in the hood, looking down.

Joe did not appreciate being mocked. "Who are you?" he responded gruffly.

"Ah, well, as any mystery man worth his reputation, I've gone by many names, but presently Victor serves. Victor Morosoff," He pulled his hood back, revealing a man in his late twenties, though his thick red beard and mustache and long, nearly white blonde hair made him look quite a bit older. "And you are Josarik Mactoni, but most know, or will come to know you, as Screamin' Joe Blade."

"How do you know — Did Carnesh send you? That's it, isn't it? You're one of the Balconsul's dogs. You're not dressed like a chackler, so you must be a bounty hunter. What am I worth these days?" Joe inched slightly closer, close enough to strike Victor with the sword if he should make any sudden movements.

"500 gold, and you're right, I'm no roving judge and jury, a 'chackler,' as you say, but I'm certainly not a bounty hunter either. Are you always so jumpy? Calm yourself and sit." Victor patted on the spot next to him where Joe had been sitting moments ago. "What I am is here to help." Joe didn't sit, but he eased his weapons down slightly. "Did the Crystal Master send you too?" he sneered in a disbelieving tone.

"Too?" Victor looked surprised. "Well, that's going to complicate my weekend."

Just then, a piercing screech came from above the two men. Joe wheeled around, looking up in the direction of the noise; his knife arm went back, ready to launch the deadly little weapon if needed.

"Stay calm, Mr. Blade," Victor said quickly. "She's with me." He held out his right arm. A strange-looking little creature dropped from the sky with swooping grace, landing on his arm. Its head looked like a snake, the scales there being brilliant stripes of green and blue, its cat-like eyes shimmering gold. Deep ruby-colored feathers stuck out from the back of its head, while neon orange feathers covered the rest of its body, including the long whip-like tail with a fan of red-tipped feathers at its end. Rather than tucking in its wings, it actually used them to help it perch. Two tiny blue fingers with red claws stuck out from the feathers in the middle of each wing where it grasped at Victor's robe. The odd creature, no bigger than a large parrot, gave Victor an acknowledging little screech, then crawled up his arm and around his neck to sit on Victor's opposite shoulder. Its long tail draped around Victor's neck and trailed down his chest like a living, swishing scarf. "It seems you've lost your pursuers, Joe. Still, we should get ourselves inside before Goms's men start poking around these woods, and they will. My house is just a short walk past those bushes. I can tell you all about your sword there." He pointed over his left shoulder.

Joe cocked an eyebrow, puzzled at Victor's casual nature. "I'm still not convinced that you aren't a bounty hunter." He still brandished both blades, ready for anything Victor or his pet might try. Victor raised his left hand as if indicating the direction for Joe to follow, and then a tall staff, topped with a carved crystal skull that seemed to melt into the rest of the staff, appeared in that hand.

Victor hoisted himself to his feet, straightening his ragged robe-like cloak. "There's freshly roasted chicken and deep-fried potato chips," he said, shrugging as he started off toward the bushes.

Joe watched Victor walk away for a few paces, put away his knife, and hustled up next to him. Neither said a word as they wandered past the bushes.

"Next time, open with the chicken," Joe said, breaking the brief silence, and then a few steps later, "...and at a distance."

Screamin' Joe Blade's Ten-Point Guide to Life:
Point #2: Never turn down a free meal (unless it's a meat pie from a baker whose recently missing wife also happens to be a woman you had spent a great deal of mutually naked time with).

Chapter 5

Victor's 'house' was a round burrowed-out cave no more than twenty feet in diameter, hidden in the tangled roots of a large oak tree that had grown on, through, and around the stump of an even larger fallen pine. The doorway was only four feet high and masked by a living sheet of vines that swept back into place when the small wooden door was closed. There were no windows. The room was illuminated by a cluster of large orange crystals embedded in the ceiling. The walls of Victor's den appeared to be entirely made of the surrounding roots of the oak, save for an eight-foot portion that seemed to be the remains of the outer wall of the pine stump. Bricks had been built up along this portion of the wall, protecting it from the large cast iron stove that resided there. The stove's exhaust pipe ran, with a slight bend, into a hole in the wall. Joe wondered where the chimney emerged. He had not seen any smoke outside. The air above a large pot of oil on top of the stove rippled dangerously with heat. Inside the stove, illuminated by the orange flames that licked at it from below, a chicken on a spit rotated magically under its own power.

Victor grabbed a nearby wire basket full of freshly cut potato strips and dipped the basket into the oil. The oil bubbled and sizzled ferociously, letting off a puff of steam.

Joe had seated himself on one of three chairs around a hefty but simple round oak table on the opposite side of the room. These furnishings were the only decoration in the room save for a square, woven, multi-hued blue rug that covered most of the ringed pine-stump floor and a detailed tapestry that Joe could swear depicted, in an almost comical stylized way, the various communities of Midgorn; it was essentially a map.

"That stove looks trall-made," Joe said, fishing.

"It is, you're right," Victor responded quite casually. "Do you like it?"

Joe ignored the question. "You are from Midgorn, but that's not exactly true either, right?"

"I don't know what you mean." Victor's tone was that of exaggerated false innocence.

"Well, for one thing," Joe started, "there's the map of Midgorn on the wall."

"Quite observant, do go on," Victor interjected sarcastically as he inspected the progress of the potatoes.

"Second, you call them elves; the danuwan, that is, you call them elves. Only iconic priests and their followers call them elves, and everyone knows that most iconic priests claim to be from some 'outer world.'" Victor was about to say something, but Joe just kept going. "Which brings me to what's on your feet. Nobody but so-called outerworlders wears anything like that. What are they even made of?"

Victor hiked his cloak up a bit, examining his shoes as though he were seeing them for the first time. He was wearing high-top sneakers, one red and one white. Dropping the cloak back down, Victor pondered for a moment. "Hmm, you might have something there." he offered.

"Might have something?" Joe sounded a little exasperated but laughed despite himself. "I'm going to have to join that crazy cult myself now. I mean, this is it, isn't it? The 'Outer World'."

"Not exactly. I mean, yes, it is an outer world, but it's not the outer world." Victor turned to face Joe, a contemplative look on his face. "The truth is, I'm not even sure what world this is exactly. The locals call it Modnar, but I suspect it's a version of my outer world, which we outworlders call Earth. Still, it is quite different in far too many ways, so I really don't know what to make of it. I found it some long while back by accident, not unlike yourself. The falls, right?"

"Ya, that's right, so you're stuck here too." Joe could feel his hopes of getting back to Midgorn fading.

"Well, not truly stuck, but I'll get to that. The thing is that Modnar doesn't even fit into the time patterns of Earth. It almost seems to be a place where all of the stray bits of time go whenever someone makes a change that doesn't fit into the proper flow of things. I'm sure if I looked around hard enough, I'd find the woman that used to do Kermit's voice."

"Whose voice? What? You've lost me. Time? Stray bits?" Joe could feel his brain shutting off and just wanted to eat. He pointed at the stove slightly, "How's that chicken coming?"

"About another ten minutes, but the fries should be ready." Victor pulled the basket of sliced potatoes out of the oil, giving them a couple of shakes before carrying them over to a low, wide, wooden plank shelf, a few steps away, that served as a countertop. "Ah, perfect." Using two wooden spoons as tongs, he scooped out two heaps of the fries into a pair of wooden bowls, dowsing them with a generous amount of white vinegar and then sprinkling them with salt that he kept in a large glass jar with holes drilled into its metal lid.

"The secret is in the oil," he said, handing one of the bowls to Joe, placing his own on the opposite end of the table. "Tell me what you think. Careful though, they're still ridiculously hot." with that thought, he returned to the counter. He grabbed a brown bottle, pouring its contents into two plain metal goblets. "It's not the best pairing, I know, but a little dwarf mead from Kursik should cool your mouth if need be."

"Dwarf? You are an iconic priest, aren't you? Why do you iconic priests call the trall 'dwarves' or the danuwan 'elves'?" Joe was talking through the fries stuffed in his mouth.

"I'm not a priest, I'll assure you of that, and we outerworlders call them that because they very much resemble the dwarves and elves that we are told stories about right from when we are very little children. In fact, the interactions of their ancestors with ours, the humans' ancestors, is exactly what led to those tales."

"So you're a memory keeper then, or more likely a memory seeker if you found yourself going over the falls in Beedo. I did some work for a seeker once. Did you work out of the city of Orter before you got stuck here? These potatoes of yours are great, by the way." Tiny bits of potato spat out as Joe spoke. "Maybe you're one of those fancy moshans from Advan."

Victor tossed a fry to the strange reptilian bird that sat patiently in its own chair. The bird caught the fry effortlessly with its mouth, gulping it down and giving a happy little screech of a chirp. "No, not a memory keeper either, or a chef or moshan, as you say; certainly not of Advan caliber. I'm just a man who's made a home here in the forests of upper Senuvia, and I'm here to help you." The bird squawked, and Victor, rolling his eyes, pushed his bowl of fries over to the creature. Stretching its neck out, it began devouring the contents of the bowl, making contented little chortling sounds.

"Help me how," Joe questioned absently, mesmerized somewhat by the spectacle of the bird making short work of the fries, its long turquoise tongue now lapping up the soup of oil, vinegar, and salt.

"That sword of yours. It's more than it seems." Victor leaned in slightly, his voice growing a little more serious.

"Oh yeah?" Joe's attention was reeled back in. "worth something, eh? Looking to buy it from me, maybe? You don't think that king or that danuwan fellow will be coming for it? He is danuwan, right?"

"I'm sure they will, and yes, Baron Solvar is an elf. By the way, they do call them elves here. Solvar, however, is genuinely a danuwan of Midgorn, stuck here just like you. The thing is — can I call you Joe, or do you prefer Screamin'?

"Joe works. You seem like a square stone."

"Fair enough, Joe, then. They won't be looking here for the sword; they will still be chasing after you." Victor gave him a sly smile that made Joe a little uncomfortable. "But, since they will be chasing you, we might as well give them something worth chasing after. I have no interest in the sword."

Joe suddenly found himself wanting to be rid of the thing. "What do you mean you have no interest in the sword? You seemed to be all about it back there. What's so special about it? You said you were going to tell me about it, so let's hear it."

"Well, in all fairness, it's not the sword itself that is all that special. The sword is really just the messenger. It's the stone in the hilt of the sword that is special. May I?" Victor reached for the sword, which Joe had propped against the table. Joe nodded his approval, curious about how valuable the roughly shaped black gem in the hilt could be.

Victor eyeballed the gem, then examined the blade. He stood up and gave the sword a few swishes in the air, testing its balance. It was clear that he was familiar with handling a sword. "Don't get me wrong, this sword is no ordinary blade either. It's elven forged, so in addition to being ridiculously strong and sharp, it's likely got some hidden extra or two, but it's still just common steel. No, the sword that this stone truly belongs to is a far less elegant weapon, but could likely cut through this sword, the person wielding it, and the bunker they were hiding in all in one swing, and that's without the gem. The sword this stone belongs to is one of thirteen swords forged from ultimorite.

"Never heard of the stuff." Joe shrugged.

"You wouldn't have. It's only found here on Modnar, as are the beings that made the swords; thirteen god-like beings known as xenomods. Each weapon was infused with the power of the god that forged it. I'm not enough of an expert to recognize which sword this particular stone powers." Something about Victor's demeanor made it seem like he wasn't being entirely honest. Joe didn't call him on it. Most of the people he dealt with were far from entirely honest. Regardless, Joe was finding the sword far more interesting.

"Well, if the stone is so special, why doesn't it give this sword any god-power." Joe was on his feet now, anxious to play with the sword.

"Oh, it probably does. As I said before, this is an elven blade, which alone could mean it's full of tricks, but it's no accident that the stone is in this sword; it was designed to carry this crystal shard. It most certainly draws some sort of particular ability from it." Victor held the sword out for Joe to take. "I'm sure you'll figure it out along the way."

Joe felt very conflicted. He very much wanted to take the sword back, but he had a sinking feeling that he was somehow being roped into something that he really didn't want to be a part of. Hesitating slightly, he took the sword by the handle.

"What do you mean 'along the way'?"

Victor chuckled a little. "Well, you can't stay here forever. For one thing, I only have the one chicken, and for another, Goms isn't the only one who will be looking for you."

"Right, right, I know, that Solvar fella is going to be wanting his sword back, but the man is clearly no threat."

"You're quite right, I don't mean Solvar. As skilled as Solvar is, truly it's Goms that you need to fear and another. I'm not sure Solvar was aware of Goms's intentions, at least not at first. He was probably under the impression that his prowess as a swordsman and the curiosity of him being from another world was what had landed him in Goms's favor. Make no mistake, though, Goms only means to unite the stone with its rightful sword. It's the only reason the wayward elf was welcomed into Goms's court at all. What I wonder is whether the Baron was sent to Modnar intentionally, or did he fumble his way in as you did." Victor opened the stove, instantly filling the room with the roasted chicken's delicious aroma.

"Wow, that smells great!" Joe nearly lost his own train of thought but quickly pulled his thoughts back on course. "Then who's this other person I should be concerned about?" He was squinting at Victor as though somehow he might be able to bring Victor's secrets into focus.

"Nashtar. He's a powerful wizard who holds the ultimorite sword that the stone belongs to. He, of course, will be after you for the stone as well. Or at least his conjured minions will be."

"Whoa, wait, I didn't sign up for no conjured minions, or for that matter, sword-collecting wizards and kings. I just want to go home. You can keep the sword and deal with the crazies. Consider it payment for the chicken."

"No, no, you don't understand yet." Victor turned his attention back to the chicken, his voice echoing into an unseen depth as he spoke, "MANOKAN, VISCRATA!" Then, pointing at the counter, "ERPLASIN VOLEN STATICAN!" All at once, two plates removed themselves from the small stack at the end of the counter while the roasted chicken shot out of the stove hovering above the counter. The plates set themselves down beside each other on the countertop as the chicken neatly exploded into carefully carved slices, two drumsticks, and two wings, each half of the chicken coming gently to rest upon its own plate. The remaining bones of the chicken, still floating in the air, then shot back into the stove. The stove door slammed, and the fire roared. Victor picked up the two plates and walked them over to the table. "There we are then."

Joe had sat back down, looking a little stunned. "You're…" he stared blankly, searching for words, "Nashtar?"

Victor laughed as he set the plates down on the table. "No, not at all, and I have no interest in acquiring any of the swords." He tossed a slice of chicken to the bird. It caught it as easily as it had the fry earlier and gulped it down just as quickly, giving a satisfied screech. "Settle down, enjoy the chicken." he motioned to Joe.

"What you did to that chicken a moment ago," there was a little apprehension in Joe's voice and demeanor, "you can do that to a person, too, right?"

"Is that what has you bent out of sorts." Victor laughed, giving Joe a dark smile. "Eat, eat." He encouraged again. "No. Magic on the living is far trickier, if you'll pardon the pun. It's why fire magic is so difficult. The council tried to have it banned, you know?"

"What, magic on the living?" Joe found himself easing up again with the conversation.

"Well, that would have made a little more sense, perhaps, but no, I was referring to fire magic. I think ultimately it was the mashun guild of Advan that had convinced the council that a ban on fire magic would adversely affect their food preparations."

"I'm not sure I'm entirely following this conversation. Weren't we talking about the sword?" Joe said, focusing on eating the chicken.

"My fault entirely." Victor offered. "You'll need to be on your way soon, so let me sum things up for you and point you in the right direction of things."

"That would be - wait, what do you mean soon?"

"I believe we've already covered that, but once you're done with your chicken, and we this conversation, then you must be on your way for things to play out the way they should. Now, now," Victor held up a hand, stifling Joe just as he opened his mouth to speak, "before you go asking questions that get us off track again, let me just tell you what you need to know."

Joe frowned a bit. "Fine, I'll just be over here enjoying my delicious chicken. It really is delicious, by the way; I wasn't being sarcastic. I mean, I was, but I wasn't, y'know?"

Victor simply stared at Joe for a few moments, reconsidering telling this foolish man anything. "Uh, thanks. So, to the point, then. Goms is after the stone in your sword, and so is the wizard Nashtar, who presently possesses the sword that the stone rightfully belongs attached to. Once either of them has both items they will seek out the temple of the Xenomods, for legend has it that only there can the two be combined. If it is the sword that I suspect it to be, then it will be your means of returning to Midgorn."

Aha, Joe thought; Victor did know more than he was letting on earlier. The more he could keep Victor talking, the more he might let slip. "Well, I suppose anything's possible. Nothing in the legend saying just how exactly the sword is supposed to take us to Midgorn, is there?" Joe took a big chomp out of his drumstick.

"Us?" Victor puzzled. "Oh no, no, I won't be coming with you. I have business elsewhere." The bird creature squawked then, and Victor tossed it another large morsel of chicken, talking directly to it as if the bird had just said something. "That's right, we have business elsewhere, and no," he turned back to Joe, "the legends that I'm aware of don't say how exactly the sword is used or even how the stone and sword are to be merged. But it is a sword, after all, so I imagine it's used in some sort of swordy fashion, and given that the joining ritual is to be done in a Xenomod Temple, I'd wager a mountain of gold crits that a bunch of magic and some sort of blood sacrifice is involved. More mead?

"Now, hold up right there. Screamin' Joe Blade doesn't do blood sacrifices." Joe waved the bone of his drumstick with the authority of a judge's gavel for emphasis.

Victor just stared at him for a moment, a slightly puzzled smile on his face. "Your name; you realize that it practically says 'Hi, my name is Joe; expect a horrific bit of bloodletting,' right?"

Joe was taken aback somewhat. "Well, ya, I suppose you put it that way, but I'm not about to just dice someone up to patch together some toy sword of the gods."

Remember, that toy sword will be your key to getting home. Since Nashtar has the sword, and he's likely to seek you out once he hears that you have the stone, it would probably save you both a lot of hassle if you just went straight to him. After all, who better to throw around a bunch of magic, if necessary, if not a wizard."

"Wait, wait, wait. Why not you? You could throw around the magic, right? 'Sides, this Nashtar fella is likely to nominate me as the blood sacrifice, and if not me, then who?" Joe punctuated his question by popping an especially large piece of chicken in his mouth.

Victor gave Joe an amused smile. "I'm sure you'll work it out, but now it's time to be on your way." With his gaze fixed on Joe, he reached out to the side with his left hand. His staff flew across the room to meet his grasp. The crystal skull capping the staff began to glow with a dull blue light.

"Um, go? Now? But I haven't even finished my chicken." Joe pointed at the few scraps left on his plate.

"Sorry," Said Victor flatly, "but I have a date for tea with a certain queen whom I would hate to disappoint." He began to motion towards Joe with the staff, and Joe cringed a little, but then Victor paused. "I almost forgot. What was the name of the person that helped you out of your cell?"

"What?" Joe relaxed a little. "Oh, ya, ya, she said her name was Vicki, no wait, it was more like Vera; no, no, Vella! That's it; her name was Vella. Said that breakin' me out of my cell settled her debt with the Crystal Master."

"Hmm," Victor responded, shrugging; the name Vella clearly meant nothing to him. "Well, in any case, you'll need this." He tossed Joe a small red crystal, nearly identical in shape but twice the size of the one Vella had provided him. A cap of gold, looking much like a spider web, attached it to a thin black leather necklace.

Joe looked a little anxious as he caught it. "Hey, this thing isn't going to explode, is it? Wait, you're him, the Crystal Master!"

"No," Victor smirked, "it won't explode. At least, it's not meant to. You might want to grab that." He motioned toward Death Seed.

Joe picked up the sword, "Sure, but…" The room flashed with bright blue light, and then Joe was gone.

Victor hoisted himself out of his seat with the staff, the blue light in the skull dimming. "You don't recall a Vella, do you?"

In the chair, where a moment ago the reptilian bird had been perched, sat a very attractive woman. Her skin was a light caramel color, and her lips were naturally a deep red. She had green eyes that nearly glowed with neon brilliance and deep crimson hair cut short into a sassy winged bob that swung and bounced about easily with her slightest movement. She wore an equally crimson, skin-tight one-piece mini-skirt that sat just off of her shoulders and shimmered with opalescence as she shifted in her seat to face Victor. The dress almost looked to be made of liquid and left little of her athletically curvy body to the imagination. A slender emerald crystal on a short, elegant gold chain hung around her neck. On her feet, she wore four-inch, red-strapped, stiletto heels, the bindings of which ran halfway up her calves. She sat very demurely with both her feet tucked off to one side together and twirled a lock of her crimson hair casually with her left hand.

"Nope," she said, shrugging.

Victor frowned at her, a little frustrated with her short response. "Invaluable counsel as always." He grumbled. "And you might want to put something on; we are having tea with the Queen."

"Ah, Jinxy don't care," she said with a dismissive wave of her right hand. Her voice was delightfully feminine, her intonations smooth and silky but with a girlish playfulness. "Besides, it's the elven sky caves. If anything, I'm over-dressed. You, however…" She finished her sentence with a disapproving look up and down and yet another dismissive wave of her hand in a figure-eight directed at Victor's well-worn attire.

"Right. Right, you are. We'll make a stop at the mall. What year would you prefer?"

She smiled slyly, leaning forward rather provocatively, "oh, you know me," she purred seductively, "always 2025."

Victor rolled his eyes. "Malls are all but dead then, and we are not stopping by the bookstore this time, Lisa." He walked over to the tapestry that looked like a map of Midgorn and pulled it aside, revealing a large metal iris doorway.

Lisa gave a quick little mock pout that had just a hint of a conniving smile. "We'll see."

"Indeed, but first, I need something from home. Will you do the honors?" he said, bowing to her slightly.

"Of course, m'lord," she said mockingly. Standing, she gave Victor a demure little curtsy, then slinked over to the iris, hips swaying hypnotically like a golden age movie starlet, her heels clicking on the floor with each step. She gently unlatched the necklace from her neck as she walked. Her movements were unnaturally smooth. As she approached the iris, the emerald crystal began to glow. She touched the crystal to the iris, and immediately, the door's twelve metal plates slid open without a sound, revealing a brilliantly lit room beyond. Its walls and ceiling were ornately sculpted solid gold, while the floor was a checkerboard of five-foot square, gold, and black marble tiles. Lisa poked her head in a little, examining the forty-foot by forty-foot room.

"As secure as we left it." She said, smiling a bright white smile that almost seemed a little unnaturally wide. "So, he makes it this time?"

"Yes. I think so."

"So we're done here then, or are we coming back again after tea." She tapped an impatient toe, one hand on her hip as she leaned against the opening.

Victor twirled his staff as he walked toward Lisa and the door. He gave an absent wave of his free hand, magically snuffing the fire in the stove. "Third time's a charm, they say. You showing him the library this time around should have it all on track."

"Technically, that hasn't happened yet." Lisa corrected him.

"It should be all sorted now." Victor paused in the doorway. "I'm pretty sure we're done here. He has the sword for sure this time." There was a slight bit of uncertainty in his voice. He cleared his throat and shrugged himself into a better state of confidence. "We'll find out when we see the Queen, I suppose." He motioned for her to go ahead. "Ladies, first."

She put the necklace back on as she stepped through. Victor followed close behind, letting the tapestry fall back into place. The iris closed without a sound, and then all in the room was darkness and silence.

Chapter 6

Joe had been walking along the heavily forested path for two hours now. He had no idea where he was headed or which direction he should take. For that matter, Joe didn't even have a real destination. According to Victor, the Crystal Master, if he could be trusted, he should try to find the wizard Nashtar and acquire the powersword in his possession. He still had a feeling that Victor was actually Nashtar, though if that were the case, why didn't he try to keep the crystal shard, and why give him the necklace. Joe didn't contemplate it too much. He learned long ago not to try to figure out the motivations of wizards. They just didn't think like normal folk.

When he first appeared on the path, and it was immediately apparent that neither direction seemed to hold any indication of anything significant, he decided which direction to take by tossing one of his knives in the air and seeing which way the blade pointed when it landed. Unfortunately, the dagger's direction would have taken him off the trail and into the woods. He discreetly nudged the dagger a little with his foot until it pointed in the direction that he had been secretly cheering for, subtly enough that his subconscious might not shame him to guilt should any grievous pitfalls befall him in the falsely indicated direction.

The bright ball of light and heat was still high above, though he was starting to get the sense that it was moving. Indeed, it was higher above than earlier when he had escaped the castle and far higher than when he had been on the beach the day before. What a strange, chaotic world this is, he thought.

Despite the deep shade offered by the massive trees that lined the well-worn dirt and gravel road, the walk made him overly hot. Only half an hour into the walk, he had found himself having to shed his black leather jacket, tying the arms around his waist. He re-slung the bandolier of throwing knives across his black sleeveless shirt, undoing the lacing near the neck of the shirt to open it up as much as possible. He would have considered shedding the leather pants as well, but as it was, minus the jacket, he was being constantly bitten by tiny flying insects. Midgorn had its share of bothersome insects, some terrifyingly large, but here, small flying insects of a staggering variety flitted about. Many of them seemed intent on draining him of his blood, one tiny droplet of a meal at a time. He had spent much of the walk in frantic fits, swatting at the critters buzzing about him in the air and smacking at the little beasts whenever he felt a bite.

It was during one of these vain thrashing battles that Joe first heard a high-pitched chortling sound coming from somewhere high up in the dense canopy of leaves and branches above him. At the time, he had taken it for the sound of some sort of bird, and being terribly occupied with fending off the bugs, he paid it little mind. Three more hours passed, his battle with the insects as ceaseless as the curses he alternately muttered and shouted in gapless succession. All the while, the high-pitched chortles from the treetops continued, and with every other sounding, it was joined by another, adding slightly to its volume.

The big ball of light was low on the horizon then, peering through the trunks of the trees with an orange-red light, distorting the appearance of everything in long colliding shadows. The air had grown much cooler, the bugs far fewer, and Joe's attention a little more focused on his surroundings. The high-pitched warbling cry came again from the deep, dark ceiling of leaves, but now it was made up of so many voices as to be nearly deafening. Joe had a terrible sense of foreboding then, and though he still had no idea where he was going, he decided that it would be better to get there a little quicker.

He had just picked up his pace when there was a rush in the leaves above, like the sound of heavy rain. Instinctively, Joe began to run, but it was too late. Hundreds of furry red puff balls, each roughly the size of a fist, fell all about Joe. Some fell directly on Joe, sticking to him, while most of the others hit the ground with a grunting chirp sound, immediately leaping back into the air toward Joe. Joe ducked, spun, and ducked again, dodging many of the hostile little puffs with incredible agility and slicing many of them in two with Death Seed, spattering the nearby tree trunks in a rain of bright blue blood and goo. Soon, however, Joe was overwhelmed by the little beasts. There were simply too many of the chortling and chirping balls of fluff coming at him, sticking to him; before long, all that could be seen of Joe was a large writhing mound of contentedly burbling red puff balls.

A horrendous metallic clatter arose in the surrounding forest, a cacophony of pots, pans, chains, metal tankards, swords, and even a large gong all being banged together. A harmonious, angry squeal answered back to the noise from the collective puff ball clustered around Joe. The clattering and banging grew more intense, and now an older woman, whose dress and shawl were shabby shades of green, stepped from the shadows onto the path. She carried a long, shiny, spiraling black horn on a thick yellow leather strap. The clatter from the surrounding bushes continued. The puffballs continued to squeal and were shaking violently.

The grey-haired woman in green held the horn to her lips, blowing gently. A loud, deep, rumbling bellow burst from the horn like a wall of water smashing through a stone dam. The trees shook, leaves tumbled all around, and even the ground seemed to tremble. The squeal of the puffball cluster rose, and then the mass exploded into its individual balls, shooting up into the shelter of the leaves, the individual squeals of each ball fading into the distance in all directions as the balls fled somewhere high above. The clatter from the surrounding forest diminished, and the woman stopped blowing her horn.

Joe was thrashing about on the ground, covered in an orange-colored goo. He clawed at the dripping, clinging globs covering his face, clearing the area around his mouth, gasping for air.

"That should hold it off for a day or two." the woman said as she walked over to Joe. Her hair was a wiry tangle of various shades of grey. By the wrinkles and cracks in her face, she might have been eighty or ninety years old, but she had the stride and body of a woman forty years younger, and the clarity of her eyes spoke of the quick mind behind them. She grabbed Joe by the arm and hoisted him to his feet with surprising strength. "At the very least, it will go hunting elsewhere for a meal tonight." She turned to the surrounding bushes then, raising her voice. "See that he's cleaned up," she ordered.

From the shadows, ten men emerged. They were a motley bunch.

Some were large, some small, some fat, some skinny, but all had dark black curly hair, and all but one had some style of mustache. Each was dressed in elaborately colorful but dirty and well-worn clothing. The man without a mustache puffed on an enormous pipe that he held clenched in his teeth in the left corner of his mouth. They all looked to Joe like the street performers who would entertain the crowds in the filthy market square of Cur. More often than naught, those performers were simply a distraction from their partners, many of whom were children or wily old folk like this woman in green, who would discreetly slice the purses and pockets of the spectators. Joe had been one of those children. He would have been more on guard if he wasn't so thankful for their arrival, and he found himself more than a little distracted trying to scrape the goo off of himself. He was starting to tingle wherever it had got directly on his skin, which was nearly everywhere on his upper body.

The old woman seemed to sense his concern, both of the goo and her men. "Don't you frimble any now, young man. The spordikan was just trying to calm you down. It's the green slime you have to worry about. Once the beast gets that on you, you're as good as slime yourself."

"Beast?" Joe sputtered through the orange goo dripping from his face. "There were hundreds of those little things."

"No," said the man with the pipe then, "The spordikan is a single beast who spreads itself out to hunt or protect itself. Most aren't so large as to be brave enough to attack a person, but this one's old. It has stalked these woods since before my grandfather." The man was standing next to Joe now, and just like the woman in green, Joe could see that this man was much older than he seemed to carry himself. His face wasn't as wrinkled as the woman's, but it was creased with lines and wrinkles in every direction.

"A single beast?" Joe found that his mind was a little foggy, indeed, getting foggier, but mostly, what they were saying about the little puff balls just didn't make any sense to him.

"You aren't from around here, are you, boy?" the old woman started. "From Westerlan, I'd wager by those clothes of yours. Mighty creepy the way you all walk around inside the skins of others. Is it true what they say about you eating people too?" There were snickers from the other men who had gathered closer, encircling Joe.

"You won't eat us though, will you, son." The old man said more than asked, punctuating his sentence with a puff of smoke from his pipe. "After all, we're your friends, what with us rescuing you and all."

"Yes, I mean no, not eash, I mean eat, not eat." Joe's vision was starting to swim as much as his speech, and he was getting dizzy. The crowd of men closed on him a little as he swayed. He went to swing Death Seed to hold them back but realized only then that he had not been holding the sword for some time. He could also have sworn he had some other sort of weapon or weapons, but it just wasn't coming to him.

"He's going down." said one of the men casually.

The woman said something then, but for some reason, Joe couldn't hear what it was, couldn't hear anything, really. The world around him seemed to spin and swim, and then all was darkness."

Chapter 7

The sound of lively music roused Joe from his second goo-induced slumber, a squeeze box of some sort accompanied by a tiny pipe and a booming, thumping drum. Joe was in a very small room lit by a single candle. Pots and pans of various sizes, along with a wide assortment of strangely shaped bottles, all hung from the thin rafters of the room on leather strings. Some bottles were filled with liquids, some with powders, and others with dried-out bits of this and that. This and that mostly being tiny body parts from an assortment of small animals. It took Joe a moment to notice in the dim light, but someone was sitting in the corner of the room by the door.

"You don't want to get up too quickly." Said a soft feminine voice from the corner. "There's some tea just there, on the table next to you. It will help clear your head."

Joe leaned over, sniffing at the tea. The sharp odor of putrid, regurgitated horse meat and cinnamon masked in some sort of fecal potpourri filled his nostrils. He choked down the tiny bit of vomit that swelled in his throat and politely declined the tea.

"No matter. Really, you're only supposed to smell it anyway. Feeling a little better, I trust?" She was right. The horrible stench had shocked him to a higher level of alertness.

"Ya, a little. I've gotten used to blacking out lately." Joe realized just then that beneath the bed sheets, he was completely naked. "Um, so, how did I — what, exactly — where — "

She mercifully cut his fumbling short. "Moiren had a couple of the men clean you up. I had them put you in here. Your things are here." She patted his neatly folded clothing in her lap. "I'll leave them here on the chair for you. They've been cleaned as well. You'll want to get dressed. Moiren wants you by the fire; wants to know what brings you through this forest."

With that, she stood up, placed his clothes on the seat of the chair, and stepped out the door. She had remained mostly in shadow, but Joe caught a glimpse of vibrant, fiery red, curly hair in the candlelight before she closed the door behind her.

Screamin' Joe Blade's Ten-Point Guide to Life:
Point #3: If you wake up in the proximity of a redhead with no memory of how you got there, assume everything has been going very right.

Joe hoisted himself out of the bed and walked across the room to gather up his belongings. At first, he thought he was still feeling the toxic effects of the goo on his equilibrium, as the room almost seemed to sway a little with his every step. A few of the dangling bottles clinked together above him, causing him to instinctively wheel around to face any possible threat trying to sneak up on him. It was clear then that the room itself was actually moving. His sudden motion caused the room to rock a little more noticeably, and that, combined with the last remnants of the toxins that were still in his head, made Joe a little dizzy. He stumbled back, sitting on his clothes and slumping down in the chair, but his back hit something metallic. The shock of the cold sensation made him bolt upright. It was the hilt of one of his throwing knives. His bandolier was slung across the back of the chair. It was then that he noticed that Death Seed and the amulet that the Crystal Master had given him were both missing.

Joe slapped his clothes on quickly. He was still trying to pull on one of his boots when he emerged, hopping from the back of the caravan, stumbling down the three steps but never entirely losing his balance. The clatter had caught the attention of the entire group gathered around the large bonfire. Even the musicians had stopped.

Joe was still in the middle of composing himself and straightening his jacket when he noticed that all eyes were upon him. He paused momentarily and then righted himself, taking on the air of having just called together an important meeting.

"Good, right, so, which of you has my sword and my necklace?"

The man with the pipe stood up from his seat around the fire. He had

Death Seed in his hand. "So the sword is yours, is it?" Smoke puffed out of his mouth in billowing clouds as he spoke. He began walking over to Joe. "Seems to me that there has been some zeshian dandy running about with a sword just like this beauty."

"Let's not be rude to our guest now." came a familiar feminine voice from among those still sitting around the fire. Though she had her back to Joe, he picked her out of the group immediately. Where everyone else had hair black as a raven's feather, this woman's hair was a dazzle of red, orange, and blonde, as fiery as the flames that now illuminated it. "Introductions should be made." Then she stood and turned around. Her features were again cast in shadow, but the silhouette of her body in the yellow glow of the bonfire more than hinted at her potential beauty.

"Of course, m'arm, t'was rude of me. Would you be so kind as to do the honors?" The man with the pipe bowed low to the woman in an exaggerated manner, and his overly polite tone made it clear that he was not one to normally regard social etiquette.

"Come, stranger, step into the circle so that we may all be known to you and you to us." The woman motioned for Joe to step into the circle, and a couple of the men shuffled themselves over on their makeshift log bench to make room for him.

Joe hesitated for a moment but then realized that if they meant him any actual harm, they could have done him in while he was unconscious. He cleared his throat. "Sounds good," He said. As he walked past the man with the pipe holding Death Seed, Joe paused slightly and muttered, "But I still want my sword. The man chuckled slightly, pulling the sword behind his back, making it clear that the sword would be staying with him for just a little longer. Joe frowned at him and kept staring at the man even as they both continued on to the fire to take their seats.

Once they were settled, the red-haired woman, standing directly behind Joe, spoke again. "Since you're already making friends, let's start with you." She put a hand on each of Joe's shoulders, giving them a gentle pat to let him know she was speaking to him.

Joe craned his neck back and forth, trying to get a look at her, but her face was always just out of view. He looked around the group. All of them were men, save for the old woman who had saved him from the puffballs with her horn. They were all in the same colorful but worn-out clothing. He puffed himself up a bit and then leaned forward. All eyes were on him. His right hand went to one of his knives in a blur of movement, and in an instant, it was spinning on the tip of his index finger, a dazzling spectacle in the firelight.

"They call me Screamin' Joe Blade." He said with a well-practiced swagger.

"Never heard of ya." responded an extremely obese man with short-cropped hair and a huge, curling mustache. "They call me Big Tom, and not because of my belly," he said, giving his enormous harlequin-clad belly a hardy slap that made the entire mass shake and jiggle.

"Nah, it's because of that fat head of yours," said the man with the pipe. The entire circle, save Big Tom, burst into laughter. Joe sheathed his knife and chuckled too, though nervously, unsure if it was quite his place to do so yet or if it was particularly wise to poke fun at someone so large.

"Quiet, you lot!" barked the old woman, standing. "The stranger – Joe," she corrected herself with a nod to Joe, "don't care who you mangy bunch o' brookshins are." She wagged her finger around the circle. "The only name you need concern yourself with, lad, is ol' Moiren." as she said her name, she swayed her hips, running one hand seductively down her torso while the other flirtatiously tossed the tangle of grey hairs on her head. Although her ancient face made the spectacle off-putting, Joe could not help but think that she must have been the cause of many a bar fight back in her day and was probably still far more than any man her age would be capable of handling.

"Emphasis on OLD," added the man smoking the pipe.

Moiren waved her hands dismissively at the old fellow. "Still too much for your old thumper, Vokar." Again, the group broke into laughter, and Vokar gave a slight nod and salute with his pipe that suggested he didn't disagree. Joe could hear the woman behind him giggle quietly to herself.

The introductions continued more rapidly then. Some stood as they said their names, but most just raised a mug, or drinking horn, or whatever random object they were drinking from, as they stated their name; Tulex, Velunsk, Korsan, two men each of the name Zolfung, Buleg, Kritsolf, Rudenz, Miromol, Petrux, Tomars, Billanov, Cormot, Klumid, Dombler, Fiff, Gregor, Bartalox; and there were the four musicians, Nooch on the bone pipe, Freshnir on the drum, Pox on the squeezebox, and Pronz on the fiddle.

With all but one of the introductions made, Vokar clapped his hands loudly twice, bringing the group, that had grown rowdier and louder with each name, to silence. "Well, go on, "he plucked the pipe from his mouth, pointing it at the woman still standing behind Joe. "Your turn, girl."

She stepped around Joe into the light of the bonfire. The forest itself seemed to have gone silent then, and the crackle of the fire seemed to fade somewhere into the distance. Joe still wasn't able to catch a glimpse of her face behind the luxurious mane of fiery curls as she passed by. Her hair almost seemed to writhe with a life of its own as the air currents generated by the bonfire's heat played through her locks. There was a gravity to her, as though the air, earth, the tiny whirling embers, even the light from the fire, everything around her was part of some subtle fluid dance that was her every alluring step. Her body was undeniably captivating. She was curved in nearly exaggerated feminine proportions. It was not that her hips were overly large, but that her waist was tiny enough that if an average-sized man were to hold her by the waist, his thumbs and fingertips would touch. It was also clear that, despite the enticing smoothness of her curves, she was not a soft woman of leisure. Where her flawless caramel skin was exposed from the side cuts in her short green v-shaped skirt or her bare midriff beneath the rough, yellow cotton blouse tied tight beneath her ample breasts, she was solidly toned. Her exquisite, slender muscles flexed and rippled with her every motion. She seemed an element of nature, flame and stone forged into a perfect animal of ferocious beauty. The Kodin priestesses of Midgorn would have called her an embodiment of the Guardian Flame of Havwen, but to Joe, far from being a spiritual man, she was just unbelievably hot. Reaching the far side of the fire from Joe, she turned around.

Joe's entire state of consciousness seemed to shift into another dimension, separated from anything physical. Her face was radiantly beautiful with eyes like smoldering golden embers, drinking in the firelight and lips whose delicate, seductive shapes matched the sensual curves of her body.

It seemed to Joe that the surrounding forest, the group of people around the bonfire, all the world, save for her face, framed in dazzling flame, had momentarily ceased to exist. He was fully mesmerized and found he was unable to draw a breath, but somehow, that was okay, for breathing might disrupt this silent moment of perfection.

"I am Runara Tessep." She said, staring intensely into Joe's eyes across the undulating, flickering flames, a sultry demon goddess tempting him into the fire.

"Runara!" barked Moiren, breaking the spell of the moment. "You know better than to be giving out your house name! It is sacred. It is secret. How can you trust this stranger so quickly?"

"Well, we've all been introduced," Joe interjected, "and one, or more of you, has scrubbed goo off of my naked body, so I'd say we're anything but strangers now." Runara smiled a small, knowing, unashamed smile, giving Moiren a glance and a tiny defiant shrug of her shoulder.

"But the man looks to be from Westerlan. He may know of your family." Vokar grumped in support of Moiren. "You're likely the wisest of us all, but you don't think with the sense the wind blows through the flowers."

"Be I the wisest, and be the other true too, then I'll take your windless words for what they're worth, Vokar." Runara punctuated her words with a sharp little smile that quickly disappeared, letting Vokar know she hadn't appreciated his insult. Vokar rolled his eyes and gave his pipe a few puffs. Runara then motioned for the men behind her to move over to allow her to sit, which they quickly did.

"Look at his black hair, Vokar." She said as she sat. "He could be a brookshin himself."

Someone from the group then bellowed, "Brookshins!" The entire group took the cue, holding their drinks aloft and shouting the word back, followed by laughter and long swigs.

Nooch, Freshnir, Pox, and Prons, feeling the introductions done and the conversation dull, returned to their music, though at a hushed volume. Soon, all the conversations that Joe's presence had interrupted resumed where they had left off. One of the Zolfungs put a mug in Joe's hand. "Drink up, Screamin. You're lucky to be alive, and another day alive is another day of possibilities."

Vokar came over then, using Death Seed like a cane as he eased himself down onto the log. "Y'heard the man. Drink up, lad, you're alive another day, and that alone is enough to celebrate." Coker slapped Joe on his shoulder, distracting him from sniffing his drink.

"What? Oh, ya. Ya, lucky. Most days, luck's all I need." Joe shrugged.

"Fortunately, you lot came by while my luck was off having a piss." Now Zolfung was slapping him on the back laughing, holding his mug up in a toast to the jest, and throwing back an extra large swallow of his drink. Joe just smiled and nodded, holding up his drink but still hesitating to partake.

"Well, I'd say the only real luck was us hearing the spordikan stalking you," Vokar added, puffing a cloud of smoke around Joe as he spoke. "Ol' Chuckler tends to hunt down people more often than critters, and most times, before we manage to catch up, he's already had his way with his prey. Nothin' left for us most times than a few amusing trinkets." Vokar stared at Death Seed, turning it about slowly, watching the firelight glint off the gems embedded in the handguard. "We're scavengers, to be sure, but not so heartless as to stand by and watch a poor soke like yourself be eaten alive."

Joe leaned over, grabbing Death Seed with a bit of a jerk. "And I thank you for saving my stuff as well." His words were said with nothing but charm in his voice and a friendly smile, fully contrasting the message of annoyance in his quick grab. Vokar didn't resist in any way, immediately releasing the sword.

"I trust you have kept my necklace safe as well?" Joe was examining the sword. It looked freshly forged, just as before; not a notch or fold in the blade, not a scratch to be seen.

Vokar signaled to another member of the group nearby, who produced a rigid scabbard and handed it to Vokar.

"Here, you'll be wanting to keep that monster in a box." Vokar handed Joe the scabbard. "or you'll cut yer own head off tripping on a root out there. Made out of dried tarboc hide. Only thing that can contain a blade like that." The scabbard was nothing special to look at, just one solid length of hardened light brown leather. The seam's length had been decorated with a short black animal hair fringe. A similar animal hair also seemed to be the material used in the belt cord. It was clear to Joe, by its size and shape, that the scabbard had been custom-made to fit Death Seed. Such craftsmanship, and done so quickly, left Joe a little amazed. It was singularly the nicest thing anyone had ever given him, willingly.

Joe just gave Vokar a thankful nod. He wasn't used to people just giving him things of their own accord, so he wasn't entirely sure how to react.

"Where did a man of weapons happen upon a pendant of such a nature?"

Runara suddenly stood beside Joe. Joe hadn't seen her move from her spot across the fire, and her voice next to him made him jump a little. Zolfung got up, offering his spot to Runara, and wandered off, quickly joining the carousing of others nearby.

"Do you work for Nashtar?" she asked before Joe could answer her first question, sitting down as she spoke. She moved with the smooth grace of a cat.

"Nashtar? No, just learned of the man today, but as it turns out, I am looking for him, or at least—"Joe stopped himself, reconsidering just how much he wanted to tell these people. For all he knew, they were the minions of the wizard that Victor had mentioned.

"At least, what?" Vokar prodded with a puff of smoke.

"Nothin'; just want to talk to the man, is all." Joe was a horrible liar—he always had been. He was also fully unaware of his lack of talent as an equivocator, the knowledge of which would have found him playing cards far less frequently and substantially more wealthy, or at least less poor.

"I think you're after a little more than a chat." Vokar chuckled. "The way I see it, lad, you were hired to bump off that zeshian fella what owned that there sword. Talk has been in these parts that the wizard has been wanting the zeshian's weapon, but he's been havin' a hard time in the taking of it. Let me know if I'm off the mark with any of this." Joe just nodded his head somewhat self-consciously. He didn't want to come across as knowing as little as he did, but he didn't want to let on to anything Victor had told him either. The internal conflict was manifest in some rather awkward body language.

Runara could see right through it. He was no assassin, at least not hired by the wizard, but she couldn't figure out where he had acquired the crystal pendant. It radiated with an intense, invisible magical energy, more powerful than anything she had ever encountered. It had to be the work of Nashtar, but she perceived no sense of Nashtar's darkness from either the pendant or Joe.

Vokar simply accepted Joe's awkward nod and continued. "So the problem the wizard's been having is that the zeshian is the right hand of King Goms. As powerful a wizard as Nashtar is, he's wise enough not to underestimate the magic of an elf. Also, the zeshian is a fierce swordsman. He's never been known to lose a fight and never lets a man walk away with his ghost attached, if you get my meaning."

"Ya, well…" Joe puffed his chest out a little bit, his usual arrogant swagger back. He turned to look at Runara, expecting to bask in what must be piqued admiration but instead met with an unrestrained expression of unimpressed amusement. He tried not to let it deflate him, and he focused his attention back on Vokar. "Came away with a little more than my ghost, I'd say, if you know what I mean." He jabbed the sword into the ground next to him, holding it like it was some sort of grand scepter.

Vokar conceded a slight nod to Joe. "The wizard also fears Goms, himself." He continued.

"That's not entirely true," Runara corrected. "It's more that Goms doesn't fear Nashtar, at all, and that is enough to make Nashtar think twice about confronting him, at least in person."

"True, true girl. Either way, that, we figure, is where your lot comes in." Vokar pointed his pipe at Joe, blowing a little smoke ring at the end of his sentence. "We've seen Nashtar's hired goons and conjured monsters head off to the king's castle plenty of times, and many, I'd say, seemed far more of a fright than you, but not one has ever come back. 'Course, we didn't notice you on your way to the castle. Did the wizard fly you in? Teleport?"

"Does this necklace have something to do with how you got into the castle?" Runara was wearing the necklace and pulled the crystal out from beneath her blouse, where it had been hidden deep within her cleavage.

She had Joe's full attention now. "Um, the castle really isn't that hard to get into." Joe's voice trailed off as he stared at the crystal, which evolved into staring at Runara's breasts. With her index finger, she pulled his view up by his chin, back to her half-smiling, half-sneering face. It snapped him out of the spell and back into the conversation. "I only recently acquired the crystal, so, no, it didn't help me get into the castle, but I'm told it will help get me home." Joe offered truthfully.

"I told you, girl, he's no wizard," Vokar said gruffly. There was an odd, sullen moment then as Vokar and Runara exchanged stony looks.

"So…" Joe said uncomfortably, breaking up the awkward moment. "Ya, no, not a wizard. I'm not sure where that Solvar fella got his reputation, though. I've fought five-year-olds more dangerous." Joe wasn't exaggerating. Back in Midgorn, he had a run-in with a group of wolgar toddlers. The

Wolgar are a race of very large, very ugly, and very strong people. A five-year-old wolgar is generally taller than the average adult human. Joe had stumbled upon what was essentially a wolgar preschool and made the mistake of trying to take away one of the children's toys; a solid gold skull. The result had been Joe nearly losing his own and going through a rather emotionally and physically scarring apology session with one of the mothers. "And you've called Solvar both a zeshian and an elf. Elf, I know, what's a zeshian?" Joe questioned Vokar.

"You must be from Westerlan." Vokar chuckled. "Elves in Senuvia call themselves the Zesh, and no human with any sense goes wandering into the land of Gizesh, to the north, without an invitation; not Nashtar, not even Goms Ethdab."

"Yes, but with Solvar being a welcome member of Goms's court, an alliance between the elves and him can't be far off if it hasn't already been established," Runara added, then put a hand on Joe's shoulder to gather his attention more fully. "Respect for the power of the elves is all that keeps King Goms from setting his troops out to take your Westerlan, and Gizesh is the only portion of Senuvia, aside from Estobrex, that Goms hasn't conquered."

Joe smiled. "Lots of elves in Westerlan, then? Well, don't you worry your pretty little head about my lands. I'm not from Westerlan, and as long as I have this here sword, from what I'm told, Goms won't be getting to where I'm from." He rested his hand on her bare knee as he said this, thinking it was an appropriate reciprocation of the physical contact she had initiated a moment earlier. Instead, she returned a frown and shuffled her knees aside, out of his reach. Joe just kept talking. "So why do you lot care so much about whose lands this king takes or who he's allied with? Doesn't it benefit your people the more successful he is?"

Vokar sputtered at this, which quickly evolved into a coughing fit. Then Joe became aware that the entire circle around the fire had again gone silent and was looking at him.

"You must be from far off indeed, m'boy, if y'be thinking we share any love for the likes of Goms." Moiren spat her words harshly through gritted teeth, her fists clenched at her sides. Kritsolf and Petrux were actually holding her back.

Runara then, her own voice agitated but much calmer, leaned into Joe, speaking softly. "The people that now occupy this land may call us, and the few other small bands like us, 'brookshins,' but we were once the true inhabitants of North Eastworld. Moiren's grandfather ruled this land."

"And a kinder ruler there never was," Vokar added, contemplatively staring into the fire. "And the elves were our friends then. Our people share the elven love of nature, more comfortable out here in the forest than in any castle."

"Aye, they may not call us friend now, but no elf but the king's lap dog would dishonor themselves by harming a brookshin," piped up Cormut from across the fire.

"To be shar Cormut, and soon 'nuf y'll be pickin' flowers in the zeshian pleasure field, whisperin' sweetness in the elf queen's pointed li'l ears," jested Tomars making a rather lewd gesture with his crotch that implied more than innocent courting or flower picking would be going on with the elf queen. The bits of laughter from the group broke the somber tension that was becoming terribly uncomfortable for Joe. Again, the music started, and the interrupted conversations and carousing resumed. Moiren was still looking menacingly at Joe, though others around her were trying to distract her.

"Don't mind her; she's always been a bit of a thistle." Vokar patted Joe on the back. "But, we've yet to hear your story, lad. Are you one of Nashtar's men or not?"

Moiren's glare was making Joe uncomfortable, and the conversation wasn't getting him anywhere. He needed his necklace from Runara, and he needed to know the way to Nashtar's castle. It was time for him to take control of his circumstances with his particular brand of Screamin' Joe Blade charm. He responded to Vokar in a loud voice dripping with attitude.

"Look, I don't want to shake your snake basket. Seems you lot got a raw deal with this Goms fella, but for all I know, your granddaddies were assholes and not the delightful booze-swilling do-gooders that your time here in the forest has obviously made the lot of you." Again, the music and conversation stopped. Joe had expected it this time, had anticipated it, and stood up now that he had the group's attention once more. "Don't get me wrong, I'd love to just take some time and hang with all o' you for a while, blowing horns, chasing away fur balls, and whining about how mean the pasty-faced king is, but I plan on getting back to my world and to do that I'm going to need that necklace," he pointed Deathseed at Runara, "and a guide to the big, bad wizard's house." The entire group just stared at him. Some looked angry, some skeptically interested, some amused, others just blankly drooled. Big Tom was just engrossed in the contents of his mug, staring into it, taking another drink, and then staring at it some more.

Vokar spoke then. "What do ya want with Nashtar if you're not one of his hirelings? It's not like that old wizard is just going to help you out of the kindness of his hard, black, shriveled heart."

"It's the necklace," Runara answered before Joe could speak. "He means to give the necklace to the wizard as payment. I think it would be a mistake." She had a dark, troubled look on her face.

"Listen to me!" Joe first shouted, then paused, rethinking his tactics, and started again softer. "Listen to me. I'm not giving the wizard anything. I need something from him, a sword, and I need my necklace."

"And just how are you going to get this sword you're after from a wizard the likes of Nashtar? Going to storm the castle all by yourself, lad?" Vokar's tone had grown gruff. "If it were that easy, Goms would have kicked his door in long ago."

"I have a plan, but I'll need a few men to help me, and I promise them all of any plunder to be had, except for the wizard's sword, naturally. It's the only thing I'm after."

Moiren spoke then, venom in her voice, "Nashtar is a bushel of thorns fer Ethdab, always has been, but leaves us brookshins be, mostly. You'll have a hard time finding a brookshin willing to risk his life fer somethin' that might make life easier fer the king. I'm already regrettin' that we saved your hide from Ol' Chuckler. Take yer damned necklace and get out of my camp. Aint no brookshins here gonna follow you on yer dead man's errand." She spat then into the fire in Joe's direction, shooting Runara a sharp look as she did.

Runara stood up, taking off the necklace and placing it around Joe's neck. She held the red crystal pendant for a moment, trying one last time to make sense of its strange energy. She didn't say a word, but the look on her face—her beautiful, enchanting face—told Joe that his brashness had been foolish and that she didn't want him to go to Nashtar, at least, not alone.

"Sorry, lad," Vokar said, puffing on his pipe. "Nothin' to be done for it. Moiren wants you gone. You best be on your way. He touched the side of his nose and pointed in a direction just over Joe's shoulder. Joe understood that he was pointing in the direction of Nashtar's castle. "Best of luck with your plans, boy. You'll want to find yerself a boat, passage on one leastways, in the city of Loncodi."

"Real nice way to make friends," Joe said, annoyed, rotating to address the entire group. "And thanks for saving my life. The women of Modnar and Midgorn will be very grateful." He took a final swig from his mug before handing it to Vokar, to whom he gave a respectful nod. He turned back to Runara, giving her an overly polite bow and taking one last long lingering look to burn the image of her firmly into his memory. Finally, he turned to Moiren, bowing deeply and adding a sarcastic "By your leave, Majesty" as he did so.

Again, Moiren spat into the fire in disgust, waving impatiently for him to be on his way already. With that, Joe straightened himself proudly and left, pointing and nodding to various individuals as he went as though they were long friends or fans, generating bemused looks in response. Eventually, he disappeared into the darkness of the woods, and the group returned to their carousing

Deep among the trees, on the other side of the camp, two shadowed figures eased themselves away further into the darkness. Nobody in the camp noticed, too distracted with their carousing. So distracting was their revelry that they and the two shadowy figures also failed to notice a third, dark, hulking figure lurking in the dancing shadows cast by the camp's firelight. It continued to linger, watching all, just a few feet from where the other two shadows had been.

Chapter 8

Joe had been walking through the dark woods for five minutes before coming to a large grassy clearing. The grass here seemed to glow a bright grey, but it was the illumination from above. In Midgorn, when the ceiling crystals go dark at night, the darkness is absolute. Were there no street lamps or, as in some of the smaller communities without such amenities, if you didn't have your own candle, lamp, or torch, the night meant darkness so complete that one couldn't see their own hand held just an inch in front of one's face. Here though, on Modnar, the night had a grey-blue illumination. He found this puzzling until he looked up. He was so dazzled by the spectacle of the Modnarian night sky that he tripped and fell.

He lay there on his back, drinking in the wondrous beauty of it. The entire sky was lit up with an uncountable number of tiny little lights, as though someone had spilled a bag of luminous flour across the sky. One of the little dots of light streaked across his line of sight and winked out. It was all so alive. That would have been enough, Joe thought, to light the way, but there was more.

Three other huge lights hung in the sky. The first of these objects hung low on the western horizon, just above the trees. It was a slightly yellow color, with dark patches scattered across it. It seemed to Joe, given its size, that this must be the dimmed form of the light that hangs in the sky during the day. The second was larger, hanging fairly high in the southern sky. It was sickle-shaped and a deep red, the color of blood, Joe thought. Its surface was covered in dark patches and circles like the much smaller yellow one. The third was in close proximity to the second but further to the east. It was about twice the size of the first but still less than half the size of the second. It was a brilliant turquoise color; its entire surface twinkled and shimmered as though it were covered in diamonds. Joe thought it was the most beautiful thing he had ever seen, next to Runara.

The thought of Runara made him regret the way things had gone with the group of brookshins. He was used to not making friends, to always moving on, but he thought it might have been better to have a little more time around Runara.

He heard someone shouting in the distance then, echoing through the empty night of the forest. Then, more voices came, louder and growing louder still, followed by the unmistakable clatter of battle and then a piercing horn. By the time the horn blew, Joe was already running back to the camp. Then came the screams.

* * * * * * * * * * * * * * * * *

Runara had decided to turn in for the night immediately after Joe disappeared into the forest. She gave Uncle Vokar a kiss on the forehead as she went. Her thoughts were filled with Joe, wishing he had been able to stay, but with him falling out of favor so quickly with Moiren, that just wouldn't have been possible. She couldn't help but think about the crystal, too. Such a strange magic it had, and in the short time that she had worn it, the crystal touching her skin had affected her physically somehow. Her body was tingling from head to toe. It had her more than a little concerned, and she decided that a cup of healing tea would be wise before bed.

She had been inside her caravan for no more than a few minutes. The pot of water she had put on the tiny one-burner wood stove in the corner of the room by the door had just begun to boil when a commotion came from outside. At first, she assumed it was the usual night's carousing getting a little out of hand, but the voices now were shouts of anger, not drunken jubilance. She was about to go back outside to break up whatever nonsense the men were up to when the clatter of weaponry started. Then she knew that there had to be outsiders involved, bandits likely. Brookshins never draw weapons on one another. If a dispute needs to be settled between two brookshins, it is done with fists if a large log and a lake are not handy.

She looked about her room, frantic for a weapon of some sort. Suddenly, a symbol flashed through her mind, or had it been floating a few feet before her face. She couldn't tell for sure, but its image was burned into her memory. The symbol was made of four thin concentric circles with a large dark circle in the middle, resembling a flower, with eight tiny rectangular petals, and between those petals, long forked spearhead-like projections pointing inward. At the center of the dark circle were two more symbols, like letters perhaps, that she did not recognize. Runara didn't have time to contemplate it, still needing a weapon, but all she had was a large cooking knife. She lunged for it and spun around just as her door burst in. A burly man in black armor, his head wrapped in red silk, stood in the door. He was brandishing a large curved sword.

"No!" was all she managed in her panic, thrusting the knife out in front of her.

A billowing ball of fire burst from the knife, hitting the armored intruder with the force of a charging bull, throwing him back outside and turning his head into a torch as the silk wrapping caught fire. The knife made a horrible squealing sound, glowing bright white with heat, and then shattered. A flying shard sliced a deep, instantly cauterized gash in her left cheek.

The sounds of the fight flooded in from outside. Amongst the commotion, the man she had flung from her caravan screamed for a moment as his flesh burned away from his skull. Runara didn't have any time to contemplate where the fireball had come from; she was no sorceress. Other such men would be coming any second, she feared, and the fireball had caught her caravan on fire as well. She quickly grabbed a satchel and flung the strap over her head and across her chest. It was her healing bag. There was so much more she wanted to save, but there was no time. The fire was already up the walls of the dry little wooden caravan.

She ran out the door, leaping from the caravan over the body of the soldier that she had somehow blasted out. His head was a black smoking char, but this passed her notice as she was too horrified by the spectacle over by the bonfire. There, more than half of her band of brookshins lay slaughtered, many of them horribly dismembered by the small band of sword and ax-wielding armored men. There had been ten soldiers; there were seven now and ten brookshins.

Vokar, brandishing a small handaxe with blindingly fast skill, was parrying the increasingly labored sword swings of a particularly large soldier.

His ax, however, simply didn't have the reach to get in a strike of his own. Out of the corner of his eye, he saw Runara burst from the flaming caravan. His heart skipped a beat with joy at her still being alive, and he could not help but look to see for certain that she was okay. That tiny moment of distraction was enough to let the soldier swing through Vokar's defenses. The monstrous blade cleaved Vokar nearly in two from his left shoulder to the middle of his abdomen.

Runara had seen the whole horrible moment. All rational thought left her then; there was no stifling the screams that burst from her throat.

* * * * * * * * * * * * * * * * *

Screamin' Joe Blade's Ten-Point Guide to Life:
Point #4: Never walk into a fight.

Screamin' Joe Blade literally dove into the battle, his battle cry seeming to fill the forest. He had sprung himself off a stump at the edge of the camp and dove, headlong, Death Seed thrust ahead of him, at an enormous armored man, well over six feet tall and nearly three hundred pounds. The man was relentlessly bashing his sword against the defensive blocks of Big Tom's large, rough wooden club. Chips of wood flew off of it with every blow.

Death Seed sunk into the man as though he hadn't been wearing armor and was made of nothing more solid than wet mud, slicing through flesh and bone with the same ease. Joe's momentum knocked the man over, taking Joe, hanging on to Death Seed, with him, flinging Joe like a catapult as the soldier crashed to the ground dead. Joe flipped in the air, Death Seed sliding out of its victim, leaving an enormous gash as it came out both in the man and his armor. As he came down, Screamin' Joe flung three daggers at another armored man in his path. Two of the daggers bounced harmlessly off the man's armor, but one found a space near the man's right elbow, causing the man to wail in pain and interrupting what would have been a deathly blow on Tomars. Landing, Joe made a sweeping slash with Death Seed, taking off the same arm at the shoulder he had just hit with the dagger. The armored man staggered back, spinning in shock, blood spraying everywhere. Joe spun around; Death Seed took off the man's head.

Tomars, now free from his own opponent, rushed to help Billanov and Klumid finish off a soldier who was struggling but managing to fend the two of them off. Billanov and Klumid each had swords, and Tomars, having taken the sword from the fallen guard, now had one as well. The sword was immensely heavy, however, and Tomars was having an awkward time with it. He found it so heavy and clumsy that his swing at the soldier, as he ran over, went in a steeply downward sloping arc. He had intended to take the man's head off. Instead, he sliced through the man's right Achilles tendon. Screaming in pain, the man lost his balance as his ankle went over. Instinctively, he tried to catch himself from falling with the same leg. He came down hard on his ankle, and a distinctive loud crack indicated that some portion of his leg had now broken. At that same moment, Klumid lopped off the man's arm just above his left gauntlet while Billanov thrust his sword into the man's throat, stifling his cry of anguish from his various, near-simultaneous injuries.

Joe, meanwhile, spun around to see that Tulex and Zolfung were just managing to fend off a soldier who was wielding a sword with amazing speed. Buleg and Gregor were managing to evade two others, tumbling about and dodging their every swing, and with every swing, the two soldiers grew wearier. Buleg's evasive tumbles brought his opponent in the proximity of the soldier that Tulex and Zolfung were confronting just as Joe leaped in, sweeping Death Seed down on Tulex and Zolfung's foe. The soldier's reflexes were unbelievably fast, and in one smooth, multiple arcing sweep, sliced Zolfung's inner thigh and not only blocked the assault from Death Seed but also wrenched it from Joe's grasp, sending it flying. Joe managed to jump aside just in time to avoid being gutted by the man.

Buleg happened to be ducking the ever-slowing swing of his opponent just as Death Seed flew over, missing the top of his head by less than an inch. It shot through the soldier's shiny black armor like a projected missile, the blade bursting out of his back and throwing the man back against a nearby tree as the handguard hit his chest. Death Seed sunk easily into the wood, pinning the man's lifeless body upright, blood flowing out from beneath his armor.

Buleg whipped around to see Joe rolling out of the way of the speedy soldier's deadly swing and Zolfung collapsing, screaming and clutching at his leg as blood flowed from it at an unstoppable rate. Joe let fly a dagger as he rolled, catching the soldier in a gap in his armor just above his right knee. The pain stunned the soldier just for a moment, but it was enough, and both Buleg and Tulex tackled the man. Tulex bashed the man's helmeted head against the ground repeatedly while Buleg took the man's sword, telling Tulex to jump aside as he finished the man off.

Joe managed to gather up the two daggers deflected by one of the other soldiers' armor moments before. Things seemed to have calmed somewhat. Big Tom, Tomars, Bartalox, Gregor, Klumid, and Billanov had managed to form a circle around the remaining three soldiers. The three men had their backs to one another, constantly testing the circle with small jabs and swipes. Neither they nor the remaining brookshins surrounding them seemed to want to take the risk of striking out. It was something of a standoff. Joe took the moment to quickly retrieve his two remaining daggers, though he had to look for a moment extra to locate the one lodged in the dismembered arm.

One of the soldiers spoke out, "We have no quarrel with you; we came for him." He pointed at Joe.

Through gritted teeth, Billanov growled back. "Look around, spade. Trust me, there's a quarrel."

Bartalox whispered fairly loudly then, as though it might keep the soldiers, or Joe, from hearing. "We should just kill them and the stranger."

Joe felt compelled to jump into the conversation at that point as he pulled Death Seed out of the soldier pinned to the tree. "Um, not a stranger; we were all fully introduced, Curly Locks, was it?"

Runara's sobs washed over the group then. She was sprawled across her uncle's body, crying uncontrollably.

It was more than Billanov could take, and his rage finally spilled over. He lunged at one of the soldiers, leading with a sword he had taken from another soldier. The whole group then attacked. The clash was over the same instant it began. Billanov was dead, but so were the three soldiers, each having taken a deadly sword blow.

Suddenly, a wave of force, something physical, large, and as hard as a metal battering ram, crashed into the group of the remaining seven brookshin men. An earthshaking boom, like the crack of thunder, exploded in the midst of the campsite and a gust of air all but blew out the large campfire. Klumid,

Tulex, and Buleg had been struck by the object's full force and were sent flying to their death, breaking necks, spines, skulls, and ribs as their bodies were dashed against nearby trees or rocks. The other four were also sent sprawling but were mostly unharmed.

A chrome-skinned horse, eyes glowing a deep red, stood among them now. The creature was enormous, like a large workhorse, with a build somewhere between that and a racing steed. One of the dead soldiers lay beneath one of its massive hooves, a hoof that looked as though it were made from a large chunk of brushed steel. The dead soldier's torso, at the right shoulder, was utterly flattened beneath the beast's weight. Upon the chrome horse, clad in gold, scaled armor, skin as pale and stony as white marble, sat the King, Goms Ethdab. He was staring directly at Joe.

"Give me the sword, boy, or shall I have the entire forest killed for it?" Gom's deep voice seemed to echo through the whole forest.

"Wasn't yours," Joe said with great flippancy. "Belonged to that danuwan fella. You know, the elf, or what do you call 'em? The zeshian."

"And he's paid the price for his incompetence in keeping it for me," Goms replied coldly.

"Give him the sword," grunted Bartalox, with rage and weariness in his voice. He was glaring at Goms but shot an equally hateful glance at Joe as he spoke.

"Not gonna happen. What d'ya say we take back your people's land instead." Joe offered. He casually flipped Death Seed end over end in his right hand, taking a few steps towards Goms and his steed."

"Be the shortest revolution in history." came Big Tom, huffing for breath between words. He stepped up alongside Joe, his badly chipped-up club over his shoulder.

"Ya, come get some of what we gave yer spades, ya filthy twacker," added Gregor, and now he was alongside Big Tom. Tomars joined them, saying nothing but exchanging a knock of fists with Gregor. They all took a step toward Goms and his steed.

The chromed-skinned horse shuffled anxiously, further trampling and crushing the bodies of the soldiers beneath it. The sounds of the compacting armor, breaking bones, and sucking, blood-soaked flesh-mush was sickening. Steam shot from the horse's flaring nostrils as it rocked its head up and down.

Goms firmly held the heavy, polished, iron chain link reins and leaned back casually in his war saddle.

"Steady, Tyrant," he commanded the horse, and Tyrant calmed. "I'll ask only this one last time, boy. Give me the sword, or you, and what's left of these pathetic," he searched for the word "brookshins, will die." The disdain in his voice was heavy.

"No!" Runara shouted, her voice hoarse and cracking from crying. She was on her feet now, and her body shook with anger and hatred. "You will not have the sword." Her hair began to rise of its own accord as though a strong breeze blew directly up from her shoulders. "You will die!" she screamed with an impossible volume. A wave of force blasted out before her. Bodies of brookshins and soldiers alike blew aside from the force, hitting the King and his horse. Before either could react, Goms was thrown from Tyrant while the horse, nearly unaffected by the blast, was compelled to take a slight step sideways to maintain its balance.

The remaining men, quickly recovering from their amazement, rushed at Goms, even Bartalox. Joe was still staring at Runara. She looked as though she were going to collapse, her eyes rolling back into her head. He bolted to her side just in time to catch and ease her to the ground.

Tyrant, meanwhile, charged at the on-rushing band of brookshins, lowering its head. Its metal skull hit Big Tom hard, breaking both Tom's nose and his jaw and sending the large man sprawling, mind-numbing pain radiating from his face. The other men dodged past the beast, descending on the fallen King.

Unharmed by his fall from Tyrant, Goms rolled back away from the men, landing on his feet in a crouched position. It afforded him an extra second or two before they could reach him. He held his right hand out to the side in a fist, and a glowing green blade appeared out of nowhere, seemingly bonded to his hand by a crackling green field of energy. Tomars, wielding the sword he had taken from the soldier earlier, swung the large, curved weapon down hard. Goms blocked the slow attack easily with the ghostly green weapon that weighed nothing. A cluster of vines was now swirling up Goms's arm, growing at a lightning pace, forming thorns and small leaves. He knocked Tomars's sword aside, taking Tomars's arm off with one smooth movement.

The screams of Big Tom came then, mixing with Tomars's, first as Tyrant crushed Tom's legs with his massive hooves and again, a half second later, as he bit into Tom's massive belly, rending fabric, flesh, and fat. Joe reacted to it all, launching a flurry of four daggers all at once with only his left hand, his right arm still cradling Runara, Death Seed in his right hand. Two daggers flew in the direction of Tyrant, bouncing off the creature's skin with loud metallic clatters. The other two shot towards Goms, who was already, save for part of his left leg, covered in an armor of vines and thorns. One dagger sank deep into the King's chest, the other into his left hip. He reacted to neither.

Goms stood up then, entirely covered in the armor generated by his green powersword, blocking the attacks of Gregor and Bartalox, knocking the two men aside. Tomars staggered back, still screaming, clutching at the stump where his arm used to be. There was no blood; the wound was fully cauterized. Goms swung the glowing blade at Tomars again, but Gregor grabbed the King's arm. Holding back what would have been a deadly blow. Goms Grabbed Gregor's arm in turn and flipped the man over his shoulder. At that moment, Bartalox stabbed Goms with the long dagger that he had been wielding throughout the confrontation. Unlike Joe's knives, the King seemed to feel the bite of the blade in his back, and he swung around swiftly, cleaving Bartalox in two at the chest and taking off one of the man's arms in the process. Horrified but keeping it together, Joe let go of Runara as he let his last two knives fly. Both found their mark in Goms's chest, but the King did not react to their impact like the two before. Instead, he spun back around to Tomars, swinging his glowing sword in a deadly high arc. Tomars reflexively tried to block the attack with his remaining arm, but the blade simply sliced through it, continued through his skull, and got halfway through his torso when suddenly his body exploded in a burst of bright green light. Tiny green embers flitted about everywhere. They were all that remained of Tomars.

It was far too late for Big Tom as well, who had gone silent with death, his innards being flung about by Tyrant in hideous arcs of blood and bloody clumps.

Joe stood then as Goms turned slowly toward him, plucking out Joe's throwing knives with his free left hand, tossing them aside to the ground. New growth quickly filled in the gashes to the armor that Joe's knives had left.

"The sword, boy, and I think I'll have a use for the girl now too." Goms's voice was cold and calm but somewhat muffled beneath the tangle of vines that completely covered his head.

"What was that?" Joe asked mockingly with a hand to his ear. "You'll have to speak up. It sounded like you just asked for the sword again. You specifically said that you weren't going to." Joe's demeanor was smug and far calmer than Goms would have expected; it was even a little calmer than Joe had actually expected. Joe gave Death Seed a little swish before him and assumed a defensive stance.

Growling then in frustration, Goms took long, aggressive strides towards Joe, nearly running like someone about to kick a ball. Joe's left hand went instinctively to his bandolier, but there were no throwing knives left, and then Goms was on him, the glowing green sword coming down fast. Joe blocked the assault with Death Seed, which, to Joe's surprise, actually stopped the King's magical blade of light. He wasn't, however, fast enough to block Gom's fist, which caught him square in the chest. The hit staggered Joe back and winded him. The green blade came at him again and again, and though Joe managed to parry each attack, it was becoming increasingly difficult, and he wasn't finding a moment to literally catch his breath. He was going to pass out again, and he noted to whatever divine powers might be listening that he had quite enough of blacking out.

There was a large popping sound then, followed in rapid succession by three similar but slightly deeper and more hollow pops. Goms flew sideways with a muffled grunt, much to Joe's confusion, leaving Bartalox's dagger, which had remained in Goms's back, tumbling to the ground. It gave Joe the moment he needed to finally suck in a deep breath of air as he stumbled down onto one knee.

Tyrant was now making a horrendous noise. Its angry, ear-piercing whinnies were a mix of the sound of tumbling boulders and metal scraping on metal. Both of its back hooves and one of its front hooves were covered in putrid yellow, foamy goo that was rapidly expanding. The more it struggled against the sticky stuff, the more entangled the horse became. Soon, its struggles caught up its previously free front hoof, and then it made the mistake of trying to nip at the goo on its front hooves with its sharp, rust-colored teeth. Its snout was then stuck to the expanding goo as well.

Some sort of net propelled through the air by four spear-like bolts had initially hit Goms. The force of the net hitting him had thrown him off his feet and against a nearby tree, pinning him to it as the net wrapped around the tree. The fine, translucent mesh of the net had given way immediately around the powersword, simply dissolving where it touched the glowing green spirit blade. It left Goms's sword arm free. He was about to cut himself free when the second impact came. A ball of goo, identical to the sticky globs that had hit his steed, struck him in the right shoulder, partially sticking to the tree as well. It quickly expanded up his arm, across his chest, and entirely up his neck. Between the net and goo, there was nothing Goms could do. He was completely immobile.

Having finally caught his breath, Joe looked in the direction that the restraining projectiles had come, holding Death Seed before him to slice through anything that might come hurtling his way. Nothing came, but Joe could make out a hulking shadow on the edge of the firelight among the trees and bushes. He knew that shape. It wasn't of this world but from Joe's world, Midgorn. Joe was one of the few people from Midgorn still alive who could claim to have seen the shape before. It was a mander, and seeing it here meant his ability to claim he had seen a mander and lived was probably about to be revoked.

Joe scanned the ground for the dagger that had just fallen from the King's back. Scooping it up, he quickly looked about but could not see any of his own knives. Two, he quickly remembered, were still in Goms. Joe spun around, dove, and rolled, coming up right in front of Goms, pulling the two knives from the King, who continued to strain against the goo and the net. He wheeled around again, ready to throw the knives at the silhouette. The entire move had happened in the blink of an eye, but by the time he turned around, the silhouette was gone.

Something rustled in the leaves above. Joe's instincts had told him to dodge to the side, but, as was often the case, his curiosity won out, and he found himself looking up to see what it was instead. He turned his face skyward just in time to have a mander sleeping sac, a round, porous, leather pouch full of several strange swamp herbs mixed together and ground to a fine powder, hit him full in the face. Royal blue powder puffed in a cloud around his head as the sac rolled off his face, dropping to the ground, creating another blue cloud as it hit the ground.

"Yup, thought so," Joe said solemnly to himself. As he drifted into blackness yet again, he wondered where one had to go to lodge a complaint against the local divine powers.

Chapter 9

Screamin' Joe Blade woke to the sensation of his face repeatedly smacking against a brown furry surface that smelled of rotting turnips. He tried to right himself, but it quickly became apparent that his hands were tied behind his back. His feet, as far as he could ascertain, were bound as well from his ankles to nearly as high as his knees by the feel of it. He was draped facedown across the back of some sort of beast. From what he could see of the ground scrolling below him from his left, he appeared to be traveling along some sort of gravel road. The stones of the road were starkly white. It was a very bright day, he thought. He looked to his left, expecting to see the head of the creature. There was nothing. He looked to his right; still nothing. Despite this creature's apparent lack of a head, the most surprising thing that struck him just then was that he was still alive.

"Hello? Helloooo? Can we pull over? I gotta piss." Joe wasn't lying. He had suddenly become acutely aware of his uncomfortably full bladder, which he was finding harder and harder to contain with every step of the whatever-it-was that he was on.

"Hey, what the hell is this thing? Where's its head?" he shouted. "Hello?"

"They're bailodants," Runara's voice came from a direction somewhere over his right shoulder. Her tone was quiet and sullen.

"Bailodants huh? Well, this Bailodant is going to be smelling like piss any moment now."

The beast suddenly came to a halt, and Joe felt a massive hand grab him by his jacket, hoisting him up and off of the bailodant.

"It might be an improvement on their smell." The voice of the person pulling him down from the bailodant was deep with a ratcheted rasp. Joe's blood ran cold as he suddenly remembered his predicament just before being knocked out. He felt the twine that bound his wrists give, and then two large hands grabbed him by the shoulders and spun him around. It was, as he had feared, a mander.

Though he had been to the heart of their hidden city, he had never had the opportunity to get such a close look. If he had, it was likely he wouldn't still be alive, and he was pretty sure his life expectancy was presently growing shorter and shorter.

The mander had an incredibly intimidating presence. He was huge. Height-wise, he wasn't much taller than Joe, just a little under six feet, but he was wide. From shoulder to shoulder, the mander was three times the width of Joe and all muscle. His torso was long, and his powerful legs were disproportionately short, with broad, flat feet and four toes on each foot. In contrast to his legs, his arms, each nearly as big around as Joe's body, were disproportionately long, his fingertips almost reaching his ankles without bending over. His hands, like his feet, had four digits each; two out of the four digits on each end were opposable thumbs. Its hands were nearly big enough to wrap entirely around Joe's head.

"Why haven't you killed me, or her, yet?" Joe questioned as the mander cut Joe's legs loose with what appeared to be one of Joe's own throwing knives. The mander didn't answer. "Just seems odd that you got all dressed up for a hunt just to take us sightseeing."

The mander was dressed for a hunt, but that's just how manders dress. He wore a long, sleeveless vest, belted at the waist, and his pants ended in tatters at the knee. He wore nothing on his feet. The vest and pants were made of various soft leathers differing in color from a substantial number of previous prey, pieced together, forming something of a camouflage pattern. His shoulders were covered by a large, black leather, hooded cowl. Presently, he wasn't wearing the hood. Among the pieces of leather that made up the cowl, Joe could make out the stitched-closed features of a stretched-out, flattened human face on the mander's left shoulder. Belts and straps crisscrossing the mander's whole body held utility pouches, weapons, tools, and contraptions that Joe couldn't identify. The mander was a walking arsenal. It made Joe feel terribly inadequate with his empty bandolier.

The mander's skin was a smooth, shiny, mottled, deep green, and black. His head was wide and flat like a frog's, but his eyes did not protrude quite like those of a frog. They were set more flush with the slope of his head, and though they were nearly on the sides of his head, the eyes were angled forward. Aside from the direction he was facing, it was impossible to tell where the mander was looking. Mander eyes are translucent orbs that come in a variety of colors. This one happened to have eyes of deep red with wispy black veins that ran across their surfaces and throughout the depths of the eyes in all directions. Joe found the mander's eyes to be mesmerizing, as they almost seemed to glow the way light danced around inside them, but their directionless gaze was also very unsettling. Mesmerizing or unsettling, either way, Joe decided that it was probably a good idea to avoid this predator's eyes. The mander's mouth was as wide as his head, and when the mander spoke, Joe could see that he didn't appear to have normal teeth but two long, curving, yellow bony ridges that had a similar appearance to teeth.

"I saw you speaking to the Crystal Master on the log," The mander said as he stood upright. "Either he's going to be returning to take you back to Midgorn, or he told you how to get back. Go, piss." He pointed to an area just off of the road by a set of bushes. "Do not wander too far off. Stay in sight."

Joe smiled his broad, charming smile as he walked over to the bush. "Not a problem," he said, "I've got nothing to be shy about." He gave a knowing look to Runara, but to his disappointment, she was looking distantly off in another direction, seemingly oblivious to the exchange between the mander and him.

"Show some respect, fool," the mander growled. "And hurry. We need to keep moving."

"Keep moving? To where? From who? You did kill the King, right? I wonder, does that make you king? I'm not up on the rules of royal government." Joe volleyed the questions as he found a suitable spot to do his business. The mander ignored his questions, leaving an awkward moment of silence, so Joe thought he would try another.

"So I get that I'm your ticket back to the swamp, but why did you keep the girl alive, and why not just torture the information about how to get home out of me?"

"Torture is for witless cowards who like to hear lies." the mander replied harshly. Joe was pleased to hear that torture was off the to-do list and was even happier to have the mander talking again. Silence from your homicidal kidnapper was never a good sign. "And the girl has a blood quest of her own. To kill her now would bring dishonor on all of my kin."

"Blood quest?" Joe questioned as he relieved himself. "What would any quest of hers have to do with you or your equally as attractive, I'm sure, kin."

The mander was staring at him now. Joe couldn't make out the expression on his face. It might have been contained rage well peppered with hate. It might have been a case of uncomfortable flatulence. It was impossible to tell which. In any case, the silence was making Joe uncomfortable. Runara was still lost in her own somber world of thought.

Joe was just about to say something to break the silence when the mander finally spoke. "I failed to end the killer of her kinsmen, the one you call King. Had he died, I would have had no reason to bring the girl with us, but I am bound now to assist her in any revenge she seeks against the man until either he or I is dead. A hunter always finishes his kill."

"My name is Runara, not 'girl.'" Runara's tone was sullen but angry. She had taken both men by surprise, and they each turned to look at her. Her gaze was still somewhere off on the horizon, and she had grown quiet with her sorrowful contemplations once again.

Joe finished his business by the bushes and tucked his shirt back in as he walked back. He was just now really noticing the three bailodants. They were essentially large balls of brown fur on what looked like a giant bird's powerful, scaled legs, but they ended in three-toed hooves. They had no apparent heads or tails, though two large ribbed horns sprouted from the fronts of each of the beasts, sweeping back, conveniently forming natural handlebars for their riders. The mander was holding a tuft of grass that he had pulled from the side of the road and was holding it in front of one of the bailodants, and though Joe couldn't make out a mouth clearly from his perspective, it was apparent by its noises and motions that the bailodant was eating the grass.

"So let me get this straight: you tried to kill the King, but what, you missed? Was he too hard of a target for you, pinned to a tree? Prefer your targets moving? I get it. I mean, I prefer them standing still myself. You don't need to lead your shots so much, but hey, everybody's got their thing." Joe's sarcastic humor was lost on the mander.

"Of course, I didn't miss. I ran him through with that sword of yours four times. He didn't even bleed. There must be something wrong with your puny sword." The frustration was evident in the mander's voice. "I would have tried taking his head with his own sword, but it wouldn't come free from his grip, and I could hear more of his men approaching before I could try anything else. Should have just snapped his neck." The mander's voice trailed off a little as he grumbled this last thought contemplatively.

"Maybe you just didn't try hard enough for his sword. Maybe the guy is stronger than you. He is taller." Joe was all smiles. He was enjoying this exchange with the mander immensely. He giggled like a young girl inside at the thought of the tales he would have later of actually speaking to a mander, let alone seeing one up close. How delightfully normal this mander was! Nobody would believe him.

"I heard the man's arm snap, and still he held on." The mander grumped back.

"The only way to remove a powersword is either by the will of the wielder or to kill them." Again, Runara's voice startled both men and again, she immediately retreated back to her own thoughts. Joe noticed then that she was wearing his crystal pendant and had Death Seed slung across her back. Given the apparent mood of both Runara and the mander, Joe decided to wait to bring up the topic of returning his possessions to him.

"As I said," the mander was nearly growling, glaring at Joe. "He would not die."

Joe's thoughts clung to Runara's words, or rather, one word, "powersword." It was what he was told Goms and Nashtar were trying to form with the crystal in the hilt of Death Seed. If it were a powersword keeping Goms from dying, Joe thought, then it would make sense that he wouldn't want anyone else in the kingdom getting their hands on another powersword, especially an apparent rival like Nashtar. Not dying seemed like a nice perk of owning a sword. Joe found that he was suddenly more on board with the idea of putting the powersword together, and now, not just to get back to Midgorn. He felt a little sorry for the mander; he seemed like someone he could like in some handy-to-have-in-bar-brawl sort of way, but Runara was just too attractive to sacrifice.

"Now, arguably, as you said, you didn't try breaking the man's neck; if it's true that this king can't die, I don't see how there's much chance for revenge." Joe's observance seemed to go unheard by both Runara and the mander. Even Joe's attention was only partially attending his words, half of his mind was on the powersword, and most of the other half was trying to figure out how to get back up on his bailodant. The beast's legs alone were nearly as tall as Joe, and the top of the beast was about two and a half feet beyond that. Joe fumbled at trying to clutch at the bailodant's fur to climb up, but it was impossible to find any proper leverage to even begin to pull himself up. The bailodant clearly didn't like being pawed at either and kept shuffling sideways, making strange, short, deep grumbling sounds, adding to the impossibility of it all.

The mander chuckled at the spectacle in a low, croaking, snorting way. "Just pat the thing's leg twice, just below the bend."

Joe did, and immediately the bailodant crouched and sat down. Joe climbed onto the creature, straddling it and grabbing hold of the handlebar-like horns. Satisfied that Joe needed no further assistance, the mander quickly mounted his own bailodant.

A few more instructions on communicating one's intentions to the beasts, a tap of the foot here, a tug on a horn there, and the three of them were off down the road at an astonishing pace.

"So, you can't kill the king, and you don't seem to mean to kill either of us, so where are we off to?" Joe's voice warbled from the jostle of the bailodant's pace.

"We're off to see the girl's great-grandfather." the mander said.

"Who's that then?" Joe asked.

Runara spoke then, looking at Joe, her face sullen and seething, with a quiet, disturbingly calm anger. "Nashtar."

* * * * * * * * * * * * * * * * * *

Screamin' Joe Blade's Ten-Point Guide to Life:
Point #5: Poking fun is just another way of showing that you're paying attention.

Joe found the mander, whose name was Kord, to be far more talkative than he expected mander folk to be. Bringing just that thought up to Kord produced a response that was a little more in line with what Joe would have expected. As Kord explained it, not many manders have bothered speaking to their prey.

"Getting to know your kind will make hunting your kind easier." Kord had said flatly.

Although unsettling, Joe could appreciate Kord's candor. It was, at least, far more honest than Joe was being with either he or Runara. He was still rolling over in his head how he would approach the whole sacrifice situation when the time came.

They had been traveling for nearly three days with no sign of being pursued by the King's men. Even though the road had been clear of other travelers, it helped, Joe thought, that they had left the main road after the first day, making their way through the forest. The bailodants moved much slower on the uneven ground and brush of the forest but managed well enough.

Runara began speaking on the second day. Kord had been questioning her about Nashtar and how she had come to live out in the forest if her great-grandfather lived in a castle. Her explanation was something of a history lesson.

Very long ago, when Nashtar Tessep was a young man, fresh from the barbaric continent of Westerlan, he was the grand court wizard to King Mazeze Nathak, Moiren's grandfather. The King relied on Nashtar greatly, for never had there been a more magically talented wizard nor a wiser advisor than he. Nashtar was treated as a royal member of court along with his wife Karsera and their son Neskroff, residing in one of the towers of the King's castle.

In Southern Senuvia, Goms Ethdab, then just an ambitious warlord, had begun his campaign of conquest, and his success in conquering two smaller kingdoms had the other eleven realms considering a coalition, or as some were suggesting, an alliance with the powerful King to the north, King Mazeze. It was an opportunity for Mazeze to extend the reach of his kingdom into the south, peacefully. Diplomats had been dispatched, but several of the lesser kings of the south were insulted and would not meet with anyone they felt was below their standing. King Mazeze would have to go himself. Taking an impressive military host, as well as several representatives from the elves, Mazeze's closest allies, Mazeze set out on a diplomatic mission to the south, unsure of how long it would take to visit all eleven kingdoms, negotiate a union, and if possible stop Goms Ethdab in his conquest.

King Mazeze's wife, Falim, was known for her seductive, flirtatious demeanor. Mazeze, however, never doubted her faithfulness; by all accounts, the King and Queen had always seemed very close and affectionate. With the King absent, the Queen had Nashtar take over many of the King's tedious administrative tasks and had him represent the King's interests at public events. For the most part, he was well-received. Such social gatherings always put him in close company with the Queen. Flirtatious as she was known to be and certainly friends with Nashtar, nothing about their interactions was the least bit inappropriate, and being occupied with Nashtar's company kept her out of trouble with the many noble, would-be lovers that constantly followed the Queen around like lost kittens.

One such pursuer was the very brash and very single Duke of Estobrex. A man with an incredibly thick head of always mischievously disheveled blonde hair and a curiously raven-black goatee and mustache. When he wasn't drinking, he was making sexual advances upon one woman of court or another. More often than not, however, he would simply combine the two pastimes. For the most part, his fellow courtiers found him lewd but more entertaining in some instances than the tedious juggling of the court jester. Seldom successful in his pursuits of the women of the court, from time to time, he would manage to bed one of the servants, and this was more than enough to encourage his behavior. Though usually restrained and quite nearly polite in his interactions with the Queen, one day, during the Queen's birthday celebrations, with a belly and head full of alcohol and the King still absent, the Duke found himself far less inhibited.

His comments had gone far beyond inappropriate, and when politely asked by the Queen herself to apologize, he became quite belligerent, making a few more salaciously bawdy retorts. Nashtar stepped in then, demanding that the Duke not only apologize to the Queen but to the rest of the court, who had paused in their merriment to take in the spectacle. When the Duke then suggested that Nashtar should undertake the role of a lumbering hellgoat suppository, Nashtar transformed the man into a snail, much to the shock and delight of the entire court. He placed the Duke in a glass box and offered it to the Queen as a gift, which she graciously declined. The Duke of Estobrex was never seen again.

Three months into the King's absence, the Queen made fewer and fewer public appearances and left the entertaining of court primarily to Nashtar. By the fourth month, she would not be seen at all. Rumors began to circulate around the court of the Queen's health, and many began fearing how the King might react should he come home to find his Queen had perished. Some rumors, however, were far more accurate, suggesting that the Queen was with child, and with that came speculation as to whether or not that child had been conceived by the King.

On the twenty-first day of Alexorum, eight months since he and his diplomatic entourage had departed, the King returned. His mission had been far from a success, though not a complete failure. Many of the kings of lower Senuvia were inclined to make an alliance with Mazeze for the potential support of his great army. All but two, however, had no interest in peace with the other kings of the south. A union of the Southern realms was not to be. Though much of the south was likely to fall victim either to Goms or wars among themselves, Mazeze had, at the very least, established a strong alliance between himself and the two closest bordering kingdoms. The King returned in good spirits.

Greeted by his pregnant wife upon his return, King Mazeze was elated at the prospect of a fourth heir. Learning of the conduct and fate of the Duke of Estobrex, the King rewarded his faithful steward for defending the Queen's honor by making Nashtar the new Duke of Estobrex and, with that new title, granted him the former duke's lands and keep. The King then sent an armed garrison to the keep to remove the former duke's men and staff while also sending a troop of newly handpicked servants to prepare the keep for Nashtar and his family, a task that would take several months.

Two months passed before the Queen gave birth to a son, and Mazeze had moved on from concern at his wife's seemingly long overdue pregnancy to realizing the truth of the matter. His suspicions of who the unborn child's father was were actually directed at one of the Queen's personal guards until Nashtar approached the King with news of the birth and went so far as to suggest a name for the boy. The King realized in that moment that at no time had his most trusted advisor mentioned concern over the Queen's lengthy pregnancy. The rest of the court, meanwhile, had spent the past month twittering their more accurate suspicions amongst themselves.

Never had anyone seen such anger in Mazeze. Even Mazeze was unaccustomed to his own anger. Where other kings, more comfortable with dispensing their wrathful thoughts, would have ordered the deaths of the two lovers, he ordered his guards to remove Nashtar, Queen Falim, and their new son Toreks from the castle.

"Toreks?" Joe interrupted, "Why not Nashtar Junior, Nashtar the Second?"

"Toreks," Runara explained, "means 'Lord of Secrets' in a very ancient and lost Modnarian tongue, used now by only a few who are well schooled in the ways of magic."

"Fitting." croaked Kord.

Joe scoffed. "Fitting? How is it fitting? What secrets is a newborn going to have or even be able to tell, or are there those schooled in the language of cries and drool?"

"In your question is your answer, rooter." Kord chuckled, "Not only is he not likely to tell anyone anything he might know, but one can be sure that the child had not said a word to anyone for many months before."

Joe rolled his eyes at the nonsense of it but gave a slight laugh. He ignored the racial slur and smiled, happy that everyone was talking, marveling at having heard, no, made a mander chuckle. He apologized for his interruption and encouraged Runara to continue the tale. She didn't return his smile but gave Joe a polite nod and picked up her story where she had left off.

A group of the King's guards escorted Nashtar, Falim, and the baby, Toreks, forcibly from the castle. All along the way out, both the Queen and the baby cried inconsolably; the Queen called for her husband's mercy while Nashtar pleaded for a chance to speak with the friend and King that he had regrettably betrayed, but all of their noise was in vain. They soon found themselves left in the wilderness to fend for themselves. It's uncertain what happened next, but it is said that the three, making their way to the keep at Estobrex, were set upon by brigands. Some stories even have it that the brutes were the previous guards of Estobrex. Both Falim and Toreks were murdered. Nashtar was nearly killed himself, cut and beaten to the edge of life before managing to use his magic to escape.

Reaching the keep of Estobrex, he placed a powerful spell upon the new guards there. The guards at Estobrex, ultimately loyal to Mazeze, were not yet aware of Nashtar's fall from favor. The enchantment would ensure their loyalty to Nashtar to the extent that they are bound to serve him even beyond their deaths.

"Beyond their deaths?" asked Kord.

"Yes," Runara confirmed, "their corpses march the walls, halls, and grounds of the keep, and many are no more than skeletons now."

Kord made a dismissive croaking sound. "Dead is dead. You're either alive, or you are meat. That is the way of things."

"Maybe in your world," Runara offered solemnly, "but the layers of existence in Modnar, this world, is a complex, tangled mess of possibilities born of the wandering imaginations of child gods. It is even possible, perhaps, that your world is just another layer of this one."

Kord only grunted as a response.

"So, if Nashtar and his dead guards are still at the keep, then the King must have forgiven him, right? Probably feeling guilty about sending his wife out into the wilds to her death, right? I'm right, right?" Joe questioned, wanting Runara to continue with the story. She did.

Mazeze had quite the opposite reaction one might have expected when he learned of Falim's death. He was heartbroken. Though she had betrayed Mazeze, a part of him still loved Falim. He blamed Nashtar for her death. The rage over her betrayal, mixed with his profound sorrow, festered into an unimaginable fury. What followed was a war between him and Nashtar that would leave much of the land in tatters and a great portion of the population homeless.

The wizard's conjured minions, hideously transformed servants, and undying soldiers were never a real threat to the well-fortified castle of the King. Nashtar made no attempt to attack the King's castle for this reason, and also his own family still resided there. He did not wish any harm to come to his wife and son. Nashtar's abominations, however, were enough to hold off the King's army, and the King sent wave after wave of his men to try to take the keep at Estobrex. Mazeze turned to his allies, the elves to the North in Gizesh, but they refused to become part of what the elven Queen called a "petty matter of jealous men."

Just a year into the war, Mazeze took Karsera as his new wife and Queen, and although not officially a prince of the realm, her son Neskroff was treated as one of the royal family. He was well-loved by his adopted father and siblings, being particularly close to the King's youngest daughter, Mortrell, who was only younger than him by a month. By the end of the war, Neskroff was eighteen, had been fighting in the battle against his true father for three years, and was married to Mortrell.

The war between Mazeze and Nashtar had lasted for ten years and would not have likely continued much longer. Nashtar's keep was already in dire disrepair. His armies of foul beasts and the dead were so few in number then that he no longer made attacks upon the King's lands, but simply concentrated on fending off the King's own much reduced and feeble army. Mazeze's once numerous and powerful forces were little more than a few militias scattered throughout the land. The King had also lost his taste for the war with the recent death of his eldest son, Mazeze II, in a minor skirmish that had gained nothing for either side.

The prince's widow, Princess Katria, was pregnant with Moiren at the time, adding to the feelings of guilt festering in the King.

In the south, meanwhile, Goms Ethdab had conquered the remaining eleven kingdoms, including the two that had allied with Mazeze. In the end, Mazeze, so obsessed and invested in his war against Nashtar, ignored the calls for assistance from his allies to the south.

Goms's forces were so numerous at that point that he took the last two southern kingdoms with little resistance. Goms, his armies, and his various beasts and machines of war arrived in Northern Senuvia ready to face the great King of the North in a conflict that would immortalize all involved in story and song, regardless of who won. He had not anticipated how much the war with Nashtar had ravaged the once-powerful nation. The battle that followed then was not epic; it was pitiful.

Goms gutted every town and village, every castle and keep. His men wiped out most of the population of Northern Senuvia, replacing them with people from the south looking to make a new life for themselves after the wars brought by Goms through their own territories.

Goms had even tried to take Estobrex, but when several garrisons of men met the same fate as Mazeze's men, he decided it best to simply leave the dark wizard be. By the time he marched on Mazeze's grand castle, he had already replenished any lost men and supplies.

Mazeze's end came quickly. The castle was completely unguarded; all of Mazeze's men had died trying to hold lesser keeps or the town below the castle. Mazeze stood alone in the courtyard, the gate wide open, and called Goms out as his troops approached. Goms's men filled the courtyard, but all were ordered to leave Mazeze be. When Goms pushed through his men to confront Mazeze himself, he found the King simply standing, not ready for a fight, not defiant, or even looking defeated, merely standing there looking at Goms as someone might casually pay some mind to a stranger approaching them amongst a bustling party. Mazeze had no weapon and wore no armor.

"The wizard will ruin you, too," Mazeze said without malice in his voice or expression of emotion.

Without a single word, Goms slew Mazeze, striking him down with a single blow of his glowing green blade. He claimed the castle as his own from which to rule his now vast kingdom, which he renamed Eastworld.

As inglorious as the conquering of the north had been for Goms, he had no need to be the subject of songs to be immortalized. Over the ten years of his conquest of the south, Goms had acquired one of the thirteen swords of power, perhaps, in some ways, the most powerful of the thirteen; the Green Sword of Life. Just possessing it, legends say, makes him immortal.

"I told you he would not die." Kord turned to Joe, grumbling.

"Shhh!" Joe retorted, motioning to Runara to continue her story, and he urged his bailodant to hurry up alongside hers to hear her better.

When Goms's forces first quickly swept into the northlands, Mazeze sent his family from the castle into hiding. Much of his court did the same. These noble men and women, their children, and their servants became wanderers, brookshins. Koliks, Mazeze's remaining son, a pretty and vain young man, not suited for a life outdoors, worn to the bone by his harsh new life, fell ill within a few months of being out in the wild. He was dead before a year had passed. He had left no heir, no wife, as he had a taste for the company of other men.

"Ah, he was a broon," Kord commented with an air of understanding. "My mother was born broon. It can be a hard life."

"Um, your mum? I don't think what she's saying and what you're thinking are the same thing." Joe chuckled a little. "First off, this Koliks fella was, well, a fella."

"So was my mother at first," Kord said gruffly; obviously a little insulted by Joe's tone. "Some of my kind is born broon."

Runara and Joe simply stared at Kord, not understanding. Joe looked at Runara. Seeing that he was not alone in his confusion, he looked back at Kord and shook his head, shrugging his shoulders."

Kord gave a frustrated huff and already regretted that he had shared anything with these two, who should have just been his prey. "Broon, born with horns." He said it with a tone that suggested that it should be obvious. "They are trained from birth to become the most fierce and powerful warriors, but they are never to know the hunt, and they have no taste for women. Though they are both feared and celebrated, they are shunned by most. In their later years, they undergo the change. As females, their strength is greatly diminished, and many even lose their horns after laying their eggs." He smiled then proudly, "My mother never lost her horns; even today, she could rip the arms off of any of the young broon."

"So, who's your old man then?" Joe asked overly cheerfully, hardly believing the tales he would be able to tell about this mander and his sex-changing mum.

"I have no father." No child of a broon does. As women, the broon lose their taste for men and only keep company with other broon that have gone through the change. Broon eggs hatch without a male's life milk."

"Life…milk." Joe was laughing so hard now that he had a hard time staying on his bailodant.

Kord snarled, fully regretting now having shared anything with the laughing fool. "Finish your story then girl." His voice was a low, menacing rumble.

Runara suddenly felt terribly uncomfortable and shifted her position atop her bailodant. She cleared her throat to get Joe's attention but mostly to get him to stop laughing before Kord did something horrible. Joe struggled, but he reigned himself in, giving a little uncontrollable chuckle every few minutes, for which he would quickly apologize. Runara continued her story.

The brookshins wandered the land, living on the generosity of local farmers and townsfolk here and there. Increasingly, though, the brookshins found fewer and fewer refuges as Gom's people took over the lands and towns, either killing the former residents or driving them out, forcing them to become brookshins too. To make things worse, Gom's men made sport of hunting down brookshins. Between being hunted by Gom's men and feared and hated by the new residents of what was now called North Eastworld, the brookshins had no choice but to live their lives in hiding. Some fled to the mountains; many hid away in the forests, moving around as much as possible.

"What about the elves?" Kord asked. "I thought they were friends to your people. Staying out of the King's quarrel with the wizard, I understand, but it makes no sense to let one, such as this Goms, slaughter their allies."

Runara looked like she was going to cry. "I don't know, she…" she murmured through a tight-lipped grimace, her thought unfinished. "They may not help us outright or allow us into their lands, but elves have saved bands of brookshins from Goms's men many times, only to disappear without a word. That's why so many brookshins live here on the border of Gizesh."

"Well, if they're anything like the elves back home, they like to keep to themselves and don't have much regard for others." Joe piped up. "

"The same could be said of we manders," Kord said with a smirk. "I've never had the honor to hunt an elf."

"See. Keep to themselves; that's just the way elves are. Kinda full of themselves, the way I hear it, too. Not nearly as good looking as you manders either." Joe added sarcastically. Kord simply nodded in agreement, which made Joe smile. He turned to Runara then. "So why didn't you mention earlier that you're the heir to the throne?"

Far more emotion than had been seen from Runara since the confrontation with Goms suddenly swept across her face as she sputtered her response. "I — I'm not — Moiren — I'm just — I mean — "

"I'm a little new to this whole royal family thing. There hasn't been a king or queen in Midgorn for hundreds of years, but if I'm following your story, and Nashtar was your great-granddaddy, that makes Neskroff your granddad and what was the King's daughter's name again?"

"Mortrell." there seemed to be a little defeat in the sound of her voice.

"Right, Mortrell. So Mortrell is your grandmum. Right? So, did they have a son or a daughter?

"A daughter, just one child, my mother."

"So there you have it. Unless Moiren's got some brothers or sisters out there or kids."

"No, they're all gone. My family, too. Any family I had left was murdered back at the campsite." Runara's voice trailed off at the end to the point of nearly being inaudible.

"Well, bust my arse over a vorv's spine. What d'you think of that Kord ol' pal we are traveling in the company of a genuine queen."

"I am NOT the queen." Runara protested loudly, her smooth voice cracking with anger and grief.

"And I am not your 'pal,'" added Kord at a far more civil volume than Runara in his usual gruff tone. Kord gave the air a sniff, stopping his bailodant. Joe and Runara also brought their bailodants to a halt, wondering what had Kord so concerned.

"Odd," he said in a hushed tone, "it almost smells like a human, but" Kord's voice trailed off as he sniffed the air again.

"What?" Joe asked, puzzled by Kord's comment. "Like a human butt? What smells like…"

"Behind you! Down!" Kord shouted. Runara gasped, seeing it too, but it was too late. The coconut hit Joe square in the back of the head, knocking him out cold.

Chapter 10

"I think he's waking up." Joe felt like he was at the bottom of a deep well, and somewhere, far above, there was a little circle of light. A young, sharp, feminine voice was faintly echoing down to where he was. The harder he tried to listen, the closer the light-filled opening seemed.

"Should I slap him? I hear it's good to slap them."

Joe tried to say, 'Don't slap me,' but nothing came out. He continued to struggle toward the light.

"You already hit him with one of your blasted coconuts, I think that's enough." A low, gravelly voice was speaking now. Joe blinked his eyes. His vision was nothing but a blur, and his eyes were slightly crossed. He blinked again and then a third time before his eyes finally focused. The vision of a skull face hovered sideways a few inches before his face.

"I've always been told that Death comes wielding a sword or a scythe. What is a coconut?" Joe asked, becoming aware now that he was lying on the ground.

The brown-eyed skull hovering above Joe blinked and, then, turning to some unseen companion, spoke with a great deal of concern in the same feminine voice that he had heard from the bottom of the well of his mind. "Oh-oh, I think I beaned him a little too hard. He doesn't even know what a coconut is."

"He wouldn't. Neither of us is from here." croaked Kord's familiar voice from some distance," but if you mean this battapod, I think you could have hit him a little harder."

Runara's face appeared above Joe then, as several hands hoisted him up gently into a sitting position. "He'll be fine," Runara said, looking at Joe with the scrutiny of a doctor. "Here, eat this; all of it." She handed Joe a palmful of black-colored moss. "It will help with any injuries we can't see."

Still feeling a little dazed and directionless, Joe munched down the dry, bitter plant.

"You'll need a little o' this too, m'boy." Another face of death was before Joe now; this one with a wide, snaggletoothed grin nested within an even wider, more ridiculously toothy smile. Joe was having difficulty making out just what he was looking at. The figure was holding out a wineskin, however, and that he comprehended clearly. Taking the wineskin, Joe gulped down the fluid within greedily. He hadn't realized how thirsty he was until that moment. The potent home-brewed alcohol instantly took his breath away. He was gasping for air, which quickly evolved into coughing. "Thanks," Joe finally managed to wheeze.

"Are y'all daft?" said the low, gravelly voice Joe had heard earlier. "This young lady is trying to heal the man, and you lot just keep trying to kill him."

Joe stood up then. The coughing fit had actually made him far more alert, and he was aware then enough to start taking in his surroundings. A motley spectacle filled his vision. He was in the company of a circus troop consisting of three clowns, a mountain of a man who was clearly their 'strongman,' and he assumed the man standing atop some enormous beast was the animal trainer. Joe had never seen an elephant before, but since no one else seemed to find the presence of the monstrosity troubling, he played it cool as well.

When Joe was a very young boy, he and his older sister had snuck into a circus show in the city of Ter-Merrow. Orphans, he and his sister were street rats, stealing what they could to get by, and a circus crowd made for an easy night of cut-pursing, but Joe had been dazzled by the performances that night, and his take was a tenth of what it should have been. Joe was in awe of the agility of the acrobats, wondered at the menagerie of strange beasts brought from the deepest tunnels of the Core Cave, but was most mesmerized by a man dressed in the red and black leathers of an Armidon guard. He was a tall, wiry man with thick blonde hair slicked tightly back and a large blonde mustache that stuck out straight a couple of inches on either side. The man would twirl his mustache as he spoke to the audience, introducing his next feat. His assistant, a woman with long blonde hair who wore a doll-faced mask and not much more than a blue corset, would be strapped onto a large upright wooden disk. The mustached man would then set her spinning and, walking quite some distance away while donning a blindfold, would proceed to throw what seemed like an endless number of knives at the woman and the rapidly rotating disc. With all the knives thrown, the man walked back to the woman, bringing the disc to a stop. The woman was completely unharmed, her body perfectly outlined by the knives stuck in the wood around her.

Joe promised himself at that moment that he would become a master of knives and one day join the circus, too. It seemed now like he might have the opportunity to keep the second part of that promise to his seven-year-old self.

There were two others in the circus troop before him whose roles Joe could not immediately identify. One was a woman who was striking, if not typically beautiful, with hard, angular features to her face. She was dressed in finery that was more typical of the manner of men in the Midgorn city of Advan: black silk slacks, ruffled sleeves and collars, and a long black coat with a vibrant yellow silk lining. Her black hair was pulled back in three tight braids that formed a single ponytail in the back. She was leaning on a decorative walking stick that could possibly double as a mace, and Joe suspected that was precisely what it truly was.

The other was a man, all in shades of purple and black; he was dressed in the heavier garments of a merchant, though going by their grimy state, he wasn't a well-to-do merchant. His ankle-length coat ended in tatters, and many of the once fifteen gold buttons were either missing or had been replaced with wooden bobbles. Half his shirt was untucked and stained with the remains of many previous meals and drinks. Evidence of these same past meals could be found in his large, bushy brown mustache that continued back along his jowls, becoming equally bushy sideburns. The sideburns disappeared beneath his floppy, flat, round, brimless purple hat. What really caught Joe's attention, though, was that the man's skin seemed one size too big for him. All of his facial features sagged. His eyebrows seemed to sit too low over his eyes, and even his ears seemed to be hanging at odd angles. Whenever he spoke, his jowls and neck skin would bob and shake as though they would fall off if he moved too suddenly. He was the man with the gravelly voice and apparently in charge of this little troop.

He introduced himself as Host, owner of the circus. The woman in yellow and black, he explained, was Dicesh, the circus's ringmaster, or rather, ringmistress. Dicesh bowed deeply, giving a little flourish with her cane, and then she took over the remaining introductions. When she spoke, her face lit up with exuberant emotion, somehow making her more attractive despite her hard features. She had a charisma to her that made it hard to look away from her as she spoke.

She pointed to the man on the elephant. "Subduer and grand puppeteer of the will and purpose of all beasts, Adriga the Great." Adriga, dressed in simple cotton and wool garments of drab blues and greens, gave the group a subtle nod. He was a clean-shaven man whose leathery caramel skin had seen more than its share of sun. His head was wrapped in a brightly colored but dirty orange scarf. The elephant, whose shoulders he stood upon, at that moment, seemingly without prompting, stomped one thunderous step forward as it gave an earsplitting trumpet blast from its upturned trunk.

Joe and Runara both jumped, and Joe even took two steps back, catching himself before actually hiding behind Runara.

"And my companion, here," Adriga added with a sly smile, happy with the reaction he had gotten out of Joe and Runara, "is Kotep." the elephant flapped its massive sail-like ears and gave his head a shake. It seemed a little agitated. "King Kotep, that is," Adriga added. The elephant gave a satisfied huff and calmed down, much to Joe's relief.

Dicesh rolled her eyes but broadened her smile and continued her introductions. "In all of Senuvia, you shall not find a more dynamic exemplification of resplendently robust, brawny magnificence as our mighty Drix," Dicesh made a dramatic sweep of her arm, directing everyone's attention to the man Joe had already assumed was their strongman. He was a massive, muscular individual, reminding Joe of the intimidating presence of the King. His square-jawed face was almost exaggerated in its manly handsomeness. He had a mane of chocolate-brown hair, which hung loosely, save for two thin braids in the front that fell just past his shoulders. A nearly black beard, almost as long as his hair, was neatly bound into a single braid, with a skull bead carved from some sort of bone adorning the end.

Seemingly lost in some other thought, Drix suddenly became aware that everyone was looking at him. There was a brief awkward moment while Dicesh stood stuck in her dramatic pose, her smile frozen as well, waiting for

Drix to present himself with at least a portion of the sort of flare that Adriga and King Kotep had. Drix just blinked, took a bite of the large roasted bird leg he had been working on for some time now, and shrugged his shoulders. "It's a living." Bits of meat spat from his mouth as he spoke.

Dicesh's face and posture drooped a little. Obviously frustrated, she casually motioned in the general direction of the people just to the side of Joe.

"And then there are our clowns. Unfortunately for you," Dicesh spoke directly to Joe, "you crossed the path of our juggler and acrobat, Crash."

Beside Joe was the girl that had apparently hit him with the koli, or coconut, as these modnarians were calling it. Her face was painted in black and white makeup that resembled a very fanciful skull. Decorative black swirls and dots made it more whimsical than frightening. Her hair was a starburst of short, brilliant green ponytails pointing in every possible direction. She wore a tight-fitting leather bodysuit, half white, half black, that left little of her athletic, acrobat body to the imagination. A loose-fitting leather jacket that she wore provided a small degree of modesty. It was cropped rather jaggedly, mid-torso, and was a patchwork checkerboard of green and black diamonds. Joe imagined that at some point, the green probably matched the striking color of her hair but was now just a dull, faded hue. A large leather satchel, made with a matching diamond pattern, was at her side; the strap went across her chest beneath the jacket.

She shot out a hand in greeting with such exuberance that Joe flinched a little, thinking at first she was going to slap him.

He reluctantly shook her hand while rubbing the sore lump on the back of his head with a little contemplation. "Well, you've certainly got the most suitable name of anyone I've met."

"Really sorry about the coconut. It just got away from me." Crash's apology was accompanied by an overexaggerated pouty face, which the two clowns behind her mimicked, somehow making it seem a little less than genuine.

Crash introduced the two clowns behind her as Ugor and Chenoval. Their faces were painted with similar skull designs, but their clothing was absurdly oversized in contrast to Crash's body-hugging leather.

Ugor was short, approximately four feet tall, a dwarf, or as Joe knew them to be called in Midgorn, a trall. His outfit looked like five striped balloons linked together. The stripes were royal and midnight blue. The largest of the balloon-like portions covered most of his upper torso while each upper arm, from shoulder to elbow, and his upper legs, from his waist down to his knees, made up the other balloon portions. His hair was swept back in seven large blue spikes. His was the double-smiling skull face that had given Joe the whiskey.

Chenoval was tall, a little less than seven feet, with a long face and pointed chin. His skull facepaint was nearly identical to the Ugor's, but the design's teeth were painted in an exaggerated frown, with a tiny black teardrop below his left eye. Joe thought his red and black striped clothing looked like the lapelled suits the bankers of Advan wore back in Midgorn but with ridiculously over-padded shoulders. The suit ended in tatters at the elbows, knees, and waist. His hair, too, was swept back in similar spikes to Ugor's, but his hair was a deep wine-colored red.

Joe started to make his own introductions, but Host quickly interrupted him.

"No need, m'boy; Miss Runara here was polite enough to make the formal presentations while your soul was busy scurrying about, gathering your senses back together."

"What's a circus doing roaming about the woods?" Joe asked.

Host looked at the others, whose gazes were all suddenly very distracted in every direction but Host's. It was clear that he would not be getting any assistance in answering the simple question. He opted to tell the truth.

"Well," he started. There was a long pause as he contemplated what he would say. "We ran slightly afoul of some of the King's men. They started laying down some blather about traveling shows, such as ours, requiring special permits or some such rubbish like that. When I explained that I had never heard of such a requirement, they threatened to confiscate our belongings and poor Adriga's animals."

"Animals?" Joe asked, puzzled. "He's got more than one of these things?" He pointed at the elephant, "Where have you got the others hid?"

Runara realized then that what she had thought were animal skins draped across the elephant's back were actually two enormous sleeping tigers.

"Koobara!" Adriga shouted. A moment later, a large black panther leaped like a living shadow from the surrounding bushes. It landed with the slightest bit of sound just in front of the elephant, a low rumble in its throat. It was looking at Kord intently. "Koobara! Hup."

The cat looked like it was getting ready to pounce, ignoring the animal trainer's command. Kord shifted slightly and cocked his head, looking at the beast with curiosity more than anything else and sniffing.

"Koobara!" Adriga shouted sternly again, and this time, there was the loud crack of a whip just above the beast's head. Adriga had seemingly produced the whip out of nowhere while everyone was distracted by Koobara. "Hup!" Crack, came the whip again. Koobara did not move, continuing to stare at Kord. "Hup!" Adriga shouted again, louder this time, cracking the whip a third time.

Without warning, the cat leaped into the air, twisting sideways and backward towards a nearby tree. It pounced upward off of the trunk of the tree and landed on the back of the elephant. The nearest sleeping tiger raised its head slightly, giving a growl of protest. Koobara gave the other beast a little respectful room before laying itself down across the elephant's back.

Joe looked around then, wondering how many other beasts might be prowling about as he questioned Host further. "Okay, so what does your run-in with the local authorities have to do with you being in the woods?"

Chenoval spoke up then in a slow, deep, bone-rattling baritone. "Easier to hide the bodies."

Joe simply blinked at the honesty.

Host was next with a question. "And what would you three be doing riding such road beasts through the forest? But before we get to that, more importantly, what are you?" Host asked this last question directly to Kord.

"Similar problem, and what I am is none of your concern," Kord answered in his usual gruff tone.

"How rude." Host made an exaggerated gesture of feeling affronted, like a bad stage actor, but the look on his face said that he found Kord both amusing and fascinating and wasn't, in the slightest, insulted.

Joe, not being the best at reading people, felt the need to explain to avoid things turning into a confrontation. "He's not used to having to talk to people. Where we're from, he usually just kills them. All manders are like that. Scary bunch."

"Where you are from? And that would be where exactly?" Dicesh questioned. She was circling Joe, Runara, and Kord then, clearly sizing them up, giving her cane a theatrical swing or a twirl with each step. "Wait, no, let me guess." She paused in front of Runara, leaning in with both hands on the studded ball of her cane. "Hmm, garishly bright colored clothes, but a bit ragged; mhmm, you have the curls of a northerner, but I've never seen any with hair so vividly red. Still, this one is surely a brookshin, probably a fortuneteller or a witch, both, most likely. She has an earthiness to her." Dicesh said as she leaned in even closer, giving Runara a little sniff.

Runara clearly didn't like being scrutinized in such a manner. She took a little step back from Dicesh with a frown and simply nodded, indicating that the ringmaster's guess wasn't wrong.

Off to the side, Crash jumped up and down, clapping and exclaiming, "Do me next! Do me!"

Dicesh rolled her eyes and moved on to Joe. She squinted, looking him up and down. "Much like our enthused young clown," she began, a finger to her chin in contemplation, "the suppleness of your black leathers says that you are from Westerlan, and their simple cut probably makes you a mercenary, but…" She paused there, looking around, quite puzzled. "But your friends carry your weapons." She pondered this for a moment more. "You seem small for a berzerker from… Rigtor?"

Crash laughed, "No way he's a berzerker. No way he's from Rigtor."

"Nope," said Joe, "Miss Crash is right. I don't even know what a buzzlicker is, but it sounds like they're snappy dressers." He took a few steps over to Kord then. "My friend Kord, here, although not as stylish as I," Joe made like he was inspecting and adjusting Kord's garments. Kord quickly swatted his hands away with a deep scowl and a guttural rumble that seemed far more menacing than a simple growl, "is from the same world, a place called Midgorn. As for my friends carrying my weapons…" Joe turned around. His bandolier was suddenly full of all six of his knives, having just been deftly lifted from Kord. He walked back to Runara, relieving her of Death Seed with a slight bow. She didn't resist, not wanting to make a scene in front of the strangers. "I'm new to riding these beasts and my good friends here," his tone was both full of sweetness and sarcasm, "just didn't want me hurting myself, should I fall, but I think I have the swing of it now." He gave Runara a wink.

Crash burst out a hysterical laugh that almost sounded like a bad case of hiccups. Everyone looked at her, not quite getting what was so funny. Crash's laughter subsided to a giggle as she looked around at the others. Seeing that she was alone in seeing the humor, she shrugged her shoulders. "He's saying that he has the swing of it, but we just found him lying on the ground." She juggled three coconuts as she spoke, including the one she had accidentally hit Joe with earlier.

Everyone stared at her, waiting for her acknowledgment of her participation in Joe's dismounting. Crash just looked around, perplexed that nobody else found his comment the least bit funny.

"What? What?" she asked of the staring group as she continued to juggle, not once looking at the coconuts. "He was on the ground. What?"

Dicesh rolled her eyes and turned her attention back to Joe." A bladesman." Dicesh said with a large, hungry smile, a hand on her hip as she inspected Joe like he was for sale.

"The sword is really just kind of a souvenir. I favor my knives," Joe said, removing one of the knives from the bandolier with a fluidity that made it hard to truly catch the move. He casually began twirling it about his left hand and wrist. It almost looked as though the knife was attached to some sort of pivot point.

Host gave Dicesh a pat on the shoulder as he cleared his throat and approached Joe. "I think that our young clown's errant coconut may have been guided by the hands of Fate herself. It happens that our recent disagreement with the authorities and the inexplicable disappearance of our mime has left us several members short of our usual numbers. If we're to put on a proper show, we'll need a few more attractions, and a master of knives would be a wonderful addition, not to mention a brookshin witch and a, well, whatever you are. I could fill a city square just with people wanting to see you." he motioned toward Kord, giving him an unusually broad smile. Host's teeth seemed too large and too perfectly rounded.

As difficult as it was to read Kord's emotions, it was clear that he was somewhat annoyed. Runara's annoyance, on the other hand, was unmistakable.

Host seemed unaware or chose to ignore the festering attitudes of the witch and the beast. He turned back to Joe. "How's your aim with those things, lad?"

Joe laughed, falling back into a reverse summersault, rolling twice, then springing upright, three feet into the air and back, landing right beside Crash. His hands and arms were blurs, the knives flashing briefly in the sunlight as they seemed to launch themselves from his chest. Dicesh didn't even have time to flinch as all six knives found their mark in the shaft of her mace cane.

Host shook with a deep, gravelly laugh. The skin of his face shook so violently that it seemed it might pull away from his skull. Dicesh looked a little annoyed at first at the knives having embedded so deeply in her cane but gave a deep bow of respect, simply saying, "Impressive." The others were clapping, though none with the same exuberant enthusiasm as Crash, who was also patting Joe on his shoulders and back between rounds of clapping.

Runara felt the need to stop things before they went too far, speaking up then. "We are not joining your circus," she said, trying to tinge her stern, angry tone with as much politeness as possible.

Joe skipped over to her, grabbing her by the elbow and pulling her aside, whispering in her ear. "This could work for us. We just need to convince them to head to your granpappy's place."

"What?" Runara exclaimed in only a half-whisper. "What wou–"

Joe cut her off. "Trust me, he's going to vaporize us, or whatever evil wizards do, if we just show up on his doorstep waving around the sword and the crystal, but if we show up as part of a circus…" He left his sentence unfinished, stepping back towards Host and the others, his arms wide open, with a broad smile on his face. He nodded to Runara as though his plan was obvious. It wasn't, and the truth was he wasn't even really sure what good taking the whole circus to the wizard would be, but it would be the fulfillment of his childhood dream. Plus, it just sounded like a lot of fun to him. All his best plans, in addition to presenting themselves, as this one clearly had, started out as something fun, or rather, the ones that didn't start with being thrown through a window or a wall or unexpectedly detonating an explosive crystal.

Before Runara could protest any further, Host spoke up.

"The Mystical Magim, Runara, has made it clear that she is not fond of the idea of joining our circus, but let me offer this; travel with us as far as the city of Loncodi. We all seem to be headed in that direction anyway. We are to put on a show there in two day's time. All I ask is that you do that one show with us. If, after that, you still feel the circus life is not for you, we'll simply give you five gold each for your trouble, a more than fair wage, and go our separate ways. Reasonable?"

"Done," said Joe. Given that they were all headed to Loncodi, it was hard for Kord and Runara to protest, as they would be continuing on in the circus's company, one way or another.

* * * * * * * * * * * * * * * * * *

Traveling to Loncodi together now, the group moved through the forest just off of the road, not wanting to attract the attention of any of the King's men. The trees this close to Loncodi were massive pines, their lowest branches nearly fifty feet up. There was almost no undergrowth, just the odd fern, flower, or the occasional old dead fallen tree covered in moss and mushrooms or sprouting a new sapling. The forest floor was covered with a blanket of massive dead, rust-colored pine needles that crunched beneath the steps of the group's various beasts and the wheels of the clowns' cart.

Drixosu, the strong man, had no beast to ride but seemed content to run along with the group, seemingly tirelessly so. At first, he tried to chat with Runara, but when her one-word responses did not lead to any further conversation, he contented himself to simply run alongside her and her bailodant. He did manage to catch Runara briefly smile at him out of the corner of his eye and that was enough encouragement to keep his pace next to her, even if it was in silence.

Joe more than made up for their lack of loquacity.

Dicesh and Host's riding beast was almost as fascinating to Joe as the elephant. It was a robust but lanky camel, a little shorter than his bailodant, fitted with a canopied houdah. A great deal of the trip's initial conversation had been spent on not only the camel and the elephant but the beasts of Modnar in general. Adriga found Joe's descriptions of the beasts of Midgorn equally bizarre and fascinating. The two of them entertained one another with story after story about their countless, near-fatal encounters with a vast array of the native fauna of their respective worlds.

Joe's fascination did not stop with the beasts, finding the very concept

100

of the world of Modnar to be a source of endless wonder. Being that they seemed well-traveled, he rained question after question upon the circus troop about every aspect of Modnar.

He asked Crash, who had insisted on riding on his bailodant with him, about the land of Westerlan, and she was more than enthusiastic to regale him with tales of her homeland. During the course of her stories, Joe learned that it was just one of three other continents besides Senuvia, though Crash seemed to know little to nothing of the other two. She filled Joe's head with tales of wondrous Westerlan creatures, a race of enormous warriors called ogres that rode on the backs of flying, fire-breathing dragons, and entire elven cities that floated among the clouds. Joe found the very idea of the vast oceans separating the continents staggering and was looking forward to seeing the enormous boats she said were used to cross them. He also latched on to the concept of the flying elven cities, noting the similarity to the lofty abode of the Danuwan, the elves of Midgorn. Their kingdom resided up an extreme vertical cave, interestingly referred to as the Sky Cave. Crash, in turn, seemed entirely fascinated by Joe's descriptions of his world entirely encased in rock.

"Why don't you just dig your way back home? She asked, being fully serious.

Joe thought for a moment, not entirely sure that her idea was without merit. "That seems like far more work than I'm willing to put in, and honestly, I'm not sure Midgorn is down there. I fell down a very big waterfall to get here."

Crash's eyes widened at this, and she looked straight up, lost in deep, awestruck thought.

Asking her why she left Westerlan brought her back but resulted in her telling a rambling, convoluted tale involving a stuffed bear, a witch, a group of time travelers from the distant future, and a battle between a strawberry-flavored blob and a monster entirely made out of a substance she referred to as cotton candy. The explanation of why she left Westerlan or how she came to be in Senuvia as part of the circus was so obscured in the tale, if it was there at all, that it escaped everyone's comprehension. Her story only seemed to overlap with Ugor's version of Crash joining the circus in that they met during an arm wrestling match, which Crash had won. Ugor defended his loss, saying that he had been unusually intoxicated and Crash had been far too naked at the time. Rather than confuse himself further, Joe just let it be. Crash only reacted with a shrug and nod of agreement to Ugor's contribution to the tale.

Crash's story was only slightly stranger than the topic of the circus's former mime. Most in the troop seemed reluctant to touch the subject at first, save for Host, and even he started with, "Creepy lot, aren't they? Never wise to speak their names." Everyone seemed to agree, silently nodding, except Kord, of course, who was just as in the dark on the subject as Joe.

"But they sure can draw a crowd. That's how they hunt, you see." Host said with a wink.

Suddenly, Kord's attention was fully focused on the conversation, and he broke his run of silence. "They are hunters, these mimes? Fearsome things are they?"

"Oh no, not at all; dangerous, yes, but not fearsome. They can almost be kind of likable," Host said flatly but then gave a shiver, making all his loosely hanging skin shake and sway. "But they're silent."

"They do not speak?" Kord questioned.

"Aye," answered Dicesh. She leaned out of the houdah a little towards Kord. "They don't speak; they make no sound at all. Not if they cough or sneeze, not a footstep. Not even if you slapped one would you hear the smack of your hand on their disturbing little black and white face."

"But you don't dare slap a mime." Host shook his head violently, his loose flesh seeming to move a second or two behind his movements. "Remember how we found ol' Baylobar."

"What? How did you find ol' Baylobar?" Joe asked, having no idea who Baylobar was and sounding like a child being told a ghost story by the campfire.

Nobody responded. Crash just turned around to Joe and shook her head, letting him know it was not something to speak about.

"All mimes are as dangerous as this mime of yours?" Kord asked Host.

"Most I've seen anyway, but they're just little scrawny things, lookin' a bit like our clowns here, 'cept their faces are just naturally black and white; no need for makeup. Always dressed in black like they're headed to a funeral."

Joe cleared his throat at that point.

"My apologies, bladesman, I meant no offense. Your leathers are not nearly so off-putting; mimes are cloaked in living shadows, you see. Linger too close to a mime for too long, and you're as likely to end up a meal for their clothing as you are for the mime, if there's any difference between the two. Plus, it's not so much what you see with a mime that is so unsettling as what you don't."

"That infernal invisible dog of his kept spooking my beasts," interjected Adriga from above on the other side of Joe as King Kotep strode past the others, taking the lead of the pack. His cats, save for Koobara, were napping as before on the elephant's back. Koobara had run off, as was its way, as soon as the group set out.

Chenoval followed directly behind the elephant, riding a sizeable shaggy workhorse, adding in a monotone full of pathos, "And he was always tripping me with his invisible rope. Not funny at all."

Pulled by Chenoval's horse, Ugor rode in a small agile cart with tall wheels. Jugs of home-brewed alcohol surrounded him. The still that he used to make his alcohol ate up a quarter of the space in the cart, wrapped in a canvas tarp next to him. As the cart went by, Ugor leaned over awkwardly, only half whispering in Joe's direction, his breath thick with the stench of his hooch, "It WAS pretty funny. I miss the weird little bugger."

Nothing more of the mime was discussed.

Riding between the handlebar-like horns of Joe's bailodant, Crash had been looking at the sky throughout the entire mime talk. She turned to Host and Dicesh riding next to her and Joe. "Gonna rain tomorrow," she said matter-of-factly. "We should be to the city before then," she added, squinting back upward, "if we get back onto the road."

Joe looked at the clear blue sky. It rained in Midgorn as well; that is to say, water would fall like rain from holes in the vast domed ceilings above the major communities of Midgorn and in some of the larger wild caverns. In the communities, it fell at predictable intervals, as though regulated by some giant clockwork. The rain would fall more often in some communities than others, but always on the same schedule. Many of the timekeeping devices in Midgorn relied on this regular fall of water. That it rained in Modnar was comforting to Joe in a strange way.

"So there is a torvug up there somewhere, then." As he said this, Joe felt a little clever, convinced that he had figured something out about this world that its own inhabitants didn't even understand.

"A tor-what?" Crash asked, craning her head around to look at Joe.

"A roof, a ceiling that holds the other parts of the world above this area. It's where the water comes from." Joe explained as clearly as he could.

"Ceiling?" Dicesh laughed. "Nothing more pitilessly endless than the sky, my friend. I knew a woman, an odd, pink-skinned gal with glowing blue eyes; never seen the likes of her since, but she rode around in a magnificent, metal, flying skyship. All bluster, smoke, and thunder that mechanical juggernaut of hers. Said she and her ship came from another world, up there somewhere. The way she told it, if you fly upward far enough, you'll find other worlds beyond count. Sounds to me like you fell from one of them yourself. I'm surprised you survived. Ever try high wire?"

"Um, no," Joe answered slowly, confused by almost everything Dicesh had just said.

"Well, whatever's up there," Crash said flippantly, "rain is coming out of it tomorrow. Gonna be cold tonight, too."

"How can anyone tell? How do you?" asked Joe, finding this world more and more perplexing.

"Learned a few things from my papa. He was a knower, 'fore he blew his self up," she answered matter-of-factly. "'Course, I guess, he's still a knower, just a blowed up one."

"Blowed up?" Joe asked hesitantly, not entirely sure that he really wanted an explanation.

"Ya, you know…" Crash made a throaty rumbling sound as she spread her arms, her hands fanned out to depict her father's explosive end. "Caroline, Papa's lady friend, was pretty sure that he had just run off to be with Ma. It sure sounded like a 'splosion from the field. That's where I was, tendin' the sheep. When I run up, the house is gone, nothing left but Papa's boots, and they were pretty burnt up." Crash shrugged. If the incident had affected her emotionally, it wasn't evident.

"What happened to your ma?"

"I was too young to remember, but Papa said that she accidentally walked into a glowing hole in the world one day while she was feeding the chickens." She shrugged as she said it. "Hole closed up before he could go after her."

"What?" Besides the part about feeding chickens, Joe wasn't following any of it.

"Happens." Offered Host, having been listening to their conversation.

"Happens? What happens? People just disappear?" Joe asked, a little concerned.

Dicesh was the one to answer. "Usually, you'll see a hole already formed, just floating a little above the ground, but sometimes they sneak up on you. Especially just before Gatal is full. The thirteenth is a bad day for travel."

"Who is Gatal? The thirteenth?"

"Ya, you know," Crash pointed at the sky toward the smallest of the three moons. It was the only one still visible in the daylight as a small white half-circle against the blue sky. "Gatal is full on the fourteenth of every month, and the day before it turns full, the holes get tricky. Doesn't happen often that someone gets gobbled, but then it only has to happen once, right?"

Joe nodded in agreement, still not entirely sure what it was they were talking about.

"And godlings help you if a celeston crawls out of one of those holes," Dicesh added. "Nasty creatures. Come in all shapes and sizes they do, and no telling what manner of magic each monstrosity might wield."

"I heard a wizard once caught a celeston in a bottle," said Host. "Ooh, to have that for our show."

"That's nonsense, and you know it," grumbled Dicesh. "Not one celeston small enough to fit in a bottle."

"Where do the holes go?" Joe wasn't as much interested in whatever the celestons were, but what if one of these magical holes could lead home.

Host chuckled at the question. "If you're lucky, you'll just pop out another hole somewhere. That's what happens to most folk, least ways; end up on the other side of the world. Some, though, just never come back."

That might be grim, but it's still promising, Joe thought.

After a few minutes of a lull in the conversation, while everyone considered the possibilities of walking through randomly appearing tears in reality, the conversation for the remainder of the evening tended to revolve around food. The topics were mainly along the lines of 'What would they have for dinner?' or 'What was the weirdest thing you ever ate?' It was clear that everyone was getting a little hungry. Kord's eventual detailed participation in the discussions resulted in another more extended conversational lull. No one enjoys hearing about his or her own species described as food. His story was particularly gruesome, detailing a dish his mother would prepare for him, which consisted of parts of a freshly killed human woman fried in a batter made from her unborn child.

"So easy to find pregnant humans," Kord began to explain, then noticed that everyone was just staring at him with varying expressions of disgust or alarm. He judged their silence to be confusion, so he continued to explain. "It's just that your kind doesn't have a set mating season. It's just babies, babies, babies all the time." He licked his lips and rubbed his belly at this. "I can almost smell Mother's cooking now," he said, closing his eyes as he became lost in the memory.

Joe heard Dicesh comment in a low voice to Host, "And we thought the mime was frightening, but no worse than us, I suppose." Joe was simply left feeling repulsed and guilty for every critter he had ever eaten, made all the worse by a sudden craving for fried chicken.

Before sunset, Host suggested that the group stop and make camp, which, for the most part, consisted of nothing more than building a small fire. This was the task of Drixosu. While the others fashioned minor shelters from fallen logs and pine branches, Drixosu was busy twirling a sharpened twig into a curved portion of bark, trying to generate an ember among a tangle of grass, twigs, and pine needles. Runara, used to nightly camp preparations with her fellow brookshins, took it upon herself to gather firewood.

She was happy for the time alone, away from the chatter of the others, away from the chatter of her own mind as well. The task required enough of her concentration to keep her mind focused but was mundane enough to let her thoughts drift away. It was the first time since the incident with the King and his men that she felt something other than rage and despair, even if that something was nothing. With all the kindling and wood that they might need for the evening in her arms, she headed back to the campsite, and as she returned, so too did her thoughts of the horrors of the massacre of her family and friends, but now, with a slightly more objective perspective.

She was thinking about the first few moments of the attack, the way that she had fended off the soldier in her caravan. Even now, she could feel a warmth building in her hands as the feeling of anger and fear boiled within her memories. She dropped the kindling next to Drix and stared at the palms of her hands. They were glowing, very faintly but noticeably in the twilight.

Drix was still struggling to produce more than a few puffs of smoke, and his frustration was showing on his face.

"It's usually not this difficult," he said, looking up at Runara. "I think the wood might be a little wet."

"Let me try something," Runara said, motioning for him to scoot aside. Seeing the glow coming from the palms of her hands, he quickly shuffled out of the way, giving her nothing further than a cautious nod.

Runara knelt down, placing her hands just above the ball of grass and twigs that Drix had been trying to get to light. She stared intently at the little bundle, trying to will it to burn.

"You need to feel the heat in your hands, feed it with rage, passion, fury," Dicesh whispered from behind her. The slight surprise disrupted Runara's concentration only a little. "The emotion doesn't matter, but it must be intense. Picture something you love, something you hate, both together if you can." Dicesh added with a slight snicker.

Runara's mind went again to the soldier, but she could feel her hands cooling. Then she thought of the King, her dead family, and friends all about him as he sat upon his chrome horse. The heat in her hands grew. Drix backed away slightly, feeling the waves of warm energy emanating from Runara's hands. The air around her then was rippling from the heat being projected from her.

"Good, good," Dicesh whispered encouragement closely in Runara's ear; her hands were on Runara's shoulders then as she leaned in for a closer look. Dicesh's sudden presence, strangely, had not startled Runara. Her voice was somehow soothing, yet simultaneously sent Runara deeper into the emotions of her memories. "Whatever you're thinking about, focus on it. Focus on the core of that emotion, the root of everything that made that moment, that emotion, real."

Runara's thoughts turned to Joe's arrival in her camp.

An enormous ball of flame burst from her hands with an audible 'WOOMPH!' Dicesh jumped back in surprise with a triumphant laugh. Drix jumped back as well, his beard singed, parts of it still glowing and smoking.

As the rest of the group ran over to see what had happened, Dicesh turned to Host, saying with a broad smile, "I think we'll have her doing more than reading people's cards."

Joe was the only one who hadn't run over to see what had happened. He had looked up briefly, and aside from Drix having somehow lit his own beard on fire, nothing seemed to really be out of sorts, he thought. As Joe yanked on the makeshift sapling ties, tightening together the three logs of his amateur-grade teepee, he smiled and took a step back to admire his work. Crash had started to show him how to do it, but he interrupted her, assuring her that he knew how to tie a knot. A distinct sense that he had somehow avoided being knocked unconscious washed over him, and he let out a small, satisfied sigh.

Chapter 11

The summer sun beat down on the sand-colored stones of the catwalk, five stories up, joining the top of Loncodi's city hall to the deck that wrapped around the midpoint of the Tower of Laws. The shaded street below bustled with people using the main thoroughfare, coming from or going to the palm tree-lined market square. The noise of the market, one of the largest in North Eastworld, could be heard even up here on the catwalk, six blocks away.

Three men stood on one end of the catwalk, leaning against the wall, staying in the shade of the Tower of Law's archway canopy. Another man, tall, his long wavy black hair pulled into a loose ponytail, was on the other end of the catwalk, talking to a raven-haired woman who clutched a large stack of papers to her chest, her back against a wall. Her free hand self-consciously went back and forth from fiddling with her hair, pulled into a tight bun, to adjusting the tight-fitting knitted skirt of her formal, royal blue clerk's uniform. The man had one hand on the wall by her head, leaning in casually, closely, as they spoke. His words were making her smile and blush.

Nooch was in no mood for any of it, or any other delays, for that matter. It had been hard enough, taking most of the day, to get an audience with the local convenor to make arrangements to use the market square. Now, they needed to have the permits notarized, and Freshnir's flirtations with the town hall's filing clerk were only slowing things down.

The door to the Notary's office was right next to where Nooch leaned against the wall. He was tempted to go in without Freshnir as the office would be closed soon, but all four men needed to be there as each had requested a separate permit. In Loncodi, any individual can request only one permit per day, and their employer needed all four. He ran a frustrated hand through his thinning, greasy, black hair. He had already asked Freshnir twice to hurry it up and got nothing more than a smile and a wave each time.

"Drummers, always on the make, eh?" Pox gave Nooch a little nudge with his elbow, knowing full well how irritated Nooch already was.

"Aint that the truth." Pronz agreed on the other side of Nooch. The wiry, short little man twirled one end of his downward curling mustache as he waxed nostalgic. "What was the name of that girl back in Boxwater?"

"Who knows," Pox chuckled, his entire large, stalky frame shaking with the merriment of his memories of their time in the small swamp community.

"He's an ass." Nooch huffed.

"Nearly as pretty a thing as our Runara, she was," Pronz said, ignoring Nooch as he gave Pox a playful tap.

Nooch made a dismissive sound. "Hardly. Not a flower in this whole world will ever be half the beauty our Ru was."

The three stood silent for a moment, the reality of what had happened to their band of brookshins washing over them. Each wrestled with his own version of guilt over running away when the attack had begun to turn grim.

"Still," Pox said, breaking the uncomfortable moment, stroking his exceedingly long black beard contemplatively. "The girl was attractive."

A large clack sound came from the notary door just then.

"No," Nooch said with a low breathy voice of concern. He scuttled over to the Notary door. It was locked. "No, no, no, no, no!" he exclaimed tugging vainly on the door handle.

He turned, collapsing against the door as though he had just run a marathon. "We've failed. One simple task, and we failed it. We'd best start looking for a place to play for some coin lads 'cause I'm pretty sure we're out of the circus."

Freshnir came striding casually across the catwalk with a broad smile across his face. He turned briefly, giving a final quick wave to the clerk, who returned his wave. She disappeared into the dark archway of the city hall. A loud clunking sound echoed across the gap between the two buildings as she locked the door behind her.

"What's up, fellas?" he said jovially as if he had just happened to meet them there.

Nooch lunged toward Freshnir, shaking both of his fists in anger. "You, horny fool, you've cost us our jobs! Do you have to go chasing every pretty ankle in the land?"

"I'm really more of a breast man," Freshnir said, a swarthy look on his face, pointing a thumb over his shoulder. "And I don't know if you were looking, but she is…"

"GAAH!" Nooch blurted, frustrated beyond coherence.

Pronz and Pox laughed.

Nooch wheeled around, giving Pox and Pronz both an icy look.

"But…" Freshnir had tried to speak, but Nooch was too angry to hear any more of his blather.

"The three of you fail to understand the weight of our situation, but go on, make light of it if you will. See this?" Nooch dug frantically in one of the pockets of his grubby brown and yellow striped pants. The others smirked but waited patiently. Finally, his hand emerged. He held it out, showing three silver coins.

"You see?" He turned to show Freshnir as well, who simply rolled his eyes. "This, these three little coins, this is all we have. Enough to buy us three meals tonight, the only meals we'll have had all day, and guess which one of us is going hungry."

"Don't worry, Nooches, I'll share some o' mine with ya." Pox's voice was innocently sincere.

Nooch all but growled and was about to go into a rant but was cut off by a thought from Pronz.

"So, about them meals. How we gonna get them?" Asked Pronz. Nooch just blinked at him, his mind running in stray directions from anger and frustration, trying to fathom what part of purchasing a meal was eluding Pronz. "If the Notary is closed," Pronz continued, "and if I'm not mistaken, Freshnir's latest admirer just locked the door to the City Hall, how are we supposed to get down from here? The way I see it, lest we get down, none of us will be gettin' fed."

The other three were silent as they each came to grasp their predicament. Nooch's eyes grew wide, astonished that anything further could go wrong with the day. He turned and pushed past Freshnir, going to the iron railing at the edge of the deck right by the catwalk, and looked down the five stories to the street below. His whole body tensed with anxiety and rage.

"On a better note," came Freshnir's voice from behind, empty of any sort of concern, "I was trying to tell you. That lovely Miss was nice enough to give me our permit before she left. It gives us full use of the market square, not just the performance papers we were going to get. Look." He pulled the neatly folded sheet of paper from the bright yellow woven vest he wore instead of a shirt. "Gold city seal even. Said we wouldn't need the Notary."

Nooch's body relaxed as his temper gave way to a comedic sense of ironic defeat. "Well, good job, lad," he said, turning around. His voice oozed with sarcasm. "Let's get to the market then."

* * * * * * * * * * * * * * * *

As they rode through Loncodi's massive stone gate, carved from an impossibly large single stone monolith, a sight that had Kord mesmerized, Joe was preoccupied fingering at the painful bumps on his head. One lump, of course, was from Crash's rogue coconut; the other was a little newer. He had been knocked unconscious the night before. The dried vine he had used to bind the logs of his would-be teepee let go, dropping one of the logs on his head as he watched the commotion around Runara and the campfire. He was out for the night, waking in the morning as though he had simply been sleeping. Aside from being a little sore, he actually felt remarkably well-rested.

Crash was once again sitting between the horns of Joe's bailodant for this leg of the trip. She twisted her upper body around, nearly facing Joe, and observed his preoccupation with his head lumps for a few moments. "I knew this guy once, got whacked in the head by a gnome with a magic stick."

"Ya? This gonna be some sort of dirty joke?" Joe questioned, wincing a little as he pushed on one of the lumps a little harder than he ought to have.

"No, no. Straight as the arrow flies." She said.

"Arrows fly in an arc," Kord grumbled from his bailodant alongside them, still mesmerized by the enormity of the stone gate.

Crash frowned slightly at the interruption. "Well, no joke, leastways." She waved a dismissive hand at Kord and continued with her tale. "This fella had a lump on his head; started out small, just like yours. Six days later, it was so large he had to have his buddy hold his head up for him."

"Um…" was all Joe could muster as a response, wondering if that was all there was to her unlikely story.

"Ya, so a few days of walking around with his buddy holding his head up, the lump falls off, the guy's brains fall out, and a couple of little critters, kinda looked like tiny little dragons, pop out of the lump. Oh, they were such little cuties, chasing each other's tails, and then fwoop off they flew. Never saw 'em again."

"What?" Joe exclaimed. "And what in Kodin's arse is a gnome anyway?"

"No worries," Crash said flatly. "Gnomes are just little fellas, like Ugor, but smaller. Most of 'em pretty nice, too. Sooner bake you a muffin than give yer head a wackin'."

Joe had no response; he simply frowned as he continued to rub one of the bumps on his head. He could swear it was throbbing a little more than it had been a moment ago.

"Stop touching them. You need to let them heal." Runara commented from behind them on her own bailodant. There was no concern or compassion in her voice, only stern annoyance.

Adriga's elephant, King Kotep, just behind Runara, trumpeted then, startling Runara slightly. She turned frowning but cracked a rare smile at the sight trailing her. They had just barely entered the gate, but already there was a group of fifteen or so children running and laughing alongside King Kotep. Adriga was waving at the children and encouraging others they passed, adults as well, to join what had become an impromptu parade with Host and Dicesh bringing up the rear on their camel. Drix, still on foot, picked up two of the children, putting one upon each of his shoulders, much to both children's delight. The young dusty-haired boy in the ragged clothes of a child of the streets on Drix's left shoulder alternated between waving at others and flexing his biceps like some sort of mini strongman. The young girl on Drix's right shoulder, her clothing in better condition than the boy's, likely the daughter of a street merchant, reached out and patted King Kotep's rough grey skin. King Kotep seemed to approve and let out another trumpeting blast from its trunk. It was much to the young girl's delight and Runara's annoyance, but despite the earsplitting noise, Runara found herself sincerely and, surprisingly, still smiling.

Crash laughed and clapped at Kotep's second blast, then hoisted herself with surprising grace to her feet, standing with her arms open wide, more for flair than for balance, between the horns of Joe's bailodant. Joe laughed, and even Runara let out a little giggle. The festive atmosphere that was building was becoming infectious.

Kord was not feeling it. Though his face was expressionless, it was clear that he was uncomfortable with all of the attention that this spectacle was bringing. Everywhere he looked, there was prey, unafraid, smiling, cheering, and even waving at him for his attention. It wasn't natural.

Joe noted Kord's discomfort, making him laugh more than he was already. "Don't worry, ol' hunter, I'll keep you safe from the children." Joe snapped out one of his knives, twirling it about his hand in the seemingly gravity-defying manner he often did when bored. There were a couple of "oohs" from the crowd as they marveled at the dexterous display. Joe flashed a broad, charming, cheesy smile and, catching the eye of an attractive young flower vendor in the crowd, gave her a wink as he tossed the knife high into the air. As the knife came back down upon Joe, there were gasps from the crowd. Joe leaned well back and to the side a bit. The knife shot, blade-first, into its respective holster in his bandolier. Joe bolted upright, arms wide, with a smile to match. Cheers came from the crowd, drawing others to line the street. Joe was living his dream and wondered why he had never tried to join a circus earlier.

"Do you see what's going on?" Host asked Dicesh, leaning out of the houdah trying to see around Kotep's immense butt, giving the occasional absent wave to the crowd.

"No," she said. "I assume it has something to do with one of the new recruits." She was beaming, her hand making constant circles in the air, waving to the people lining the edges of the wide thoroughfare to the market as though she were some sort of royalty. "This is going to be a magnificent show."

* * * * * * * * * * * * * * * * * *

Garen Relok breathed in deeply the aromatic steam wafting from the simple white ceramic cup full of vibrantly green vericberry tea. Something about the color mixed with the aroma always reminded him of his youth. He couldn't quite place the emotion or the moment connected to it, but it always

114

made him smile. This was his favorite part of the day. The grand market merchants were just beginning to gather their goods and close shop while the clatter, rumble, and chatter of the day's shoppers and vendors trailed off in the distance to a nearly imperceptible murmur. The city would almost go silent for an hour or so before the night's revelers begin boisterously staggering through their various drunken, celebratory journeys from one tavern or inn to another. The sun was not yet set but so low to the horizon that its light was changed, if not exactly diminished. Garen felt a certain magic in the twilight, as though there was a thinner veil between the realm of man and that of the godlings. It was a chance to commune with the divine if only he could quiet his mind enough to listen.

Closing his eyes, he exhaled, reveling in the calm. He began quieting his mind, sweeping away all the distractions that had assaulted his thoughts throughout the day. His body, too, as it relaxed, seemed to be physically releasing the stresses of the day. It felt as though the tension was pouring off of him like a heavy, smoky vapor. Garen could almost swear that it made him feel lighter, but this was another distraction he needed to let go of.

He was having a little more trouble focusing on nothing today, however. During his prayer rituals in the morning, he had bound his left arm just the slightest bit too tight in the black leather-covered ropes that made up his traditional Zanxian monk arm braces. He couldn't tell yet if it was now cutting off his circulation or was simply just a little uncomfortable. He opened his eyes briefly, looking at the five-headed gold image of the godling Zanx that served as a buckle for the arm binding, and contemplated for a moment if it was something he could easily adjust. No, even this he could not allow himself to dwell upon, and closing his eyes again, let it go with the rest of his thoughts.

Somewhere in the distance was the clatter of falling wood and shouting voices that quickly trailed off. It seemed to be the last bit of the day's commotion. Garen's mind let go. A lone raven uttered a deep, croaking call that echoed among the taller neighboring buildings before fading into silence. It seemed to echo in his emptying mind as well.

This is how it was for him every afternoon and had been for ten years, save for the days it rained, which were few. He would make his way from a window on the third floor of the temple across the rooftops and precariously placed wooden planks that served as makeshift bridges between the building tops of the western quarter to the rooftop of the magician's guild.

Unlike the flat-topped roofs of the mostly mud and stone buildings of Loncodi's western quarter, with their rafters visibly jutting from their exteriors, the magicians guild's roof was a beautifully masoned dome covered in opalescent, blue stone tiles. Originally, the dome's apex had been adorned with a decorative, gold, anthropomorphic rabbit statue brandishing a wand and a staff as though it were casting some magnificent spell. Having been fashioned of solid gold, however, it quickly became the property of the thieves' guild, or at least so it was rumored.

Whatever the fate of the rabbit, what its absence left behind was a small, flat, yellow stone top to the dome about the radius of a large pie. It was just enough of a surface for Garen to rest his tea-filled cup and to hold himself in his usual meditative stance. The pose would not have been his first choice, but the Grand Master had insisted that it must be so if Garen were to have any success. Though physically demanding at first and making it an extra challenge to drink his tea, he came to find that standing on his hands, with his legs crossed, lotus style, gave him a wonderful perspective of the city. Looking down his body into the endless depth of the sky gave him a sense that he was flying. That sensation somehow made it easier to slough off the distractions of the day.

If the city guards ever noticed the bald monk with his black arm bindings and blood-red borakin, the traditional loose-fitting shirt and pants of the monks of the House of Zanx, they never bothered him. However, few people would be foolish enough to bother a Zanxian monk or nun. Members of the order were both loved and feared by most, known as much for their beneficence — feeding the homeless, cleaning the streets — as they were for their ferocity as warriors. Every monk or nun of the House of Zanx is trained from the age of three in damina kazo, the second oldest and perhaps most lethal form of martial arts in all of Modnar. In the ten years that he had spent upside down on the roof of the magician's guild patiently waiting for some sort of sign from Zanx, the five-faced godling, as to his true life's purpose, never once had anyone ever disturbed his meditation.

"Hey, hey you! HELP! HELLO?" The voice ripped through the silence with all the subtlety of an ax hitting a rhinoceros in the ass through a pane of glass. The sound shocked Garen's eyes open and nearly caused him to lose his balance. Maintaining his handstand, he shuffled himself around to face the direction from which the voice had come.

"Yes, YES! He sees us! He sees us. Thank the woods! Please! Please help us!"

Garen was having a hard time discerning exactly what he was observing. Being upside down, of course, was not helping, though he had grown used to looking at things from this perspective. As much as he could tell, however, down the slope of the dome, at the edge of the roof of a neighboring building, there was a large two-headed man with extremely long arms trying to strangle a headless, armless monkey that, in turn, was holding a large red ball with its feet. Although not entirely unlikely a situation in Modnar, Garen was still quite confident that his perception was far from accurate. He flipped to his feet, gliding down the slope of the dome to a thin ledge close to the frantic apparition.

Seeing the spectacle upright and much closer now, Garen immediately understood the desperation in the man's voice. Across the alley, on the roof of the building next to the Magician's Guild, two men in garishly colored striped clothing were leaning over the edge of the roof, holding another, equally garishly dressed man by the ankles, who in turn was holding a fourth man, of the same questionable fashion, by his head. This fourth man had both of his hands occupied, clutching the straps of a large backpack.

Garen scrambled back up the dome.

"Hey, wait, where ya goin'?" cried the same man as before.

Garen had no intention of leaving these men in peril; in fact, as a Zanxian monk, he was obligated to try to help them in any way he could. Almost back to the top of the dome, he turned around and took three running steps, then skidded down the dome at an alarming speed. Almost at its base once again, the monk jumped, launching himself into the air and executing a tight double somersault. He seemed to nearly fly between the two buildings.

He landed, nearly soundlessly, on the ledge of the other building near the precariously struggling men and immediately undid the gold buckle of the black leather and twine rope that made up the wrapping on his left arm. The relief to his left arm was immediate; he gave it a quick shake to help the circulation fully rebalance itself and then went immediately to the task at hand.

He stepped down onto one of the jutting rafters and quickly fashioned a lasso as he sat down, straddling this tiny portion of the large wooden beam.

"Stick your leg out if you can," Garen shouted down to the balding fourth man clutching the bag.

"But I ca—" Nooch flailed both of his legs. His face was a bright red, growing darker by the moment, with veins bulging hideously from his forehead and temples.

"Stop squirming; I can't hold on to your greasy skull much longer." groaned Freshnir, trying to tighten his grip on Nooch's head.

"Lucky for us, ol' Nooch don't have no neck," Pox grunted, readjusting his hold on Freshnir's squirming left leg.

"Ya, that noggin is locked on tight," Pronz added, seeming strangely comfortable with his half of the load. "Take more than a little neck stretchin' to pop our Nooch."

"Will you two shut it!" Nooch growled, his head turning a deeper shade of red. He continued to flail as he tried to raise a leg for Garen.

Garen's lasso flicked down at Nooch, effortlessly catching one of the random movements of Nooch's left foot. Garen gave the binding a flick, wrapping it twice around his forearm to prepare for the weight. The loop of the lasso closed tightly around Nooch's ankle.

"Drop him," Garen said calmly to Freshnir.

"Okay." Freshnir's compliance came almost too quickly.

Nooch cried out, terrified, "Wait, no!" but it was too late. He was falling.

Somewhere to the east, in the city, an elephant's trumpeting call echoed through the calm of Loncodi's early evening streets.

* * * * * * * * * * * * * * * * * * *

Screamin' Joe Blade's Ten-Point Guide to Life:
Point #6: Given the opportunity, always join the circus.

The market square in Loncodi, like many in Modnar, was precisely that, a large square, but where many squares in Modnar would have a well at their centers, the Loncodi market had an enormous fountain. It was a thirty-foot tall, sculpted stone depiction of the Tree of Life. Water sprayed out in flat discs from the end of every little stone twig, giving the illusion of a leafy canopy that poured down like a huge, watery, weeping willow. The thick roots of the tree writhed and twisted in their shapes like the tentacles of a group of tangled octopi dipping in and out of the large circular pool below. They nearly entirely masked a serpentine shape hidden among them. Within the roots, below the trunk of the tree, just above the pool's surface, one could barely make out the sculpted form of one of Modnar's oldest myths. The mother of dragons, forever trapped beneath the undying Tree of Life, endlessly gnawing at the undying roots of the tree, feeding upon its energy, even as the tree's roots fed upon her own immortal writhing, twisting body.

Loncodi was a wealthy city and the primary hub of all trade by land or sea in North Eastworld. Its wealth was reflected in the lavishness of such things as the size of the square itself, the market fountain, or the self-lighting torches and lamps that illuminated the square and fountain. These various flaming luminosities, even the strings of tiny orange lamps that dangled above the four street openings to the market, were no feats of magic but the works of Loncodi's ancient knowers, whose knowledge of their workings had been passed down for millennia to, and maintained by, the members of the present local knowers' guild. This and countless other fragmentary arcane secrets were kept in the library of their guild hall.

Visitors to Loncodi would be impressed not only by the fountain or the sixteen large lamps carved in the shapes of towering palm trees from the stone sides of the four tall buildings that lined the market square but also by the very streets. Bricks, fashioned of gold, silver, and even large cut gems, were woven in complex geometric patterns among the more typical stonework. In the market square, these patterns took on swirling shapes that radiated out from the stone bench rim of the fountain pool, reaching the very edges of the market square. The precious metals, stones, and crystals reflected the market's firelight in a twinkling display that made it look like the fountain was radiating light across the surface of the market floor. One would expect such bricks to be easy pickings for opportunistic thieves, but the streets of Loncodi were well patrolled by the city's guards, and the penalty for both stealing and vandalism in Loncodi was immediate death by beheading. As a result, Loncodi was incredibly pristine for such a busy metropolis.

Word had quickly spread throughout the city of the arrival of the circus.

By the time Joe and the rest of the circus troop arrived in the square, a large crowd had already gathered. So large was the crowd that the circus would have had no room to perform, but Adriga and King Kotep quickly corralled the crowd, packing them to the edges of the square. At the same time, Koobara slinked along behind, having only to give any stragglers the slightest rumbling growl to spook them into joining the rest of the crowd.

Seeing that some sort of performance was brewing, a few city guards began helping to corral the crowd to the edges while one younger guard was sent running down one of the side streets by his commanding officer.

Keeping the atmosphere light, if not entirely manic, Crash bounced along behind Koobara, clapping her hands above her head with great jubilance, doing a cartwheel or two, and making ridiculous faces. It was all much to the delight of the little children in the crowd. In a surprisingly loud voice, Crash shouted encouragements to the crowd to clap and cheer, which they did. The crowd was now suitably enlivened but well-contained along the edges of the market square. Crash proceeded to do a series of cartwheels and backflips, pulling the crowd's attention toward the fountain.

Host and Dicesh watched from their houdah atop the camel. It was going to be time to start the show, and still, there had been no sign of the minstrels they had sent on ahead to get the permit to perform. That troubled Host for two reasons. First, they would need the permits before more city guards show up, looking to shut the performance down. He might be able to talk his way around this first concern, but the second point was more of an issue. To perform without music would make for a weak show. Music can sway the mood of a crowd, and a happy crowd lets go of more money than an unhappy, or worse, bored, crowd does.

"Where are those fool minstrels? I know we shouldn't have trusted those brookshins with our gold," Host's whole face shook as he grumbled. "The four of 'em are probably face down in some tavern, drunk, and our gold spent on women and booze." a little droplet of blood streaked down his face from his left eye.

Dicesh produced a handkerchief and dabbed at the blood, cleaning up Host's face. "Now, now, my love. They'll show," she said consolingly, pocketing the handkerchief and holding his face in her hands to examine her work. "They may be fools, but they have honest souls. Don't go falling apart on me now." She kissed his cheek gently. "You can't be getting yourself worked up like this. It is nearly time for you to change."

"And there's that," he said, sounding a little defeated.

"No worries," Dicesh winked, sitting up a little, straightening her jacket, and brushing lint off where she could. She gave Host a knowing, sly smile. "We've drawn a large audience tonight; there's bound to be someone suitable. Or we could always use the boy with the knives." She climbed out, standing on the edge of the houdah opening. "He is more pleasing to the eye than the last, at least."

Host gave a disapproving grunt, to which Dicesh laughed. With that, she vaulted herself high off of the houdah, somersaulting down with all of the jungle-cat grace of Koobara, landing into an impossibly straight-legged, noble stance onto the fountain rim. Her gloved hands were folded neatly over one another on her cane, centered before her. There were a few gasps and "oohs" as the rest of the crowd grew quieter, their attention drawn to Dicesh's agile display. Crash cartwheeled past her, laughing maniacally.

Joe looked over at Runara to see if she had seen Dicesh's leap, and the look of both astonishment and confusion she was giving Joe confirmed that she had found it just as inexplicable. Joe couldn't catch Kord's eye as his attention was entirely focused on Dicesh, which was confirmation enough for Joe that he, too, had witnessed Dicesh's perplexing agility. Drix, standing between Runara and Joe's bailodants, offered Runara a hand down.

"It just gets weirder from here," Drix said in a hushed tone to both Joe and Runara as he gently lowered her to the ground. He held onto Runara's hand for a moment after. He could sense her tension. "Don't worry, you'll be great. We'll be up pretty soon, though, so we should make our way over. Joe, you can hang back here with the audience until Dicesh introduces you. Try to make your entrance dramatic if you can. The louder the crowd cheers for you, the bigger the chance Host will throw you a few bonus coins."

Joe nodded, hopping down from the bailodant and joining the nearby portion of the crowd. Among the curious onlookers surrounding him was a young girl, no more than fourteen.

"I'm Screamin' Joe Blade," he said, giving her a little wink as he flashed his cheesiest smile.

The girl responded with an unimpressed expression but tried to give

Joe a polite smile. It made her look even more unimpressed somehow. Joe, feeling a little uncomfortable then but undeterred, fueled by his excitement to be part of the circus, pointed to his bandolier as he looked about at the others around him in the crowd.

"I, uh, I throw knives."

An older woman just over the girl's shoulder nodded her understanding. Joe responded with a similar nod and a smile, folding his arms as he puffed up his chest a little, trying to look regal in some fashion as he waited for his moment in the show. He still wasn't sure what exactly he was going to do. The others had been practicing, going over routines while Joe was unconscious. He was utterly unprepared, though sure he would end up doing something pretty fantastic. Still, he was feeling uncharacteristically nervous. This was the closest thing Joe had to a life's dream, and he really didn't want it to go the way most things in his life tended to go. At the very least, he didn't want it to end with him flying through a window of some sort. Crash cartwheeled by, giving him an idea of what he wanted to do.

Dicesh, meanwhile, was busy strutting around the rim of the fountain, pumping up the crowd with promises of amazing feats from her gaggle of unusual performers gathered from all parts known and unknown around the world. The way she went on made Joe wonder if there were other members of the circus with them that he had not seen somehow.

In true clown fashion, Chen and Ugor were trying to corral the bailodants without much success, stumbling over one another, nearly being trampled at times, and dragged along in various unflattering positions. The bailodants did not require any corralling until Chen and Ugor approached them and very intentionally managed to spook the beasts. It was all very much for and to the amusement of the crowd. Eventually, Crash tumbled over to them in a series of backward handsprings, playing the part of what seemed to Joe an ironically sensible hero saving the two clowns from themselves.

King Kotep lowered Adriga to the ground, gently curled in its trunk. With the clowns safely out of the way, Adriga cracked his whip above the bailodants twice to catch their attention, bringing them to a halt. Koobara silently stalked nearby, making sure that none of the three bailodants tried to run away from Adriga or toward the crowd. It laid itself down, its front paws out regally before it, its head held high and alert, watching for any sudden movements from the nervous beasts. The bailodants, still a little skittish from the antics of the clowns, shuffled away from Koobara and closer to Adriga. Adriga made a few strange clicking sounds with his tongue. All three bailodants made a honking, grunting sound in unison and then gently sat down as though waiting for a rider to mount them. Adriga made a few more clicking sounds approaching the bailodants, giving each one a hardy pat, then turned to the crowd with an arms-wide flourish and bow.

There were smatterings of clapping and cheers from the crowd, but the entire audience hadn't been won over yet.

"Adriga!" Dicesh boisterously announced, strutting around to that side of the fountain. "There is no beast, large or small, that will not bend to the command of the greatest animal tamer on Modnar!" Dicesh twirled her mace-like cane like a baton. She had hoped to stall for more time, to give the minstrels a chance to show up, but the crowd would grow restless soon if they did not begin an actual performance, and there was no sign of the minstrels. The next thing to worry about would be getting shut down by the local authorities. She quickly scanned the crowd, hoping to see even just one of the minstrel's faces. Seeing no sign of them, she looked back toward Host, looking for approval to continue. He gave a reluctant nod.

"Citizens of Loncodi," Her voice bellowed at an unnatural volume, echoing off of the four buildings surrounding the square and gaining the full attention of every member of the crowd. "We are the Surco Gorra Monsarri!" A sudden fanfare of music punctuated her address, echoing as loudly as her voice in the square. Dicesh looked up to see the four brookshin musicians they had sent ahead and what appeared to be a Zanxian monk perched on the edge of one of the buildings lining the market square. She shot a quick look and a smile back to Host. He looked very pleased and was motioning for her to continue as he compelled the camel to lower itself so that he could exit the houdah.

Runara was beside herself with elation, so surprised, so thrilled, to see her friends. "They're alive!" Runara exclaimed in an excited whisper, more to herself than anyone else around her. She was trying her best not to burst into tears.

"I thought they might be part of your band of brookshins." Drix could see that she wanted to run to them if she could. "Don't worry, you'll get to talk to them soon enough; for now, it's the show."

Runara turned to Drix, Dicesh's words just now filtering down into her thoughts, "Surco Gorra Monsarri? That's ancient Modnarian for," she paused to make sure her translation was correct. Few in Modnar, other than scholars of arcane knowledge, still spoke the old language, but she had been schooled in the language by Vokar, and many of her medicine books were written in it. "Circus of Monsters?"

"Something like that. I did say it was going to get weirder." He said it with a charming smile that was somehow reassuring, though only slightly so. Drix still had Runara gently by the hand. "We're up. Come on," he said, leading her out in front of Dicesh.

"Behold, good people of Loncodi," Dicesh bellowed with a broad sweep of her cane in Drix and Runara's direction. "From the oldest, darkest woods of North Eastworld. The fire witch RUNARA!" the band missed their cue, looking at each other in disbelief. Nooch, gathering himself, signaled for the others to play. Pronz fiddled out an eerie progression, accompanied by Freshnir, suggesting distant rumbling thunder on his drum. Runara thought her heart would burst with joy and excitement. The deep red crystal nestled between her breasts began to glow slightly.

"Here we go, just like we practiced last night," Drix whispered in her ear. He grabbed her by the waist with both hands and, with a quick movement, tossed her straight up in the air. She gave a little surprised scream from the shock of the sudden movement, even though she had known it was coming. There were a few startled little screams from the audience as well. Drix's ridiculously strong, meaty hands caught her well above his head, just above her ankles. His grip alone did most of the work to keep her balanced, but Runara flailed her arms a little and completely stiffened her legs to keep herself from tumbling backward.

She swallowed hard, closed her eyes, and raised her arms high, bringing the heels of her hands together far above her head, palms facing the sky. She felt a tingling sensation in her chest emanating from the red crystal pendant. Energy surged through her arms, and an enormous fireball erupted from her hands high into the air. It made a loud woomph sound, and Joe, like the others in the audience, could feel its heat. There were many "oohs" and "aahs" from the crowd.

Drix, still holding Runara high, now began walking around the fountain, displaying her for all of the crowd to see. She let off another two fireballs as they made their way completely around the fountain. Many in the crowd were clapping then. Others were cheering. Crash continued to tirelessly cartwheel around the fountain close to the audience in the other direction, laughing maniacally.

Ugor lagged behind her with a shallow wicker basket, holding it out to generous-looking people in the crowd. Chen was doing the same on the opposite side of the fountain. There was a specific skill to the collection baskets. One didn't want to bully people into giving money, and one didn't want to look too needy. The first trick was to get someone to look you in the eye. From there, it was all about finesse. Without saying a word, you had to convey a message like, "Hey, isn't this fun we're having." If you could squeeze a smile out of them they were as good as got, but you couldn't just thrust the basket out. You had to make slight subliminal movements, and if you did it just right, the person would have their hand out with a coin or two before you even held the basket out. Ultimately, though, it came down to reading people, and sometimes shaking the basket in front of them did the trick. Some even wanted you to banter it out of them. Chen was all about silent subtlety, but Ugor was a master and would engage the crowd in whatever manner it took to coax the coins out of the people. Still, it was just the beginning of the performance, and people were reluctant to relinquish their money so early.

Seeing some of the people part with some coins, Runara found herself smiling and glanced up at the musicians on the roof, who nodded or waved as their instruments permitted as they played. She looked back down at Drix then, ready for instruction.

"Now, the other thing," he encouraged with a smile.

She closed her eyes and put her arms straight out to either side, her palms facing out. Drix let go of her right leg, holding her aloft then only by a single firm grip above her left ankle. She folded her right foot behind her left knee as Drix began to rotate. Again, she could feel the energy rise within her. She had marveled the night before at how Dicesh was able to coach her on exactly how to use her newly discovered ability to conjure fire, but everything worked as Dicesh suggested; precisely, in fact.

As spouts of flame shot out four feet from both of her hands and Drix slowly rotated her, each spout of flame left a fiery trail at its farthest-reaching point. Slowly, the two trails formed a floating ring of fire. It was something impossible, and the audience gasped and went quiet even before the ring was finished. More coins started to be dropped into the baskets of Chen and Ugar as they went about the audience.

Drix gently lowered Runara down, holding her close in both arms, face to face, a little longer than was necessary for Runara to regain her footing on the ground. The music reached a little fanfare as Drix and Runara took a bow beneath the still-burning ring of fire. The music trailed off shortly after, each musician seemingly playing completely different bits of music from one another. It was clear that the music was being entirely improvised, and the band had no idea where things were going next. King Kotep filled the silence with a blast from his trunk. Adriga, back on the shoulders of King Kotep, shouted a short command, and Kotep began lumbering over to Drix, Runara, and the ring of fire.

The two tigers on King Kotep's back rose from their constant napping, roaring, and pawing toward the audience menacingly. There were cries of alarm from the crowd.

"Fear not, good citizens of Loncodi! These beasts will not harm you, though surely either could dispatch you with a single stroke of its paw. Adriga has the beasts well under his control, even as he commands the beast that prowls at your feet." Dicesh pointed her cane in the direction of Koobara, who was slinking along the edge of the crowd. Many had not even noticed it on the move again, so focused on the ring of fire and the tigers. There were many gasps of surprise and concern, and everyone took a step or two back as Koobara came by, just as intended. Audiences had a tendency to shuffle in closer and closer if they weren't encouraged to keep back, making it potentially more dangerous for both them and the performers. Koobara only needed to give the slightest of huffs or growls to encourage anyone not moving back immediately. It crossed paths with Ugor, who made a comical, stumbling point of mock fear and respect, giving Koobara a wide berth to do his job and the audience a much-needed chuckle to relieve any tension.

"Kruliza! Azilurk!" Adriga shouted the names of the two tigers. The two cats instantly calmed at the sound of his voice. Kotep was alongside the ring of fire then. So tall was King Kotep that the ring, having not moved from where Runara had created it, hovered nearly two feet below the level of Kotep's back. "Ota! Kruliza, Ota!" Adriga commanded, pointing at the ring of fire.

Kruliza shuffled slightly, adjusting her footing on Kotep's back, then leaped out toward the crowd and down through the ring. There were gasps from the crowd as the tiger jumped, even more so when she landed. Kruliza was no longer a tiger. She had transformed. Rising from her crouched landing position, Kruliza was now a young woman, looking approximately eighteen years of age. Her orange and white hair was cropped short and slicked back. She wore a loose-fitting tunic, seemingly made of her former tiger skin, tied with a belt that a moment ago had been her tail. Though entirely human in appearance, there was something vaguely cat-like about her face; her eyes almost seemed to glow yellow with an inner fire, and tufts of white hair sprouted from her ears. She gave the astonished crowd a pleasant but mischievous smile.

Runara had gasped in shock along with the crowd. "I didn't do…I… did…did I do that?" she exclaimed in an astonished whisper to Drix.

"No, no, though I expect you could, in time. Nope, that's just their nature. I told you it was going to get weirder." Drix gave Runara a playful nudge with his elbow.

"Azilurk, Ota!" Adriga shouted, commanding the second tiger to jump.

Azilurk gave a rebellious roar and pawed slightly in Adriga's direction. Adriga, instead of shouting the command again, simply responded with a stern look and a slightly raised left eyebrow. The tiger gave a frustrated, growling chuff and leaped off Kotep's back through the ring of fire. Like his sister before him, his form altered the instant he emerged through the bottom of the ring, landing in a crouched position, completely human. He was nearly identical, in his lean, muscular appearance, to his sister. Kruliza approached him, taking him by the hand as he stood and raising their hands together in a triumphant manner.

"I give you Kruliza and Azilurk," Dicesh's voice boomed. The music from the nearby rooftop reached a dramatic crescendo as the two took a bow. The audience cheered and clapped. "Among the last of Southern Senuvia's animons!" The two began walking the perimeter of the market to give all in the market a proper look. There was still a cat-like smoothness to their stride and demeanor. With far less coaxing required, Ugor and Chen's baskets filled with far more coins.

Without warning, Azilurk and Kruliza stopped their promenade. Kruliza, still holding her brother's hand, made a few short strides around her brother and then kicked out with both legs. Several audience members closest to them cried out as her feet swung past their faces. Her brother swung her around three times like a great war hammer and then arced her high into the air, her momentum suddenly halting as she came to rest in a one-armed handstand, balancing with her left palm flat against her brother's right. Gravity dropped her tunic to her waist as she slowly executed a full split with her legs.

"By the Woods!" Runara exclaimed with a shocked gasp.

Drix chuckled. "Well, they are cats. Not much into undergarments. Great acrobats, though."

"Now THIS is a circus!" someone shouted, clapping, from the crowd. It was Joe. There had been gasps and chuckles from the crowd, but this quickly erupted into full laughter and applause.

Kruliza went straight into a fantastic series of backflips, rotating above her brother's head, touching his hands with each flip briefly enough to propel her into the next flip. It didn't seem to be a physical strain for either of them. Their stony expressions didn't hint at discomfort or pleasure, and aside from pausing for a dramatic flourish to get a cheer from the crowd, they went from one amazing acrobatic feat to another, hardly seeming to acknowledge that there was an audience there at all.

Joe was enthralled by their performance, clapping very loudly with each extraordinary move and applause cueing flourish. He prided himself on his own agility; it had gotten him out of more than a few nasty situations in the past, but these two made him feel like a clumsy drunk. He made a mental note to get the feline siblings to teach him a new move or two later when they had a moment.

A squat little man in a heavy knit, grubby, dark grey jacket was beside Joe. He hadn't been there earlier, having wriggled his way into the spot, clearly trying to get a better view from wherever he had been. It was hard for Joe not to take notice of him as he was clapping and cheering nearly as vigorously and loudly as Joe. His heavy body odor also played a good part in being noticed, and a portion of the crowd had pushed back from him somewhat. Joe didn't care much; he had been around much worse, had been much worse himself from time to time. The smelly little man had bushy eyebrows resembling two spiny-backed black caterpillars butting heads above the bridge of his bulbous nose. His squinty, extremely dark brown eyes, nearly looking black, blinked at a distractingly frequent rate, with every third or fourth blink pulling his whole face into the action. Greasy strands of black and grey hair were swept across the top of his head in a poor attempt to conceal its balding. The nearly shoulder-length hair on the sides and back of his head was thick, however, and looked as though it may have been combed once a very long time ago. His equally tangled, hedge-like sideburns all but completely hid his tiny little ears. They had been left to grow down his cheeks, where they eventually met under his nose, forming a woefully mismanaged mustache, the hairs of which poked out in every possible direction.

"Flexible little puss." The foul-smelling man commented with a sleazy little snigger as he clapped loudly with his pudgy little hands. Kruliza had herself bent backward, holding her ankles forming a nearly perfect circle, while her brother, on his back, propelled her around and around in the air with his feet in a running motion. "And did you see the kegs on that fire witch?" The little man continued, puckering his lips, "Makes a man want to join the circus, eh lad." he nudged Joe with an elbow.

Joe looked down at the man, still clapping. He couldn't help but give the man a smile and a nod, then leaned over slightly to him. "I am with the circus!" Joe made the exclamation with a boyish bit of over-enthusiasm in his voice. The young girl on the other side of him just rolled her eyes and took the moment as a cue to shuffle herself a few people further away in the crowd. "But mostly, it's her fault." Joe added jokingly, pointing at Crash, who was still touring the edge of the audience in a tireless set of cartwheels."

The little man gave a hearty guffaw at that. "Are ya lad? Aye, that little rabbit would keep a man up for a night or two, I'd wager, if you get my meaning." The man laughed hard at his own comment, making a needless and more than slightly inappropriate gesture with his fist and forearm to help explain.

Joe laughed, but his laughing trailed off as he started to find the man's lewd commentary on his new friends a little off-putting. It was a surprise to

Joe. Conversations such as this had been quite common in the past and often initiated by Joe himself. He wasn't used to having friends or having to defend them. Joe was always on his own and always found his own way. Being part of a group was going to take some time to adjust to, and he suddenly found himself wondering if, in the past, he had come across as offensive as the fuzzy little man in grey. At the very least, Joe assumed others found him far more charming and handsome than this sleazy little man. He then remembered the young girl beside him, who probably didn't need to hear the man's comments. Seeing that she had gone, he was relieved and hoped that she hadn't been too exposed to the inappropriate exchange between him and the lewd man, not just for her sake or the sake of his friends, but because he was going to be part of the show soon. He didn't want someone in the audience to dislike him before they even saw him perform. If he could, he hoped to be as inspiring to some young kid as the knife master in the Midgorn circus had been to him. An extremely little voice in the back of his mind started to rise in protest, citing the ridiculous mess of brawling, womanizing, thievery, murder, and booze that his life had been, but that was soon drowned out, as it always was, by his thoughts of how awesome things were going to be in just a few moments.

Another voice was shouting then, somewhere beneath the noise of the crowd. It was slowly cutting through the other noise as the roar of the crowd diminished.

"Stop! Stop, I say!" Roared the angry voice from behind the crowd, down the main thoroughfare. The crowd parted as a troop of ten Loncodi guards in royal blue gambesons and gold breastplates ordered them aside. Their captain strutted in angrily behind them, shouting again. "I command you to cease! Who is in charge of this troop?" He strode into the middle of the market, staring at the floating ring of fire. "And who is responsible for that! Stop it. Stop it all now!" The firelight danced off his breastplate, which was fashioned to look like the scales of a great lizard. His men were dressed similarly to him, but their breastplates were made up of small interconnected hexagon shapes rather than the scale design, and whereas the captain had only a short sword at his hip, his men brandished pikes and small forearm shields. Also, unlike his men, he wore no gold helmet. His face was not exactly handsome, crisscrossed with the scars of many a melee, but he had a strong jawline, and his thick, well-groomed, short, wavy grey hair gave him an air of handsomeness.

"I SAID STOP!" The captain's voice echoed throughout the market square, though nowhere near the impossible volume that Dicesh's voice had earlier.

The musicians stopped playing. Kruliza and Azilurk stopped their acrobatics. Chen and Ugor paused in their basket-waving activities amongst the crowd. Runara gave a subtle wave of her hands, causing the ring of fire to fade to nothing. Crash continued to tumble along, laughing maniacally, as she had been doing all along. Everyone watched in silence, seemingly mesmerized by her cartwheels of insanity. Somewhere in the crowd, someone cleared their throat just as she tumbled up to the captain of the guard. His face was stern, not quite at a point of seething anger, as he stood fully in her path, making no attempt to avoid the laughing, tumbling juggernaut who seemed oblivious to his presence. She stopped up short of kicking him in the face, coming to an incredibly sudden halt, planting her feet toe to toe with his, and once upright and still, lifted herself up on the tips of her toes, flashed the captain a huge smile, and quickly planted a small kiss on the end of his nose. The audience erupted in laughter.

An old man wearing the robes of a merchant reached over Ugor's shoulder from behind and tossed a coin in his basket. "Best part of the whole show so far." he croaked in a grumbled tone that clearly wasn't used to saying anything positive.

The captain of the guard held up his hand, and the audience seemed to understand that he wanted their silence. The laughter stopped, and the din of conversations trailed off to a quiet few.

"Who is in charge here, girl?" the captain's tone was a low, forced calm.

Crash bounced on her heels slightly as she pointed toward Host, who was already walking toward them.

The captain straightened his already stiff form, apparently trying to make himself as tall as possible. It was unnecessary as he was already several inches taller than Host.

"Why, sir, are you disrupting the flow of my earnings?" There was an amicable tone to Host's mock gruffness.

"You must gather your performers and vacate this square immediately."

The captain said. He hardly looked at Host, constantly scanning the crowd and the other members of the circus for any activity that might seem suspicious.

"With all due respect, that simply isn't going to happen. We have our permits, and we will complete our show. You wouldn't happen to know where I might find some dancing girls, would you? I'd prefer them with spear-dancing experience, but any talent will do. We just recently lost our gals, and the show just doesn't feel right without them." Host's drooping face registered nothing but innocent inquiry?

The captain huffed with frustration. "We received no notice of your performance, not for today, not tomorrow, not at all. Where are your notes of acquiescence?"

Host fumbled about momentarily, patting his coat pockets until he remembered the musicians. He cleared his throat, hoping nobody noticed his moment of uncertainty, and turned, looking up at the musicians on top of the building across the square. "He wants the papers," Host shouted up to the four-man band.

Freshnir immediately produced the paper from the pocket of his brightly striped vest, waving it above his head. "Got it right here," He shouted down to Host and the Captain.

The captain gave Host an unimpressed look. "Get him down here. Now."

Waving his arms to gather his small troop of performers, Host assured the captain that they would have them right down. He excused himself from the captain and huddled with Dicesh, Adriga, the twins, and Drix. After a few moments of discussion, they broke. Dicesh scuttled herself back to the fountain. Her voice boomed at an unnatural volume once again. It made the captain and nearly everyone else in the market square jump slightly.

"Our apologies, good people of Loncodi, but we will have this matter with the local authorities resolved shortly. We thank them for their diligence in ensuring the safety of everyone here tonight and all that they do to make Loncodi such a magnificent city. Please put your hands together for the brave men of Loncodi's city guard!"

The audience erupted into applause. The captain of the guard looked a little annoyed at first, glaring at Dicesh, but as the applause and cheers continued, he noticed his men smiling even as they continued to hold the crowd in their place, and his stern countenance softened slightly. He even gave the crowd a small, self-conscious, acknowledging wave. Not entirely taken in by the ploy, though, he shot Host a stiff-lipped look, brows furrowed, and pointed at Freshnir, indicating that he still wanted to see their papers. Host responded with a large smile, holding his hands up in a gesture of reassurance. He then gave a signal to Dicesh.

Once again, her voice boomed, quieting the audience. "If I could ask you to direct your attention to the mighty King Kotep as he assists our musicians from their lofty abode among the stars down to the ground with the rest of us mortals.

Adriga, Drix, and the twins stood around King Kotep, directly below the musicians' location. A portion of the crowd had cleared away for them. Adriga motioned for his fellow performers to step back and give the elephant some room.

"Toma!" Adriga commanded. King Kotep seemed reluctant, shaking his massive head. Adriga jumped back slightly to avoid being hit by Kotep's enormous, curved tusks. Kotep gave a small trumpet from his trunk, further protesting the request, and took a rebellious step toward Adriga. Adriga held his ground this time, giving Kotep a stern look.

"Don't pretend you haven't done this before." Adriga was staring the giant beast down. He was trying desperately not to crack a smile. "Toma!" He tried the command again.

King Kotep snorted his trunk, flinging a splatter of mucus that covered Adriga's head and shoulders. The audience immediately surrounding them broke into laughter. Crash, too, was jumping up and down, clapping.

"Funny," Adriga said quietly, scraping as much of the dripping elephant snot off his face. "Now, if you're finished, would you mind?" he made a motion with one hand as he spoke, indicating a direction toward the building and up.

Kotep trumpeted in such a manner that it quite nearly sounded like laughter. The elephant then shuffled itself around, positioning itself facing the wall. With great effort, it pushed itself up onto its hind legs, propping itself up against the wall of the building with its front legs. Adriga made a half-hearted one-armed flourish. The crowd clapped while their laughter over the elephant mucus continued.

Azilurk and Kruliza were moving then. Kruliza crouched, cupping her hands and launching Azilurk as he ran toward her, up and onto the back of King Kotep. She then quickly scrambled up behind using Kotep's tail. Kotep let off a disapproving blast from his trunk but held his position. Azilurk climbed up to Kotep's head with ease and reached out a hand to assist Kruliza, who was right behind him. Kotep wrapped his trunk around Azilurk's legs as Azilurk smoothly hoisted Kruliza into a standing position on his shoulders. Kotep raised the two of them as far as his trunk could extend. The crowd clapped, but the trio still fell nearly eight feet shy of reaching the rooftop.

Drix stepped up then. He gave each of his arms a stretch as he crouched down at Kotep's feet. Without so much as a grunt, he lifted the elephant by its back feet to his chest level. The crowd was astonished; many gasped, but most had simply gone silent. Drix shuffled his feet a little, finding more stable positions, then with a slight grimace, Drix gave three short puffs and, in one quick, incomprehensibly strong motion, lifted the elephant and the twins, straight-armed, above his head. It was another impossible feat, on par with Dicesh's leap earlier.

The crowd remained silent for a few more moments as the people tried to process what they were seeing. Someone started clapping. It was Joe. Then, the entire market square erupted in applause. The clapping and cheering were nearly deafening. Kruliza took a moment to give a little flourish. Then, on her tiptoes, peeking over the edge of the building, she gave the band a wave, trying to encourage them to use her and the others to climb down. The band seemed reluctant to do so, but Garen stepped up, still feeling responsible for their safety, and carefully made his way down. Kruliza offered one hand as a foothold while she steadied herself against the building. The monk had no trouble at all making the climb down. The hardest part was the drop from Kotep's butt to the ground, but he accomplished this with a dextrous roll. Popping upright a few feet away.

"You're not part of the band," Drix said with a little grunt.

"No, I am Garen," the monk replied.

"Well, Garen," Drix shuffled a little, readjusting his stance under the crushing weight of Kotep and the twins. "Nice rollout. Ever consider joining the circus?"

Garen looked around as though he were sizing up what the life of a performer might be like. "No. It is not our way." His voice was genial enough, but his face betrayed no emotion.

Drix grunted a little as the weight of Pronz making his way down was added to his load. "A monk, huh? Well, you might want to help the others down from the King's ass. I figure that our musicians don't have your agility."

"Of course." Garen gave Drix a deep bow, then positioned himself to catch the others as they came down.

Host and the captain of the Loncodi guard were walking over to the wall then.

"As my Mistress of Ceremonies said, we'll resolve this matter shortly." Host reassured the captain.

"You best because the list of fines I'm about to slap on you is growing every moment." the captain said sternly. A few steps later, his stern character broke, unable to hold back his astonishment. "How is he doing that?" referring to Drix's impossible feat of strength.

"It's really all about leverage." Host offered, shrugging as they continued toward the strongman. The captain didn't seem convinced by the answer, frowning and looking more than a little puzzled.

Sensing a lull in the performance, the scrappy little man beside Joe gave Joe a nudge with his elbow. "So, where the lot of you off to from here?"

"What?" Joe had been as distracted as the rest of the audience by Drix's lifting of King Kotep and the twins. "Uh, oh, I'm not sure. I mean, we haven't worked that out just yet." Joe was stumbling over his own words. "It's, well, it's complicated."

"Of course, of course." the little man nodded as though he completely understood. "I don't imagine you would have made the trip to Loncodi if you hadn't intended to head out to sea to reach your next stop, am I right?"

Joe wasn't sure how to answer the man. From what he understood, taking a boat would cut the travel time to Nashtar's keep, but he didn't want to let this man know about his plans. He didn't even know the names of any communities in that direction that he could bluff about as the location of their next show.

"What are you getting at?" Joe tried to deflect the man's query.

This triggered a broad smile from the man, which Joe found a little disconcerting. It felt like he was walking into a trap. "Well, it just happens that I have my own ship," the little man began.

"What's a 'ship'?" Joe asked, having no such thing in Midgorn.

The little man just laughed, assuming that Joe was playing with him. "Me and my crew just dumped some cargo here in Loncodi, but a deal we made with a local merchant went belly up, so now we'll be weighing anchor with an empty hull."

"Sorry to hear that." Joe offered, not entirely following what the man was talking about, but he was able to surmise that a ship was some sort of water-faring vessel large enough to transport a large number of goods. "So, you're offering the circus and me a ride, is that it?"

"Well, 'offering' for a reasonable fee. Can't pay my crew with an empty ship or good intentions, eh, my friend?" the little man gave Joe another playful nudge of his elbow.

Runara walked over just then. "Staying out of trouble, I hope?" She was only half joking with Joe, but Joe was glad to hear any degree of humor from her. She was even smiling.

The little man was nearly drooling as he eyed Runara up and down. "Well, now, friend, you must introduce me to this fiery beauty." He was clearly proud of his weak play on words.

"Uh, sure. Uh…" Joe realized that he didn't know the little man's name.

"Cap'n Maktura Krag." the little man quickly jumped in, wiping his right hand on his coat before offering it out to Runara.

Reluctantly, Runara shook the man's hand, sure that she would be contracting some sort of illness in doing so. "Runara," she said flatly.

"Most just call me Cap'n Mak." He was staring directly at her breasts as he spoke and continued to shake Runara's hand for a moment longer than she found comfortable. Runara found herself having to pull her hand away. "And what's your name, lad?" He asked, turning back to Joe.

Joe's chest puffed a little as it did whenever he introduced himself. "Screamin' Joe Blade." He crossed his arms, trying to strike as heroically phlegmatic a pose as possible.

The man simply blinked, apparently void of any opinion or reaction. He turned his attention back to Runara. "So, I was telling your friend, Screamin', here, that there's room on my ship for you and your circus."

"Really?" Runara leaned in. Capn' Mak suddenly had her attention. "We need to get around the mountains to the north," she quickly went on. "Can you take us to Cravenhuddle?"

Joe had no idea what she was talking about but assumed that this Cravenhuddle place must be along the way or close to Nashtar's keep. He arched an eyebrow and looked off in a random direction, trying to look slightly disinterested.

"Cravenhuddle, you say?" Mak's eyes lit up. "Seems we may both be in luck. We had no plans to stop in a port so small as Cravenhuddle, mind you, but we are headed northward. S'pose I could give the lads a banyan 'long the way and drop you lot off while we're at it. Won't be cheap, mind you. Two gold a head, including the black cat. He's not a shifter like those other two, is he?" Mak pointed toward the twins, who were helping the musicians down.

Pronz was down. Pox was having a hard time clambering his way down Kruliza and Azilurk. At the top, Freshnir and Nooch seemed to be arguing about who was going next. At the bottom, the captain of the guard was clearly agitated that Freshnir was still not down with the papers.

Runara looked back at Mak and shrugged, hands on her hips. "Not really sure if that cat changes or not, to be honest."

Mak laughed. "He'll have to stay in the orlop; the other two as well if they're going be stalking about as tigers."

"What about the other animals? Are you sure there's room enough?" Runara motioned an arm in the direction of the camel and the bailodants. "Are you equipped to carry an elephant?"

"Not a concern, Miss. As I started to tell your friend here. My ship, the Harmaton, was set to ship forty head of boggorats."

"Boggorats!" Runara was astonished. "Don't the males breathe fire. Terribly dangerous cargo, isn't it?"

"Oh sure, sure, but the man assured us there would be no males, just a heard o' docile gals carrying prime-grade meat sacs ripe for pluckin'." Mak cleared his throat then, realizing he was getting a little off track. " But as I was saying, we'd already loaded up the food and bedding for the beasts when the merchant shows up saying his entire herd has been stolen. So now I'm stuck with a hold full of open hay and feed that I can't sell. You'll be doing me a favor bringing along your big breasts — er beasts." the little man's face blushed at his blunder, but he kept talking before either Runara or Joe could react beyond the snicker he got from Joe. "I won't even charge you for transporting the steeds, even the elephant."

"That's great news, right," Joe said excitedly, entirely blowing his already feeble attempt at seeming stoic. He had no idea what a boggorat was but was glad for their timely misappropriation. Soon, they would be on their way to the wizard, and here he was, part of a well-received circus. What a great day this was turning out to be, he thought, not at all the way his days usually go. Nobody had even tried to hit him yet today. He looked around to see if the good news would get a reaction out of Kord, but he was nowhere to be seen.

"Have you seen Kord?" Joe asked Runara.

"No, haven't seen him since we began the show," Runara said absently, still focused on Cap'n Mak. She appeared to have ignored the captain's word-slip. "Look, I'm going to go and mention your offer to Dicesh, the ringmaster." She pointed at Dicesh. "If she and Host are up for it, they'll be the ones paying our way. Will you be right here?"

"Actually, lass, I have to be gettin' back to my ship." Mak oozed an insincere sadness. He was absentmindedly rubbing his hands around one another like a greedy tax collector. "With or without you, we set sail at midnight tonight. You'll want to show up well before then to get settled in if you're coming." He started to push back through the crowd then. "We're at the far south end of the wharf, last ship on the widow's pier. Look for the ship's name; she's called the Harmaton," he reminded them in case they had missed the name the first time.

"Thanks," Runara offered, as Mak disappeared into the crowd. She turned back to Joe, her polite smile immediately dropping. "I'll have a talk with Dicesh about that little pervert's offer. You should get yourself ready. Once they clear things up with the authorities, I think Dicesh wants you up next."

"Well, look at you all part of the circus," Jack said smugly. "Lady, I'm always ready." His left hand flashed to his chest. It flashed back out, spinning one of his knives on the tip of his forefinger. He punctuated it with a smooch in the air and a wink in her direction.

Runara rolled her eyes and spun around quickly, walking off to talk to Dicesh.

"Ya, she loves me," Jack said hungrily, watching her hips sway as she walked away.

Crash tumbled by, seemingly out of nowhere, slapping Joe across the face and grabbing the spinning knife all in one smooth movement, cartwheeling away, her maniacal laughter apparently ceaseless. Joe stood a little stunned, watching her spin away. The crowd immediately around Joe was laughing; a few were even clapping.

"Hey, that's my knife," he exclaimed, holding his cheek. He started chasing after her. The crowd laughed even harder. The laughter followed Crash and Joe through the crowd as he pursued her clockwise around the perimeter of the market square.

As Joe scrambled after Crash, he noticed a man in the crowd clad in black armor with a red head wrap. He was one of the King's men; there was no doubt. The black armored man didn't seem to be about to cause any trouble, but his presence there in the market was potential trouble enough. Joe stopped, looking back in Runara's direction, hoping he could catch her attention. Where in Kodin's name had Kord got off to, he wondered. It was no good; Runara was too caught up in her conversation with Dicesh. It seemed he couldn't get anyone's attention. Host was busy keeping the captain of the city guard occupied while Freshnir was finally making his way down. Nooch was still trying to figure out how he was going to get down from Kotep's butt, and Drix was helping him out with that by finally putting Kotep down very slowly. Chen and Ugor were busy keeping the market-filling audience from walking away with their antics, while Crash just continued her cartwheeling madness. Joe was frustrated; he could feel that things were about to go sour, and he couldn't get the attention of any of his companions. Koobara was suddenly standing beside him, perfectly silent. It was staring directly at the King's guard.

"Well, at least someone else sees him. A little more subtlety might be in order, big fella," Joe said in a muffled tone for Koobara's ears only.

A menacing rumble came from Koobara in response.

"So how do we let the others know without being too obvious?" Joe was looking around again, hoping for an opportunity to present itself. Instead, what he saw made his stomach twist a little. There were others now. More of the King's guards were in the audience. They hadn't been there a moment before; he was certain.

Host and the captain of the town guard were walking over to Dicesh then. Joe started toward them himself.

"Come on, Koo—" Joe had started to summon the large jungle cat to follow him, honestly not expecting the cat to pay him any mind, but not only was it not paying him any mind, it had already slid away as silently as it had appeared. A little boy in the audience who could see Joe's bewilderment waved at Joe and pointed toward the fountain. Joe looked where the boy pointed but couldn't see the cat.

"Creepy," Joe muttered to himself. He gave the boy a little nod, just the same, which made the boy smile. "Gotta play this cool," he muttered further to himself, and he started walking over to the others again.

"This farce of a circus is done!" shouted a new voice from a spot in the audience not far from Drix and the musicians. Joe was on the opposite side of the fountain, unable to see who was speaking. It wasn't the captain of the guard, for his familiar voice boomed in response.

"By whose authority?" the captain of the Loncodi city guard commanded as he held high the permit sheets that he and Host had retrieved from the musicians. "I'm the authority here, and their papers are in order." The captain of the guard had expected cheering from the crowd, but instead, the crowd seemed oddly pensive. His men were gathering to him then, and it was just then that he noticed the King's men dispersed throughout the crowd.

"By my authority." Shouted the new voice. The crowd before the main thoroughfare parted again, revealing Baron Solvar. He was wearing a deep crimson patch over his left eye now. "Oh, and the King, but I'm sure you've figured that out already."

The captain of the city guard pushed past his men and marched angrily toward Solvar, his voice echoing through the square as he walked. "Even the King must provide the proper documentation to overstep my authority here."

Solvar appeared incredibly bored. He raised his left arm, holding up his hand as if to signal the captain to halt, but then there was a loud crack of thunder and a flash from Solvar's palm. The captain of the Loncodi guard stopped in his tracks, a small dark spot in the center of his forehead. He collapsed then, lifeless, blood gushing from the tiny hole in his forehead.

There were screams from the audience, followed by mass pandemonium as the entire audience tried to scramble in any possible direction that took them away from the scene or the nearest King's guard.

"Take them!" Solvar's voice shouted over the turmoil.

Joe was being buffeted on either side by frightened city folk rushing past him. He had lost sight of Runara almost immediately when the audience first got out of control. He called for her, but it was near hopeless to be heard now above the screams of the people and the barking communications of the King's men, who seemed content to hack down anyone that got in their way, and from there, as citizens began to fight back, it all broke down into a complete riot.

Joe managed to hop up onto the lip of the fountain. Dicesh was still on the lip on the other side, but Runara was nowhere to be seen. Forty more city guards poured into the square from the northern street exit.

"CHEN, UGOR!" Dicesh's voice boomed at an impossible volume above the noise.

Though Dicesh was mostly obscured by the fountain between them, Joe could see one of the King's guards closing in on her location. She didn't seem to be aware of him. Joe shouted at her, frantically looking in all directions, trying to avoid being snuck up on himself. It was useless, though; she couldn't hear him. He ducked down, getting a better view of her through the fountain's downpour. The black-clad guard was wielding, with both hands, a menacingly large double-headed ax, already drenched in the blood of a couple of Loncodi citizens. He was bringing the weapon down hard upon Dicesh. At the last possible moment, she whipped around with an uncanny instinct, moving in close to the man in a blur of movement. She stopped the assault, catching the handle of his weapon with the handle of her mace. Her free hand ripped the helmet and its wrappings violently from the man's head. The guard swung his ax back in one hand, attempting a second attack, but Dicesh opened her mouth wide, revealing a menacing set of long fangs, two above, two below. She lunged forward, biting down hard on the man's exposed neck. The guard stiffened instantly, dropping his weapon, his face contorted in silent pain and horror, apparently unable to produce a scream.

Joe nearly lost his balance from the shock of the spectacle. He decided she wasn't going to need his help and jumped back into the panicked crowd. He needed to find Runara.

Dicesh tossed the guard's limp body aside into the fountain, the blood pouring from his neck quickly turning the water red. She turned back toward the sea of frightened scrambling citizens, looking for Host. Instead, she saw Solvar making his way toward her, a menacing smile on his face. For the briefest of moments, she found herself thinking how distractingly handsome the one-eyed elf was. She shook it off but still found the moment disconcerting. It had been centuries since she had been mesmerized by anyone, used now to being the one who did the mesmerizing, whether of a crowd of patrons or a victim of her blood thirst.

Solvar raised his arm, ready to fire another round from the gun built into his recently acquired mechanical appendage. Dicesh was about to dodge but then smiled. It was not the reaction Solvar had expected, and he realized just in time that something was wrong. Instinctively, he ducked and turned to confront the skull-faced tower that had nearly managed to get the better of him. Chen had narrowly missed taking Solvar's head with the sword of one of Solvar's very recently deceased men. Gears whirred, and plates shifted with grinding squeals as a long, sharp-pointed blade sprung from the forearm of Solvar's mechanical limb. Solvar easily parried a second attack from Chen, leaving the tall clown open. The King's one-eyed elf quickly seized the opportunity and sunk his blade deep into Chen's midsection. It stopped the clown's assault momentarily, but instead of dropping, the giant simply made a moaning groan and, with his free hand, clutched Solvar by the throat, easily lifting Solvar off the ground. Solvar, strangling but with the calm of a seasoned fighter, pulled his blade from Chen's torso. In one smooth movement, he blocked another swing of Chen's sword and flashed the blade above the arm Chen was throttling him with. Chen's eyes rolled back, and he began lowering Solvar, whose face was turning red. Solvar's toes barely touched the ground when Chen's eyes suddenly rolled back into focus, an expression of rage clearly visible through the clown's paint. He jerked Solvar back into the air. Solvar's eye went wide. He didn't understand.

"But —" was all Solvar managed to say through Chen's strangling grip, and he stabbed the giant repeatedly in the chest in desperation. Still no reaction, no blood.

Chen made a sound then that was close to but not quite like a hiccup. His head rolled back and fell off. Chen's body went limp, dropping Solvar and collapsing. The Baron recomposed himself and turned back toward Dicesh just in time to see her leaping toward him. She was practically flying. He fired his arm gun at her, catching her fully in the chest no more than three feet away. She collapsed onto Solvar's blade, impaling herself through her midsection. The force of the impact knocked Solvar to the ground, Dicesh's limp form on top of him.

There was an angry blast to the right, then from King Kotep's trunk. The massive beast was crashing through the crowd, buffeting aside and crushing beneath its massive feet, both guards and citizens, making his way toward Solvar. Adriga, riding Kotep, had a crazed look on his face. He gave a guttural cry as he repeatedly cracked his whip in the air.

A massive royal guard wielding an immense war hammer stood his ground partway between the approaching elephant and the Baron. A city guard attacked the giant of a man from the left, swinging his sword in a deadly arc toward the royal guard's neck. Barely moving, the royal guard raised his hammer in the sword's path. The sword shattered, shooting deadly fragments and wreaking havoc among those in the surrounding crowd. The royal guard shot out with the hammer, without a windup but with incredible force, catching the city guard in the face with a horrible crunching sound. The city guard collapsed, his helmet and face pushed in, his neck broken. The royal guard again turned his attention toward the charging elephant, winding back with his hammer, preparing to hit the beast full force.

Kotep lowered his head, preparing for the impact with the large royal guard. The guard swung his hammer, putting all his strength and weight behind it. Kotep twisted his head slightly at the last minute, reacting to the man's defensive assault, blocking the hammer with one of his log-sized tusks. The tusk broke with a thunderous crack but succeeded in dissipating the hammer's energy. The pointed end of the broken tusk, propelled by the force of the impact, punctured the armor on the guard's right thigh, passing through his leg and bursting through the other side. The enormous man grunted but almost seemed unaware of the grievous injury. He was already pulling his hammer back for another swing as Kotep crashed into the guard, grabbing him, at the same time, with his trunk. The guard's hammer narrowly missed crashing down upon Kotep's skull as Kotep flung the man across the market, dashing the man against the wall of one of the surrounding buildings. As his body hit the ground, a group of citizens descended upon him, pummeling and savaging his lifeless body further.

Adriga looked down from Kotep into the chaos below as Kotep arrived at Dicesh's limp form. Kotep swung his head back and forth, keeping an area clear around Dicesh. A scarlet spider web was expanding beneath Dicesh's face-down body as her blood flowed out through the spaces between the bricks of the marketplace floor. Ugor arrived on the scene at that moment as well. To Adriga's frustration, Baron Solvar was nowhere to be seen. He hadn't even noticed the elf run away.

"Is she gone?" Adriga shouted down to Ugor.

"Can't tell," Ugor responded as he turned her over. "There still may be time." He was holding a hand over the blade wound in her belly, but blood still poured from the gash where the blade had emerged from her back and the small hole in her chest.

"I need to get her out of here!" Host's voice caught them both off guard as he burst from the surrounding crowd. "There's a boat on the docks!" He was a nightmare vision of blood and gore. A large flap of skin that had been his left cheek dangled from his jaw. His clothing was shredded and soaked in blood; large, sliced wounds in his flesh were clearly visible. "The witch spoke to its captain," he croaked, huffing, out of breath, "the Harmaton." He placed a hand on Dicesh. "She's still here. Go! Get her to the boat." his voice was weak but stern as he clutched at Ugor. "I'll follow when I can."

"I'm not leaving without the cats." Adriga was scanning the mayhem even as he shouted.

"What about the others?" Ugor asked meekly.

"I'll gather them if I can, but you must go now!" Host growled.

With surprising strength, Ugor lifted Dicesh, cradling her in his arms. Her feet were dragging slightly as he disappeared with her into the chaos.

Another royal guard suddenly leaped out of the surrounding melee, lunging his sword at Host. Kotep slapped the man down hard with his trunk, stepping on the guard's head as he hit the ground.

Then came a burst of flame to the right and howls of pain as flesh cooked within black armor. Two armored, smoking bodies went flying across the crowd, still screaming, into the fountain pool, producing a hissing cloud of steam. Runara and Drix burst forth into the safe area being created by Kotep's vigilance.

"The others?" Drix asked with a relaxed tone that seemed out of place in the havoc. Aside from a few rips in their clothing, he and Runara looked almost entirely unharmed.

"Chen is gone; Ugor and Dicesh are headed to the boat. Haven't seen the bladesman or his beast friend. And the minstrels ran off at the first sign of the King's men." As he spoke, Host tried to push the flap of skin on his face back in place. Thick blood oozed from the edges down into his already blood-soaked beard.

"Oh!" Runara put a hand to her mouth in shock at the sight of Host.

"Hold it together, girl," Host said gruffly as he picked up the sword of the guard with the crushed skull. "We're going to the boat. The others will just have to find their way." Blood spattered from his lips as he spoke.

"But," Runara tried to protest, knowing that her fellow brookshins had no idea about the boat, but Drix had her by the arm.

"Ja! Ja!" Adriga shouted, cracking his whip and slapping the top of Kotep's head on the left side. The elephant lurched to the left, sweeping people out of the way with its trunk. As Kotep skirted the fountain, moving toward the market's east end, people cleared out of his way. Two of the King's guards made an attempt to halt the beast. One was wise enough to get out of the way; the other fell victim to Kotep's remaining tusk and was carried for a distance impaled upon it. The gruesome spectacle made others more inclined to get out of the way until Kotep flung the man some distance into the chaos of the ongoing riot. Host and the others followed closely behind in Kotep's wake.

It was chaos, though; in addition to the city guards and the citizens fighting the royal guards, in the frenzy of the riot, citizens were attacking other citizens, and as a result, city guards were also fighting with citizens. This simply turned further citizens on the city guards. At one point along the trip across the market, Drix knocked out a large man with a single punch as the man tried to grab Runara. Host, meanwhile, lashed out with the sword he had picked up by the fountain at anyone who got too close. Kotep was an easy mark to follow, however, and as the group got closer to the eastern exit, a group of the King's men was working their way through the mayhem toward Kotep and the others.

More city guards had shown up as well. The situation was getting worse rather than better. However, the mayhem was primarily contained in the market. The narrow street leading east from the market to the city docks was completely empty.

As they arrived at the street opening, Adriga turned Kotep around, completely blocking the exit to the street and shielding the others from the mayhem within the market.

"What are you doing?" Host demanded of Adriga.

"I told you. I'm not leaving without the cats. Crash is still out there, too.

"I understand, but we don't have the time. They might already be de—"

"They're not," Adriga interrupted Host through gritted teeth. "Go! We'll be behind you."

Host stared for a moment, trying to devise an alternative plan. Kotep lurched, fending off the first of the King's men to reach them. Host could see more guards growing closer through Kotep's legs.

"GO!" Adriga pleaded.

Drix put a hand on Host's shoulder. Realizing that there was no alternative, Host simply gave Adriga a relinquishing nod and turned down the street. Drix followed. Runara stood a moment more, tears in her eyes.

"I'll try to find your friends too, Runara, but save yourself now. Go." Before Runara could protest, Adriga turned back to the crowd, scanning for his cats and the others. Runara wiped at her tears, giving the mayhem one last look before turning and running to catch up with Drix and Host.

✱ ✱ ✱ ✱ ✱ ✱ ✱ ✱ ✱ ✱ ✱ ✱ ✱ ✱ ✱ ✱ ✱ ✱ ✱

Joe had tried to make his way to Kotep and the others as they made their way around the fountain but had got caught up in a fight with a particularly persistent city guard. By the time Joe managed to toss the man into the fountain, Kotep was already at the east exit, and Joe found himself distracted by further attackers. Death Seed had been getting a workout, and though he was not typically one for brandishing a sword, he found that he very much liked the speed and agility of the long, narrow, impossibly sharp blade.

He had been fending off one of the King's guards when he underestimated just how sharp the blade was despite his previous experience with the sword back in the woods. Old fighting tactics and habits were hard to adjust. What should have been a much lighter thrust as he ran the man through turned out to be a little overzealous. So easily Death Seed sliced through metal bone and flesh that Joe sunk the sword to its hilt, and the sword, protruding quite some distance out of the man's back, sliced into the arm, slightly, of a citizen.

This particular citizen was part of a trio that had been busy kicking a city guard they had brought down just moments before. They immediately turned on Joe, leaving Joe little choice but to dispatch the three townsmen as well. No sooner had he dealt with them, in a gruesomely deadlier way than he had hoped, when he was confronted by a city guard. The man, seeing the body of a fellow guard at Joe's feet, assumed that Joe had done the deed and immediately tried to exact some vengeance for his fallen comrade. For the first time ever, Joe found himself trying desperately not to gravely harm an opponent. He was failing in a spectacularly bloody fashion. What should have been a block of his sword against the guard's metal gauntlet ended up taking the man's hand off just above the wrist. Death Seed continued on its path unimpeded, lopping off a good portion of the man's right cheek and ear, along with that portion of the man's helmet. The guard was more than a bit distracted by his sudden injuries, and Joe took the opportunity to remove himself from the situation.

"Sorry, sorry," Joe shouted back as he went.

That retreat, however, meant pushing through the surrounding melee and having to injure even more people, whether intentionally or not. Joe fended off two more citizens, which distracted him from keeping his eyes on Kotep. By the time he had a chance to look up again, Kotep and Adriga were gone. He assumed they must have continued down the eastern street, but he had no way of knowing whether Runara was with them.

It was just then that, through the chaos, Joe spotted the brookshin minstrels and the bald fellow they had with them on the rooftop earlier. The bald fellow was a blur of impressive defensive fighting flurry, but the brookshins were just doing their best to avoid being hurt, using their instruments, if they could, to block any attacks. Joe decided that if he could save this last remnant of Runara's massacred band, he would. He knew he owed it to them and to Runara, and he hated owing anyone anything. Joe crashed through the crowd in the band's direction, his battle cry echoing off the market square walls, clearly audible above the noise of the rest of the riot.

* * * * * * * * * * * * * * * * * * *

Garen and the brookshins had made little progress maneuvering through the crowd. They had started to flee toward the southern exit when the King's men arrived but were caught in the crowd of panicked citizens running in every direction but the southern exit. City guards, arriving from the south street, were already trying to restore order while the King's men attacked people seemingly at random, both citizens and city guards, fanning the flames of chaos.

When the band saw Adriga and Kotep plowing their way toward the eastern exit, they tried to follow.

Garen had used his martial skills to blaze a bit of a path without inflicting any harm on other fleeing citizens, but it still seemed unlikely that they could cut through the market frenzy in time to meet up with the others. They had yet to make much progress through the crowd and were still closer to the southern exit than any other street. As much as any action can make sense in the midst of a riot, it made sense to turn back and aim again for the southern street.

They had nearly made it when their progress came to a complete stop. There was a cluster of four of the King's men, whose presence blocked the southern exit; nobody was getting out that way without a fight. Before Garen and the band could choose a new direction or forge a plan to slip past the royal guards, one of the black-armored men pointed at them. Trapped by the surrounding mayhem, Garen and the brookshins had nowhere to go, at least not soon enough. The four guards were quickly upon them. None of the guards seemed interested in Garen, much to his advantage.

Before the four guardsmen could react, Garen lashed out with the speed of a striking viper, the pointed fingers of one hand finding the gap between chest plate and helm on one of the guards, striking him hard in the throat. His trachea crushed, the guard staggered back, clutching at his throat. In an unbroken chain of movement, Garen stepped past the suffocating guard, spun low, sweeping out a leg, hitting the next guard hard in the back of the knee, dropping him face-first to the ground.

Garen then had the other two guards' attention, now distracted from the damage they were inflicting on the musical instruments that the minstrels had been using as shields.

A blood-curdling cry, like the wailing of a restrained madman, resounded throughout the square then as Joe came crashing down upon one of King's men. The momentum of Joe plummeting into the guard sent them both tumbling into the surrounding melee, bringing down three other men with them like a set of dominos.

Garen was a swishing blur of movement, stripping the helmet and sword from the remaining guard while also spinning him around and kicking him headlong into the hole punched into the crowd by Joe's tackling of the other guard.

The stumbling guard's face rushed straight into the extended fist of Joe, who had already recovered from his bullish battering of the other guard with the agility of a leaping monkey. The guard was out.

There was a brief moment of respite as the chaos continued around them. Joe gave his punching hand a little shake. The last impact had been a little harder than he expected, but it was nothing he was not used to.

"You guys all right?" Joe asked with a tone so casual he might have just been strolling by.

"Sure, sure," Nooch responded, sounding extremely frantic. The rest of the band simply nodded, traumatized beyond words.

Satisfied that the band was unharmed, Joe turned to Garen then. "Do you have to shave every day, or is it just like that?" he asked, pointing at Garen's head.

"Neither," Garen responded without hesitation. "My meditations keep it from growing back."

"What, really?" Joe was incredulous.

"Bladesman!" a voice cried from the surrounding mayhem, prompting Joe and Garen to spin around. It was Solvar. His remaining eye was fixed on Joe as he hacked and punched his way through rioters and city guards, seemingly unstoppable in his approach. In the wake of the one-eyed elf, there were two more black-armored King's men, finishing off anyone maimed but alive. Solvar's charge gained momentum as he grew closer.

Garen calmly went into a defensive stance. Joe knew better than to waste throwing knives on Solvar. Giving Garen a sideways glance, he tried to mimic Garen's well-trained martial pose.

"You should get a sword," he suggested to Garen, nodding toward Death Seed as he swished it subtly in the air as an example.

"Not necessary," Garen said solemnly, his eyes fixed on the approaching assailants.

Solvar punched a man hard in the face as he bullied through the riot, breaking the man's nose and hurtling him toward Joe. Joe was forced to throw the man aside, lowering Death Seed in the process. Solvar was on him in an instant, the tip of his arm blade narrowly missing Joe's head as Joe reflexively leaned backward, dodging the attack. Solvar kicked out, catching Joe in the stomach and knocking him to the ground.

Garen fluidly dodged the assaults of Solvar's two guards. As one lunged at him with a sword, he swiftly sidestepped, grabbing the man by the sword arm and guiding him directly into the other guard with a crashing clatter of armor. The two men stumbled together into Solvar just as he was about to shoot Joe, knocking the shot wide by only a few inches. The shot ricocheted off the market floor, catching Nooch in the thigh. The musician cried out in pain.

Joe took the opportunity to roll back and up onto his feet, simultaneously giving a sweep of Death Seed as a defensive measure. It worked. Solvar had lunged at him but was forced to stop short to avoid the tip of the ridiculously sharp sword that had once been his.

Garen leaped then at Solvar's rattled guards, spinning in the air and landing a kick to one guard's head. The force was enough to break the man's neck, and he crumpled to the ground. That made the other guard pause and rethink his next move. Garen landed in a defensive posture, ready for whatever the guard would bring. Three more royal guards arrived, bashing their way through the crowd.

Death Seed rang as it clashed against Solvar's arm blade, sparking as it took tiny nicks out of the edge of the elf's surprisingly strong weapon with each defensive block. Defense was all that Joe was managing. The few opportunities during which Joe could attack were invariably blocked and countered, putting Joe back into a defensive role. This wasn't his style of fight. He was all about the quick, surprise attack. Solvar would eventually win this fight if it carried on much longer. The smile on Solvar's face told Joe that he was only being played with. Solvar was simply biding his time until

Joe might give him an opening. The elf pushed in with three quick slashes.

"You owe me an eye and an arm," he growled at Joe.

Joe didn't understand how he was responsible for Solvar's missing eye and arm. Besides, the arm wasn't even missing anymore. At best, all he owed the man was his sword and that he had stolen fair and square. Whatever the case, Joe was too busy trying to parry Solvar's rapid attacks to argue the point.

Although outmatched, Joe was able to deflect two of three flashes of Solvar's blade, being forced to lean back and to the side to avoid being skewered by the third. Joe was more agile than most in a fight, but the move had left him vulnerable. Solvar quickly flicked his blade in a small arc, trying to convert his miss into a hit. Joe twisted his best to avoid the extra strike but was already too off balance. Solvar's blade just managed to catch Joe on his exposed weaponless arm. The badly nicked blade barely chewed through Joe's black leather jacket before inflicting a wide, shallow gash on his arm just below his shoulder. Joe took two quick steps back before somewhat regaining his balance. He tried to ignore the pain, but his momentary focus on the minor wound had already made him sloppy. He was still open.

Solvar's blade was already arcing to take Joe's head off when, with a roar, Koobara seemed to drop out of the sky. The Baron whipped around just in time to see not much more than teeth and claws slashing at him, and then he and the shadowy cat crashed into the surrounding mayhem.

Koobara let out a blood-chilling scream that sounded almost human, leaping off Solvar but then stumbling. Blood poured almost invisibly against the blackness of its left front leg but left a stark red trail on the ground.

Solvar was struggling to get up, having difficulty finding a foothold on the equally struggling heap of bodies he and the jungle cat had taken down with them. He was covered in blood. It was hard to tell if it was all his. There was a bleeding set of wounds just above the shoulder of his mechanical right arm where Koobara had bitten him and slashes across his chest and legs as well. He quickly gave up trying to stand and chose instead to finish off the cat with his arm gun. Koobara's bite had made it impossible for Solvar to raise the mechanical arm on its own. He was forced to use his other hand to lift and aim it toward the gravely injured cat.

Joe lunged toward Solvar but smashed into something solid, or rather, something not quite soft but certainly much harder than the air ought to have been. The invisible, whatever it was, knocked him back, causing him to stumble and fall at Nooch's feet. Nooch and Pronz pulled Joe inside of the minstrels' defensive back-to-back huddle.

Thunder burst with a flash from Solvar's mechanical arm, creating a strange spatter of blue fluid in midair between him and the prone form of Koobara. The air blurred and rippled between the two, and then suddenly, Kord's hulking shape appeared. His enormous upper right arm trickled blue blood from the small wound that Solvar's little bullet had inflicted.

Mirroring Solvar, Kord had his left arm raised at the elf. He was aiming a series of bamboo-like tubes that poked out from the leather and binding twine that made up the bulky gauntlet on his left forearm. Kord's expression was as stony as ever, but something in the corners of his mouth almost seemed to be smiling.

Voop, voop, voop, came the sound from his forearm, throwing Solvar back with the impact of three large darts. One had stuck into the barrel of Solvar's arm gun in the palm of his mechanical hand, the second had caught him in his upper left arm, mirroring Kord's wound, and the third had embedded in the leg that Koobara hadn't slashed a moment ago. Solvar was writhing on the ground like an upturned turtle, unable to effectively use any of his arms or legs to pick himself up now. Kord reached over his shoulder, pulling out a wooden cylinder long enough to accommodate both of his massive hands. Leather and twine formed a grip. There was an audible clicking sound as he brought it down in front of him. A spike of hardened, black wood nearly the length of the cylinder dropped from the bottom, while two small, hooked, steel ax blades snapped up from the sides at the top. It was a traditional mander hunting weapon called a gorsrog.

From Joe's perspective over Pox's shoulder, events seemed to unfold in slow motion. Garen was spinning, jumping, bending, doing everything he could to fend off the group of the King's men. There was already a heap of them at his feet, but these last four weren't giving him an opportunity to strike. One of the royal guards, a large man wielding a heavy single-bladed war ax, noticed Kord moving to strike Solvar with the long spike of his weapon. He broke away from the futile assault on Garen and lunged at Kord, ax in both hands above his head. Joe called out, trying to alert Kord of the coming assault. It wasn't necessary. Kord had already seen the man, but it was too late for the mander to avoid the attack. As the guard's ax crashed down onto Kord's arm, Kord was reaching over with his other hand to keep hold of his weapon. He was too slow; the man's ax sliced through Kord's forearm, sending the gorsrog clattering to the stones of the market floor.

There was a loud crack, like wood being split, as the ax cleaved through Kord's bones, which had been enough to slow the ax from finishing its job. Kord's arm swung wildly from his elbow, connected only by some thin strands of muscle and stretched flesh, as Kord whipped around to face the man. Kord grabbed the guard's ax, just below the blade, with his remaining hand. Before the guard could react, Kord ripped the weapon from the man's hands, bashed him in his helmeted face, and spun the ax around. With a flick of his wrist, he cleaved the guard's head from his shoulders.

Without a grimace of pain or show of emotion, as the man's body slumped and dropped, Kord used the ax to finish slicing off his own dangling arm. It was as though it had simply been some annoying torn piece of clothing. Kord's blood, the same color as the blue sky here in Modnar, had been spurting everywhere when initially sliced, but it had already stopped bleeding by the time the arm fell to the ground.

Kord turned back toward Solvar, drawing Joe's attention in that direction as well, but Solvar was gone. Despite the noise around them, a sudden clatter drew their attention back toward Garen. Apparently, Kord's distraction and dispatching of the fourth guard were what Garen needed to gain the upper hand with the other three guards. All three were now part of the heap of other unconscious or dead royal guards strewn about Garen.

Joe broke out of the minstrels' defensive huddle and headed over to Kord. Kord had already turned his attention to the unmoving form of Koobara, kneeling and putting his remaining hand gently on the large cat's side. Compared to Kord's massive frame, the jungle beast nearly looked like nothing more than a huge house cat.

Garen was close to them now, too, his back to them slightly, defensively, looking around. People were running in a frenzy now more than fighting, trying to flee the square in any direction they could as a troop of twenty or more royal guards marched into the square from the main thoroughfare to the west. City guards, in similar numbers, were rushing in from the market's north exit.

"It's going to get real ugly now," Joe said anxiously, but there was just a touch of excitement in his tone. The whole situation greatly reminded him of his home city of Cur, back in Midgorn. The population of Cur was made up primarily of criminals and people of questionable moral values. Even the local farmers all had some sort of side hustle going. The easily triggered citizens were prone not only to barroom brawls but also gang wars and street riots. The market riot had Joe feeling more than just a little nostalgic. "You gonna be okay there, big guy?" he asked Kord. "I mean, your arm, it's been — " Joe didn't feel he needed to finish the thought.

Kord responded as though he hadn't heard a word from Joe. "This beast is still alive," he said as he gently slung Koobara's limp form over his shoulder without effort.

"We gotta get out of here!" Nooch's voice cracked as he shouted to the others. His fellow musicians were emphatically nodding in agreement.

"Where's Runara?" Pronz asked.

"I saw her leave safely with the strong man and the others," grunted Kord. "We must follow." There was something a little calmer but still panicked to Nooch's tone.

"There!" a royal guard shouted over the crowd. He was pointing through the rush of people in their direction.

"There's a large boat of some sort on the docks," Joe explained quickly. "It has a name, like Harm Upon or something. It's waiting for us." He turned to Kord. "Keep the fellas safe. Baldy and I will keep the guards off your trail. We'll meet you at the boat once we ditch the guards. Joe slipped something into the left pocket of his coat as he spoke.

Kord simply nodded and grunted. With Koobara still motionless over his shoulder, he pushed past the musicians, who looked at one another wide-eyed, each trying to assess if they were all on board with the plan to follow the scary, giant frog man. None of them directly objected, so each, starting with Nooch, reluctantly followed Kord as he bee-lined through the chaotically stampeding crowd toward the eastern exit.

Garen had already taken down yet another guard by the time Joe turned his attention away from the departing musicians.

"Some assistance would be welcomed," Garen said, his voice calm and unlabored, as though the fighting thus far had not required the slightest bit of exertion. "That is if you're done stealing gems from the market floor."

"Caught that, did you? Sorry 'bout that," Joe responded casually as a man from the crowd ran headlong toward Joe from behind. Garen nodded to Joe, drawing his attention to the fast-approaching man. Joe spun around just in time to punch the man in the face, knocking him out, and sidestepped slightly to let him fall. "I'm Joe, by the way, Screamin' Joe Blade," he said, turning back to Garen with a huge grin.

"Garen," the monk said solemnly, giving Joe a quizzical look. He found Joe's smile puzzling, given the surrounding turbulent and grim circumstances. "I'll not be joining you and your friends on the boat," he said simply.

"I think you're going to have to. I'm pretty sure you're on their list now," Joe pointed at the guards strewn about them. A look of quiet defeat fell across Garen's face. "You didn't see where the one-eyed elf got to, did you?" Joe asked as he jabbed the tip of Death Seed into the market floor. A small green gem popped into the air at chest level. Joe quickly caught it with his free hand and stashed it in his pocket with the others.

"No." Garen's tone was one of barely restrained annoyance. As he spoke, he backhanded a man in the face who was about to slash him with a knife. He broke the man's nose, sending him sprawling, without interrupting his glaring look at Joe. The man was quickly trampled by other fleeing and rioting citizens.

Joe chuckled. "I like this guy." He seemed to be speaking to a young man nearby who was stumbling over the bodies of the fallen guards. The stumbling man paid Joe no attention, however, and was quickly lost in the chaos of the churning crowd.

"Hold!" came the voice of a royal guard not too far away in the mayhem. A large group of the King's guardsmen was cutting through the crowd in a widening wedge-shaped formation, leaving a corridor of relative order and crowd-trampled bodies in its wake.

"Time to go," Joe said, sheathing Death Seed, his smile broadening, waving for Garen to follow. Joe turned then, waving his arms at the King's men, ensuring he had their attention. He also drew the attention of several other royal guards scattered throughout the crowd. They were all approaching Joe and Garen then. "He's with me, Joe shouted as loud as he could, pointing to Garen."

Garen let out a deep sigh of resignation and followed as Joe pushed and punched his way through the buffeting crowd to the southern exit.

Chapter 12

The roughly cobbled streets of Loncodi's southern quarter were claustrophobically narrow, barely accommodating people to pass two abreast. It was the oldest part of Loncodi, the original, much smaller city. Despite its primitive age of origin and being the smallest of the four quarters, it was comprised of the tallest of Loncodi's structures. Though an impressive sight in its day before the city's population boom as a trading hub, the simple, towering, unadorned, dark grey brick buildings could not compete in splendor with the newer, more decorative portions of the city. Unlike the brightly burning oil-fed lamps of the rest of Loncodi, the streets of the southern quarter were barely illuminated by strange, dimly glowing green tubes dangling in the middle of coiled cords that zigzagged twenty feet above the street.

It was rare to meet someone other than a beggar in this part of the city on a normal day, but word of the chaos in the market had managed to reach these quiet streets, and even the beggars had made themselves scarce.

As Joe and Garen charged along, randomly turning down this street or that, window shutters slammed shut; some at street level, some several stories up. The citizens and shopkeepers here wanted no part of or to even be witness to whatever was spilling over from the market.

The ruckus of the market square faded in the distance as the two men ran, and only the clatter of the men chasing Joe and Garen remained. The two were starting to put some distance between themselves and the group of guards chasing them. It helped that the guards were slowed by their heavy armor, but Joe was starting to tire. He began to ponder finding a place to hide to catch his breath, a tavern preferably, but the southern quarter was almost entirely absent of inns or taverns.

"I'm going to need to stop," Joe huffed breathlessly to Garen, who was not even sweating at that point.

"You can not," Garen said in a perfectly even tone as if he were simply out for a stroll.

Despite the widening gap, Goms's men were still too close, always just managing to see them turn a corner. If only they could duck into a building, Joe thought, but the men were too close behind to risk slowing up to check a door that might turn out to be locked. As the two of them rounded another corner, he looked back.

"Dammit!" Joe exclaimed, huffing. One of the guards had just come around the corner a block back. He had to have seen Joe and Garen make the turn.

Something swooped past Joe's head just then; an odd-looking, reptilian bird with orange feathers that almost seemed to glow in the darkness. It made a small squawking sound like a crow with a sore throat as it flew around a corner ahead.

"Follow…the…bird," Joe huffed. Garen gave him a puzzled look. "Know…owner," Joe managed to say as they approached the corner.

Taking the direction that the bird had flown, they saw it sitting patiently on an ornate, peaked frame of a building entrance with large double doors made of the same grey stone as the building.

Having seemingly boundless energy, Garen sprinted forward, arriving at the door well ahead of Joe. Roughly fifteen feet tall, the doors were menacingly studded from top to bottom with four rows each of three-inch rusted metal spikes. Large metal rings in the middle of each door served as door handles. Garen yanked on one of the doors and nearly fell backward when it swung open with almost no resistance. He waved Joe in. Joe paused briefly outside the door looking up at the red bird whose green eyes sparkled as it looked down at him from the top of the door frame. It was unmistakably the deep-fried potato gobbling bird he had seen with the mysterious wizard, Victor.

"Thank…you!" he said breathlessly to the bird. It answered with a tiny hissing screech ending in a cheerful chortling sound, then flew away. Joe dodged into the darkness of the building.

Garen gave one last quick glance back down the street to ensure the guards he could still hear in pursuit hadn't rounded the corner. Satisfied they had not been seen, he jumped inside, closing the door behind himself as quickly and quietly as possible.

"Can I help you, gentlemen?"

Joe and Garen both jumped at the echoing voice coming from somewhere in the immense, dark room they found themselves in.

Outside, the clattering sound of the armored King's guards running by filled the narrow street. Neither Joe nor Garen said a word, waiting until the sounds faded around some distant corner further down the street.

Somewhere in the darkness of the room, there was a loud metallic clack sound followed by sharp cracklings as large stone-like pillars, previously invisible in the dark, flickered into luminous orange columns of light. The light from these forty-foot columns, with floral stone caps, was so much brighter than the dim green lights illuminating the street outside that it took a moment or two for Joe and Garen's eyes to adjust.

"The library is closed; you'll have to come back tomorrow. We open upon the tenth bell."

Despite the light, they still couldn't determine the source of the voice. They were, indeed, by appearance, inside some sort of library. Between the columns were equally tall bookshelves. Some shelves held neatly organized volumes; others had books of varying sizes and shapes lined up side by side or stacked in whichever way they would fit. Other shelves, which looked more like diamond grid wine racks, were full of scrolls of various sizes. The room was enormous, stretching back well over a hundred feet and a little over fifty feet on either side of the entrance. Ornately fashioned metal mesh catwalks ran along the shelves and between the rows on four levels above. The voice seemed to be coming from somewhere above Joe and Garen.

"Uh, no, we uh, is Victor here?" Joe's words stumbled randomly from his adrenaline-addled mind. He was hunched over, hands on his knees, needing to catch his breath. Speaking while trying to gather his thoughts was not his strong suit. It was a hard enough task, thinking while talking under non-exhausted conditions. He needed to devise a plan for getting to Captain

Mak's boat. Hopefully, Victor would be here and could just blink him to the ship or something.

"No Victor here. You'll have to go." The male voice came echoing from somewhere above.

"Yes, we should go." Whispered Garen. "This is the library of the Knower's Guild. They'll call the guards on us if we linger."

Joe ignored Garen, continuing to address the disembodied voice from above. "Victor, Victor Morosoff. You're sure he's not here," Joe asked again. "I mean, his bird was —" Joe's voice trailed off, not really sure where he was going to take his explanation, realizing it would sound a little crazy, especially if the person had no idea who Victor was and maybe even then.

"Morosoff? Well, now that does sound familiar." A slender, balding man with a stubby little round nose and a face that seemed pudgier than fit the rest of his frame poked his head out from around the second-story catwalk on the column nearest Joe and Garen. His tiny ears only made his head look that much larger, and he seemed to be in a permanent state of squinting. He made his way to a nearby tightly winding iron staircase, speaking as he made his way down. "Can't quite place the name, but it's right on the edge of my memory. Something I've read. Yes, yes. That's it. Something I've read." He laughed a little then. "Of course," he said, gesturing at the surroundings, "something I've read. Who did you say you were?"

Joe righted himself, still huffing a little but putting his chest out the best he could. "Screamin' Joe —"

"Blade!" the man finished for Joe with a bit of astonishment and question in his voice. Joe gave Garen a smug look and a wink. The man was walking toward them then. "But that's simply not possible. He's just a story, as is this 'Victor' you mentioned. Well, Joe is not even a story, really, is he? Screamin' Joe Blade is just someone mentioned in a story. Not sure how the likes of you would know any of that, but you're clearly trying to have a laugh. Now, who are you really, before I call the authorities."

"It is true," Garen spoke up then. "This man is known as Screamin' Joe Blade, at least by his companions, and I am Garen of the Zanxian order here in Loncodi. My sincere apologies for barging in here. We will leave immediately, of course." He gave the librarian a slight bow of respect.

The man looked Garen up and down. Garen's garb clearly made him out to be a Zanxian monk, as he had said, but the man was still having trouble accepting Joe's identity.

"Hmm." the man had a bemused smirk as he looked Joe over once more. "No need for you to go just yet, I suppose. Joke or not, you have me intrigued, and there's nothing more delightful than the intriguing." He waved a dismissive hand at Garen, indicating that he wanted Garen to step back while he continued to look Joe over. "Quite a claim to be a character from a story. How did it go again? Ah yes, tore a man's arm off and beat him to death with his own limb? Truly gruesome nonsense."

"Wow," Joe said, having finally caught his breath, "news gets around here pretty fast, but I wouldn't say that I 'tore' the man's arm off, exactly." Joe's demeanor had developed something of a swagger, making little attempt to hide the pride over the apparent notoriety he had already managed to establish in this new world.

Garen was frowning at Joe now, hardly believing the tale himself.

"What?" Joe turned to Garen, feeling his disapproving stare. "I had to use something to make the man let go of me, or I'd still be sitting in your King's dungeon."

The three stood in silence for a moment, Garen and the librarian staring at Joe, both in their own flavor of confusion.

"Well, now, this is a curiosity," The man said, a finger tapping his chin. "My name is Tosh, by the way." He gestured in a way that seemed like he was going to offer to shake hands but brought his own other hand up to meet it, folding them neatly together in front of himself. "Word certainly does travel fast around here, and I have heard of the grizzly scene left behind by a man recently escaped from the King's keeping, but I would never have associated it with —"Tosh left his thought unfinished, reaching past Joe and Garen, to pull on a large metal ring on the door. A loud metal thump came from the door and echoed through the library as the large doors locked. "Follow me," he said, tucking each hand into the wide sleeves of his heavy, purple robe. He then turned, walking down a nearby aisle and deeper into the library.

Joe looked at Garen, shrugging, and then followed after the man. Garen's head dropped as he let out an audible sigh, relinquishing himself yet again to whatever path it was Zanx was putting before him.

"For every kindness, there is at least one consequence." Garen muttered to himself the simple lesson that had been among the first he learned as a young monk. "but for every inaction, a hundred things never learned." He put his fingertips together and gave a little nod in respect to the long-departed old master who had first spoken the words to him.

It was just then he noticed something odd at his feet. At first, he thought the bright red little creature was some sort of small lizard, a gecko perhaps, with the tips of its long little toes bulbous like that of a wall walker, but its body tapered into a long whipping, swishing tail, like no gecko he had ever seen. Also, the little creature had six appendages rather than four. The extra two spindly limbs sprung from the middle of its torso, looking like bat wings without the webbing membrane that would have made them proper wings. These odd extra limbs that it crawled about on, like the legs of a spider, were not the most unusual feature of the little beast, which was no more than the length of Garen's forearm from tip to tail. Its head was what truly caught Garen's attention. The entire head seemed to be taken up by one large, very human-looking eyeball with a bright green iris.

"What manner of beast are you, little one?" Garen questioned the creature, taking a cautious step back from it.

"Grrrrrtok," chirped the little creature as if it were answering his question, tiny little gill-like structures vibrating on its neck. Its single, unblinking eye stared up at Garen.

Garen bent down, sticking a probing finger out to the odd little being. It skittered back and forth nervously for a moment but then, seeing that Garen apparently meant no harm, jumped up onto his hand, perching there like a bird. Garen smiled at the odd little thing as it gently wrapped its tail around his wrist for more stability. It started making a satisfied little cooing sound.

"You comin'?" Joe shouted, turning back to Garen before following Tosh around the end of one of the bookcases.

Garen hustled along to catch up, taking the little creature with him.

The library was much more extensive than it first appeared; its size was masked by endless rows of crisscrossing bookshelves. After a few turns down similar-looking halls of book-burdened shelves, Joe and Garen were quite lost, unsure of the way back to the door. Joe and Tosh arrived at an open archway with a small, winged, smiling gargoyle carved into the pointed peak of the arch. It had what looked like a feather quill in one hand and a wand or perhaps a leafless twig of some sort in the other. A narrow staircase beyond the archway descended into the darkness of the level below. Tosh proceeded into the dark, quickly disappearing. Joe followed but stopped short just a few steps down as a baritone but strangely androgynous voice boomed from the unseen depths of the staircase. Garen, who had fallen behind a little, now simply followed the sound of the voice. It was quickly evident that he had made several wrong turns.

"Greetings, Knower Stokko," said the voice. "Will you be needing access to the Well of Wisdom tonight or the Curiosity Archive?"

"Just the Archive tonight, thank you, Umadda," answered Tosh.

"Excellent!" The voice thundered. Joe could feel the stone of the staircase vibrate beneath his feet from the exuberance in the disembodied Umadda's response. "May your evening be one of discovery, Knower Stokko."

"Thank you, Umadda."

"Wait!" The voice boomed again.

"What is it?" Tosh's voice came from the darkness of the staircase, sounding more annoyed than concerned, though certainly a bit of both.

"Are these others to enter as well?"

"Yes. Yes, of course." Tosh responded.

"All of them?"

"Yes," Tosh responded again, starting to sound genuinely annoyed.

"I could have them vaporized if they're giving you any trouble." Umadda's voice had dropped in volume somewhat and almost sounded a little hopeful.

"Uh," Tosh hesitated, looking back at the shadowy form of Joe in the dark, curving stairwell. "That really won't be necessary; thank you, Umadda."

"You are sure?"

"Yes!" The annoyance in Tosh's voice was fully unmasked then.

"Very well, but do shout out if they become a problem."

"Um, I'm not going to be a problem." Joe chimed in, feeling the need to have some input on whether or not he was to be vaporized.

"Of course," Tosh said, half speaking to Joe, "of course," he repeated louder for Umadda's benefit. "Now, the door?"

There was a blue shimmering in the darkness ahead of Tosh, and then suddenly, a doorway blinked into existence, pouring light into the lower portion of the staircase. The room beyond was full of glass display cases, some rectangular, which looked as though they could be opened, and rounded blown glass cases that appeared to be permanently sealed. Connected to these display cases were one or two drafting-style wooden writing desks. An additional row of desks ringed the outside edges of the immense room, and beyond those, lining all four walls, floor to thirty-foot ceiling, were bookcases filled with books, which, just by their worn spines, appeared to be very old.

Tosh motioned for Joe to follow him inside.

Garren had rounded the corner of the aisle leading to the stairs just in time to see the top of Joe's head descend into the darkness of the stairwell. A sound from behind made him pause for a moment. At least he had thought he heard something, almost like footsteps behind him. He stood still momentarily, straining his ears against the silence, trying to hear anything.

"Grrrrrr-TOK!" the little creature in his hand chirped loudly. Its voice echoed down the aisles of the library. The sound nearly made Garen's heart skip a beat. He gave the little creature a slight frown, quickly followed by a grin as it cocked its little eyeball head questioningly, looking up at him. Garen looked back the way he had come.

"Hearing my own footsteps, eh, little one?" Garen held the little red creature up to his face. He threw one last glance over his shoulder down the empty aisle and then hurried over to the stairs to catch up with Joe and Tosh.

As Joe walked into the room, he turned around to see if Garen had caught up. However, he was surprised to see a perfect image of himself looking back instead. The archway he had just walked through was entirely covered by a mirror. To the left and right of the mirror stood two odd-looking suits of red armor, each standing just over six feet tall, and something about their body frame reminded him of Kord. The armor didn't appear painted. It seemed as though the metal itself was actually red; scratches here and there revealed nothing but further red metal. The helmets were broad and shallow, hardly looking like they could accommodate a human head. The dome of the helmets appeared to be made of a single bulbous piece of black glass, with a single strip of metal running up the middle, which seemed meant for some protection. Joe questioned its usefulness and could not imagine being able to see out past the bar. The wide metal strip had tiny spiked metal rivets running the center of its length. The metal plates, if they could be called such, that made up the rest of the armored suits were seamless pieces connected by what looked like some sort of black leather at the elbows, waist, shoulders, and knees. The chest, shoulders, and knee pieces were large round metal bubbles, while the shin and forearm guards were cones, narrow at the elbows and knees, widening toward the hands and feet. The metal shoes, spiked similarly to the helmet, were as wide as the base of the shin guard cone. Each suit held in one of its metal gauntleted hands a four-foot black metal staff. Each staff was topped by a deep green, egg-shaped crystal, slightly smaller than a human fist. The bottom end of each staff was attached by what looked like a thick, black leather, spiraled cord looping to a connecting point in the back of the suits.

Joe almost found the two ominous suits of armor flanking the door more distracting than the conundrum of the impossibly mirrored doorway. Still, it was his mirrored image that recaptured his focus. He was a handsome scoundrel, he thought, and really no worse for the wear of all he had been through lately. He took a moment to practice his most disarming smile. The mirror certainly seemed real enough. He was about to reach out to touch the mirror to confirm its reality when Garen came walking through, looking like a ghost passing through a solid wall.

"What are you doing?" Garen questioned, ducking Joe's outstretched finger as he entered the room.

"Nice trick," Joe said, jumping back out of Garen's way and turning back to Tosh. "How's it done?"

Tosh ignored Joe, quite certain that Joe wouldn't understand even if it were explained. Instead, he simply encouraged both Joe and Garen to continue following him. He led them past the various display cases to a bookcase in the back of the archive. Tosh began to reach for a book among a set of very worn, ancient-looking books but paused, turning back to face Joe.

"Now, where did you say you are from," Tosh queried.

"I don't think I did," Joe answered. He felt a little uncomfortable trying to explain that he was from another world, but this man was being incredibly accommodating, so he decided to just be straight with the fellow. "I'm from a world called Midgorn. Doesn't have a – what d'ya call it – sky; solid rock, like a sensible world."

Rather than the confusion he was expecting to see on the man's face, Tosh instead smiled broadly.

"Fascinating," Tosh said quietly. He appeared a little mesmerized.

Joe could feel Garen staring and turned to him. The monk had the look of confusion on his face that he had expected from Tosh. Joe just shrugged, having nothing more to offer the monk, as he had no explanations for it all himself. It was then that Joe noticed the odd little red creature wrapped around Garen's hand, and then it was Joe's turn to shoot a confused, where-did-that-come-from look in Garen's direction. Garen simply shrugged.

Tosh pulled down a very old, worn book bound in black cloth. It had no writing or outer markings save for an embossed spiral on the front cover.

"What do you make of this now?" Tosh opened the book to a seemingly random, yellowed pair of pages. The edges of the pages were rough, ripped in some places, missing small chunks in others. The page on the right actually had a jagged hole in it the size of a large coin in the upper right quarter of the page.

Joe looked the pages over. The passages in the book appeared to be handwritten but in no alphabet that Joe recognized, and indeed, the midgin alphabet was the only alphabet he knew. His sister had taught him to read when they were kids. He wasn't sure where she had learned.

"Not much," Joe shrugged. "What is it? Is it that story about me?"

"It is," Tosh said, simply taking the book back. "Now, I'm sure you haven't been down here or have seen this book before, but have you seen anything like it, perhaps in another library somewhere?"

"Nope," Joe offered simply. Tosh examined Joe intently as he answered.

Again, Tosh smiled. "So interesting," he said, speaking to himself more than to Garen or Joe. He flipped to the back of the book to a badly torn page. "Now, how about this?"

What little was left of the top of the page, Joe could make out easily. It was written in the midgin alphabet, and Joe read a portion of it out loud. It was something about the rightful resting place of the book. Joe found it all quite dull. It didn't seem to mention him, or anyone for that matter, but he couldn't help but feel a little excited to see something of Midgorn, other than himself or Kord, here in Modnar. It made him feel a little less crazy. Tosh looked astonished.

"So you believe that my world, Midgorn, is real?" Joe handed the book back to Tosh.

"Beginning to," Tosh said, cocking a quizzical eyebrow. "Until now, most of us, myself included, believed Midgorn to simply be a fanciful tale. And, up until a few moments ago, I was one of only six others in all of Modnar that could read any of the creator texts."

"Creator texts," Garen scoffed. According to his beliefs, Modnar was formed and held together by the energies of the godlings, beings who were not prone to leaving such mundane traces of their existence because they simply are all existence. Even Zanx was a creation of the godlings, an avatar, and the only true testament to the nature of reality. However, there were those in Modnar who believed in a creator god or gods whose very thoughts gave form and substance to Modnar. Such gods often left behind writings or enchanted objects as proof of their existence or to help some true believer hero smite some sort of evil. As far as Garen knew, all such stories were simply myths passed down from one misguided heathen to another.

Tosh smiled. He had an audience, and it was a rare audience indeed. Zanxian monks were noted for their scholarly pursuits, albeit religiously tinctured, but knowers and monks rarely exchanged insights. Joe, meanwhile, would make a suitable addition to the archive if he were truly from the mythical world of Midgorn. Unfortunately, there was a specific rule against the curation of people and creatures, at least live ones.

"Yes, creator texts. It has been recorded that many of Modnar's greatest heroes and at least one of its greatest villains, the Mad Architect of Doom, as he came to be known, could read and write in the odd glyphs found in this book. Some of these legendary heroes even claimed to be the avatars of the creator himself. Many among my colleagues believe these heroes to be members of a secretive cult, and this book is simply the ancient work of one of their more imaginative members, perhaps even one of the founding members."

"That seems to make sense." Garen agreed. "How old is the book?"

"Well, now, that's what makes your friend here so interesting." He put the book back in its place on the shelf and turned back to Garen and Joe. "The book is well over five hundred years old. Well, that's when it was found. It's thought to be much older than that. It's really quite remarkable that it is still in the shape that it's in, and if you are, in fact, THE Screamin' Joe Blade, it seems unlikely that you should be in the shape that you are in."

"Surely then, the names are a coincidence," offered Garen.

"Yes, of course, except that this book apparently described the scenario which our Screamin' Joe Blade, here, went through no more than a week ago. More perplexing is Joe's claim to knowing another character from the book, Victor Morosoff."

"Nothing strange about that," Joe asserted. "I met the fella in the woods; him and his bird."

"His bird?" Tosh was gobbling up every word Joe spoke. "It's little things like that that have me believing you, or at least convince me that you aren't entirely making this up. You see, there's no indication in the Journal of Midgorn – that is what the book is called – that Victor knows Joe. Still, this may all be coincidence, but tell me, do you know this man by any other name?"

"Matter of fact, I do. Back in my world, the fella is known as the Crystal Master. Kinda has a nasty reputation, actually, but he seemed nice enough to me. Roasts up a mean chicken and some pretty great potatoes, too." Joe rubbed his belly as he thought about the best meal he had experienced since his arrival in this world.

"Remarkable! In the book, too, he is called Crystal Master." Tosh said, analyzing Joe's face. "You really aren't lying about any of this, are you," he added rhetorically.

"Nope."

"That may be so," Garen interjected, "and I'll grant that the coincidences are seeming more unlikely, but that's still not enough to make Joe and this Victor person the characters from some ancient cultist's book."

"Still, your friend here couldn't have read this ancient text, and if it's some elaborate prank being played upon me by my colleagues, well, it's either the most complex or the most ill-conceived hoax ever perpetrated. I really wouldn't see the point." Tosh could see the uncertainty on Garen's face as he spoke. "I'm also under the impression that neither of you intended to come here tonight and that the two of you have just met as well. True?"

"Yes," said Garen. "Both correct." Joe nodded in agreement but honestly just barely heard the question; he was starting to get bored and was looking around the room at the display cases, hoping to see something of interest. There was a cube, made up of gears, springs, and metal plates, in a nearby case that looked like someone had crushed down a large clock. It was almost interesting, for a fraction of a second. Nothing fun there, Joe thought.

"Then, practical joke eliminated, I can only conclude that our man Joe, here, is a man not only outside of his own world but somehow outside of his own time as well, and there may be a bigger problem with that than him simply being lost."

"Hmm, what problem," asked Joe, only half listening. "You mean the guards chasing us? Ya, I think they've lost us. Thanks for that. Hope we don't get you in trouble for helping out a couple criminals on the run."

Tosh shook his head, approaching Joe slightly so as to keep Joe's focus. "No, you clearly don't understand. In the book, you are one of a handful of heroes in a war between the humans and elves of Midgorn that give the humans and dwarves hope."

"There's no war in Midgorn. Hasn't been a big bash-up for centuries, ever since they stopped having kings and queens. And I don't think there's ever been a war with the Danuwan if that's who you're talking about. Maybe it's just a, what did you call it? A coincidence. Maybe it's just a story."

"No, I'm not convinced, especially with you having just referred to the elves of Midgorn as the Danuwan, just as they do in the book." Tosh was shaking his head negatively again, "I don't think you belong here, and given that this book is here in Modnar as well, I suspect that the histories of our two worlds are tied together, and unless we want existence or at least what we know of history to unravel, we need to get you home to become the hero you're meant to be. I have a feeling that Victor and his little bird may have directed you here in the hope of rectifying the situation."

Joe hadn't heard much other than "get you home" and "hero you're meant to be," but it was enough to snap him back into the conversation.

"Well, now we're talkin'," Joe said, slapping his hands together. "So what about Victor? I mean, his bird led us here." Joe leaned in, his face very close to Tosh's. "You aren't Victor, are you? One of those abettors you were talking about."

"Avatars." Tosh corrected.

"No, I think he had that right," Garren said with a slight bit of sarcasm.

Joe ignored them both. "If you are Victor, you need to blink us to Runara. She has the crystal, or better yet, you could just blink Runara and me both to her great grandpappy's so that we can make the sword and get me home."

"What?" Tosh was trying to follow Joe's rambling. "Grandpappy's? Sword? What sword? Crystal? Who's Runara?" It was then that Tosh noticed Death Seed hanging at Joe's hip. He began to point at it, but before he could ask, Joe interrupted him.

"No, not this sword. The other sword, the one that gets me home. I'm not even sure why I'm telling you all of this. Look, you've been a big help just letting us hide out here for a bit, but if you aren't Victor, then we should be getting back to our friends."

Garen nodded in agreement but had no intention of continuing with Joe to the docks. All he wanted right now was the sanity and sanctuary of the Zanxian monastery.

"Ah, but I might be of more help." Tosh offered. "Tell me more about the sword you are trying to make."

It was Joe's turn to examine Tosh for any ill intent. He could sense nothing deceptive about Tosh. Still, he found the man's openness to potentially criminal strangers terribly suspicious. "My friend, Runara, she called it a powersword. One of —"

"Thirteen!" Tosh finished Joe's sentence for the second time. Joe found it a little annoying. "They're thought to be as much the stuff of legend as you and your land of Midgorn."

"No legend. King Ethdab was swinging around a green one. Saw it myself," Joe said flatly.

"Yes, yes! I have heard tell of the King wielding one of the thirteen as well. Most of us just put the stories off as tall war tales or propaganda to fill his enemies with fear. But I'm no expert regarding the swords of power. We can certainly look up anything you might need to know. You believe that one of these swords has the ability to take you back to Midgorn?" It was evident that Tosh was struggling to contain his excitement.

Garen was finding all of it a little hard to accept. "So, him, you're some sort of expert on, but the 13 swords of power, a common legend in all of Modnar, that you have to look up?"

"We all have our interests." Tosh's response was followed by an anxious chuckle, which made him a little self-conscious. He cleared his throat as he tried to regain his composure. "Unfortunately, I will have to charge you for the library's service."

"What?" Joe found Tosh's sudden need for compensation surprising, considering his apparent interest in helping Joe get back to Midgorn. Conflictingly, it also made him feel a little more at ease around Tosh. He always found people of a purely charitable nature suspicious. Joe looked over at Garen.

With a pleasant smile, Garen quickly stopped Joe's silent request. "Although I would be honor-bound to assist you, fortunately for me, I have no money."

"Yup, me too, I'm afraid," Joe said, turning back to Tosh. "We'll have to owe you."

Tosh couldn't tell if Joe was trying to make a joke or not. "I wouldn't ask, but if the other guild members were to discover that I've been handing out the guild's services for free, especially after hours, well, I'd have to start looking into another profession. You understand, right?" It was clear by his demeanor that Tosh really didn't want to be asking for payment. "Look, it doesn't have to be money. You are, potentially, from an entirely different world, right?"

"More than potentially, I'd say." Joe sounded somewhat affronted.

"Right, right. So if you had something from Midgorn —"Tosh's eyes darted briefly back to Death Seed.

Joe caught the look and intercepted Tosh's thought. "Sorry, pal, got the sword here. Plus, I'm going to need it to get home. I think. Part of it, anyway."Joe was patting himself down then, vainly checking empty pockets and pockets that didn't exist while conveniently ignoring any of the market floor gemstones he had managed to lift. "I honestly don't have anything else, other than my clothes and my knives, but I'm kinda using my clothes, and there's only one way a person gets one of my knives."Joe paused for dramatic effect, trying to muster his most intimidating tone. "and trust me, you don't want to get one of my knives."

"How about this" came a familiar voice from behind.

Joe turned around just in time to see Kord's hand fill his field of view and slap him hard in the face. The blow knocked him to the floor.

"What the — Who are you! How did you get in here?"Tosh's voice was a combination of shock, fear, and anger.

Garren had taken a defensive stance instantly but was already relaxing.

Joe looked up from the floor, Kord's severed arm lying on his chest like a fallen log. "Crash?"

Crash stood above him, flashing her wild, brilliant smile as she fished at something inside her jacket. "Here, you left this." She tossed down the knife that she had swiped from Joe in the square before the riot. Joe caught it in one hand just before it struck him in the throat.

Joe made a sheepish chuckle. "Thanks, great to see you again. Help a fella up? Anyone." Joe had his hands in the air, waiting for assistance like some helpless child. Both Garen and Crash hoisted him back to his feet. Kord's arm flopped to the floor with a sickening wet plop sound; thick dark blue blood oozed onto the floor. Joe brushed himself off a little with one hand, mostly just making sure there wasn't any severed arm goo on him, while he gave Tosh a gentle slap on the back. "Y'know, you really ought to look at building up the security in this place."

"What in the world is that!" Tosh ignored Joe's comment and bent down, marveling at Kord's severed limb.

"Payment," Joe said quickly as if the idea had been his. He shot Crash a quick sideways glance. She had her hands clasped in front of her, rocking on her heels, her infectious smile frozen on her face. She seemed very pleased with herself. Joe looked back to Tosh. "You wanted something from Midgorn; well, you wouldn't find a rarer item from Midgorn than this arm, even if you were dealing with a Manrian shadow-market body merchant."

"Manrian," Tosh repeated Joe's word in a breathless chuckle. The random reference to a Midgorn community that Tosh recognized just further confirmed Joe's identity. "But what is it?"

"That, my friend," Joe said, slapping a hand on Tosh's shoulder, "is the hand of a mander, one of the scariest groups of brutes in all of Midgorn. Even the wolgars don't mess with the mander."

Tosh wasn't exactly sure what Joe was talking about other than having a vague idea that wolgars were some big ugly race from midgorn, at least according to the journal. He simply nodded at Joe, picking up the arm. It was even heavier than he expected and seemed a little slimy.

"This — this is more than I could have hoped for. Is this man, uh, creature, uh, dead?"

"Nah, seemed fine." Crash answered before Joe or Garen could say anything. "Don't think he misses the thing, either."

Tosh blinked in amazement, stared at the arm a moment more, and then looked up at Crash. "Are you from Midgorn too?"

Crash just laughed.

"I'll have a hard time explaining this to the guild, but the others will be impressed by it just the same, I'm sure. N-none of them will have seen, uh, anything like it." Tosh was so excited that he stumbled over his words. "The book you'll need to reference is right over here, but I am going to have to leave you while I preserve this specimen immediately. I shouldn't be too long, but you'll need me to unlock the library before you can leave, in any case, so please be patient if you finish up before I'm back." With that, Tosh led them across the archive to the far left portion of the room, pulling down a massive white, leather-bound book and placing it on a nearby desk. He then excused himself, thanking the three profusely as he left, nearly at a running pace, out through the mirror with Kord's massive forearm and hand cradled in his arms.

Seeing that they would be here a while longer, Garen also considered excusing himself. The opportunity to access information from the knower guild's library, however, was something that a lowly Zanxian monk could not pass up. If that was not compelling enough, here he was, without supervision, not only in the guild's library but in their special archive.

Joe opened the book but, flipping through just a few of the thick parchment pages, quickly realized that there would be a problem. He couldn't read even a single word that was written. The glyphs of the common Modnarian alphabet were utterly foreign to him.

Crash pushed Joe aside and started feverishly flipping through the pages. She paused on a page for a moment, examining it intently and silently, and then flipped further into the book, deeply examining yet another page.

Joe had to admit to a bit of excitement at the prospect of learning more about the possible way home. "What are you finding?" Asked Joe, looking over her shoulder.

"Oh, nothing," Crash answered quickly, "I can't read; I just like looking at the pictures. Look at this one," she said, pointing and laughing. "That's so silly; they don't even have teeth." The illustration appeared to depict an enormous duck-like creature devouring an armored man.

"Seriously?" Garen made no attempt to hide his frustration with both Crash and Joe's lack of education. He knew that he wasn't likely to have the chance now to browse through any of the other books here in the archive. He motioned for Crash to move aside, which she did reluctantly, making an exaggerated pouty face. Garen's tiny red, one-eyed pet had crawled up onto his shoulder a few moments earlier. Against Garen's garments, the little creature was nearly invisible. Its little eyeball head scanned back and forth, almost as though it were reading the words in the book. Garen noticed this, and it made him smile. "At least someone here can read." He muttered to himself. "Powerswords, correct?" he asked Joe.

"Yup," Joe confirmed.

Garen flipped through the book, trying to absorb as much information as he could from the pages he was having to pass by. There were two pages devoted to a mask that supposedly allowed the user to take on the guise of others and another page about a cube-shaped puzzle box that granted the possessor access to alternate planes of reality. That page had a map of Westerlan and seemed to indicate the location of a pyramid-shaped building, but he didn't have enough time to tell if this was where the box had been or where it was supposed to be. If Joe truly was from another world, then such a device, if it were more than myth, might be the key to finding a way back.

Joe noticed Garen lingering on the puzzle box page. "That's a box," Joe said, being painfully obvious. "We are looking for swords."

"Yes, yes, of course." Garen flipped further into the book, not wanting to waste energy trying to explain the box or get pulled any further into Joe's problems. He flipped past images of a goblet, a spear, a flying castle, and a black orb. From the little portions of text he managed to skim and some of the names he saw associated with these objects, he became aware that all these items were linked to gods of one variety or another. The theme of the book essentially seemed to be the gods of Modnar and their ridiculous toys.

A little past halfway through the book, he reached a section entirely devoted to the powerswords forged by god-like beings known as godés. There were thirteen swords, each associated with a color and a particular esoteric realm over which they held influence. Anyone picking up a powersword would absorb it into their essence and would be able to call upon an ethereal form of the sword that would glow in its associated color. According to the book's texts, someone couldn't possess more than one of the swords at a time or, more accurately, absorb more than one sword. Calling forth an absorbed powersword also summoned up a magically formed suit of armor unique to that particular sword with special properties associated with the abilities of the sword itself.

The orange sword, for example, granted the possessor control over fire and covered the wielder, head to toe, in a protective layer of fire. Crash particularly liked the illustration of this sword in use. The colors were pretty, she thought. Joe agreed, but Garen had a hard time seeing the beauty past the images of the charred and burning bodies of the orange sword wielder's foes.

Garen began reading out loud much of the information on the swords for Joe and Crash's benefit. Each of the thirteen powerswords had a page with an illustration and description of what was known of that particular sword's powers or what abilities it granted its wielder. The different godés associated with imbuing each sword with its unique attributes were also depicted with each sword. Most looked very human, but some looked monstrous, having some physical characteristics of beasts. In the margins, in various handwriting styles, notes had been written in the margins of nearly every sword's page. Most of the notes consisted of a name and a range of years. This, Garen quickly surmised, indicated individuals thought to have possessed any particular sword and the length of time it had remained in their possession. One of only three entries for the green powersword confirmed this to some measure. The first was "King of Azizoo," who apparently had the sword for a period spanning four thousand years. The second was a woman known as "Empress Ulma, Devourer of Men," who had kept the sword for one day shy of six hundred years. The final entry had an open-ended date range listing "Goms Ethdab, Warlord, Conqueror, King" as the green sword's current holder. Garen found it interesting that despite this documentation by what had to be one of Tosh's colleagues, Tosh considered the powerswords to be nothing but a myth.

Three of the swords were relegated to a special section, all of their own. They had been the focus of a great war among the godés involving many of Modnar's mortal races as well. The war was finally brought to an end by an outside force. The book's wording made it unclear if this outside force was a singular being or another race, simply referred to as "the Akar," but whatever, or whoever it or they was, their arrival brought the war to an end by destroying nearly all life on Modnar. Then, strangely, they left. The godés that had survived, or in most cases that had slowly reconstituted their bodies over millennia, decided to dismantle the three forbidden power swords. The swords themselves, forged from ultimorite, could not be destroyed but, through very specific arcane methods, could be separated from the crystals in their hilt from which their powers sprung. Similarly, odd and difficult methods could be used to fuse them back together, should the need arise.

Unlike the crystals in the hilts of the other ten swords, which were the appropriate corresponding color, cut as fine translucent gems, the crystals of the three forbidden swords were rough black shards. They were the three broken pieces of a larger opaque black shard that had been a powerful item in its own right. The origins of the large black crystal and its power are foggy, but it had once belonged to the elves of Westerlan and was taken forcibly by the godés. An illustration of one of these forbidden crystal shards confirmed that the black stone in the hilt of Death Seed was, in fact, the crystal of the red powersword.

"Are you listening to any of this," Garen asked in frustration as Crash danced around the immense room, pausing only to look at the various curiosities in the glass cases, here and there. At that point, she was at the far end of the room and could barely hear Garen.

"What?" Crash shouted back and then went back to dancing before a response could be given.

"It's okay," Joe offered, "She doesn't need to know anyway. This is my thing. As long as you can tell me how to put the crystal thing back in the other sword, then I'm as good as on my way home, and we'll be out of your hair." Joe stared at Garen's bald head momentarily as Garen glared at him, doing his best to quell his disdain for Joe. "Well, you know what I mean," Joe said in an apologetic tone, trying not to look at Garen's bald scalp. He quickly pointed then at a random spot on the page, mustering up as enthusiastic of a tone as he could, "Hey, what's this say?"

"I already read that part." Garen's tone was flat. The little creature on Garen's shoulder made a little chirp.

"What is that thing?" Joe leaned around Garen's back, trying to get a look at it.

"I'm not sure. It seems to like books, though." Garen smiled a little as he gave the tiny creature a sideways glance. He resumed reading where he had left off.

The description of the dimensional rift opening capabilities of the red powersword did seem to suggest that it might be able to get Joe home. However, there was no documentation for any of the three forbidden swords about where the individual crystals and swords might have been scattered.

"Not a worry, pal. Already have the two crystals, right? Well, Runara has the other anyway, and we know where the sword is." Joe gave Garen a little pat on the back. "Now we just need to know how to put 'em together."

"I think you only need the one crystal," Garen said, pointing at Death Seed.

"That's not what Victor seemed to think," Joe said with a shrug, "and they do call the guy 'Crystal Master', so I'm going to assume he knows the what's what of it all."

The other two forbidden swords were the grey and black swords. Joe felt compelled to point out that the black sword still had a color-matching crystal. Garen couldn't argue the point but still found the comment slightly irritating for a reason he couldn't quite put his finger on. He simply nodded and continued reading. The grey sword gave the possessor the power of lightning and invention. The black sword's entry was curious compared to the other two. It gave no actual description of its power or associated armor, only a simple sentence. "Death walks in the wake of the black sword." The illustration was of a solitary, somber, disheveled-looking man sitting on a tree stump by the side of a road, head down, leaning on the physical sword with both hands as though it were a walking stick. The caption below the image read. "The Hand of Death."

"Boring!" Joe punctuated his exclamation with an exaggerated, fake yawn. "How do you put the crystals back in the swords. Do they just snap into the ends, or what? And what does the second crystal have to do with any of it?"

Garen flipped the page. "Here," he said. "This is the bonding ritual for the red sword; it says,

With the last breath of Nolis,
The wand of the triputhon glows,
As the child of old magic dies,
As the blood of Kronus flows.

In conjured flame and ichor
The forlorn blade bathes so silent
Dreaming to rend the infinite
Raging, it craves the violent.

New magic's progeny speaks,
Initiates the tine shapers,
Waking the ancient metal,
Making all before it like vapors.

Still untamed, still such fury
Annihilating all who reach.
A droplet then, one of three
Death's heart gift spent, in blade's hilt breach
Bound by fire, bound by blood
The red sword, reality's foe.
By the traveler now borne,
Unbound wherever they go.

"And then there is this last line here. It looks like it's written in some language I don't recognize."

"Wait, what?" It was almost possible to hear the crickets chirping within Joe's mind. "What was that, a poem?"

"Yes, I suppose it —" Garen's response was cut short as Joe threw up his hands.

"Well, that's useless!" Joe was getting more frustrated with every word he uttered. "What does that jumble of flowered kruptan crap even mean? That's no instructions." Joe was pacing back and forth, looking for something that didn't look too expensive to break, but found he lacked the necessary appraisal skills or the frame of mind.

Garen felt the need to calm Joe down, if only to silence him, but wasn't sure how short of knocking him out, and such an act would be inappropriate. He tried reason instead. "Well, Nolis is thought to be the father of all dragons, and —"

"So, what, now we have to find the father of dragons? What? No! Victor didn't say anything about dragons. I don't do dragons. It didn't take a dragon to get me here; I'll get home without one, too."

Crash came bouncing over, a heavy, old, brown leather-bound book in her hand. "I liked the poem. Read it again, monk boy. And I happen to think dragons are fab. Such little cuties! Just makes me want to— Look out!" Before Garen could react, Crash brought the book she was carrying down hard on his left shoulder. The little red creature perched there only managed a shrill chirp before being crushed by the heavy tome. Translucent yellow goo from its flattened eye-head oozed down Garen's shoulder.

In a lightning flash of movement, grabbing Crash by one of her wrists and giving it a slight twist, Garen had flipped Crash off her feet, leaving her lying on the floor, flat on her back. She was laughing like she was being tickled.

Garen's movements ceased as quickly as they had begun, feeling the incredibly sharp point of Death Seed at his throat. A thin trail of blood already trickling down his neck.

"Do it again!" Crash breathlessly squeezed out between snorts and giggles.

Let's say we all calm down for a moment before anyone does anything rash." Joe's tone was flat, serious, and measured, greatly contrasting his ranting from a moment before.

"Yes, that would be splendid," Garen agreed, trying not to spin too much sarcasm into his words.

Joe pulled Death Seed back and away slowly from Garen's neck. Garen sat back down at the desk, trying to wipe away the remains of his recently acquired pet with one hand as he stemmed the bleeding from the knick on his neck with the other. Crash sat up and leaned back on her hands, seemingly content to remain sitting on the floor.

"Good," Joe began, pointing Death Seed to the floor and leaning on it like a cane, "So, what just happened here?"

"It was a grotok," Crash said, pointing up at Garen's shoulder.

Garen stared at her blankly, then looked to Joe to see if he was comprehending what the skull-faced clown woman was talking about. Joe, however, was simply a mirror staring back with the same questioning expression. Joe shrugged, shaking his head.

"Aw, c'mon Joe, you know." Crash whined. "I told you about them before. Wizards make them by whackin' people in the head with their magic sticks." She pouted then. "Shame to have to squish the poor little guy. Didn't even have proper wings, but he was reading that book."

"Don't be absurd," scoffed Garen.

Joe cleared his throat. "She gets paid to be absurd."

"I mean," Garen continued, "that the little creature, the grotok, as you call it, was only curious, as many little creatures are. It seems unlikely that it could read. You two can't even read."

Joe and Crash both frowned a little.

Crash shook her head, saying, "No, I didn't mean the creature was reading; I meant the wizard that made it was reading through its cute little eyeball." She punctuated this last part by scrunching up her face, one eye closed, and gesturing in a manner that suggested that her finger was shooting out of her eye.

A thud sounded from a distant part of the archive toward the entrance.

"Did you hear that?" Joe asked as he raised Death Seed in preparation for whatever.

Garen waved a hand, indicating that Joe should lower the sword. "It's probably just Tosh coming back to kick us out of his library, as he, assuredly, should have done in the first place."

Joe made no acknowledgment of Garen's words, continuing to hold Death Seed at the ready. He went straight back to their conversation about the squashed grotok. "Hold up. That might have been one of Victor's pets! "Joe slapped a hand to his forehead. "What have you done? The guy was likely trying to help us."

"Or, perhaps, not. What interest would the wizard have in helping you acquire the sword or even reaching this other world of yours? A powersword, especially one of the three 'forbidden' swords, is quite a prize," Garen offered. "What do you know of this wizard?"

"Well, he does have a bit of a bad reputation back in Midgorn, but he doesn't seem evil at all."

"Yes, yes, and he roasts a chicken well, as you've said. Seems to me like he seeks the sword for himself, and you are simply his errand boy."

"I've seen the King wield his powersword. I don't see how anyone would go about taking it from him. Seems like it would be a bad plan to send someone else to get one of these swords for you. Besides, he already had the crystal that he said I need to use, and he could have taken this thing," Joe held up Death Seed, showing Garen the hilt, "back when I was in his lair. He would have an easier time getting the sword from Nashtar than I will, too, I'd wager."

"Wait a moment," Garen said, astonished. "Did you just say Nashtar has the sword?"

"Well, ya," Joe shrugged as though Garen should already know. "That's where we're headed once we get out of here. Y'know the guy or somethin'?"

"Everyone knows of Nashtar," Garen said gravely. He looked down to Crash for some confirmation. She nodded in a strangely silent agreement. "Right," Garen continued, turning back to Joe. He looked at the wet scraps that remained of the tiny creature that had been on his shoulder. "If this little beast was his minion, we may have made a terrible mistake."

"We?" Crash said in an affronted tone. "he was your little buddy."

"Well, it's not like the book told him anything, is it," Joe huffed. "That poem is useless."

"It's not." Garen argued, standing up from the desk. "you only need to understand the meaning hidden in the words."

"So you know how to do it then?" Joe seemed skeptical.

Garen could feel himself getting trapped into helping this man far further than he wished, but his honor as a Zanxian monk demanded that he answer truthfully. "No, but a little more research and some meditation on the matter, I am sure I —"

"Aggressions in the Archive are prohibited." the unexpected, hollow, mechanical voice made all three jump. They looked in the direction of the voice, Crash peering around the side of the desk. The two suits of armor from the entrance of the Archive were now standing a few displays away. Each was pointing their stick with the now glowing, green, bulbous ends; one at Joe, the other at Garen. Joe immediately took a defensive posture, brandishing Death Seed in front of him.

Both suits aimed their sticks at Joe then, and again, the mechanical voice came from one of them, though it was impossible to tell which. "Relinquish your weapon or be immediately neutralized."

Joe maintained his stance. "Nootra what? Are there guys inside those things?"

Garen spoke as calmly as he could out of the side of his mouth, trying not to make any sudden movements that might provoke the two menacing metal men. "I don't think they —"

Before Garen could finish his thought, Joe made a slight swish of his sword, arrogantly inviting the metal men to try something. In that same instant, several flashes of green light erupted from the ends of the sticks, filling the vision of Joe, Garen, and Crash, and then all was darkness.

Chapter 13

Screamin' Joe Blade's Ten-Point Guide to Life:
Point #8: Always make time to get a good sleep.

Joe woke to the sensation of being repeatedly thumped in the back of the head. This was an interesting experience; he was far more used to that sensation preceding the darkness. These moments of unconsciousness were beginning to wear on him, but this time felt a little different. It was much more like he had simply been in a very deep sleep, and aside from a dull pain in his extremities and a soreness in his left hip, he felt remarkably well-rested. He opened his eyes to find the order of things restored, as there was only more darkness. That had him a little concerned, thinking that he might be back in the King's repaired dungeon. There were hints that this wasn't the case.

For one thing, the floor he was lying on was wood, not stone. There was also something very troubling about this wooden floored room. It was vibrating, rumbling with the occasional thudding jolt, like the one that had woke him. It was like an endless earthquake. Still, nothing seemed to be crashing about him, so he assumed he wasn't in any real immediate danger. It was a common assumption he tended toward in situations such as this, and he had come to accept that it was most often incorrect. This bad habit, however, did help him get through each day a little calmer. He groped about his immediate surroundings and himself, trying to get more of a bearing on his situation. He still had his bandolier of knives, his clothes, even Death Seed, nicely tucked away in the sheath the brookshins had made for it. Not a prison, he thought, but then where?

"I think he's awake." Crash's voice whispered from the darkness to his left.

Joe felt a swift kick to his left hip. "OW! What the —"

"Yup, he's awake."

A curtain pulled back at Joe's feet then, washing him in the gently strobing green illumination of the street lights of the southern quarter passing by above. Joe was lying on the floor of a cart with a grey canvas canopy held up by a boxy wooden lattice frame. He could see Garen and Crash now, seated on wooden benches on either side of him. Tosh was past his feet, through the opening, driving the cart, and he looked back at Joe briefly.

"You'll want to stay back there until we get to the docks, I expect," Tosh said over his shoulder in a shouted whisper.

He went on to explain that the suits of armor, back in the archive, were really automata, recovered from an ancient tomb centuries ago and repurposed to protect the archive. They had been referred to as "GET"s in writings found on the tomb walls, so the Knower's guild still referred to them as such. Umadda had alerted Tosh to the situation, and by the time he got from his lab several floors above back down to the archive, the GETs had arranged Joe, Garen, and Crash's unconscious forms neatly at the archive entrance. Tosh had managed to easily rouse Crash and Garen, but the same spices waved beneath Joe's nose had no effect.

Garen and Crash had explained their situation fully to Tosh, and Tosh agreed to help get them and Joe to the docks, with the condition that they take him along. Having briefly examined the biological wonder that was Kord's arm and hearing what Joe planned to do regarding putting together the red powersword, he could not resist the opportunity to record and document all of it. Tosh hoped the brief note he left behind with Kord's severed limb would be enough for the guild to excuse him for abandoning his duties as library keeper. He had even left an additional note to be delivered to the Zanxian monastery to explain Garen's absence. Crash quickly agreed to take Tosh along, and Garen seemed pleased to have another intellectual with whom to ponder the riddle of the red powersword's assembly. Garen, however, was not entirely thrilled to still be caught up in the chaos of these strangers. He reminded himself that helping these insane people was among his duties as a Zanxian monk, the simple Zanxian rule being that if you can help, you must.

The sound of the cart as it raced through the brickwork streets was strangely muffled. This was in part due to the inflated flexible coverings on the wheels. Additionally, the soft padded feet of the domesticated tarboc pulling the cart made almost no sound as it ran. Tarbocs made excellent hauling beasts for smugglers, and the Knower's Guild, whose members' various experiments required a variety of questionably legal or ethically moral goods, always needed to do some smuggling. Such activities were frowned upon by the Loncodi Thieves Guild as it potentially impinged upon their realm of operations, but since the goods being smuggled by the knowers were usually those acquired via dealings with members of the thieves guild, business wasn't terribly impacted, and the thieves were happy to leave the risk of transport to the knowers.

In any case, tarbocs were not easy beasts to obtain and far too dangerous for any sensible thief to try to bother with. They also needed to be fed a unique concoction, known only to the Knower's Guild, to keep tame. The size of a horse, their powerful cat-like bodies were built for speed and didn't draw attention with clattering noise the way horses and other hoofed and shoed animals did. Should anyone take note of them, however, the sight of the highly venomous fangs of a tarboc's cobra-like head was usually enough to deter any curious people from getting too close or nosing about.

Generally, tarbocs were the color of sand, with black spots or stripes, but it was the far more stealthy and rare all-black colored tarbocs, like the one pulling Tosh's cart, that were sought for the purpose of smuggling.

This tarboc knew the way to the docks well; so many times had it made a run for the knowers. That night, however, Tosh found himself having to steer the beast more often than usual. The King's men seemed to be everywhere, down every street, every turn, but so were the Loncodi guardsmen.

Most of the small groups encountered were too busy fighting with each other to notice Tosh's black cart and tarboc zip across an intersection or quickly turn down another street with little more than the sound of a strong gust of wind. The few that may have actually noticed paid the smugglers' cart little mind as it simply wasn't what they were immediately concerned about.

Helping to elude notice, however, Tosh was wearing a special set of driving goggles that looked like a trio of stubby black inverted telescopes, one over each eye and the third in the middle at brow level. They were the invention of one of his colleagues and allowed Tosh to see any living beings well in advance without the need for any illumination. Through the goggles, everything appeared in varying hues of yellow and green, but still with enough detail to make out who was a friend and who was a foe. This wasn't much of an advantage in the dimly lit southern quarter, where everything visible was already in hues of green. However, it was of much more significant benefit once they reached the oppressively unlit streets of the warehouse district of the eastern quarter.

It was through these streets that they made their best time, but ironically, also where they caught the attention of a troop of the King's men, nearly running them down as they rounded a corner. The King's men pursued them angrily but, being on foot, quickly fell hopelessly behind.

"What was that?" Garen asked from within the covered cart, concerned by the clatter and angry shouts generated by nearly running over the King's men.

"No worries. No worries." Tosh said, trying to calm the monk. "Just a few of the King's guards. Doubt they'll follow. Not looking for smugglers."

Tosh reached into a satchel next to him with his right hand, keeping his left hand on the reins of his speeding tarboc. He pulled out a decorative brass box with several jeweled knobs down its left side. Thin swirling silver appliqués covering the entire exterior blended into a square of silver mesh on the front. A single, round, silver button sat centered on the box's top edge, and Tosh gently bit down on this button and pulled the box away from him. The button telescoped out into a short, silvery antenna. Still using only his right hand, he deftly spun two of the side knobs with his thumb, he pressed on a third knob, and it slid up slightly.

"I'm here," came a metallic voice from the box.

"Have you found the boat?" Tosh asked, holding the mesh part of the box close to his mouth.

"Yes, south end of the wharf," the box answered back. Looks like they're about ready to shove off, but you'll need to meet me at the third jetty. My, uh, parcel is on the R—" The box's last word was cut off by crackling noise.

"Come again?" Tosh requested.

There was more crackling and a piercing squawking sound then, "Roc's Tooth. Big, red, war voyager. Looks black in the dark but you can't miss it. End Relay."

"Got it. End Relay." Tosh retracted the antenna and stashed the box back in the satchel.

Joe, Crash, and Garen had sat silently within the cart, mesmerized by Tosh's conversation with the metal box. It was Garen who finally asked what manner of sorcery they had just witnessed, putting together that somehow Tosh had been speaking with someone who was already at the pier.

"Not sorcery, young monk, science!" Tosh flashed a wide smile over his shoulder at his passengers. "We call the devices vocasters. They are based on items that were found along with the GETs. As you heard, we'll be meeting one of my colleagues on the docks. As luck has it, he has need of the cart himself tonight, so we'll be leaving it in his care and then make for your boat at the widow's pier."

"Oh, we're going to need those!" Joe said excitedly. Imagine all the trouble a couple of fellas could get into with those things.

"Yes," agreed Garen, "like smuggling illicit materials into a city while coordinating the escape of wanted criminals by sea."

Joe just scowled at the monk, not entirely appreciating his sarcasm.

Joe turned back to Tosh, asking, "Who's your buddy on the dock?"

"Barrowmel. We call him Barry." Tosh said over his shoulder. "I'm not sure what it is that he is picking up. Some secret project of his; all hush-hush. He's been at it for months now. He is obsessed with Zeebo, though, so I'm assuming it's part of another of his crazy schemes to reach it. Nearly killed himself with that cannon of his last year."

"Zeebo?" Joe asked, not understanding.

"The sparkly blue moon, silly." Crash giggled.

"Yes," Tosh went on. "It's blue and sparkly, as you say, because it is covered with water. Just one of Barry's discoveries. What's more, he says that he saw a beautiful mermaid wave at him up there one night as he looked through his large multi-lens. Most of the guild thinks he's gone insane. I think he just had a little too much of that Westerlan ogre whiskey that he's so fond of." Tosh chuckled at this. "Probably what he's really picking up tonight."

They rounded a corner hard then, lifting, briefly, up onto the cart's two left wheels, tossing Joe, Garen, and Crash around a bit within. The next three corners were much the same, prompting Joe to tell Tosh to take it easy, as he didn't much feel like being knocked out again.

"No worries, friend. We're here." Tosh said in a hushed tone. "Stay inside until I call you out." He closed the curtain behind him, leaving Joe, Garen, and Crash in the dark.

Passing through the eastern gate of the city, the only gate that remained open at night, the cart's soft wheels made a slight rhythmic, rumbling, flapping sound as they passed over the small gaps between the dock's four-foot-wide boards. So quiet, or at least so unlike the sound of an ordinary cart, was Tosh's ride that seldom, in the past, had it roused much notice from the guards who usually stood atop the wall. A particular situation in the market square and the surrounding streets involving an unexplained attack by the King's men had the guards occupied elsewhere that night. It would make rolling onto the docks even less of a hassle, but Tosh would still need to be cautious; Loncodi guards weren't the only ones who would be curious about the contents of a cart arriving on the docks at such a late hour.

The tarboc gave a loud hiss. It had made the trip to and from the docks countless times but protested a little every time it set foot on the ancient stone-like timbers of the Loncodi dock. Getting a tarboc this close to water was a testament to the level of near-impossible obedience achieved with this beast. Tarbocs are not able to swim and will instinctively do all they can to avoid getting anywhere near water. Just getting a tarboc wet would throw the beast into a panicked rage. One never left their tarboc out in the rain unless they wanted to deal with a great deal of damage and death.

"Hush now, Sabon." Tosh reprimanded the creature in as quiet but as stern of a voice as possible.

Only a few torches here and there illuminated small portions of the long, well-maintained wooden docks. The wharf ran the length of the eastern wall and was wide enough to allow ten carts to ride abreast. Such wouldn't have actually been possible, though, as the main dock was littered with large stacks of crates and barrels, goods either having just arrived by boat, just being loaded, or destined to be loaded onto one or more ships. Without the presence of the usual Loncodi security protecting the goods, many of the shipments were presently being guarded by the local longshoremen, who were paid extra by individual captains or merchants for their services. Few thieves were likely to risk tangling with massive brutes the likes of Loncodi's dock workers.

The knowers' guild's cart, black as it was, faded into the shadows; a trait made all the more effective by the path taken by the tarboc. Without being prompted and without losing stride, the well-trained beast took a low slinking posture as it pulled the cart along, skillfully taking a serpentine route from one shadow to the next. Not a head was turned as the cart slid its way to the third pier.

The looming silhouette of the Roc's Tooth was impossible to miss; it was easily the largest ship moored in the Loncodi docks that night. The massive vessel was a multi-decked war voyager, powered by both sail and a hundred oars and armed with as many cannons on two decks. It was a ship designed for speed and destruction, with enough cargo space to transport an army. However, Its function here was more likely the protection of a fleet of merchant vessels and, apparently, the transport of whatever questionable commodity Barry was picking up that night. This particular pier was completely unlit, generally an indication that there was no work to be done or, quite often, that those working didn't want any prying eyes. Tosh brought the cart around a stack of crates, parking it out of line-of-sight of anyone save for those on the Roc's Tooth if they possessed some means of piercing the darkness.

The cart had no sooner come to a halt when Tosh's colleague, Barry, seemed to spring out of nowhere. He was older than Tosh by about fifteen years, somewhere in his fifties, and in pretty good health for a man his age, though bone thin. He was bald on top, but the salt and pepper hair around the sides and back, which matched his bushy grey mustache, was thick and stuck out in random directions. The panicked look presently on his face, though softened by the darkness and subtle light of the waxing moons of Zeebo and Gatal, only helped complete his appearance as someone potentially insane.

"You need to get out of here!" he exclaimed in a harsh whisper.

"What?" Tosh responded a little too loudly. Barry quickly prompted him to lower his voice. "What?" Tosh tried again in a much quieter tone.

"The ship is crawling with the King's men," Barry whispered frantically as he climbed up onto the cart, taking a seat beside Tosh. "Look for yourself."

Still wearing his night driving goggles, Tosh looked up to the deck of the Roc's Tooth. The ship was a mass of movement. He counted forty of the King's guard before giving up, and that, he noted, was just along the ship's rail. He could assume there was at least twice that onboard, probably far more. Then, a massive figure came into view. At first, he thought it might be the King himself, but the figure was too large, standing nearly twice as tall and nearly three times as wide as any of the guards. It was hard to make out features through the glowing, green and yellow hues that the goggles made of the figure, but Tosh quickly recognized the general shape of the massive man.

"Ogres! You're dealing with ogres?" Tosh's frantic whispers bordered on indecipherable screeches as he grabbed Barry by the collar of his black robe.

"Ogres?" came Garen's concerned voice from within the cart.

Barry pulled back the curtain. Garen was little more than a black blob in the darkness, while Joe and Crash were entirely masked by the dark within the cart.

"Oh, how do you do," Barry said in a hushed but cordial tone, as though the apparent direness of the situation he had expressed earlier had somehow passed. He twisted in his seat awkwardly, reaching around Tosh's hold on him to put his hand out to shake in greeting. "A Zanxion monk, are you?"

Garen was taken aback somewhat. How could Barry tell in the darkness?

Barry quickly explained his question, reading the monk's confused silence. "Fractaberry juice gives one the most excellent night vision with the right additives."

Tosh grunted in frustration, grabbing Barry about his collar with both hands, then twisting Barry back to face him and giving him a bit of a shake. "Ogres? Have you lost the last few scraps of your mind?"

"What's so bad about these ogre fellas?" Joe asked innocently. He turned to Crash then, "I thought you said they rode around on some sort of flying dragons, not giant boats?"

"Not just any ogres with a ship like that." Crash whispered. Her tone lacked her usual maniacal gaiety. It almost made her sound like an entirely different, serious, sane person.

"You're dealing with the Westerlan Trading Syndicate!" Tosh was having a hard time keeping his voice at a whisper level and he gave Barry a few more shakes.

"Well, not exactly, I mean, well, yes." Barry shrugged his shoulders and looked a little defeated. "But they're only involved in the transport. They're not who I'm buying from."

"Not who you're buying from? If they're involved in the transport, of course, that's who you're buying from, or who you're buying from is working for, or more likely enslaved to." Tosh pulled his goggles up onto his forehead, hoping that direct eye contact with Barry might better convey his concern and anger.

"That might be the case," Barry came back calmly. "But what matters now is that the King's men are fishing about, looking for you and your circus friends by the sound. They got some tip that you would be on the Roc's Tooth, and the Syndicate doesn't take well to having the authorities snooping about their ships. Not sure what you've got yourself involved in Tosher, but it's three leagues deeper than any trouble I have unless I'm seen with you."

Tosh pulled his goggles back down, scanning the ship again. The hulking, glowing green shape caught his eye again, but it wasn't on the boat. It was on the dock, making its way from the gangway toward the cart.

"Time to go," Tosh said to the others. "Quick, out the back of the cart!" He turned back to Barry. "I'm going to need your vocaster."

Barry didn't question Tosh's request, quickly digging out his decorative, brass, and silver vocaster from an inside pocket of his robe. "Knowledge guide you, friend."

"And you, though common sense has clearly abandoned us both." Tosh went to dodge into the cart, but he was stopped short. Barry made an odd, surprised, panicked yelping sound. A huge hand had hold of Tosh by the hood of his robe. It pulled him off the cart and tossed him onto the dock.

"Friend of yours, little thinker?" Rumbled a voice in a low, menacing tone. To Tosh, the ogre wasn't much more than an enormous yellow blob in the darkness.

"J-Just my, uh, the driver." Barry stumbled over his words a little, and it grew worse the more he spoke. "You'll, he, will, not, I mean, he won't, I mean rather, he is —"

Tosh, getting to his feet, rubbing a badly bruised elbow, and mustering up as calm a voice as he could, helped Barry out. "I will not be a problem. Really."

"Wasn't talkin' to you. Aint gonna talk to you." the ogre's voice was menacingly calm and dismissive. The threat in the tone made Tosh take a step back. "You were told to come alone. Got enough of a headache with your King's damned roseheads nosin' about. Captain isn't happy. The deal's off."

"But, Tongar, you already took the gold!" Barry protested, raising his voice without thinking.

Tongar chuckled a deep, rumbling chuckle that sounded a little like thunder on a distant horizon. "First rule of business, little thinker, don't pay 'til you got the goods in hand. 'Sides, you really want to take this up now; you gonna explain to the King's boys what yer up to." The ogre gave another menacing chuckle. "Shove off and leave the wagon behind."

"You heard the man," came Joe's voice from the darkness beside the cart. He, Garen, and Crash had already started to make their way off when they heard Barry's protest and turned around. "Time to go fellas."

Joe's tone was light, far from quiet, and had a bit of the sound of a father picking his children up from a day of playing at a friend's house.

"This is your idea of comin' alone, is it? Who's this, then." Tongar growled as he grabbed Barry by the throat, lifting him off the ground. Barry tried to speak but found his throat was too busy being strangled.

"Just some friends. How 'bout you put ol' Barry down, and we'll be off. No hard feelings even." Joe slowly stepped forward as he spoke, quietly unsheathing Death Seed in the darkness.

The ogre, still holding Barry aloft, reached into a pocket, producing a round, cut crystal. Pointing it in the direction of Joe's voice, he gave it a squeeze. A wide beam of soft, white light shot from the crystal in his hand, illuminating Joe, Garen, and Crash. Joe had the guilty look of a child caught stealing candy and tried to hide Death Seed behind him as slowly and casually as possible. It wasn't working. The ogre just looked at Joe with anger and a bit of confusion over Joe's lack of sense, but then he noticed Crash, or rather, the paint on Crash's face.

"You're them circus freaks that got our ship crawlin' with filthy roseheads!" Tongar shouted this, and the volume of his voice not only took Joe and the rest by surprise but drew the attention of everyone on the deck of the Roc's Tooth. Lamps and torches bobbed along the deck in haste toward the ship's gangway.

Seeing the ogre in the pale light of his illuminating crystal, Joe was completely rethinking his plan of attacking the man. Tongar was truly immense; nearly ten feet tall, clad in highly crafted red leather, with his shoulders, chest, and forearms covered in armor made from the enormous black scales of some sort of creature. Joe wasn't much for second-guessing his own plans, however, and giving a subtle shrug that concluded a brief argument with himself, he lashed out quickly with Death Seed, catching the ogre in the forearm of the arm holding up Barry. The sword vibrated, uncharacteristically, in Joe's hand from solidly impacting rather than cutting through the scaled armor plates on the ogre's forearm. The backlash was so violent that it hurt Joe's hand, causing him to drop the sword. The result was close to what Joe had tried for, however. Tongar dropped Barry, who immediately staggered back into the darkness, coughing and choking.

"Dragon scales," Crash was at Joe's ear. "You're wasting your time." Her hands were on his shoulders, trying to coax him into fleeing with her.

Shouts were coming from the base of the gangway then, along with the sounds of armored men running toward them. Tongar laughed, lunging at Joe, his massive hand grabbing the disarmed sword thief by the front of his leather jacket. Before Joe could react, the ogre threw Joe over his shoulder like he was tossing away a freshly emptied bottle of ogre whiskey. Crash called out for Joe in a sincere voice of concern but was helpless to do anything as his body flew off into the darkness. Tosh lurched toward her, grabbing her and telling her to run, and she did.

"There you go, boys," the ogre shouted back at the approaching King's men. Unable to see Joe's body hurtling through the darkness to avoid him, Joe crashed full force into the first few charging men, sending all four, including Joe, sprawling. The men behind them stumbled over Joe and the others in the dark with a clattering of armor until fifteen men lay on the ground, confused as to what had just happened. By the time a trailing guard arrived, carrying a lamp, Joe, unencumbered by armor like the others, had already sprung to his feet and was running, concealed in the darkness. The sound of his feet was masked by the grumbles of the fallen men trying to get up.

The tarboc didn't like the disturbance and hissed loudly at Tongar.

"Aw, poor kitty," Tongar said, chuckling as he attempted to punch the tarboc.

Despite being harnessed, the tarboc's serpentine head had enough mobility that it was able to easily dodge the ogre's slow swing. Ferocious as the tarboc was, it had enough instinctive sense to realize that being bound in the harness rendered it out-matched. Rather than fight the oversized opponent, the tarboc's instinct was to flee, and it ran off down the dock, along with the cart, toward the end of the pier. This amused Tongar greatly. He laughed heartily, flashing his light around to take in the various bits of mayhem in the shadows. Garen, who had moved to a position concealed beneath the cart moments ago, now found himself without cover, but the ogre's scanning light had not yet found him. Quickly, he rolled towards the ogre's feet, grabbing Death Seed from where Joe had dropped it. Still unnoticed in the darkness, he rolled away over to where he thought Barry was, but Barry had already made his escape. It was just then that Tongar's light fell upon Garen.

"How many of you little circus vermin are there? Over here!" He shouted back to the King's men, then turned back to Garen, who was taking a defensive stance and ready for a fight. "Better run, little monkey," Tongar said with a broad smile.

"When he's right, he's right," Joe shouted as he ran past Garen, with a bit of a limp, disappearing into the shadows. Garen followed. Guardsmen, several with lamps and torches in hand, rattled by a moment later.

Satisfied that the entertainment for the evening had concluded, Tongar extinguished his crystal and lumbered back to the Roc's Tooth. Several more guardsmen clattered past him in the dark, trying to catch up to the others already in pursuit of Joe and Garren. Tongar mumbled some obscenities and hoped that was the last he would see of King Gom's men that night, especially on his ship.

"Tongar is it?" came a voice from the shadows near the gangplank.

"Who's askin'," Tongar grumbled. The crystal in his hand winked back on and probed the darkness. "Shouldn't you be runnin' along after the rest o' your little mates?"

A man, one of the King's men by his garb, with long blonde hair and a patch over one eye, stepped into the beam of light. "I am Baron Solvar, emissary for the King of Eastworld. I apologize for the intrusion by my men onto your vessel earlier, but I expect we may need to inconvenience you further."

* * * * * * * * * * * * * * * * * *

It was a fairly typical evening at the south end of the Loncodi harbor wharf. Somewhere out in the bay, a buoyed bell clanged its slow, lonely, warning song as it bobbed in the gentle ebb tide. A light fog was just beginning to roll in, smelling of seaweed, saltwater, and the day's catch. Boats of varying sizes, some with sails, some that simply used oars, creaked in their moorings as they lazily rocked in the gentle swells of the calm waters of Freltard Bay. Among the ships waiting in the darkness this night was the Gristabell. A big-bellied, cargo, rowing vessel, it was moored in the first birth of what the locals called the widow's pier, next to the wharf. A nearby area on the main boardwalk itself, ringed by five large, permanently fixed torches, illuminated a collection of barrels and crates waiting to be loaded onto the ship. It was one of the few areas alive with activity that night.

Normally used to carry grain to various ports in Westerlan or Southern Senuvia, this night, the Gristabell was being loaded with kegs of the best Senuvian wine, as well as one enormous barrel containing nearly two thousand gallons of dwarven whiskey. It had been hauled, at great expense, all the way down from the Munwrath Mountains and, like the other barrels, had the same destination; a wedding feast in the desert land of Kil'Velhara in southern Westerlan.

The only daughter of the King of Kil'Velhara was marrying a North Westerlan prince. What misgivings the King may have had about his daughter marrying a prince of one of the most notoriously murderous northern barbarian clans was entirely offset by his daughter's own reputation.

Beautiful as she was, with raven-black hair that fell in gentle curls to just below her waist, deep violet eyes, lips naturally as deep red as wine, and skin so flawless and smooth she nearly appeared to be finely crafted from porcelain, her breathtaking appearance was rarely spoken of. No, instead, the people of Westerlan whispered among themselves tales of horror, for the princess was known for ordering the death of any servant that displeased her, torturing them herself for days before allowing them to be dispatched. It was said that she even ate the hearts of her slain female servants. The rationale for this act of cannibalism varied depending on who told the tale, but it was never more than speculation, as only the princess could know her own reasons.

Most infamous, perhaps, and the story most consistently told was the tale of the artist who had so accurately painted her portrait that she had ordered his death to preserve the rarity and value of the work. Before his execution, however, she amputated his painting hand herself, taking it off at the elbow. She forced him to watch as she had a servant roast it up and serve it to her. It was, she explained, to assure him that though he would be leaving this life behind, his talent would live on through her. The story typically ended with the servant who did the cooking eventually being killed as well for spreading the tale. It made for a delightfully frightening story to tell children around the hearth late at night to instill, however ironically, the wrongs of spreading rumors.

The princess had a penchant for violence since her childhood, torturing and killing any small animal unfortunate to find itself in her clutches. At that time, the King assumed she was reckless or too exuberant with her affections for the creatures. By the time she was twelve years old, the deaths began to include the servants. It became impossible for the King to deny that something was deeply wrong with his daughter. Yet, so fiercely loyal and lovingly sweet she was to her father that he could not bring himself to order her imprisoned and certainly not executed. His only hope of ridding her from his kingdom was to marry her off, but finding someone who had not been scared off by tales of her was hard to come by.

The first three suitors that had come around when she turned fifteen had simply assumed, much to their detriment, that the tales of her violent nature were just the tales of bitter men who had failed to woo the young lady. Each, in their turn, had hobbled back to their own realms gravely maimed in one manner or another. The first suitor's injuries nearly initiated a war when he was sent back to his realm minus one of his legs. A great deal of gold, four elephants, and six months' worth of diplomatic negotiations quelled that particular situation, and the King was pretty sure that the other two suitors that followed were truly only after a similar payoff but left, instead, happy to still have their lives.

On her eighteenth birthday, when a messenger arrived with a note from one of the twelve barbarian kings to the north expressing his wish to arrange a marriage between their children without the two having ever met, the King of Kil'Velhara jumped at the opportunity. Though he feared telling his daughter of the agreement, surprisingly, she had heard stories of the barbarian prince and seemed quite pleased with the idea. Overjoyed by this good turn of fate, the King made no hesitation in making the arrangements for his daughter's wedding and to ensure her delight with the day. No expense was to be spared. Indeed, he was nearly making himself penniless in the process, but bankrupting the entire kingdom would be worth it if he could make this arranged marriage stick.

Of course, none of the longshoremen presently tasked with loading the wedding goods onto the Gristabell had any idea why such a volume of alcohol was being shipped across the ocean to a land that surely must have its own supplies of equally intoxicating beverages, nor did any of them care. To them, it was just another job, albeit an especially problematic one.

Presently, a mere ten longshoremen were dealing with hauling all of the two-hundred-pound wine barrels, each carrying or rolling one barrel, rather than assisting one another for the sake of expedience. Meanwhile, a group of four others dealt with the variously sized crates. Initially, the bulk of the fifty-man crew had been assigned to the smaller barrels and crates, leaving the enormous seven thousand-liter whiskey keg to be hoisted by a four-man crane crew onto the boat. However, the seven-foot diameter barrel full of dwarven hooch had turned out to be too heavy for the four men working the crane's two tread wheels to budge.

The remaining thirty-two men had set to the task of figuring out a way to get the large barrel aboard the Gristabell. At twelve feet long, the barrel was too wide to roll up the gangway and would have been too heavy for the gangway to support. Had neither of those issues been a problem, they still would have been faced with the situation of being able to get no more than eight men behind the barrel, which wouldn't have been near enough manpower to roll the twelve thousand pound keg up to the ship's deck.

Instead, it was decided that they would stick with using the crane in some manner. Taking most of the evening to set up and the result of years of experience moving difficult cargos, the men wove an elaborate web of ropes and pulleys attached to the crane, the wharf, and the ship.

Hoisting the enormous keg into the air had been going slowly, but the complicated rig allowed the thirty-two-man crew to accomplish what could easily have taken three times as many men to do strength-wise. The men had formed three lines, each group pulling in a different direction but ultimately contributing to lifting the barrel of whiskey. One line ran down the widow's pier, one along the wharf away from the widow's pier, and the third cut across the wharf. The way the ropes had been rigged, once the keg reached a particular height, a series of slip knots would be at an angle to allow it to freely hang from the crane while also re-engaging the ropes that the men were presently using to hoist the keg, to then pull the keg toward and over the side of the Gristabell.

The task had been going so smoothly that the men had been laughing and joking among themselves about how the poor fellows in Southern Westerlan would get the keg back out of the boat. Their joking was a little premature, however. They had managed to raise the keg nearly thirty-five feet, about five feet shy of the height they needed it to be before it would begin moving toward the Gristabell. One of the slip knots wasn't slipping. It was a matter of manpower, but even calling the rest of the crew to join in the effort did not move the keg. Worse still, the men were beginning to tire. If they were to let go now, the keg would simply come crashing down.

It was just then that a woman, her face painted up like a skull-faced clown, came running by. She had been shouting something about ogres and something, something, with swords. Without losing pace, she had bent backward in a limbo maneuver to duck under the rope of the line of men cutting across the wharf, ran past the men down the widow's pier, and disappeared into the darkness.

A moment later, a man wearing a purple robe and some sort of metal and glass mask across his eyes came running along. He paused at the line of workers cutting across the wharf, following the line with his eyes to the crane and up to the suspended keg, taking in the engineering spectacle of the web of rigging.

"Oh," he said in a voice of subtle surprise. "Brilliant." He then ducked under the rope between two of the workers. Not having any reason to stop the man and unable to, even if they had, without the risk of letting the keg drop, they simply watched quietly and curiously as the man scurried off down the widow's pier, disappearing into the distant shadows as the clown woman the moment before.

They all stood staring in silence for a moment, wondering what it had all been about. The ropes holding the keg creaked as the keg swayed. A lone seagull cried out somewhere high above the bay. The tired men looked then to their foreman for the cue to get the keg up the remaining five feet. It was at that moment they heard the strangely subtle rumbling of a cart speeding in their direction.

* * * * * * * * * * * * * * * * * *

Joe was slowing Garen down. He was too pumped up on adrenalin to really be feeling all of the bruises he sustained when thrown into the King's men, but the pain in his left hip was acute enough that it could not be ignored. It was causing him to limp slightly.

"Run faster bladesman. They are gaining ground," Garen said to Joe as they ran. His voice was casual and steady, as though he and Joe were simply out for a leisurely walk.

"I know." Joe was gasping for air between words. "I'm hoping for another library."

They had managed to make their way off the pier where the Roc's Tooth was moored, but the run down the wharf to where the Harmaton was docked was going to be far too long a stretch for Joe to stay ahead of the guards. Joe looked over his shoulder.

"They're a good thirty seconds behind us," he huffed to Garen. "I could take a ten-second break."

"Please don't," Garen said flatly.

Joe stopped, holding his hip, leaning and bending his torso in various directions, trying to stretch the pain out somehow if he could. It took a moment for Garen to notice that Joe was no longer beside him, so he stopped and turned. "Bladesman!" He shouted back at Joe, seeing the pursuing torches and lamps nearly upon him.

Joe turned around, surprised to see how close the men chasing them had gotten, though still only visible as the torches or lamps they carried, and he burst back into a stumbling run, wincing again from the pain. His brief rest had not improved its condition.

Joe heard one of the men behind him cry out, followed by the clatter of armor. He assumed that one of them had tripped, and it made him

200

smile. He might get through the rest of the night alive yet, he thought, maybe even conscious. Joe looked over his shoulder just in time to see torches and lamps flying in various directions. Men were crying out in pain or shouting in alarm. Armor was clanging against armor and clattering across the wharf. Two torches flew over the side of the wharf, followed by the large splashes of bodies hitting the water.

Joe caught up to Garen just as a deep rumbling came from behind. Before Joe could look over his shoulder to see what was coming, it was already upon him.

"Get in!" Barry shouted as he reigned in the tarboc to a halt. Garen quickly jumped in the back of the cart, helping Joe do the same. Joe's feet no sooner left the boardwalk than Barry snapped the reigns on the tarboc. The cart lurched forward rapidly, accelerating with the tarboc's powerful strides. The shouting soldiers, those that hadn't been bit, slashed, run over, or buffeted into the bay, were quickly left behind. There would be no hope of them catching up to the knowers' speedy smuggling cart.

"Have you seen Tosh?" Barry shouted back to Garen and Joe as they sped along.

Joe poked his head out the front of the cart beside Barry, "I kinda lost track of all of you after your big pal showed me the finer points of flying.

"They can't be too far ahead of us," Garen added from within the cart.

"'There!" Joe said, pointing ahead at Tosh in the torch-lit loading space for the Gristabell. Tosh was awkwardly making his way under the rope being held by a line of workers hoisting a giant keg. A moment later, he quickly slipped beyond their view.

"The clown woman, Crash, she must be further ahead. They left together." Garren said, his head now poking out the front of the covered cart on the opposite side of Barry from Joe.

"Y'ah!" Barry shouted, snapping the reins. "I may not have got my liquid celestialite, but I will get all of you to that boat of yours."

The tarboc and the cart were now visible to the dock workers, who were actually a little confused by what they were seeing. Essentially, it was a rapidly moving black blob that didn't make the usual rattling and banging sounds of a cart nor the familiar clop sounds of a horse. By the time it became evident what it was, though only slightly less perplexing, the dock workers were in danger of being run down.

"Out of the way, you fools!" Barry shouted repeatedly.

"I'm letting go," came the call from one of the longshoremen, voicing his intentions loud enough for everyone on the line to hear.

"You can't," shouted back another, knowing that letting go now would drop the keg to its ruin.

The tarboc and cart were on them then, leaving no choice. The dockworkers dove in every direction, avoiding the charge of the tarboc and its cart until only one man remained. He was being pulled rapidly, by the sudden weight of the keg, into the path of the tarboc, but he wouldn't relent. The keg lurched, dropping a few feet as the men on the other two lines did all they could to keep it in the air. The tarboc leaped over the unrelenting worker and his line.

"No, no, no, no!" Barry's voice raised as the tarboc jumped the rope, and the front of the cart heaved with it, the front wheels raising off the dock. The dockworker ducked, finally releasing the rope.

For a moment, it seemed as if the cart had completely cleared the rope as it continued on for a few feet, but the rope had become tangled in the undercarriage near the rear axle. The cart's back end lurched violently to one side as it took the weight of the keg. The cart's momentum was enough force to hoist the keg, quickly, the few feet it needed to engage the secondary guide ropes to the Gristabell. So sudden had the barrel raised, that the unexpected slack in the ropes caused the men in the other two lines to fall backward like two lines of dominos, losing hold of the lines in the process.

The enormous whiskey barrel was now trying to make its way down the secondary rigging, being supported only by the cart and the tarboc, both of which the keg outweighed entirely. All that was holding the cart in place was the tarboc's claws anchored deep into the wood of the wharf. The tarboc hissed angrily as it tried, vainly, to pull forward.

"Get out of the cart!" Barry barked at the two men behind him.

Garen and Joe clambered out onto the seat of the cart on either side of Barry.

"What about you?" Garen asked as he jumped down, seeing that Barry wasn't making a move to get down.

"I need to get the tarboc free," Barry said back frantically as he tossed the reins out clear of the cart and leaned forward, fumbling for something on the front of the cart. Just then, the cart shifted backward violently. The tarboc hissed loudly as it slid along with the cart, its claws digging deep stripes into the wooden planks of the wharf. The unexpected motion threw Barry forward and down onto the yolk arm of the tarboc's harness. Joe was still in the seat, hanging on to the inside lip of the cart.

"How do I unhitch it?" Joe asked anxiously.

Barry wasn't responding; the fall had winded him, and he was struggling to right himself. Garen rushed over and helped him off of the cart's rigging. The cart shifted another inch, and Joe seriously contemplated just jumping off.

Shouts came from behind. What remained of the guards that Barry and the tarboc had run down earlier had caught up and would be on them in moments.

"Something in the front," Garen shouted as he and Barry scrambled clear of the cart. "He was reaching for something on the front panel."

Many of the dock workers on the other two lines had recovered and were just then pulling on their lines, easing the force being exerted on the cart. The workers who had been on the rope that was now tangled in the cart's axle were beginning to gather cautiously around the cart, not really sure what to do. It was too dangerous and hopeless to untangle the rope, and now they had the distraction of the King's men on the scene.

Joe groped around the front panel of the cart, his hand finding nothing but smooth wood. "Run, I've got this," he shouted to Garen. Garen nodded and pulled Barry along with him. Barry, who still didn't have his voice, looked back at Joe, motioning to reach lower.

Joe kept groping, but it was too late; the King's men were there, eight in all. They surrounded the cart's back and sides, shouting at the dockworkers to back away. The dockworkers began shouting back at the guards, trying to tell them that the cart was holding up the barrel. Everyone was shouting over one another, and nothing was truly being conveyed. Tempers from both groups of men were starting to rise. One of the King's men grabbed Joe by the ankle.

"Got you, you filthy brigand," he shouted at Joe.

At that very same moment, Joe's groping fingers caught the edge of a small recess in the front panel of the cart, and that edge moved a little. The guard pulled on Joe's leg, trying to drag him from the carriage. Joe held on tight to the lip of the recess, trying to hang on. The small piece of wood he was hanging on to flipped up and pulled out on a long metal rod. There was a loud metal thump sound, and the tarboc stumbled forward as the vehicle shaft of the harness rig let go from the cart. Free of the cart but surrounded by dock workers, the tarboc did not know where to run. It flared its cobra-like hood and bared its fangs, swiping a paw at any dock worker that ventured too close.

The cart whipped violently in line with the rope, slamming hard into four of the guards surrounding it, sending them flying. The guard holding on to Joe somehow managed to continue to hang on, even as the cart shot across the wharf. The dock workers on the other two lines were overwhelmed by the momentum and were sent stumbling and sprawling as the whiskey barrel zipped down the secondary rigging toward the Gristabell.

In an instant, the cart was airborne, being pulled by the full weight of the barrel up to the top of the cargo crane and swinging the cart across the thirty-foot gap between the wharf and the Gristabell. The guard hanging on to Joe lost his grip and was thrown violently into the side of the Gristabell before disappearing into the black water below with a loud splash. Joe was managing to hang on, though just barely. The cart was dangling nose down, and Joe was hanging on with both hands to the back of the driver's seat. He could feel the wooden slat he was hanging on to flexing, making the tell-tale sharp cracking sounds of a piece of wood just about to snap. Joe looked down quickly, trying to assess the likelihood of falling without severely maiming himself, hoping to aim for the water as the cart swung out. Before that could happen, the keg, now above the Gristabell, had managed to engage the rigging designed to lower it to the ship's deck, and it began to drop quickly. The cart shot up the last few feet to the crane arm. It swung forward toward the Gristabell hard enough to throw Joe upward into some of the rigging lines as the back end of the cart shattered against the crane arm. The rest of the cart crashed down, splintering on the wharf's edge.

Below, the tarboc finally found a moment to flee the situation, rolling out of its harness and darting down the widow's pier.

Joe managed to grab a rope that spanned the space between the crane on the wharf and a boom on the widow's pier. The longshoremen, back on their feet on the widow's pier, were doing their best to slow the descent of the keg, but the keg was doing a better job of pulling them along. It hit the net stretched across the hatch of the cargo hold hard, pulling the temporary bits securing the net to the deck from their post holes. It didn't stop the massive barrel's fall but slowed it just enough to avert disaster. The barrel hit with a thunderous crack sound, doing quite a bit of damage to the floor of the cargo hold. The whole ship rocked a little.

"You're welcome!" Joe shouted down to the dockworkers on the wharf and the widow's pier.

Joe quickly contemplated working his way to the boom hand over hand and, hopefully, be able to climb down from there. He didn't get the chance to try. The cart had also damaged the crane, and the rigging let go entirely. Joe did the only thing he could do; he held tight to the rope. The tangle of ropes, wooden slip-rings, snatch blocks, and Joe were sent swinging down over the widow's pier. Dock workers dove out of the way as Joe swung low across the wide dock, the rigging debris trailing across the pier, noisily, behind him.

Back on the wharf, the three remaining King's men watched Joe's high-flying spectacle incredulously as he swung off into the darkness of the widow's pier. When they realized that Joe might actually be getting away instead of suffering a horrible crashing death, they quickly scrambled to give chase down the widow's pier.

"Really?" was all Joe managed to utter before his unavoidable landing destination and the crushing pain to his testicles that came with it.

The tarboc, scrambling away from the wharf, ended up running right in the path of Joe and the crashing storm of ropes and pulleys. Joe landed hard on Sabon's back. He clung to the beast as best he could despite the pain now throbbing deep in his pelvis from the abuse his testicles took from the landing. The tarboc wasn't happy about Joe landing on its back but was too busy dodging and leaping over the crashing debris of the rigging to deal with the unwanted passenger. By the time it was clear of the chaos and the light of the dock workers, Sabon either didn't care that Joe was on its back or was simply more concerned with making an escape to a better location where Joe could be safely dealt with. Whatever her instinct, it took them in the right direction to the end of the widow's pier where the Harmaton was docked.

Joe did not notice as they passed Garen and Barry in the dark. Garen sensed Barry about to call out to the beast and stopped him, simply saying that the creature was going in the right direction, pointing to the hulking shape of the only ship at the end of the pier.

As Sabon arrived at the Harmaton, its keen night vision picked up the figure of a man standing directly in her path. The tarboc decided that with this new figure before it, it was time to dispense with her unwanted passenger. She dug her claws into the wood of the widow's pier. Stopping up so suddenly brought most of her momentum to a halt but threw the beast into a roll. Joe was thrown forward, hurtling toward the dark figure in the tarboc's path.

"Got you," said Drix calmly as he caught Joe. Joe was unable to respond clearly, as hitting Drix had been something akin to smashing into a stone wall. Joe was badly winded but glad for the presence of the strongman and, through frantic wheezing breaths, tried to express his thanks.

The tarboc had quickly righted itself in front of Joe and Drix, rearing its head back for a strike, its wide mouth gaping open to reveal its four large upper fangs. Its cobra-like hood was fully flared, though the intimidating effect of the fangs and hood was lost entirely in the darkness.

"Teema!" Adriga's voice seemed to come from the dark sky above, like the command of an unseen god.

Sabon hissed in defiance but did not attack Drix or Joe. Still feeling threatened, it began crouching, preparing to either pounce or flee. Drix quickly ran up the gangplank of the Harmaton, putting Joe down on the deck beside Adriga.

"The others?" Joe asked of anyone that might answer, as he managed to catch his breath.

"Quiet," answered Drix in a concerned tone and then added a little less harshly, "All here."

Adriga gave a humored huff. "Plus a few strays it seems." He then blew upon a small spherical whistle cupped in one hand while the fingers of the other worked five small holes on the instrument, producing a series of wondrous tones that seemed to impossibly overlap one another. It sounded like the melodic voice of a small songbird echoing up from some endless abyss.

Joe found the sound mesmerizing, and he had to give his head a little shake to free himself from its harmonic grip. Sabon was not quite as strong. The tarboc's head immediately swayed back and forth, entirely under the spell of Adriga's strange tune. Though its hood remained flared, Sabon had closed its mouth, a sign that it was, at least, somewhat calmer. It made no other movement, and it did not even seem to notice as Garen and Barry ran past and up the gangplank.

The angry voices of the pursing royal guards echoed out of the darkness back down the widow's pier.

"Time to shove off, lad," came the familiar voice of Captain Maktura Krag, the scruffy-looking little man that Joe had met in Loncodi's market square earlier that evening. He was speaking to Adriga. "Get the beast aboard, or we'll be leaving it for the King's men." His voice lacked the lighthearted candor it had back in the square.

Adriga stopped playing his mesmerizing little instrument, shouting then to the tarboc, "Hup, hup!"

Like a well-trained dog, the tarboc bounded up the Harmaton's gangplank in two easy leaps. Sabon hissed as she landed on the deck. The tarboc could perceive through the darkness the multiple sailors scrambling about the deck and ship's rigging, but also there, right before it, the familiar form of one of its masters, Barry. Any anxiety building as the effects of Adriga's musical magic faded was quelled by this familiar figure. Two sailors pulled in the gangplank, dropping it with a loud bang, startling Sabon, and her head whipped around to see what new danger was upon it.

"There, there, boy." Barry tried to console the dark shape of the beast.

Sabon turned back to Barry. It retracted its hood and bowed its head to its friend, nudging Barry gently on the shoulder.

"It's actually a girl," chuckled Adriga. "They give off a certain scent. She's needing a mate." He gave the astonished Barry a gentle pat on the shoulder.

"Get that thing below decks with the others," the captain barked at Barry and Adriga. His voice was farther away than it had been a moment ago. "Pull us out, Mr. Franz!" he shouted.

With Adriga's help, Barry led the now much calmer Sabon down a nearby hatch, which led to the various cargo levels below. Joe followed, feeling that he was a little in the way of the crew, who were working at a frantic pace.

The captain wanted the sails ready to drop the moment they were clear enough of the pier. They would also need to pull the ship around since the wind would not be with them to make a speedy tack. The King's men were shouting and cursing back on the dock as the ship pulled away.

Before the staggered, anxious arrival of his passengers, the captain had ordered four of his men out in skiffs with kedging lines attached to a pair of light anchors. They had dropped the anchors several ship lengths out into the harbor. The moment the captain had given the order to shove off, these same four men, now working the capstan near the stern of the ship, immediately started heaving on their posts, reeling in the first kedging line and pulling the boat out into the harbor. The dock boy had barely enough time to unmoor the ship from the widow's pier and climb up the mooring rope to get back on the ship. He had nearly been grabbed by one of the King's men but just managed to make the swinging leap in time.

"No sense, workin' in the dark, boys!" Captain Mak shouted. "They already got our number; it's only polite to let 'em see us wave g'bye."

With that, lamps all over the ship popped on as if by magic. Despite the illumination, the Harmaton had a shadowy presence. All of its timbers were stained a dark midnight blue, and its sails, still bound, were black. Even the rigging ropes were black.

"You there," Captain Mak growled at the dock boy as he finished coiling the mooring lines. "Get yer scrawny arse into the crow's nest. I want to be sure no one's got the idea to follow us out of the harbor. Seems the ramifications of our cargo is a little more volatile than I expected."

The dock boy didn't speak a word; he just nodded his acknowledgment and hopped to his duty.

The most striking feature of the Harmaton was a large dome defined by two intersecting, two-foot-thick arches, taking up much of the center of the deck. Black rope netting hung slack across the four curved spaces between the arches, covering what looked to be black, oiled canvas. Strange but artful gold markings ran up along the entire length of each side of both arches. It was the only flash of color or ornamentation on the whole ship. Shallow stairs were crafted into the tops of the arches, and the dock boy now quickly scaled one of these stairs on all fours, reaching the towering central mast that sprung from the top of the dome. There, he grabbed a rope and used it to run up the massive wood column. A moment after he climbed into the roughly woven rope hammock that made up the Harmaton's crow's nest, the boy gave one shrill whistle.

"You heard the boy. Alls clear," shouted the captain as he made his way up to the bridge at the stern of the ship to man the wheel. Disengaging the wheel's lock, he shouted again. "Turn us about Mr. Franz!"

"Turning about," came the immediate call back in the croaking voice of Mr. Franz from the bow of the boat. "Tits to the sea lads!" He said, turning to the two men manning the capstan at the bow of the Harmaton.

Mr. Franz was a weathered old man of the sea. His skin was like wrinkled, hardened leather stretched across his thin, skeletal frame. His eyes were deeply sunk, with dark circles around them. There wasn't a scrap of hair on him, not even eyebrows or eyelashes. That probably accounted, at least partially, for his constant squinting. His eyes were just two little dark slits. Coupled with his emaciated frame and the dark circles around his eyes, it looked as though he were some sort of eyeless skeletal ghoul. His rib cage showed through his chest, visible beneath the red vest that served as the only upper garment anyone could remember him having ever worn. Unlike many of his fellow sailors, his body was completely free of tattoos, save for a small seashell on his right cheek that looked like a teardrop at a distance. A shark's tooth dangled from his left ear, while his right was pierced by some sort of long claw.

To hear him tell it, a story he later shared with the new passengers over ales, the talon came from a harpy that had kept him as something of a sexual pet on a deserted island in the southern seas west of Westerlan. He had been a young man then, serving as steward to the captain of one of King Mazeze's voyager class exploration ships. It had wrecked upon rocks near the island that would become his home and prison for ten years. His escape from the island, which, naturally, angered the harpy, had been accomplished with the assistance of a magic-wielding mermaid. This, of course, made the harpy jealous and even more enraged. The mermaid had concealed their departure with an invisibility spell, intending to carry him to the coast of Westerlan. They were well out to sea, and their invisibility spell had long worn off when the harpy managed to catch up with them.

In the struggle that followed between the harpy and the mermaid, the harpy had managed to bury a claw deep into the mermaid's chest, penetrating the brave, magical fish-woman's heart. Before dying, the mermaid mustered one last magic spell, transforming the harpy into a wooden statue. The harpy had tried to fly away before the transformation could take hold and had broken off her talon in her haste, leaving it stuck in the dying mermaid's chest.

Franz, rather helpless in the water during the struggle, swam over to his beloved mermaid rescuer. She asked him to pull the talon from her chest so her death might come on with more merciful haste. She kissed him deeply as he gently pulled the claw from her heart. He vowed he would never love another as he watched her slip away into the dark depths. Knowing he could never make it to shore swimming, he resolved to simply let himself slip beneath the waves as well.

It was just then that the petrified wooden form of the harpy drifted up to him. Franz took it as a gift and a sign from his mermaid to literally keep hanging on. He clung to the harpy for four days before the Harmaton came along and plucked both him and the harpy from the water. He has served upon the Harmaton under three different captains ever since, as has the wing-spread form of the harpy that still adorned the ship's prow. Most are either too distracted by the fiercely fanged face of the harpy, forever contorted in a silent, angry scream, or too mesmerized by the beauty of her nude human upper torso to notice that a talon on her left raptor-like foot is, indeed, missing from the suspiciously life-like carving.

A glob of blackened spittle shot from his mouth onto the deck as Franz observed the men reeling in the second kedging line, turning the ship about. He gave a crooked smile, exposing his equally crooked teeth, browned and blackened by the black seaweed he was constantly chewing.

The moment the Harmaton was pointing out to sea, the captain gave the order to drop the ship's sails. The heavy, black canvas sails immediately caught the wind, and the Harmaton glided out of the harbor with increasing speed. The captain smiled, complimenting his crew but telling them to keep their backs into it. He looked back at the wharf. There were lights and movement on a ship docked at the third pier. It could just be dock workers doing a late-night haul, but one could never be too careful. He would have the crew maintain the ship's top speed, dousing the lights once they were out of sight of land. Then, they would make a sharp course change. If anyone did try to follow, they would have a hard time spotting them in the dark and would likely be looking in the wrong direction. Hopefully, his recent acquisitions, all obligingly below decks, wouldn't notice the change in their course either.

Chapter 14

Just below the main deck were the crew and passenger quarters. The dome on the main deck continued through this level, making a large, inaccessible chamber that effectively divided this first lower deck into two wide corridors. A closed-off room at the bow served as the kitchen. The accommodations for the crew were open along the two corridors and didn't consist of much more than bunks and hammocks. One of the two passenger quarters, closed rooms at the stern of the ship, had been designated for Host and Dicesh, while the second passenger cabin was for the remainder of the circus to share as they saw fit for the duration of the trip. Those not staying in the passenger cabin would be provided with improvised hammocks.

The animals were being kept on the next level down. Beyond that, the last level of the ship, was for cargo. As Ugor discovered shortly after boarding, the cargo level's access hatch was locked and off-limits to anyone but the crew.

Ugor discovered this shortly after boarding the Harmaton. He had just finished feeding King Kotep when he went looking for other members of the circus. Thinking he had heard voices below, he sought out the hatch to the cargo level. As he reached for the hatch's ring, a short sword came down hard, so close it knicked Ugor's hand. Ugor jumped back. A creepy, greasy, wiry sailor, not much taller than Ugor, with an unusually large underbite, was wielding the sword. He told Ugor in a sarcastically polite manner that the cargo hold was for crew access only and watched intently as Ugor departed up the ramp to the level above. Talking to the other circus members later, Ugor found that they had all experienced questionably hospitable behavior from the crew.

By the time Joe reached the ship, most of the group was well settled. It was decided that Runara and her fellow brookshins would share the spare passenger room, giving them time to catch up and mourn the loss of their group. Crash met Joe with a huge smile as he descended the ramp from the top deck.

"Guess we're on our way," Joe told her, putting an arm around her shoulders. "Where's the boss?"

Ugor was suddenly beside them. "Host's been in there," he said, pointing to the passenger room door back and to the left of the ramp. "Dicesh too. Haven't come out since we got here. They're both in a bad way, Dicesh especially. Couple of the cats are in a state too." Ugor reached into his vest, pulling out a small flask. He held it out briefly as if to offer Joe or Crash a drink, but having no immediate takers, he quickly took a swig from the flask himself and re-stashed it. "You'll want to see that big friend of yours too. Came out of that hullabaloo a little worse for wear.

He led them down a level to where the animals were being kept. Like the level above, the dome from the top deck continued here, fully enclosed in wood. None of the leathery material, exposed on the deck, was visible on either of these lower levels. The structure here indicated that the dome up top was part of a complete sphere, the base of which had to be a level below. Just as on the deck and level above, there was no way into the large round chamber that ate up so much space on this level. Odd, Joe thought, for a vessel meant for hauling goods.

The entire floor was covered in straw. Rows of chains had been strung between the beams of the ship, forming makeshift holding pens. It had been meant for the shipment of boggorats but now made suitable accommodations for the circus's small collection of beasts. The camel and bailodants were already sleeping in stalls down the ship's left side.

King Kotep, being kept in the large open area near the stern of the ship at the base of the access ramp, his head in the rafters, shuffled a little as the trio walked by. He reached out to Crash with his trunk, and she gave it an affectionate pat. The trio continued past the stalls on the right side of the level.

"Thought we lost these two as well," Ugor said in a hushed tone, pointing to the two tigers coiled up with one another like little kittens. One of them was snoring quite loudly.

"As well?" Joe asked with genuine concern. Ugor ignored the question, and Joe let it go, thinking Ugor had simply misspoken.

"Azilurk got a little banged up, I guess, but no worse for it. His sister ate one of the King's men, I'm told. Can't make things any worse for us though, eh." He gave Joe a humorous nudge with his elbow as they continued to walk along. "Here's your mate, then."

Two-thirds of the way toward the front of the ship were two half walls, forming a ten-foot by ten-foot pen for securing light or potentially mobile cargo, such as barrels. Here, Kord sat on a short barrel. He was slumped over the prone form of Kubara, his remaining hand resting comfortingly on the sleeping cat's side.

"Okay there, buddy?" Joe asked in as light a tone as he could muster. Despite the time he had spent around Kord, Joe still felt a little nervous around the man-hunter. That the mander was injured only made Joe a little more wary.

Kord didn't look up or acknowledge the three's presence.

Despite his better instincts, Joe pushed on. "Crazy back there, huh?" Still no reaction from the mander. "I mean, how's the arm? Has anyone looked at it for you, or —"

Kord turned then slightly to look at Joe, the low lamplight of the cargo hold glinting off of the depths of one of his expressionless red crystalline eyes. "It will grow back." He growled in a low tone.

He held up the stump of his arm. Where there should have been an ugly open wound, a fresh layer of his mottled green-blue skin had already grown over. At its center was a tiny hand-shaped protrusion. Kord gave a tired-sounding grunt and turned his attention back to the sleeping cat.

"I think we best leave 'em be," Ugor suggested, giving Joe's jacket sleeve a little tug. "He wouldn't even let Adriga near her."

The three continued deeper into the hold until they reached a dark little area near the ship's bow. Here, Barry, Tosh, and Adriga were discussing the proper care for the Tarboc, which was hungrily eating from a large blood-soaked canvas bag held by Adriga. In the dim light, Joe could see that Adriga had a large cut across his face. It started above his left eyebrow and ended on his right cheek just above his jawline. Deeper portions of it had already been stitched with rough twine, making it look all the more horrific.

Adriga noticed Joe and Crash staring and simply pointed at his face, saying, "Kruliza."

The group exchanged stories then about their separate and common tumultuous journeys from the market square to the boat. When the topic of Chen's grim fate came up, Ugor slipped away, saying only that he had something he needed to take care of.

"Poor fella," Adriga said once Ugor was beyond view and earshot. He lowered his head, shaking it a little in an attempt to hide his own grief, but it was evident in his wavering voice as he continued. "He and Chen been workin' for Dicesh and Host even before there was a circus. We've lost so many these past days. Can hardly consider ourselves a circus anymore."

Crash bounced over to him, planting a big kiss on his right cheek. He flinched in pain, but it brought a smile back to his face. This, too, made him cringe in pain a little. The stories continued then until Barry expressed feeling quite exhausted by the night's adventure and needed to excuse himself to find a hammock. The others then became very aware of their own exhaustion, and with that, they all made their way back up to the crew quarters to find a hammock in the area designated for them.

Joe climbed into a hammock, with little grace, just above one occupied by Nooch. The other band members were nearby as well, already long asleep. Joe wondered for a moment why the brookshin musicians were not spending the night in the room with Runara but was too exhausted to give it much thought. Despite his exhaustion, however, he lay staring at the ceiling for some time, disturbed by the rocking movement and constant creaking of the boat. It reminded Joe just how strange a world he was in. A boat the size of a building seemed ludicrous; even aboard it, he was having a hard time wrapping his head around the complexity of it or even the necessity for such a craft. His mind drifted to his times in the water hills of Beedo and the tiny boats and docks used by the merchants and fishermen there. Inevitably, his thoughts turned and fondly lingered on the small taverns that always wreaked of fish and booze. He began trying to count the serving women he had bedded over the years, not just there but throughout Midgorn. As his lurid mental tour reached the farming community of Flurin and the carnal naked images of the serving wench at the community inn — the Old Soul Box, as the locals called the place — he drifted into a much-needed happy, peaceful sleep.

* * * * * * * * * * * * * * * * * *

Joe and everyone onboard who had not already been up was woken by an ear-splitting squealing sound, immediately followed by a large boom that rocked the ship side to side. Then came shouting from the top deck. Crewmen who had been sleeping were already bolting up the ramp while Franz's weathered voice was barking from the hatchway for all sailors not already moving to take their stations, or he would be coming down to personally skin them where they sleep.

"What's going on?" Nooch stammered from his low-slung hammock as Joe clumsily dumped himself out of the hammock above.

"Got me, but it doesn't sound good," Joe said, straightening his bandolier. Nooch found the smile on Joe's face terribly disconcerting. "Let's have us a look." He patted Nooch on the chest before heading toward the ramp.

The ship was heaving badly. Joe was staggered back and forth, making little ground toward the ramp. He was thrown hard against one of the two doors of the passenger's quarters. The door swung open, and Joe dropped to the floor before he had a chance to right himself. Joe looked up to see Drix standing over him, offering a hand up.

"Hey, I thought Runara had this room last ni—" Joe stopped suddenly, speechless, as Drix pulled him to his feet.

Runara was sitting upright in the room's small single bed with a look of surprise on her face. She had just managed to pull the sheets up to her neck before Joe had seen her, but it did nothing to hide the back of her clearly naked, curving profile.

"You two?" Joe smirked.

"Get out!" Was all Runara had as a response, and taking that as a cue, Drix put a hand gently but firmly on Joe's chest and began pushing him out the door.

Joe resisted somewhat, laughing a little and continuing to drink in as much of Runara's exquisite naked form as the concealing sheets allowed. Her mane of tousled red hair and the pouty, miffed expression on her face made her all the more mesmerizing for Joe. It was just then that he realized that Drix was completely naked as well. Drix's massive, muscular form somehow changed the nature of the moment for Joe. It made the reality of the situation, of what had obviously gone on between Drix and Runara earlier in this room, far more uncomfortable for Joe to absorb. His resistance to Drix's firm push bled away, as did his laughter.

"Sorry," Drix said with a polite smile as he gave Joe one final shove out of the room.

Joe caught one last glimpse of Runara as Drix closed the door, which ruined his mood more. The look on her face had changed from one of surprised annoyance to one of what he could only read as pity.

Joe continued to lean on the closed door for a moment more, mumbling to himself. "But, I thought for sure that — and honestly, who opens the door naked?"

"Who are you talking to?" Crash said, popping up beside Joe in her usual bouncy manner, having no apparent problem moving about the rocking ship.

"Uh, no one, I just, uh —"

Another piercing squeal filled the air, interrupting Joe's incoherence. It was followed, this time, by a loud splash and another boom, louder than before. Again, the ship rocked violently, throwing Joe and Crash sprawling on the floor beside one another.

"What is going on?" Joe's voice was full of the exasperation of a man recently confronted with just how outside of his own world he truly was.

He and Crash helped one another up. Distantly above them, a cry of "Man overboard!" sounded repeatedly from one crewman to another.

"I'm pretty sure we're being attacked." Crash offered lightly.

"By what?" Joe was having difficulty processing the situation and could only imagine some monstrous beast attacking the vessel.

Tosh stumbled up beside them, clutching a nearby support beam. "Another ship. Explosive ballista rounds by the sound. There's only one ship I've seen big enough to be equipped with a weapon like that."

"The Roc's Tooth," Barry said, walking up awkwardly with both arms out for balance as the Harmaton continued to sway. "They only need to make one of those stick and we're done for."

"Why don't they get us out of the water?" Crash's question wasn't directed at anyone in particular and got nothing but confused looks from the others, who quickly dismissed the clown-faced woman's nonsense.

Joe wasn't following any of it and scuttled himself up the ramp to the main deck. Crash, Tosh, and Barry followed.

Topside, the activity of the crew seemed to be chaos. Every sailor seemed to be shouting, either communicating orders or letting others know they had completed some dire task. Men furled and unfurled sails. Ropes were being tied, untied, pulled, and wrapped. Booms swung one way or another as the Captain repeatedly changed the ship's course in an attempt to be as challenging a mark as possible for the attacking vessel.

"Get off my deck!" Captain Mak shouted the moment the group arrived topside.

None of them paid the Captain any mind. Joe, for one, was overwhelmed by the vision before him. It was the first time he had seen the ocean since he first washed up on the beach, but here, fully out to sea, with no land in sight, the sheer expanse of Modnar truly hit Joe. There was nothing but sky and water in whatever direction he looked. For Joe, it was like staring into an immense blue abyss. He found himself fighting the feeling that gravity might fail at any moment and he would fall helplessly, eternally, into the endless surrounding blue.

The constant heaving motion of the ship didn't help. Joe quickly grew dizzy and clung to the ship's railing tightly, wrapping one arm around it to ensure he was adequately anchored.

Another piercing squeal caused the rest of the group to hold their ears as a ballista bolt shot along the length of the Harmaton, just catching the bottom left corner of the mainsail, punching a hole through it like a deadly flying tree trunk. Without losing any momentum, the bolt then impaled a sailor unfortunate enough to have been scaling up some nearby rigging. Now carrying the sailor, the twelve-foot-long metal-tipped, wooden bolt continued to arc well out into the ocean beyond. A moment later, a muffled boom and a great fountain of water shot up not far from where the bolt and the sailor had disappeared into the sea.

One of the crew, a portly fellow, rushed over, grabbing a large coil of rope by Tosh's feet. "That was nowhere near as close as the others!" His voice was anxious as he looped the coil over his shoulder and mounted the nearby shroud next to Joe. "We might just make it." The sailor quickly scrambled up the ratlines.

The moment brought Joe, Tosh, Crash, and Barry's attention focused on the attacking vessel. As Barry had guessed, it was the Roc's Tooth, which looked like a small red toy boat at this distance. Captain Mak had managed, for the moment, to maneuver out of the sweeping line of fire of the Roc's Tooth's forward ballista, but the blood-red ship was closing the distance between the two vessels at an alarming rate.

Nooch, Pronz, and Freshnir appeared in the hatchway then. Seeing the frantic activity, the three paused, reluctant to step up onto the busy deck.

"Off my deck! You risk the safety of my men by getting in the way! I won't ask again." the Captain hollered at the group.

The band quickly turned and headed back below. Tosh, Barry, Crash, and Joe stayed right where they were, either too curious or, in Joe's case, too attached to the railing to go back down.

Tosh leaned over to Barry, saying snidely, "Well, it's not like he's been 'asking' at all, is it?"

The unnerving sound and spectacle of the ballista bolt had left Barry far too shaken to respond to Tosh's weak humor. Also, his mind was preoccupied and had been so for the past few moments. There was something eating away at the back of his mind since the clown girl's outburst below, something he had encountered before in his research to reach the moon Zeebo. It hit him just as Crash called out.

"Why don't we have this heap flying!" Crash shouted back at the Captain. The tone and timber came out like she was a sea captain herself.

The Captain's reaction was a face at once full of surprise and anger that also took on some degree of frustration as he looked over his shoulder at the quickly closing pursuer.

Standing beside the Captain, Franz could sense what the Captain was going to say next and felt the need to toss in his opinion before anything rash was done. "If she catches our keel, we won't have to worry about sinking."

Captain Mak started to speak, but Franz interjected one more time.

"She'll have us lined up before we even…"

"Noted, Mr. Franz!" The Captain growled the words loud enough for all the crew to hear and threw Franz a scowl that made it clear that any further comments would not be welcome. "I have a mind to hire the clown," he sneered in a voice full of menace at a volume just for Franz. "You heard her, boys," he shouted then, "Get this bitch keelbare!"

The order repeated from crewman to crewman. A sailor rushed over to Joe and the others, shouting down the hatch," Open the valves!" before hurriedly scuttling off to another task. Muffled shouts of the same command came from below.

Franz was shouting orders then. "Drop the top! Spread'er wings! Hoist the kites! A lashing for each of you if she loses a knot' fore she lifts her skirt."

Above, crewmen were dropping the fore, main, and aft royal and topgallant sails. Men were working cranks on the main deck, raising special metal cuffs high on the tops of the masts, allowing another group of men up in the rigging and down on the main deck to pull the topmasts down and back into a horizontal configuration. Booms on either side of the bow swung out low to the main deck. Ropes looped through pulleys at the ends of these booms, connected to side slats on the ship, were tightened by a set of cranks at the bow, fanning out large, multifaceted, oiled, black canvas wings.

Somewhere below deck, a mechanical chugging sound began vibrating the whole ship.

"Locking the wheel! Get 'er up, boys." The Captain shouted.

The black material beneath the netting expanded within the arches in the middle of the ship's deck until it was straining at the ropes, forming a perfect dome beneath the intersecting arches.

A call went up then. "Heads full! Empty the bell!" It was repeated throughout the crew until the muffled response of "Dropping the hammer!" came back from somewhere, decks below, and was repeated again throughout the crew.

"Brace for lift!" Franz shouted.

Joe was already as braced as he could get. The others, followed his example, save for Crash; she was jumping up and down, clapping, taking in all she could of the busy crew.

"What is happening," Joe asked, perplexed by all the frantic activity and shouting.

"Wingmen at the ready!" The Captain barked. "I want her hard to port the moment she's clear!" Two nearby crewmen then released ropes that had been lashing large levers to the front railing of the aftcastle on either side of the ship's wheel. They had simply looked like decorative braces until then.

"We're going to fly, we're going to fly!" Crash shouted back to Joe excitedly.

The whole ship shuddered violently then. Like some enormous dark tuning fork from the underworld, a rumbling, humming metallic groan came from deep within the dome in the ship's center. The Harmaton tipped violently to the left, nearly dipping the wing tip on that side into the water. Crash went sprawling across the deck, tumbling out of control. Joe, maintaining his death grip on the ship's rail with one arm, shot out with a knife from his bandolier with the other hand towards Crash as she tumbled away across the deck. It caught a portion of her leather jacket just below her left armpit, pinning her precariously to the deck for a second. The knife, well embedded in the deck, remained as Crash's momentum slid the knife straight through her jacket, and she tumbled free. It had slowed her enough that she managed to grab the railing as she went over the side, leaving her dangling over the choppy waters that sped by below.

"Keep 'er level, you worthless sea rats!" The Captain growled angrily. The wingmen worked their levers, changing the angles of the wings. The Harmaton quickly righted. Crash slammed into the side of the ship with a grunt but quickly kicked herself into a handstand on the railing, lingering for a moment, flashing Joe and the others a smile before flipping herself back onto the deck.

The distant sound of a horn came from the pursuing Roc's Tooth, which had now not only closed some distance between it and the Harmaton but nearly had the ship back in the sights of its ballista again.

The Harmaton's hull lifted higher out of the water. Soon, it looked to be skipping from wave to wave. Franz continued to bark orders as the Harmaton rose fully out of the sea, revealing a small glass-like dome directly in the center of its underside. One of the crew, wearing thick, brass-framed goggles with yellow lenses, was seated within, his hands working a collection of ball-handled levers and cranks. Initially facing forward, his seat, attached to a central metal column that also housed the controls, quickly swung around, giving the sailor a proper view of the ever-closing Roc's Tooth.

Just then, the familiar scream of an explosive bolt from the Roc's Tooth's ballista sounded. The bolt was on target, but the Harmaton was rising too quickly for it. The large metal missile ricocheted off of the glass dome, deflecting it down with little of its momentum lost. It exploded within a second of disappearing beneath the waves below, spraying the underside of the Harmaton with water. The bolt's impact had left a small white chip in one of the eight panes that made up the dome, but it was superficial. Though the dome had the appearance of glass, none of the eight curved panes actually were. Forged by elves, the material, known as gossaphyr, was truly more similar to metal in its properties. Other than a slight blue tint, it was completely transparent and was comparable to, if not stronger than, steel but lighter than balsa wood.

The man inside the gossaphyr dome pulled hard on a large dual-armed lever. The entire dome dropped down a foot, revealing a mechanical carriage that allowed the dome to pivot both front to back and side to side. The carriage consisted of two metal disc rings sandwiching a complex collection of gears, pistons, and rods. Two three-foot-long tubes popped out of either side of the carriage, and with a heavy metallic clack sound, large steel spearheads poked out the ends.

Up top, just in front of the ship's wheel, a panel in the floor opened, and a smooth gold ring, a little over two feet in diameter, popped up suddenly on a four-foot, ornately carved wooden stand. What looked like two square gold cowbells hung on either side of the stand just below the ring.

Captain Mak quickly stepped around the wheel, positioning himself between the wheel and the ring. The space in the middle of the ring, where initially there had been nothing but air, was now filled with a translucent but crisp image of the ocean and a clearly magnified view of the pursuing red ship. A glowing blue circle with a small bright blue dot at the center of the image would turn green as the image of the Roc's Tooth bobbed into alignment with the dot. Captain Mak grabbed the cowbell-like objects on either side, holding one to his ear and the other to his mouth. They were both tethered to the stand by black leathery ropes that fed out from it, seemingly as far in length as the Captain needed.

"You waste a harpoon on that monstrosity without my say-so, and I'll drop you to the sharks! Y'hear me?" Captain Mak shouted into the cowbell being held to his face.

"Aye, captain," came the tinny-sounding voice of the sailor in the gossaphyr gun pod from the cowbell at the Captain's ear.

Captain Mak dropped the communication bells with a disgusted huff. The cords of the two bells instantly retracted, snapping them back to their original position just below the gold ring.

The Harmaton had risen quickly; it was now well over thirty feet above the waves and continued to gain altitude with every passing second.

Barry was laughing excitedly, nearly as giddy as Crash, who had returned to her happy bouncing.

"What is happening?" Joe was completely bewildered. "Are we falling? Up?"

"That's almost an accurate analogy, my friend," said Tosh with a chuckle. "A very controlled fall, I suspect. First time flying, I take it? Not a lot of opportunities to fly in Midgorn, I imagine."

"No. I mean, yes, first time flying." Joe said solemnly. He looked over the edge at the ocean, now well over a hundred feet below. "Far too much water; far too much air in this world of yours." He paused for a moment, looking back up at Tosh's widely smiling face, and couldn't help but return the smile. "This is pretty amazing, though," he said, laughing then. Tosh joined him at the rail, looking down at the receding ocean, and soon, both men were laughing boisterously.

"Keelbare and clear!" Franz called out to the crew.

The crew responded with a collective cheer of "Hoo-har!"

"Free wheelin'," Captain Mak's voice sounded much more relaxed as he unlocked the ship's wheel and signaled his wingmen to swing the Harmaton to the right.

They circled the Roc's Tooth twice, jeering and shouting at the sea-bound vessel before heading on their way, leaving the Roc's Tooth helpless to follow.

Chapter 15

For the most part, the day had passed by rather uneventfully. Joe had spent a good portion of it in exactly the same location where he had been desperately clutching the ship's railing during the Harmaton's escape from the Roc's Tooth, though now his composure was far more restored. The view was endlessly fascinating for him; a never-ending sea of blue-green below, undulating as though it were alive, and a, somehow, more infinite sky of blue above and all around, full of enormous fluffy white clouds that seemed like they could be worlds onto themselves. This spectacle would have been enough for Joe, but Modnar would prove to be a world made up of the amazing.

Not long after the Harmaton had made its escape, a sailor cried out, "Leviathan!" Below, Joe could see what looked like the dark shape of a large fish just below the water's surface. Tosh, still standing beside Joe, seemed very excited, much to Joe's confusion.

"What, you've never seen a fish before?" Back in Midgorn, Joe was used to being among the more worldly or well-traveled when socializing with others, and this small moment of being familiar with something that Tosh may not be allowed some of his usual smugness to resurface.

"A fish?" Tosh chuckled with a slightly condescending look of amusement at Joe's innocence. "You forget how high up we are, lad. Look now, quickly, it's breaching."

Joe looked back down just in time to see what he now realized to be an immense creature burst through the ocean's surface. It was dark grey, nearly black, with a row of spines down its back, the longest being more than one hundred feet. The leviathan was rising out of the ocean at an alarming rate, water streaming down its roughly scaled body like hundreds of grand waterfalls. Two black eyes, tiny for its immense form, but each nearly the size of the Harmaton, were near the top of its head and were not clearly evident until they rolled back, revealing the whites. It made the already mind-numbingly frightful countenance of the impossibly large creature all the more horrifyingly demonic. Long tendrils grew from its snout and lashed about with a mobility of their own. In the shortest of moments, the enormous fish went from looking impressively immense to obliterating the view of the ocean with its wide-open, hungry mouth. It was a deep, black abyss wide enough to have easily engulfed ten ships at once. It seemed doubtful that the leviathan ever had to truly bite or chew its meals, but making it all the more needlessly frightening, the mouth was lined with three rows of a forest of bright green, needle-like teeth, each at least fifty feet long.

Joe let out a loud grunting scream as it seemed certain that he, the Harmaton, and all aboard were doomed to be this colossal fish's meal. The entire crew had paused their work, looking over the sides of the ship. The great jaws of the fish snapped shut with a thunderous clap, and the leviathan crashed back into the sea, disappearing into the depths and sending massive waves in every direction.

The crew of the Harmaton gave a great cheer, and Tosh laughed hysterically like an excited child. Joe was simply silent and wide-eyed. His heart was racing, and he was breathing as if he had just run a marathon. The bewildered expression on his face made it clear that he had no idea how it was that they had not been eaten.

Tosh, seeing that Joe had not enjoyed the moment as much as he, choked back his laughter to offer an explanation. "I'll admit that had to have been close by leviathan measures, but that big fish had to have been shy of making us an appetizer by one hundred feet, maybe more. I've heard the tales, but that was incredible!" He patted Joe on the shoulder, hoping to rouse some enthusiasm from Joe. Joe simply nodded as his wits slowly gathered.

"One twenty-three, by my reckoning," came Old Franz's voice from behind the two men. "Rare thing for two muckers like you to see. Not many leviathan out there, and only one other, I've seen, that's a jumper like ol' Cannon Ball. Funny thing is he don't bother with the boats if'n they're in the water. Got a taste for the flyers, not just boats neither. Seen that crazy fish gulp down a flock of gulls once. Way I figure, it's all 'bout sport for that beast."

After that, the Captain ordered the crew to take the ship to a higher altitude just in case Ol' Cannon Ball decided to try a bigger leap. The Harmaton passed through a layer of cloud, which was another fascination for Joe. They continued above the clouds for the remainder of the day.

Tosh soon chose to head below decks, as he found the temperature above the clouds too cold and uncomfortable. Crash spent a few uncharacteristically silent moments beside Joe, reveling in the beauty of the world above the clouds. The Harmaton passed below a higher flying wispy cloud formation. It cast a grand shadow across the clouds below. Sunlight streamed through it in massive columns. It made it feel, to Joe, as though the Harmaton were flying through some giant, glowing, gossamer forest. The awed silence was eventually more than Crash could take.

"Well, what do you think, knife boy? Pretty, pretty, huh?"

Joe was feeling a little overwhelmed by a flood of conflicting emotions brought on by the recent events. Normally, Joe wasn't an emotional sort of man, but here, gazing out into the wondrous expanse all around him, it was almost as if his emotions were being drawn to the surface by the vacuum of the extra space around him. Though he wasn't even fully aware of it, he was being brought to the edge of philosophical concepts that he lacked the vocabulary to form into coherent thoughts. He turned to Crash, simply staring at her for a few quiet moments until managing only, "Yes…beautiful."

"Well, ya, I'm gorgeous," she said with a mocking giggle as she struck an exaggerated glamour pose. "I meant the view." She pointed a thumb out over the rail.

"So did I," Joe came back with a smiling sneer. Crash's humor had brought him back down from whatever lofty place his mind had begun to wander, making him feel far more comfortable. "It's just that…I feel so small in this world. My world, Midgorn, seems so small now."

Crash waved a dismissive hand. "Ah, it's not so big."

Joe looked at Crash with a confused look and nodded his head out to the expansive view that he felt she was clearly not taking in properly.

"Oh, ya, it's not tiny," she conceded, "but it's mostly just beautiful and scary; okay, mostly scary."

Joe frowned. "You aren't helping."

"Y'sure? You seem the sort that deals with scary better than beautiful."

Before Joe could respond, she gave Joe a wink and a deep bow, saying, "By your leave, bladesman. I'm the sort that deals with more sleep better than less." and then quickly bounced off, in her usual half-skipping way, down the hatchway to the level below.

More at ease then, Joe moved around the deck for a while, taking in sights from all directions. Eventually, he found a spot near the bow where he felt out of the way of the crew and the scowling stare of the Captain.

Throughout the day, several of Joe's companions came up to the main deck for some fresh air and to take in the view, save for Kord, Dicesh, and Host. Drix and Runara strode around the deck arm in arm; Runara snuggled in close to Drix for some protection from the cold, lofty winds. Neither said a word to Joe, and Joe paid them little attention. As they headed back below deck, Joe mumbled to himself. "You'd think she could conjure up a little flame if she was that cold." It was the extent of his thoughts on the matter. His interactions with the others were nearly as minimal. His focus was on the endless sky.

Joe's distraction with the world of the sky wasn't entirely abstract. Throughout the day, many wondrous things flew through his field of view. Most had been odd creatures that Joe had never seen before, many of them chimeral beasts, seeming assembled from several different creatures. Three things, in particular, had caught Joe's attention throughout the day, perhaps because they had not just been winged beasts.

The first had been a scantily clad woman with long, blonde, freely flowing hair. She was riding upon an enormous bird-like reptile, flying directly perpendicular to the Harmaton, and had passed just in front of the Harmaton's bow. Seated behind her was a small metal statue, roughly resembling the shape of a tiny man; it glinted like polished brass in the sunlight.

A small number of the crew, up in the sails, had noticed the woman as well and were shouting a collection of rather inappropriate suggestions that had Joe chuckling. The woman was not as amused and reined her steed to make a tight loop back towards the Harmaton, producing a large sword in one hand as she did. This only made the men jeer her more and more rudely until it seemed clear that she meant to crash straight into their midst. The men scrambled and dove onto nearby rigging, trying to get out of the way of what was seemingly an act of suicide, if not just for her, but then surely for her bird. At the last possible moment, her steed tucked its wings, and together, it and its rider shot through the gaps in the web of the ship's rigging like an enormous green missile. The woman's sword slashed sail and rope as they went, rendering one sail useless, dropping another, and heavily damaging one of the rope veils. A crewman who had been on the veil barely managed to keep from going overboard.

Emerging on the ship's other side, the bird caught the wind with its wings and banked away. As she rode off, the woman, looking back with a broad, mischievous smile, made what was clearly meant to be a defiant, rude gesture toward the ship and the crew. The crewmen, many dangling precariously from the rigging, shouted angrily after her while the Captain cursed and shouted at the crew to get things back in order.

"Oh, I like her!" Joe said out loud to himself as she diminished into the distance. Somewhere in the back of his mind, Joe found the woman familiar, as though he had seen her before, but he couldn't place where or when; somewhere in Midgorn, he thought, but that seemed unlikely. He stared reflectively for several minutes at the spot in the sky where the woman and her steed had disappeared into the distant clouds.

The second notable flying encounter was a group of colorful, glowing orbs, each slightly larger than a human head, chasing one another in dizzying loops and twists. Joe couldn't decide if they were playing with one another or fighting in some manner. Their chase took them out of sight as quickly as they had flown into view.

The third notable encounter came just before sunset. A large man, covered head to toe in thick black hair, flew quite close to the ship, heading in the same direction as the Harmaton. His arms were unusually long. Were it not for his very human charcoal-colored face, he could have been taken for some form of ape. He was riding what looked to Joe like nothing more than a decorative throw rug and was sitting on a wooden chest with heavy iron fittings. Joe could not fathom how the carpet was flying, but, for that matter, the manner by which the Harmaton was staying aloft was entirely beyond his comprehension as well. Joe simply concluded that some stuff flies here.

The carpet rider didn't immediately notice the Harmaton, engrossed in examining a large piece of paper that the wind was making challenging to hold straight. Looking up, the man, taken by surprise at the sight of the Harmaton, quickly folded up the thick sheet of paper, gave Joe a friendly wave, and darted off in a different direction toward the setting sun. Joe quickly lost sight of the strange man and his carpet against the sun's bright orange glow.

It was shortly after that encounter when Crash, done with her nap, came walking, precariously, atop the ship's railing. Joe hadn't noticed her until she did a hands-free flip over the spot where he was leaning, landing with perfect balance on the railing to his left. He shot straight up out of surprise and concern, but before he could utter a word or put out a hand to help her dismount, she had plopped herself down to sit on the ship's rail, her feet dangling freely over the side. She sat there quietly, staring off at the horizon. Joe wondered how long she had been back up here on the top deck.

"Hmm." Crash had a finger to her chin as though she were in some sort of deep contemplation. "It's totally in the wrong spot."

Joe looked out across the cloudscape. He couldn't see anything, just the sun, clouds and sky. "What is?" He asked, leaning out across the rail and squinting but still seeing nothing else.

"The sun, of course," she said, giving him a few patronizing pats on his head.

"I thought it was always supposed to be in the sky. Although," Joe looked out at the ball of fire so low in the sky now, "does it land somewhere at night?"

Crash laughed then, rocking back and forth on the rail so precariously that Joe was certain she would fall. "I like you, Joe," she said breathlessly, "you really are silly. No, the sun should be on the other side of the ship." She tousled his hair as though he was a child and flipped herself backward onto the deck. "And this world is a big ball," she added with a wink and a giggle as she turned and began walking away. Her demeanor lacked its usual bounciness.

"A ball?" Joe really couldn't even begin to imagine what she meant.

Crash paused then, looking at Joe over her shoulder. "The sun never really sets, Joe." There was an entirely different, sincere tone to her voice, more that of a woman than her usual goofy girlishness. She held him in a gaze for a moment or two, waiting to see if what she was saying was sinking in, and then quietly headed back to the hatch.

Joe stared blankly after her for several seconds, a hand absently straightening his mussed hair. Still not comprehending what she meant, he realized he was really just staring at her ass as she walked away. Any more profound thoughts immediately shifted to wondering why he hadn't taken proper notice of it earlier. With a shrug, he looked back out across Modnar's very alien, ever-changing vista.

Joe marveled then at the colors of the dusk horizon; the vibrant purple sky and the red, orange, and yellow clouds. Three bright stars were already visible higher in the darkening blue sky. The sun, now a clearly defined scarlet disc that Joe could comfortably gaze upon, looked enormous. Joe couldn't think of anything else so brilliant and beautiful that he had ever seen in his life in Midgorn.

"Bladesman," a voice whispered just behind Joe, but Joe was barely aware of it, his entire attention lost in the dazzling setting sun. "Bladesman!" The voice was louder and had a tone of insistence now and was accompanied by a tugging at the base of his jacket.

Joe turned, seeing no one behind him at first, but then quickly looked down to see Ugor looking uncharacteristically anxious. He took Joe by the sleeve and began leading him over to the hatch and down to the level below, explaining that Host was demanding the presence of all of the performers.

Below deck was a clamor of activity. The sailors who had been working tirelessly all day were now down in the crew quarters, eating, drinking, gambling, or simply trying to sleep through the raucousness of the others. A much smaller number of the crew, who had been sleeping through most of the day, was now maintaining the ship's course above.

Ugor lead Joe into Host and Dicesh's quarters. He quickly closed the door behind them. The gathering of several of his fellow travelers made the small room look a little crowded. Joe quickly noted that Adriga and Kord were not present, likely tending to the injured panther. Also missing were the non-circus members of his growing band of companions, Garen, Tosh, and Barry. Crash was just inside the door. Joe and Ugor squeezed themselves in beside her. The tiger twins were standing close together by the head of the bed, facing Joe. They stared intently at him, much like a cat stares down prey just before pouncing. They did not appear to have any injuries, which Joe thought was odd. Hadn't Ugor said that at least one of them was hurt?

Their stares made Joe terribly uncomfortable, but looking away, Joe met the smug face of Drix. He was standing next to Runara on the other side of the bed opposite the door. Trying to look anywhere else, which included the ceiling, the floor, the nervous faces of the musicians, a disturbingly blood-soaked bag in the far left corner of the room, and Runara's cleavage for a little longer than appropriate, Joe's gaze eventually worked its way up to Runara's unamused face. She said nothing; nobody was. The silence became too unsettling for Joe to take.

"What's up?" Joe asked lightheartedly, taking a couple steps into the room and positioning himself near the end of the bed. He was trying to see Dicesh or Host, who were clearly in the bed but masked by sheets and the twins. "Guess we all are, right; flying ship?" Joe looked around for a reaction to his joke but was met with only somber faces. He adjusted his posture, trying to seem a little less jovial, clearing his throat uncomfortably. "No, seriously though, what's up?"

The tiger twins stepped aside to reveal Host.

"Whoa!" Joe was at a loss for words at the sight of him.

"Is it as Crash says, bladesman?" Host's voice was even more garbled and growling than usual, and blood spat from his mouth as he spoke, spattering across the dingy yellow sheets.

Lying in the room's double bed, he looked like he was truly falling apart. His head was lying at what had to be a painful angle, resting on his left shoulder, while his right shoulder appeared to be drastically dislocated. The sheets he had pulled over him, as well as the bedding, were horribly stained with blood. His head had been wrapped in roughly torn strips of white cloth. A few strips went across his nose, and another set of bindings was wound top-to-bottom, going under his chin, all seemingly in an attempt to hold in place the large flap of skin on his cheek that had been nearly torn away back in the market square riot. Few areas of the bindings hinted at their former whiteness, being almost entirely soaked with blood, and now a thick, oozing, nearly black-colored blood was seeping through much of the bindings' edges. Surprisingly, Dicesh was not beside Host, though Joe could have sworn that a moment ago, it had looked like more than one body was beneath the sheets.

"Are we headed off course?" Host asked Joe, having received no response from his first, more abstract query. His question was punctuated with a violent fit of coughing that ended with a horrible glob of dark blood being sputtered out onto the sheets.

"Uh…" Joe looked at Crash, a little unsure of what to make of the spectacle or how Host would expect him to be able to confirm their course. Crash just gave him a little encouraging, positive nod. "Well," his mind searched for some focus. Recalling his earlier interaction with Crash, he finally answered, "The sun is off to the ship's right, if that's what you mean."

Host responded with what could only be described as a growl.

Joe, feeling very uncomfortable with everyone in the room staring at him, looked around the group, hoping someone who knew what was happening would speak and clear things up. Getting no help, he turned back to Host but was startled to see Dicesh filling his vision. She was standing right next to him in front of the bed. It was as if she had materialized out of nowhere. Runara and the band had gasped at that same moment, apparently just as surprised by her sudden appearance despite their differing vantage points. Dicesh looked perfectly healthy. A small grey parrot sat on her shoulder, preening itself.

Now, Joe was doubly perplexed. From the way the others had spoken of her condition when he got onto the ship, it sounded as though Dicesh had been near death. Then he saw the body.

"What the…Who is that?" The question had come out of Joe at an unintentionally high pitch and exclamatory volume as he pointed at the mauled and bloodied pair of legs sticking out from beneath the bed.

"Quiet now, bladesman," Dicesh said calmly. "There is much to explain and a modest share of time for it, I expect." She reached down to Host, touching his left shoulder reassuringly. "As Crash and Joe have confirmed, the Captain is taking us south instead of north. We can only guess at our revised destination, but Ugor's discovery earlier today gives us little doubt as to where we are likely pointed."

"Where?" Kruliza asked. This was the first time Joe had heard the tigress speak. Despite her voice's low thrumming, silky quality, Joe was surprised at how girlish the young cat-woman sounded.

"Ya, get to it," Azilurk followed on the tail of his sister's words. "What did Ugor find?" His voice was equally surprising to Joe; a deep, rumbling, raspy baritone that seemed to outweigh the youth's slender form. He nearly sounded like Kord. The sound made the hairs on the back of Joe's neck stand on end.

"Moilers," said Ugor.

Joe was getting used to not understanding things but still felt compelled to ask, "What?"

"Slaves?" Azilurk threw the word questioningly at Ugor.

Before Ugor could respond with more than a nod, Kruliza turned to Joe, repeating in a more matter-of-fact tone, "Slaves."

"Yes, slaves," Dicesh confirmed, "this ship is a transport for captive moilers, and the lower hold is full of fresh cargo; the inventory of which, I am certain, we are secretly, and sadly," she shot Joe a scowl, "quite voluntarily, a part of. We are likely headed for Lashers Bay, where all of you will be sold or auctioned off as moilers.

"Pfft," Azilurk uttered scoffingly. "What do you call your little pet who made the discovery?"

Joe looked at Dicesh's parrot, half expecting it to speak up, but the reaction to Azilurk's comment came from the diminutive clown. Ugor moved as though to swing a punch at Azilurk, but Crash held him back. Looking back at Crash, Ugor's temper subsided, but he shot Azilurk a scowl.

"Kruliza stepped in front of her brother, trying to further diffuse the confrontation. "What are we all? She shot her brother a sharp look over her shoulder. Have we not entrusted control of our animal forms to Adriga? Or would you rather wake to find we've massacred another village, brother?"

"And so too is the covenant held between Ugor and me," Dicesh said, giving Kruliza a respectful nod. "He chose to be my thrall and reaps all the benefits that come with that choice. Despite being bound to me, his will is still his own."

"So long as it suits you." The growl in Azilurk's voice grew more tiger-like with every word.

"Brother!" Kruliza snarled angrily in warning, turning to face her twin as she did, a hand upon his chest, pushing him back a step against the wall next to the head of the bed.

"A 'thrall'? What?" Joe wasn't following any of it.

Not one to challenge his sister, Azilurk calmed himself but couldn't resist one more rebellious jab. "Go on, tell our so-called knife thrower your original intentions for him and his freak friends, Dicesh."

"So-called?" There was a protest in Joe's voice as he frowned at Azilurk. "Intentions?" Joe asked reluctantly, turning back to Dicesh. The original circus troop members, even Crash, were looking at the floor or otherwise avoiding catching Joe's questioning gaze. Runara and the band, however, were entirely focused on Dicesh waiting for an answer.

For a few seconds, Dicesh said nothing, simply staring at Azilurk. Her stony expression showed no hint of the dark thoughts running through her mind, but the silence was enough to make everyone a little uncomfortable. Behind her, Host sputtered a little, trying to stifle another blood-filled coughing fit. Dicesh calmly turned back to Joe.

"We meant you no malice, not once we realized your potential. We assumed you and your friends were robbers, lurking about off the road the way you were."

"So… So, you meant, what? The coconut, that was intentional!" Joe could feel himself getting angry, but he was still too confused to give it much direction. Crash had a terribly ashamed pout on her face and continued to stare at the floor. "What about her?" Joe pointed at Runara. "Why didn't you peg her, or the mander, with a coconut?"

"The moment that young Runara, here, produced a wall of flame in your defense, we realized that we may have made a mistake."

"Not to mention catching sight of Kord," added Drix with a bit of a chuckle that didn't fit the tension in the room. Everyone just looked at the strongman. Feeling the room was waiting for an explanation of his levity, he quickly continued. "Seriously, the man is as inhuman as it gets, even for us."

"What do you mean 'us'?" Runara spoke up then. "Do you transform into one of these beasts as well?" she questioned Drix. She had one hand curled affectionately around one of his massive biceps, but her body language had her pulling away slightly.

Rather than taking it as an insult, Azilurk laughed, "You didn't tell her? Oh, he's not one of our sort, but he's far from being human."

"Okay, I'm not following any of this," Joe interrupted. "Drix; not a human? Ugor a, what did you call it; a thrall? And again, what were your intentions for me? 'Cause it's kinda sounding like it was a little more than whacking me with a coconut." Then, remembering they were supposed to be in some sort of secretive meeting, he lowered his voice to a half-whisper. "And what does any of this have to do with us being off course with a boatload of slaves? Because if this whole meeting is about bumpin' me off, understand that I'll be taking most of you down with me."

"Tell the boy." Host sputtered. "We can't expect friendship and loyalty if we are not going to be honest with them."

The frustration was clearly evident on Dicesh's face. "You mortals do love to prattle on, darling. We don't have time for this."

Host was a hideous spectacle as his distorted form heaved with blood-choked laughter. "We can take a moment to explain our intent. Lasher's Bay is at the southern end of Aglog. We're a good day or so away before we would have to deal with that. It is I who doesn't have the time for all this preamble. The irony of your hesitation may indeed prove to be my death. We mortals don't have the luxury of having eternity to say what we need to say."

Dicesh huffed in defeated annoyance. "Very well," she said, spinning around to catch the gaze of the four band members, Runara and Joe. "We are, without question, the Surco Gorra Monsarri, the Circus of Monsters. The twins, as you've learned, are animons. So too, our animal trainer, here, Adriga." She gave the parrot on her shoulder a sideways glance.

"The best in Modnar." The bird squawked.

"Yes, yes, the best in Modnar," Dicesh agreed, rolling her eyes, "and the most insufferable."

Runara, Joe, and the band all had stunned, wide-eyed looks on their faces.

Dicesh continued. "I," she paused, clearly not anxious to continue, but a bloody coughing fit from Host spurred her on. "I am a vampire."

Runara and the band all gasped in shocked unison.

"You see," she said, turning back to Host, "it's going to go badly. It always goes badly. Why do we always hire human musicians?"

Host coughed and drooled some sort of black fluid. "Because humans have a natural emotional affinity for music, and they don't get all distracted by how the audience might taste."

"Stop that. They don't know that you're joking." Dicesh snapped back.

"Who is joking?" Host gurgled, managing a hideous smile. "You're doing fine. Continue."

"Wait," Joe interrupted before Dicesh could continue. "What the shrok is a vampire?" His Midgorn vulgarity was lost on the room full of Modnarians.

"Cursed, evil, undead, bloodsuckers!" Nooch blurted out with a look of fear that was mirrored in the faces of his bandmates. They had all assumed defensive postures. "She's bled out that sailor, and now she's going to drain the rest of us!" Nooch pointed at the corpse's feet sticking out of the bed.

"Were such insulting words true," Dicesh said, her voice cold and cutting, a wide humorless smile, full of sweet malice, on her face, "do you really think it wise to utter such vile, degenerate, twaddle about me right… to… my… face?" She stepped around Joe and leaned in close to Nooch's trembling face with her last words. "Or that it would even matter that you knew," she added in a menacing, hissing whisper. Adriga flew over to Drix's shoulder, not wanting to get caught in the middle of any confrontation that might ensue.

Nooch swallowed hard and tried to force out a word, but nothing was coming out.

Dicesh turned back to the others, continuing as though there had been no interruption. "Drix is, was, a gold golem. Before she died, his Mistress, the witch that created him, granted her servant his freedom and gave him a semblance of a more human form, but he remained as strong and ageless as his former gold self. He's quite lost without someone to serve, however. It's his nature as a golem. We found him being used by a small thieves guild, collecting on debts."

"Worse," Drix said solemnly, adding nothing further.

"Quite," Dicesh conceded. "His free will allowed him to move on, but only if he had someone else in equal or greater numbers to pledge himself to. We offered him the perfect escape."

Runara released her affectionate grip on Drix's arm, moving a slight step away. Had she dared to look at him, she would have seen the clearly hurt expression on his face. Dicesh took notice, however, and let a subtle grimace cross her face as she shot a look back at Host. Host saw and gave her a slight, grotesque, crooked nod to continue.

"Ugor, as Azilurk brought to your attention, is my thrall, as was Chenoval. My blood flows through Ugor's veins, and so long as I live, death cannot claim him, save should someone remove his head, as that vile elf did to poor Chen."

"Wow, so Crash," Joe said hesitantly, "you're one of these thralls too?"

"No, no," Drix answered before Crash had a chance to speak, "our young Crash is quite human, just slightly crazy."

"Hey!" Crash objected loudly.

"To be honest," Dicesh said with a sly smile, "we just can't seem to convince her to leave."

Crash was looking as dejected as Drix then. "Whatever. You monsters love me," Crash said, mustering half a smile.

"She does add a certain amount of exuberance to our cast." Dicesh conceded. "Not to mention that she's boundlessly talented. All of which makes her a wonderful fit for our troop, even if she is human, and the same can be said of you, bladesman; Joe."

"As, uh, interesting and insane as all of this is, you still haven't got 'round to telling me what you had intended to do with me when Crash here beaned me with a koli." Joe had his arms crossed, trying to look stern, hoping that none of them could tell that he was trying to plot out an escape plan that didn't conclude with him leaping overboard to his death.

"Which brings us to my beloved." Dicesh continued, addressing Joe's question while simultaneously seeming to ignore his interruption. "Enol Lezad." Dicesh made a dramatic twirling sweeping gesture as though introducing one of the circus acts.

Host gave a small cough, sputtering up a glob of bloody goo, weakly raising his non-dislocated arm, giving the room a tiny wave as though he had just walked in.

"You mean Host." Joe corrected.

"Host is just the name of this body," Enol said, choking a little. "I find fewer people feel the need to hunt me down as a skin-stealing monster if I continue to use the owner's name. None the wiser, and all that."

Runara and the band were now huddled together in unbelieving silence. Joe was not so quiet.

"You mean the owner of the skin you are wearing." It was a clarifying statement more than a question, and Joe didn't wait for a response. "That is so nasty! And how is that even possible?" Joe's face fully expressed his revulsion at the very concept of it all. "Wait, me; you were going to take my skin! That's it, isn't it? The one you're wearing, what, it was getting worn out? Didn't quite fit? Who the shrok wears other people's skin? What are you?"

With great difficulty, Enol sat up a little more. The slight motion made Joe back up abruptly, banging his back against the door. One of his knives was suddenly in his left hand as his right fumbled vainly for the door handle.

Ugor was at Joe's side, holding the door shut in case Joe managed to grope out the handle.

"Calm yourself bladesman. My kind are called zomblins. We have no skin of our own and so require the skins of others to survive, but each new skin only lasts so long, depending on how well-matched it is to our body. Fortunately for you, I'm more discerning than most of my kind when it comes to picking a new form." He chuckled in a gurgling manner at this, causing the skin around his nose to sag a little. "Clearly, despite my need for a new skin, we decided you and your friends to be noble additions to our troop, even if only temporarily, by your own designs." Coughing, he held his hand up to keep Joe from interrupting. "And we are more than happy to assist you, to the extent that we can, with your own journey." Enol went into a blood-spattering coughing fit then. Dicesh was a blur of movement back to Enol's bedside, easing him back down.

"Which brings us to the matter at hand." Dicesh's demeanor changed, becoming softer and caring as she adjusted the bedding, trying to make Enol more comfortable. "We mean to take this ship; the crew's lives are forfeit, the moilers we'll set free, where we can. The question is," She looked over her shoulder at the band, Runara, and Joe. "Can we trust the others to be part of this, or will we have to deal with them in some manner."

"You mean kill them," Runara said, her voice full of venom. Drix tried to put a hand on her shoulder to calm her, but it only infuriated her more. She shrugged his hand off and turned on him, holding up a threatening hand, a ball of flame rolling about menacingly in her palm.

"Whoa! Whoa!" Joe said loudly, jumping into the middle of the room. Then, in a much quieter, calmer tone, "As crazy as everything has just become, let's not do anything we'll be too dead to regret later." As he spoke, he made an overly dramatic point of holstering his knife back in his bandolier. "Now, by the 'others,' I'm assuming you mean the two librarians and the monk because I'm pretty sure Kord is going to be pushing his way to the front of the line for any plan involving killing a lot of humans."

"Yes, we have already discussed the matter with your friend," Dicesh said, "he should already be in position awaiting our signal. But we must move immediately, Enol doesn't have much time. He will need his new skin soon."

"You mean someone else's skin." Pox corrected sheepishly, his words trailing off to the inaudible as Dicesh quickly turned, glaring at him.

"Yes." Her tone was so dark, her gaze so full of menace that Pox instantly regretted having spoken up at all.

"Pox has a point, though," Joe was searching for any way to keep things light and positive, if not for the mood and sanity of Runara and the musicians, then at least for himself. "Why not use that fella?" Joe pointed at the legs of the corpse. "You never did explain what happened there."

"He was not a proper fit." Enol gurgled.

"And dead, besides," Dicesh added. "They need to be alive when he takes their skin. This sailor, Ugor sacrificed, feeding his blood to me that I might survive."

Ugor spoke up then, explaining further, not wanting Joe or the other mortals to think he had chosen the man randomly. "He was guarding the hatch to the moilers. We shouldn't waste no more time. Someone will notice this one missing soon."

"All right," Joe said as lightly as he could muster, addressing Host and Dicesh. "All cleared up. Tell you what, give me a moment to let the fellas know what's about to go down. I'm sure they'll stay out of the way if they don't feel up to joining your rebellion." Joe pulled on the door handle behind him, but the door didn't budge, still held shut by the supernatural strength of the diminutive thrall. "Either way, I'm sure they'll be behind the plan, whatever it is; a lot of killing and bloodletting, I'm assuming, because really, who likes a slaver. Okay, sure, we have a whole crew that seems okay with it, so this particular location may not be a good example, but you get what I mean."

Everyone stared at Joe as he vainly continued to try to open the door behind him.

"Yes, yes," It was clear by her tone that Dicesh had lost her patience for this meeting. "Just go." Her words to Joe were stern as she waved Ugor away from the door. "Tell them if they will not fight with us to hide with the animals below. Kotep should keep them safe. They will die if they try to defend the crew. When they are ready, come back here and knock on the door six times. Then, head to the upper deck and immediately take out one member of the crew up in the sails. Make sure he falls to hit the deck. Whatever follows, bring no harm to the sailor who now mans the wheel."

"This is crazy. We can't fight the entire crew. How do we know what you are saying about the moilers is even true?" Runara's voice wavered. Her eyes were on the verge of tears. She looked around the room frantically for someone to offer some sanity to the moment, but now all she saw were monsters and murderous freaks.

"These are good… people, Runara." Crash's voice was soft and calm, having no hint of her usual manic tone. "They can see into your heart. They know you are a good person, too. They only mean to help you."

"Help. Always help." Adriga squawked from Drix's shoulder.

Runara looked up at the parrot but caught Drix's sad gaze instead. It filled her with a tangle of emotions. She felt the anger and fire welling up within her again and tried to push it back down. She turned back to Dicesh and Enol. "I won't be part of killing these men," she said through gritted teeth. Her hair was moving then, seemingly with a life of its own as small, subtle flames licked out from between her thick, red curls.

Nooch could feel the heat radiating from her, and upon seeing her hair alive with fire, backed away from her, pushing the rest of the band back even further into the corner of the room than they had already been huddled. The fear on the faces of her fellow brookshins made Runara pause. She put a pleading hand out to Nooch, trying to calm him, but her hand was also covered in flame, making the gesture seem a threat.

"No!" She cried out, trying to make them see she meant no harm. Even as she said it, she realized that it was only making things worse. Her flames went out, and she collapsed to her knees, her face in her hands, sobbing. It was Crash who was quickly by her side, an arm wrapped around her, trying to calm her.

"You are more one of us than you realize, child." There was a sad empathy in Dicesh's voice. Crash, see that she and the musicians are safely below with Kotep. Adriga, see to the knowers and the monk. Adriga squawked, flying over to Joe's shoulder. "Go now, bladesman."

Joe gave an affirmative nod to Dicesh and glanced over at Runara, almost looking for her permission to go, but her face was still hidden in her hands as she continued to sob. Instead, Crash met his gaze, giving him a subtle, reassuring nod and a sad smile that somehow overpowered her clown makeup's disturbingly permanent, skeletal grin. Ugor quickly closed the door behind Joe as he left.

Joe was happy to be out of the room. It had all got a little heavy for him in there. He had never been one for secret plots or righteous causes and resented a little that he had been more or less threatened into this situation. Had they just come to him saying, 'Who's up for a little mutiny?' he probably would have been more inclined to join in. He looked about the crew quarters. The air was heavy with pipe smoke, the smell of booze, and the sound of a grossly out-of-key but somehow inspiring drink-spawned song. These were his sorts of fellows, he thought. Had he not been pulled into the disturbing little meeting, he just as easily could have been through a pint or two himself, belting his lungs out with the other fools about falling on your ass, drunk, and loose women. Joe hadn't taken more than two steps into the raucousness of the crew quarters, looking about for Garen and the others, when Tosh popped up beside him. He had an enormous turkey leg in one hand and a mug of ale in the other. He had just taken a huge bite of the turkey when he came upon Joe.

"Joe!" he said, spitting out little bits of turkey. "Just looking for you. Where is everybody?" Joe tried to squeeze a response in, but Tosh just kept talking. "Do you know, these men eat surprisingly well for living on a ship. Not the slop and gruel one always hears talk of." He shook the turkey leg in Joe's face to help make the point.

Joe bobbed his head, dodging Tosh's unintended assault with the turkey leg. "Look, Tosh, do you know where your friend — what's his name?"

"Barry."

"Ya, Barry. Do you know where he and the monk are?"

"Oh ya," Tosh said needlessly loud, waving the turkey leg toward the left side of the ship. "Over there, playing cards." It was clear to Joe that Tosh was a bit intoxicated.

"Shhh. Yes, yes, that's fine," Joe said, pulling Tosh's pointing arm down. Despite Tosh's loud display going relatively unnoticed in the surrounding din of the sailors, Joe felt as though the entire ship's crew was staring at them.

"Hey, where did you find that magnificent parrot? I've never been suck…I mean, seen such a breed." Tosh pointed a finger at Adriga, trying to touch his beak. Adriga snapped at him, just barely missing Tosh's finger as he quickly pulled it back.

"Yes, the parrot." Joe shrugged the shoulder Adriga was perched on, saying, "Go on."

Adriga flew over to Tosh's shoulder, much to Tosh's amusement.

"Now, Tosh, you need…." Tosh was too busy babbling and cooing at Adriga to notice Joe trying to speak to him further. "Tosh," Joe said, his voice a little firmer but still failing to get the drunk knower's attention. "Tosh!" Joe said as loudly as he could without actually shouting. Still, he got no response. "Tosh!" He muffled his shout through gritted teeth, grabbing Tosh's face with one hand and forcibly turning Tosh's head to face him.

Joe was squeezing Tosh's cheeks so tightly, pursing the knower's lips, that Tosh looked something like a fish gasping for a breath of water as he tried to speak. "W-what?" Tosh finally managed to get out.

"Listen to me very carefully," Joe began, maintaining his grip on Tosh and giving the man's head a little shake just to make sure he had his attention. "The parrot is Adriga."

"What?"

"Don't talk. Listen." He gave Tosh's head another little shake. "That is Adriga. You do, exactly as the bird — as he says. No questions, got me?" He let go of Tosh's face. Tosh gave a hesitant, positive nod.

Adriga was already chortling away in Tosh's ear. Tosh's eyes went wide with amazement. He looked at the bird on his shoulder, scanned the carousing group of sailors, and then back at Joe. The drunken smile on his face faded into something of a forced, sober resolve. Joe just gave him a nod. Without a further word, Tosh went to find Garen and Barry.

Joe decided to wait by the door. It was close enough to the ramp leading to the cargo hold that he would see Tosh and the others make their way down, and in the meantime, he could make sure that nobody walked in on Dicesh and the others.

The door to Dicesh's room opened. Crash slipped out, followed by the musicians and Runara. Runara did not look at Joe as she walked by, heading for the ramp to the lower deck. Joe couldn't help but feel a little hurt by it but shrugged it off. Getting caught up in the emotional storms of women was never productive, but something about Runara had him a little unusually distracted. It was almost like he cared about her state of mind. He gave his head a little shake, hoping to derail whatever train of thought he was on. He continued to watch her until she and the musicians had disappeared into the shadow of the level below.

Crash leaned against the wall beside Joe, her arms casually crossed. "She'll be okay," she said with the same earnest tone she had used in the room with Runara.

"Sure. I'm more concerned about what she's going to do to Drix. They were…" Joe made a suggestive gesture with his hands, indicating the couple's sexual interaction.

Crash looked nonplussed. "Why are men so ridiculous," she said, rolling her eyes. "Anyone can tell you aren't her type."

"What?" Joe protested, sounding a little unconvincingly confused.

"I mean, you're cute enough, just a little too killy, especially for a girly man." She pushed herself off the wall, giving the right side of his face a friendly pat to punctuate her words."

"Girly man?" Joe protested as she headed down the ramp. "Killy? Is that even a word?"

Crash looked over her shoulder, flashing Joe a broad smile and giving him another of her quick, subtle winks before disappearing below.

It was just then that the door down the narrow hallway between the two guest rooms opened. Captain Mak emerged, brushing some food scraps, the remains of his dinner, from his chest with one hand while sucking a stray bit of food mush from the thumb of the other. He seemed surprised to have an audience, more so that it was Joe.

"Joe, m'boy," he said a little too brightly. "Just the fellow I was wantin' to talk to." He strode up the hall, giving Joe a hearty slap on the shoulder. Joe gave a well-acted jovial chuckle as a greeting while he desperately began strategizing how to play this encounter out. "Sorry 'bout all that shouting at you and your mates up top this morning. A captain has to run a tight ship, eh." He gave Joe a playful punch to his shoulder, laughing. Joe forced a weak laugh as he tried to discreetly scan the crew quarters for Tosh and the others. "Sides, just lookin' out for my passengers. Speaking of which, d'you think you could gather up your pals an' bring 'em right here. Me and the lads would like to have a drink with 'em, y'know, a toast to thank you all for your patronage."

"Uh ya, sure," Joe said with an awkward smile. "I'll look around the ship for them."

"That's a good lad," he said, patting Joe on both shoulders. "Knew you were good folk the moment I saw you in the square." He started to walk away into the crew quarters toward the galley. "And worth a good coin, too, eh lad?" He shouted back at Joe jokingly, pointing at him. Joe gave another weak chuckle and a nod, mimicking the Captain's pointing gesture.

No sooner had he lost sight of the Captain among the other sailors down one side of the bifurcated crew quarters than he caught sight of Tosh, Adriga, Barry, and Garen approaching from the other side. Adriga was still on Tosh's shoulder. The two knowers barely glanced at Joe before heading down the ramp, but Joe could see that they both looked extremely nervous. Garen came straight toward Joe. Joe braced himself for a confrontation that he really didn't want to deal with.

"If these men are truly dealing in moilers," Garen whispered, getting in close to Joe's ear, "then I will do what I can for the sake of the moilers' freedom. I will not hide. It is not our way."

Joe let out an audible sigh of relief. "Okay, wait right here for the others to come out, and whatever happens — 'cause I'm pretty sure it's about to get really weird and messy — don't freak out. I'm mostly certain that the circus are the good guys here." Joe waited for some sort of response from Garen, but his face was its usual stony visage. After a few uncomfortable moments that had Joe seriously wondering if Garen had somehow fallen unconscious while standing up with his eyes open, he gave Joe a slight approving nod. It was good enough for Joe. He spun around and knocked on Dicesh's door six times.

"I need to go above." Joe pulled a knife from his bandolier and gave it a casual flip as he walked up the ramp to the deck. Garen simply nodded again.

Joe spotted the man he was going to target almost immediately as he stepped onto the main deck. It was dark now, but between the moonlight of both Gatal and Zeebo, two of Modnar's three moons, and the few lamps lit about the ship, he could see quite clearly. There were three men up among the sails, but only one was the perfect mark. There was nothing particularly notable about the sailor he had picked out. He was a man of average build and appearance. He had caught Joe's attention because he happened to be standing on the boom of the forward mast, close to the mast itself. There would be no danger of the man falling anywhere but onto the deck.

Joe gave the deck a quick scan just to have an idea of who was where, should things go bad. Only a few men were down at his level. One man was near the bow, just leaning out and taking in the night sky, it appeared. A large, bald, dark-skinned fellow with scars for tattoos was on the ship's sterncastle, manning the wheel. That was the man Dicesh told him to leave be, and given his size, Joe was okay with that. A smaller man, squat but solidly built, just as bald as the man at the wheel, but with a thick beard, stood beside the man at the wheel. Six silver rings pierced each of his cheeks. The two men seemed deep in conversation and had not yet noticed Joe.

Another member of the crew, a portly man whose double chin was covered in just enough wiry, brown hair to be considered a beard, was busy carving away at a soft, chocolate-colored stone. It looked as though he was making a turtle but his intention had been to carve a bull. Unlike the sailors of the day shift, who tended to wear wrappings that covered the tops of their heads and the backs of their necks, this sailor wore a knitted beanie. There were several holes in the man's cap. Whether the holes were simply worn through or the result of the chewing activity of a small animal was hard to say.

"Hey there, buddy," the portly crewman greeted Joe cheerfully. Joe ignored him, staying focused on the man on the sail. "Nice lookin' knife you got there. Ever try carvin' mudstone?" The sailor's second attempt to gain Joe's attention was as fruitless as the first. Joe continued to stare up into the sails. The sailor looked up to see what Joe might be so mesmerized with and, still undaunted by the lack of conversation thus far, tried a third time. "Ya, never really seen the stars 'til you get above the clouds, eh?"

Joe allowed himself a quick glance at the friendly, stone-carving sailor, giving him a short nod in the hope that it would satisfy the man's apparent need for interaction. He then shot his attention back to the sailor on the mast. Joe felt a little strange about the prospect of killing a man that he had no particular quarrel with. It wasn't as though Joe had never taken someone by surprise, fatally, unprovoked, before. Quite the contrary, he had done so plenty of times, but usually, there was a more tangible prize as the driving excuse; freedom, treasure, a woman, not being killed for cheating at a game of Folsbar with a man who had also just discovered that Joe had been sleeping with the man's wife; entirely justifiable things like that. Despite the supposed looming threat of slavery, he just didn't feel imprisoned in this situation. It made him pause for a moment. He flipped the throwing knife in his hand end over end.

One flip.

"Hey, buddy." The portly man was undaunted in his pursuit of conversation with Joe. "Sorry about you and your friends, nothin' personal, right?"

The odd comment had caught Joe's attention, compelling him to pursue it, but he kept his eyes on the man in the sails. "What's that now?"

Two flips.

"Uh, I mean…" The portly sailor fumbled on his words, realizing, dull as he was, that he may have begun to reveal more than he ought to. "That is, the business with, uh, you all being — being on the run. Ya." The man's tone and demeanor made it evident that he was proud of his clever recovery. Joe almost felt sorry for the dullard.

"Slaves." Joe searched for the new word he had learned. "Moilers. You meant…" Joe dropped his gaze then fully upon the dimwitted, portly man. "Sorry about you and your friends being taken and sold as moilers."

Three flips.

"Uh, what? I mean, no. I said no hard feelings, ri—" The man's last word was cut off by Joe's knife piercing his throat. It was followed a split second later by a second knife shooting into his heart. Before the large man had a chance to topple over, Joe's right hand blurred, sending a third knife at the sailor up on the mast. It was a harder, longer shot than Joe was used to, but the flying blade still found its target. The man dropped.

"No hard feelings," Joe said, watching the man fall.

If the knife had not been fatal, his loud impact with the deck certainly was. No sooner had the man crashed into a bloody heap than Joe heard something rush through the air just a foot or so above his head. The sailor at the bow of the ship screamed out in pain and terror, a scream that faded as he disappeared into the moonlit clouds below.

A shout of "man overboard" came from one of the men in the sails, but a moment later, he too was falling, silently, following his shipmate down into the aerial sea of mist. Another unseen shot ripped through two of the sails, dropping the last lofty sailor to the deck. Joe found himself instinctively ducking down, not entirely sure what was going on.

The man at the wheel was shouting orders at his companion to alert the rest of the crew as he looked out into the empty sky, trying to find the source of the assault. It was then that Joe heard the familiar "thoop" sound he had heard at the end of his confrontation with King Ethdab in the brookshins' camp. A net burst wide open, seemingly materializing out of nowhere, engulfing the man at the wheel. It quickly tightened and rendered the man helpless. The pierced man went to bend down to assist the trapped sailor when, without warning, his head simply tumbled off, blood gushing everywhere as his body spasmed backward and fell limp.

So sudden and horrific it had been that Joe had to cover his mouth to stifle the shocked grunt he uttered. Below deck, a raucous commotion had erupted. Men were shouting, and some were screaming. A sailor came bounding up the ramp from the lower deck. He stopped short when he saw Joe's crouched form. His panicked face was spattered with blood, and it was evident that he had wet himself. He was unable to speak, simply out of fear, but he held his hands up to Joe as if to say stop, don't hurt me. A moment later, a wooden bolt was sticking out of his forehead. He fell limply back down the ramp.

Joe spun around. He knew Kord was out there, somewhere in the direction of the stern of the boat, but couldn't see him. Back in the Loncodi market square, Kord had materialized out of nowhere. He knew Kord was on his side, but the prospect of an invisible mander skulking about made him terribly nervous.

"Dammit Kord, show yourself," he said in a shouted whisper. "You're freakin' me out."

All the noise from below suddenly ceased and was replaced by a low, menacing, rumbling chuckle just a couple of feet behind Joe. Joe spun around just in time to see the hulking, laughing form of Kord appear.

"Oh, that is not right, creepin' up on me like that." Joe protested in a whisper. He wasn't sure why he was whispering. It just seemed appropriate to all of the clandestine carnage.

Kord just continued to laugh, and Joe found his uncharacteristically jovial demeanor far more troubling than Kord's usual intimidatingly solemn nature.

"You find all of this killing funny?"

"I admit," Kord answered with a wide grin, "a good hunt always improves my mood, Little Meat, but this was no hunt."

"Did you just call me 'Little Meat'?"

Kord ignored Joe's question and continued. "I've had a harder time shooting gorleander pups in a pen." He rubbed his chin contemplatively with his abnormally small right hand, which had already more than doubled in size from the evening before. It now stuck out several inches on a narrow stem of a forearm.

Joe tried to pretend he wasn't entirely repulsed by the strange little replacement appendage, but his facial expression betrayed him, giving Kord all the more reason to chuckle.

"So what, in all the black blood of Kodin, is so hilarious?" Joe demanded of Kord.

"I've come to understand the way in which you will die." Kord's uncharacteristic, unwavering grin was as unsettling as his words to Joe.

"Hey, we're on the same side here!" Joe protested a little more frantically than he would have preferred.

"So we are, Little Meat, so we are."

The large man trapped in Kord's net was shouting curses at them in a language neither Kord nor Joe recognized. The smile disappeared from Kord's face as he looked back at the struggling man.

"Not right," Kord grumbled.

"You've got to be kidding me," Joe said in total disbelief. "You were just laughing about killing me, and now you're going to express regret about offing this guy?"

"No," Kord turned his empty, ruby gaze back to Joe. "An honorable hunter never tortures his prey."

"Like you said, this was no hunt." Joe's tone was solemn. "Tonight, we're just a bunch of killers, monsters."

"Surco Gorra Monsarri," came Dicesh's correcting voice behind them.

Joe and Kord turned to face Dicesh. The image they were confronted with even caused Kord to take a step back. Dicesh was naked but covered, head to toe, in blood. Her hair, normally pulled back, hung loose, dripping in matted, blood-soaked clumps. Thick bloody strands of hair hung, obscuring much of her face, but could not hide the light emitted from her glowing yellow eyes, nor did they mask her brilliant, white, inch-and-a-half fangs as she spoke.

Kord sniffed the air in her direction. "Blood of many." He sniffed a little more. "None of it yours."

"The ship is ours. Those in the hold are free." Her voice had an intimidating hollow depth that Joe could feel in his chest.

"You mean the moilers?" Joe asked just to confirm.

"Moilers no more!" She bellowed.

The sudden volume took Joe by surprise, knocking him off balance and back two steps. The blade on Kord's left arm snapped out defensively with the menacing sound of a guillotine.

"And I will feast on the living heart of anyone who calls them such again." Dicesh took a step forward.

Kord's blade retracted. "By the silence below, I expect you have already had your fill. It is your mate that needs to feed."

"He does, and he is weak. Bring the new body here." Dicesh's tone softened a little but was still immensely intimidating, to Joe, at least.

Kord gave a subtle head nod, then sauntered over to the large crewman still struggling against the tight bindings of the net. The man spat and cursed and yelled obscenities of every sort as Kord grabbed some of the netting around the crewman's waist and picked him up. He carried the man back casually as though the sailor were nothing more than a large squirming duffle bag, dropping him at Dicesh's feet. It made her smile, and her eyes glowed brighter. Something about this happy, hungry demeanor seemed even more disturbing to Joe than her anger a few moments earlier.

"You have done well. Both of you," she said, spreading her arms as if she were welcoming them in for a hug. The glow in her eyes diminished then, her fangs retracted, and her voice, though still unnaturally loud, had returned more to its normal state. "Come, my love, your next life awaits," she said over her right shoulder.

Behind her, from the hatchway to the level below, a thin, bloody figure crawled out. Its eyes were dark, empty voids; its mouth a gaping toothless abyss seemingly frozen in a silent scream. It looked like a starved man, so thin and frail that had been skinned alive, leaving all of its gleaming, bloody muscle structure exposed. The nails on its hands were long, menacing, black talons. A smeared trail of thick bloody slime was left in its wake as it clawed across the short distance between the hatchway and the bound sailor. The sailor was screaming himself hoarse in terror as he watched the bloody thing approach.

Joe made a move to intervene. He wasn't sure what he was going to do; put the sailor out of his misery, maybe try killing the thing that had been Host, that now called itself Enol. He wasn't even sure if this horror was Enol, but it had to be. Whoever it was, whatever it was, whatever Joe was going to do, just letting the man in the net be tortured by this thing seemed wrong. Kord, sensing Joe's unrest, held out his massive left arm in front of Joe, stopping him before he even had a chance to move.

Kord's action caught Dicesh's attention, and she quickly spun her gaze from her beloved Enol to Joe. Her eyes flared with golden light as she scowled at Joe. "None of us may interfere, bladesman," she boomed.

Joe quickly put his hands up and mustered up the most innocent face he could as if to express that interfering had been the farthest thing from his mind.

Enol crawled past Dicesh, glancing up at her with his empty eyes like a pet grateful for a bowl of food just set out. Weakly, he crawled up onto the man whose screams were now nothing more than pathetically hoarse hisses. With a sudden violence and strength, Enol grabbed the struggling man's head in both hands, holding it steady. Two bloody, tongue-like appendages shot out from Enol's seemingly empty eye sockets like two striking snakes. They thrust harshly into the eyes of the sailor, pushing deep into the man's skull. The man went silent; his struggles reduced to tiny involuntary twitches. Enol began consuming the man's brain through his ocular tentacles, his toothless mouth moving as though it were chewing. Soon, the man's twitching ceased.

Then, it was Enol who began to twitch. His body began to change, to grow. His bones popped and cracked loudly as the transformation continued; within only a few seconds, he was nearly the size of the now-dead sailor.

"Interesting," Kord grumbled in a low tone meant only for himself and Joe.

"I never want to cross paths with a mime," Joe whispered back. Kord smiled.

"We must leave him now," Dicesh said in a completely human voice. "Follow me below. There is much to do."

Kord and Joe stepped around the grim spectacle of Enol's body, convulsing from the spasms of his growing form as he continued to feed. The crewman appeared to be shriveling like a raisin rapidly drying in the sun. As repulsed and horrified by it as Joe was, he could not look away, which was unfortunate. Not watching where he was going as he headed down the ramp behind Dicesh and Kord, Joe stepped in Enol's bloody slime trail. His left foot, unexpectedly frictionless, shot out from beneath him as he stepped, throwing him violently backward. He managed to utter a despairing and frustrated "Son of a b—" before slamming his head hard as he fell onto the wooden ramp. Then all, for Joe, slid into an all too familiar darkness.

Chapter 16

Joe awoke to a vision-filling panorama of creamy, caramel cleavage. The red crystal pendant nestled, enviously so, between the large, perfect mounds quickly indicated to Joe that the resplendent womanly display had to belong to Runara.

She was dabbing his forehead with a cool, damp cloth as he came to. They were alone in her passenger room.

For a brief moment, Joe considered that this may be his chance to charm the beauteous brookshin witch, but a few factors quickly crushed that plan. First, Joe tried to sit up but instantly felt dizzy. It didn't take much coaxing from Runara to get him to lay back down. Any moves he might have been planning would have to be very passive. Then he remembered her obviously physical, perhaps even romantic, involvement with the strongman, Drix. Though he had no idea what a golem was, let alone the gold variety, his experience, back in Midgorn when dealing with sorcery of any sort, was that there was simply no competing with magic, especially where romance and sex were concerned. Lastly, it was obvious that Runara had been crying, almost certainly just before Joe had awoken. Though often a prime vulnerable moment for many men to try to woo a woman, Joe had never enjoyed such encounters. They were either too disconnected, too emotional, or, more simply, not as much fun as times with women of a much more jovial, enthusiastic disposition. Joe liked to think he wasn't so desperate as to stoop to such tactics, at least, not yet.

He asked her a few questions, trying to catch up on what had happened while he had been out. It took a few minutes, but eventually, she started to answer him, mainly to keep him from getting up.

She explained that he had been unconscious for nearly three hours by the ship's clock. In that time, the others had managed to throw the bodies of Captain Mak and the rest of the former crew overboard. As far as she was aware, all of the former crew had been killed save for the young dock boy and old Franz. Franz had been found by the new crew, lashed to the harpy at the bow of the ship, but it was Crash who had been responsible for saving both of their lives.

In the boy's case, Crash had put herself between the boy and Dicesh. Dicesh reluctantly agreed to let the boy live, but as her new thrall to replace Chenoval. Later, Crash had been on deck when they discovered and pulled Franz from the bow. Runara had been there as well, and though her own pleas to let the old sailor live were ignored, Crash whispered something to Enol, who then ordered the man to be shackled and taken to the lower hold unharmed. Runara didn't know what Crash had said to Enol, but she got the distinct impression that Crash and Franz knew each other from somewhere other than this ship. Dicesh had been furious about letting the old man live, but it seemed she would not cross Enol. After that, Dicesh would barely speak to or even acknowledge Crash.

Every answer Runara offered Joe just gave rise to more questions. Who was the new crew? How long had Enol been up and about, and what did he look like? Joe was trying to imagine the large, darkly-skinned crewman but with poorly fitting skin. Was Crash okay? Runara had answers for all.

The prisoners that had been kept in the lower hold to be sold as slaves were mostly sailors, either abducted from various ports along the way or, as was the case of six of the eighteen men, picked up from a shipwreck four days earlier. Ugor had released the men from their chains in the lower hold, and, to a man, they agreed to help take the ship. Their participation, however, had nearly been unnecessary.

When Dicesh and the others heard the body drop on the deck above, they stormed out of the passenger cabin, taking many of the crew by surprise. Before the prisoners had even reached the crew quarters, Dicesh and the others had already slaughtered half of the crew, and many of those had been at Dicesh's hand, or rather, fangs, alone. Enol had been left alone to shed his former skin.

It had been offered to the former prisoners the opportunity to be dropped off at the next possible city or town, but without hesitation, they all chose to stay and serve as the ship's crew. Though the regular operations of the vessel were not a problem for the men, nobody seemed to know how to make the ship rise, descend, or operate any of the transformative flying features of the vessel. Presently, they were just focused on getting the Harmaton back on course for the town of Cravenhuddle. Once there, they would worry about figuring out how to get the boat back down into the water without dashing it to pieces.

Enol, now wearing the skin of the muscular, bald sailor that Kord had netted, had taken on the role of Captain of the Harmaton. Runara added that it was all very disconcerting, as he genuinely looked and even sounded just like the original owner of his new skin. There was little about him other than a slight change in the man's demeanor that seemed anything like the man they had known as Host. He even uses the former crewman's name, and all in the circus now refer to him as such. As far as the new crew is aware, Enol, now going by the name Morimar Braxis, started the bloody mutiny, resulting in their freedom. The former captives are more than happy to call him their Captain.

From there, the conversation deviated, and Joe regaled Runara with tales of his adventures in Midgorn. She shared stories of her life in the forest that she now missed so dearly.

Though the conversation found both Runara and Joe feeling better, hours of talking had them both feeling quite spent. There were several minutes of quiet as each, lost in their own nostalgic thoughts, began to give way to exhausted sleep. Then Joe made the mistake of breaking the silence by asking how things were between Drix and her. Runara said quite sharply that she didn't want to talk about it, and a great deal of much more awkward silence followed. With their conversation clearly over, Joe moved to get up, offering to let Runara get some sleep. She insisted that he lay back down and stay, laying herself down beside him on the bed.

"Try anything, and I swear I'll roast you alive," she said with her back to Joe.

Several clever quips crossed Joe's mind as possible responses, but surprisingly, even to Joe, all that came out was, "Thanks for letting me stay."

Runara clutched at the red crystal pendant, shedding a single tear, as she and Joe quickly drifted off to sleep.

* * * * * * * * * * * * * * * * * *

The three following days were a little uncomfortable for Joe and Runara. Their distaste for the massacre of the Harmaton's old crew was diametrically opposed to the demeanor of all of the others, save for Crash and Garen. Even Kord was in an unusually happy way. Kubara had awoken, its wounds surprisingly fully healed by whatever Kord had done to treat them. Now, Kord and the jungle cat were inseparable. Kord would spend hours petting and playing with the large predator as though it were a giant house cat. It was almost a cute spectacle to see the two ferocious hunters interact so affectionately, but Joe simply found the prospect of the newly established duo to be frightening and tried to avoid them as best he could.

Another surprise to Joe, given Runara's disposition, was the good spirits of the musicians. They spent most of their time either down in the crew quarters or midship on deck, playing requests from the crew. Nooch and Pronz even improvised a ballad about the liberation of the Harmaton's new crew by Captain Braxis and "The Circus of Heroes." Joe was even featured in one verse.

He had mixed feelings about the hero treatment. It was not the sort of reputation one wanted to have when commonly dealing with the sordid characters Joe often relied upon for his livelihood and entertainment. At least it wouldn't get back to Midgorn, he thought. Then again, for all the trouble Joe's questionable ventures had got him into during his life in Midgorn, he couldn't think of a time when death followed him so closely everywhere he went. Joe was pretty sure heroes were not so death-drenched, so his reputation was probably reasonably safe. As he watched the crew merrily working and singing along with the band, he found himself reminded that he wasn't part of this crew, or even, really, part of this circus, if there even was a circus any longer. Screamin' Joe Blade wasn't even part of this world. Beautiful as Modnar was, he just needed to return home to Midgorn. At least there, he knew who he was and his role there.

Joe and Runara were definitely in the minority regarding their hard time fitting into the new circumstances. Barry and Tosh had quickly found a matter of interest to them and potential usefulness to the new crew. They were spending most of their time in the ship's lowest level, trying to figure out the workings of the seacraft's ability to fly. On the third day, they were feeling confident enough to start experimenting.

There were three large mechanisms in the lower hold. One, the two knowers were calling the ballast pump. As far as they could discern it was responsible for inflating and deflating the large black leather-like bladder sphere in the middle of the ship. There had been some debate about whether the bladder was actually made of leather, but since neither could decide what it was or was not, they settled on labeling the substance "leather" and moved on to discerning its function.

They had argued for nearly all of the first day, after the dispensing of the former crew, as to whether the bladder's state of inflation alone was responsible for keeping the ship aloft. It had taken them much of the remainder of that same day to agree which of the devices in the lower hold was actually responsible for maintaining the bladder's inflation. They had eventually agreed that given the presence of two other machines, there had to be more to the ship's flight than the inflation of the large leather sphere.

Adding to the uncertainty of the ballast pump device's true function was the apparently contrary state of its controls. Among the various nobs, wheels, toggle switches, and push-button controls on this machine were two large levers, which seemed to be at the heart of the device's function. Tosh and Barry had agreed upon the translation of the elvish markings next to the levers, but that only confused matters. The word for one lever seemed to roughly translate to suck, while the other translated very directly to blow. The problem was that both levers seemed to be engaged.

They had questioned Franz as he was conveniently kept on that same level in the now spacious, iron-barred brig. Not unexpectedly, however, he offered no help, only suggesting they try throwing some switches and levers on the three machines and see what happens.

The second machine, a large metal barrel with three six-finned rings around it, would blast steam from two circular vents on opposite sides at regular one-hour intervals. It constantly hummed and vibrated slightly. They took to referring to it as the flight engine. They were not entirely sure what it was doing, but they were under the impression, by the ceaselessly revolving shaft that stuck out of the top of the machine and entered the base of the sphere, that it was making something within the spherical bladder rotate. The shaft of the flight engine entered the sphere through the same metal cuff as two pipes running from the ballast pump.

Given that the machine never seemed to stop, they decided it may somehow be responsible for keeping the ship in the air. Coming to that conclusion made both men afraid to fiddle with it at all.

The third machine was slightly larger than the other two. It did not seem to be doing anything at all. The main housing was a large, thick vertical ring with a tightly fitted rotating central disc. Two large cranks were attached to the central disc on either side of the machine. They deciphered the elvish labels above and below a lever on the device as "IGNITE" and "REPLENISH." After much debate and observing the top of the device, a glowing vial of glowing green liquid drained over the course of a day while another vial of glowing red liquid filled. It was decided that the device was either generating or, possibly, burning through some sort of fuel. The lever was already in the replenish position, so the men took the risk of turning the cranks. The green liquid quickly refilled as they did, and the red drained. The disc hummed for an hour afterward. They repeated this each morning for three days. On the second day, Barry suggested that they call the machine the fuel mill, and the name stuck.

Feeling confident they had gotten something right, they tried switching the lever to the ignite position on the third day. Nothing seemed to happen immediately, so they tried turning the cranks again. After two revolutions, a muffled boom sounded from the sphere's base, and the entire ship shook. The banging and popping sounds of something very large and metallic somewhere within the inflated sphere began echoing through the ship, causing a great deal of concern for everyone on board.

Garen had been meditating upside-down on the top boom of the foremast, as he had spent most of his waking hours during the three days. The shaking of the ship had caused him to lose his balance and fall. He managed to quickly save himself, grabbing hold of some rigging. With the agility of a spider monkey, he swung and leaped from rope to rope, working his way safely down.

Captain Braxis had been watching the monk's entire descent from midship and leaned back with a deep, hearty laugh as the monk touched down gently beside him. "You're sure that you don't want to join the circus holy man? Between you, the twins, and Crash, we might be able to put a trapeze act together again."

"No," Garen answered solemnly, scrutinizing the perfect caramel complexion of the smooth-faced man that had so recently been the far less healthy-looking man named Host. Garen could accept the transformation for the most part, but what bothered him most was that the man's eyes were even different from before; grey now instead of violet. It didn't seem right to Garen somehow. How then, he thought, looking a man in the eye, do you judge his honesty if he's not even looking through his own eyes? "You might concern yourself more with the state of your new ship, Captain."

The ship shook again as several loud, metallic bangs reverberated from the central sphere. The wide white smile faded from the Captain's face. Crash, who had been spending most of her time at the bow of the ship over the past three days, came running past the two men, heading down the ramp to the decks below. She nearly bowled over Joe, who was making his way up in nearly as much of a hurry.

"What in Kodin's blood is going on?" Joe got no answers to his exclamation.

The lower deck was now filled with steam, streaming ceaselessly from the so-called flight engine. A shrill bell sound had also begun ringing from the fuel mill, which was only serving to throw Barry and Tosh into more of a panic than they were already in. Their first thought was to pull the lever on the fuel mill back to the replenish position, but doing so didn't seem to change anything. Crash came bounding into the steam-filled room, colliding with Tosh and knocking him, hard, to the floor.

"Sorry! Sorry!" She shouted back as she continued, narrowly missing doing the same to Barry. She disappeared into the fog of the room. "Dammit!" her voice came back, nearly masked by the bell and the roar of the steam jetting from the flight engine. "Ouch! Dammit!"

"What are you doing, girl?" Barry shouted, squinting into the fog, trying to see her. "These machines are nothing to play with. We should probably get out of here."

"And go where?" Tosh asked, the frustration and panic evident in his voice as he picked himself up off the floor.

A noise came from the fog that sounded suspiciously like someone kicking one of the machines.

"She's gone insane!" Barry exclaimed. "Go in there and stop her before she breaks something."

"Before she breaks something? How much worse could she make it? You go in there and stop her." Tosh protested.

Then came a high-pitched squeal, the sound of metal scraping against metal under extreme forces, followed by a thunderous bang. The sound shook the ship so hard that it sent Tosh and Barry sprawling, as it did many others throughout the boat. From the level above, the angry trumpet of King Kotep sounded, followed by several roars from two of the three cats. A whirring sound began growing louder and louder with every second until it was a rumbling growl that vibrated the floor beneath Barry and Tosh.

Dicesh suddenly stood above the two men as if she had teleported there. She was wide-eyed and holding her ears.

"What are you fools doing to our ship?" She demanded.

"N-not us," Barry stammered.

"Not entirely us," Tosh amended, struggling to his feet once again.

The steam that had filled this portion of the hold began to quickly dissipate, being pulled into the now spinning, finned rings of the flight engine. Crash could be seen then flicking several switches on the flight engine and working one of the levers like a pump.

The noise and shaking had ceased. A triangular red light now glowed above the top ring of the flight engine.

In the next instant, Dicesh had Crash by the throat, lifting her off her feet. "Sabotage, girl? Give me a reason not to drain your life and toss your carcass over the side."

Crash tried to respond, but Dicesh's stranglehold prevented anything but a gurgle from coming out.

"It wasn't her; it was us," Barry said, back on his feet. Tosh was behind him, distractedly brushing himself off, mumbling something about the filthy state of the floor.

Dicesh wheeled around on Barry, keeping Crash aloft at the end of her arm. Her eyes were glowing, and the look on her face alone might have killed a man with a weaker heart. Barry and Tosh both jumped back out of fright.

"N-no, no, not sabotage," Barry vaguely corrected. "I mean, she didn't… we didn't… I mean, you asked us to…"

"I think the girl just saved us all." Tosh quickly threw in.

Dicesh dropped Crash, uttering a guttural cry of frustration, "Somebody better explain this quickly."

Laughter was coming from deeper in the hold. "Bit of a problem, lads?" Franz's muted shout came. His words were followed by another fit of laughter. "If Captain Badass is all that's keeping this heap in the air…" Again, Franz trailed off in a fit of laughter.

Dicesh grabbed Crash by the arm, dragging her along. "You two, follow," she said as she marched Crash past Tosh and Barry. Crash was preoccupied, trying to breathe normally again.

Franz was thrown into another bout of laughter as he saw the group approach. Braxis, Joe, and Garen arrived at that moment as well.

"Someone tell a joke down here?" The tone of Captain Braxis's voice was a lighthearted contrast to Dicesh's glaring, ominous countenance. "I like a good joke. Try me."

Upon hearing the Captain's voice, Franz's demeanor instantly stifled to a serious state. He eyed the man with a piercing scrutiny. "Only joke here, be the thing walkin' bout like a captain, whiles the only real Captain on this ship – well, that's quite a punchline. Seen your sort before, skin stealer. Never saw one so chatty, though. Your kind is usually too busy rippin' folk apart or diggin' up graves."

"You'll find I'm not like my kin."

Franz nodded as though he already agreed. "Still, made a mistake takin' that one's skin. Nasty piece of work he was, more like your 'kin,' as you say; lot of enemies about."

"I'm aware," the Captain said gravely, tapping a finger to his head. "Skin isn't the only thing I steal."

Franz laughed then. "No yous all be takin' boats too, is clear 'nuff. Sept, you'd be shark fodder 't'weren't for this one." He pointed a gnarled finger at Crash. Dicesh still had a solid grip on her arm.

"He's right," Crash protested, trying to wrench free of Dicesh's inhuman hold. "I just saved us all. What is your problem?"

"What is my problem?" Dicesh's voice seethed with restrained fury, "My problem is with you saving the hide of a moiler merchant like this festering old filth. Now I find both of our knowers flat on the floor, with you doing who-knows-what to the machinery holding us in the sky."

Barry looked as though he were going to say something, but a glance from Dicesh quickly stifled whatever the thought had been.

Captain Braxis gave an incredulous chuckle. "Sabotage? Seems to me the ship was already sounding like it was ripping itself apart when she ran past us."

Joe nodded in agreement, shuffling a little, positioning Braxis and Garen between Dicesh and him.

"As for this one's fate," Braxis swiftly shot an arm into Franz's cell, grabbing hold of Franz by the vest and slamming him hard against the bars, holding him there. "Well, that is still up in the air, we'll say." The swift change and deadly tone of the Captain's voice was unsettling to all but Dicesh, who actually cracked a small smile. The old sailor vainly struggled to push himself off of the bars. "Let's say you finish the punchline to your joke."

"Seems that skin's a better fit than I figured," Franz sneered. He looked, then, squinting a little, at Crash. "Surprised I didn't see it sooner. 'Course her hair's all wrong, an' she's dressed like a damned fool, but I'd wager my arse an' yours, that's Captain Badass herself under that makeup."

Braxis let the old sailor go. Dicesh kept her grip on Crash, who was now just staring at the floor.

"Captain?" Dicesh asked, giving Crash a demanding shake but directing her question to Franz. "Captain Badass? Captain of what exactly?"

Franz just laughed.

Joe interjected then, "Does everybody get a turn at being a captain in Modnar? Cause if so, I'd really like to…"

"Shut it, bladesman, this doesn't concern you," Dicesh growled.

"Just saying it would be nice…"

"I said, shut it!"

Garen shot Joe a concerned look and gave a slight head shake of no, hoping to stop Joe from provoking either of the circus owners further.

Crash let a little chuckle escape, prompting Dicesh to give her another small reprimanding shake.

"Someone other than you," Braxis said, turning to Joe briefly, "needs to start talking."

"Oh, come now, even rock huggers like you lot had to have heard the tales of Captain Badass." Franz's tone was mocking.

"Bondass." Crash corrected in an uncharacteristically small voice.

Franz chuckled, "Or as any sailor unfortunate enough t'have caught sight o' her an' the Seraphene used to call her, Captain Hotass."

"The Seraphene?" Braxis gave a hearty laugh. "The most notorious, elven pirate ship? Responsible for sinking the entire Korakan fleet during the Goblin Wars? I thought her Captain was called 'Red Tail.'"

"Red Tail, Hot Ass," Joe said, looking around at the others, "Get it? I get it."

"We all get it. Do be quiet." Garen whispered sternly.

Franz laughed and pointed at Joe. "Like that one." He cleared his throat as he turned back to Dicesh. "Whatever the name, scourge of the human fleets, she was. Only human ever to command a crew o' elves on one of their own sky ships. No little fleck like this heap either. The Seraphene was one o' them abomination class leapers. Is it true what they say, girl, that them leaper ships are alive?"

Dicesh was laughing then, letting go of her grip on Crash. "This one? Her? She is the fearsome pirate captain, Red Tail, the Flying Fox of the Seraphene? That was more than thirty years ago. What was she, a baby, you perverse, deluded old bastard?"

"I was sixteen." Came Crash's voice quietly. "The elves had an elixir…" Her voice trailed off.

Silence followed for a few seconds as everyone processed the shift in their reality.

"Ha!" Franz broke the quiet tension abruptly, "Guess that still made me something of a dirty ol' man. Clever and ruthless beyond your years, girl. Back then, leastways."

There was a look of festering displeasure building on Dicesh's face. It was born from a sense of betrayal and a bruised ego. Crash being able to keep such a secret from both Enol and her was intolerable.

"And yes, she was, the Seraphene, alive, that is." Crash offered quietly. "I preferred being called the Flying Fox, too. Thanks."

"Whatever," Dicesh growled, turning on Crash again. "You think I care about some ridiculous, enchanted, flying pirate ship and your accursed fool nickname? This filthy ship rat doesn't just know you by reputation; you also know him. Was he one of your crew?"

Franz was cackling near uncontrollably now and had backed safely out of Braxis's reach.

Dicesh's eyes flashed brightly as she grabbed Crash by the shoulders. "I lost friends in that war, to pirates, to the Seraphene, to you! Did you sell my friends off as moilers, or did you just put their heads on pikes on the prow of your precious Seraphene? I should gut you where you stand." Dicesh let go of Crash, taking a step back. Her fangs were out then, and the nails on her fingers had become long talons.

"You could," Crash responded in a calm, even voice that had taken on a sudden confidence. She took a defensive step back. "But then there will be no one left on this blood-soaked heap who knows how to fly this thing; 'cept him." She nodded her head in Franz's direction.

"Either I feast on your marrow, or I toss you over the side," Dicesh snarled at Crash, shrugging Braxis's hand off her shoulder as he silently tried to calm her, "but there's no way you or your shipmate here, are staying aboard."

"He's not my shipmate; he was one of my victims and an honorable man at that, or was. Whatever he's become since then is on me. He deserves a chance at redemption."

Braxis stepped in between Dicesh and Crash, giving Dicesh a stern look that only he could get away with. She backed down, the glow slowly diminishing from her eyes, her claws and fangs retracting. With a solemn countenance, he raised a finger to Crash. "Given your past, Dicesh is right. You'll be leaving this ship, but you have a chance to explain and save this man's hide."

A snicker came from Joe then, causing everyone to look at him questioningly. "What? He said 'hide,' and he's a…you know. I mean, he takes people's…. c'mon, that's funny." Joe put his head down, avoiding further scrutinizing eye contact with any of them. "It's a little funny," he mumbled to himself.

Captain Braxis cleared his throat, looking back at Crash, who, looking at Joe, had nearly cracked a small smile. "So, Flying Fox, let's hear your story."

Crash took a deep breath, looking at the varying expressions of curious anticipation on each of their faces, and then she dove in. "It was toward the end of the war. The Seraphene had taken quite a bit of damage, ambushed by a group of marauding dragon riders to the southwest of Kil'Velhara in southern Westerlan. We had been forced to put her into the water while repairs were attempted to the flight mechanisms. It was then that we happened upon the Kalix Glory, a voyager class ship out of Senuvia. It was an exploring vessel, not even part of the conflict with the ogres and goblins of Westerlan, so it was relatively unarmed. She was easy pickin's. One shot of the Seraphene's arc cannon and the Glory was dead in the water, her sails ablaze. Honestly, we were afraid she was going to burn down to the water line. We even sprayed her down as we approached, trying to put the fire out. No spoils to be had if she went under too soon."

"What's an arc cannon?" Joe whispered, leaning over Tosh's shoulder.

"A large round device that shoots bolts of lightning," Tosh quickly whispered back, trying not to interrupt Crash's tale. It was too late, however. Everyone was looking at him and Joe.

"Oh," Joe answered, sounding no further informed. "What's lightning?"

Crash couldn't hold back the tiniest of smiles, and she stifled a giggle.

"Quiet," Dicesh boomed. "Finish your story," she snapped at Crash.

Crash squared her shoulders and leaned back against one of the walls, getting comfortable as she settled back into her story. "Turns out the lightning cannon had done in the Captain of the Kalix Glory. A much younger version of Franz, here, had stepped into the role of speaking for the crew.

They had hoisted a white flag as we approached and made no attempt to resist as my crew boarded. He offered to talk out a peaceful solution and even had his ship's cook prepare us a meal over which we could discuss the safe passage of his crew. Franz and I managed to quickly come to terms that would have seen his ship stripped of its goods and his crew left unharmed. That might have been that, but a member of his crew took offense to one of my men nipping some of the man's personal belongings. I guess Franz's man felt that his own stuff wasn't to be included as part of the Seraphene's agreed-upon haul.

Waves or wind, the dispute between the two came to a grim end. Before I could step in to stop the fighting that immediately erupted, all but two of the Glory's men were dead; Franz and the cook. Two of my men were dead as well, and out of spite for their deaths, I ran the cook through myself. For some reason, 'parlay,' I suppose, I couldn't bring myself to harm Franz. Still, I couldn't just let him go and maintain the respect of my men, so after clearing the Glory of anything even remotely of value, we set her to sink and left Franz behind to go down with her as her new Captain."

Joe piped up again, questioning Franz this time. "Why didn't you mention her or the Seraphene when you told us the story of how you got the claw in your ear?"

Franz, much more sedate and reflective now, took a moment before responding. "Wasn't the important part of the story then, eh lad? Anyway, as she says, wind or waves. The moment I recognized her, I thought it best not to set her on my scent. I figure I might be the only man she ever left alive after a boarding. Been a long while. If she didn't recognize me, I didn't want to tip her off, and if she did know who I was, I didn't want to give the Flying Fox a reason to finish the job. Guess I should have been more worried 'bout you lot. Saving me from another bloodthirsty crew, eh girl?"

"So why; why save him?" Dicesh snarled. "Seeing what he's become, what your mercy wrought, you could have redeemed yourself and, paradoxically, kept Captain Redtail's bloody reputation intact."

"Something about the encounter with the dragons before we came upon the Glory," Crash said quietly, staring again at the floor. Silence followed for a moment, with everyone in the room unsure how to respond. Dicesh huffed with frustration. Crash felt the need to explain further. "They aren't just beasts; they're intelligent, clever, and smarter than the ogre oafs that brutally tame them into servitude. A young one, not as experienced as the others, had crashed onto the deck of the Seraphene. Even with its wings broken and its rider dead, it fought fiercely and was smart enough to never once breathe out a lick of fire. If it had, the Seraphene, damaged as she was, would have exploded like a second sun in the sky."

"Smart? Sounds like the beast was foolish," Braxis interjected. "Weren't the marauders trying to take the Seraphene out of the sky?"

"Of course not," Crash said, sounding slightly disgusted at Braxis's lack of common sense. "They wanted whatever treasures might be in her hold. Blowing up an elven ship that size would have incinerated all of them, along with any cargo we might have had. No, this beast knew enough to fight its own instincts. It wanted to live; wanted its companions to live. Have you ever seen a dragon up close?"

"Not but a few ogres who can say that with the breath of the living, girl," Franz spoke up before any of the others could simply say no.

"They are beautiful. As terrifying as they can be, they are beautiful. When they're younger, as this one was, their scales are like translucent gems. The one on my ship was still quite young, as I said, so he hadn't entirely shed his camouflage colors yet, either. He was all blues and greens, shimmering like the ocean itself in the sun, and the underside of his wings were like a midnight sky made of satin, full of stars. When the end came, and mind you, by then, he had ripped apart three of my crew, and I wanted the beast dead and off of my ship, the look in its eyes, as I approached, wasn't the crazed, panicked look of a cornered, dying beast. It was anger, it was hopeless sadness, it was thought-filled sorrow for days it would never see, fear of death, fear of having failed its comrades, fear of me. I had seen the look on many a man just before I slit their throats, and it had never made me pause, not once, but to see that look on this magnificent creature, I suddenly hated who I was, what I was.

It was bleeding out onto my deck, and its blood was quickly eating through the Seraphene, and I swear the beast knew it. Just like it had avoided using its fire, it didn't seem to want its blood to cause the ship to explode either. It tried to drag itself over the side but was too weak. It took myself and nearly every crewman who wasn't fending off the other dragons, to push it off. Instead of making some pitiful cry, as some of the others harpooned out of the sky had, this one let out the mightiest bellow I've ever heard a dragon roar; a victory roar, and it let loose with a stream of flame that engulfed its whole body. The fire found the beast's wounds, and it was completely consumed by its own flames before it ever hit the water. It died on it's own terms." She looked up at the others then, tears streaming down her face. The black makeup around her eyes was beginning to bleed down her face. The others simply looked on silently. "Don't you understand? It had fought and died with nothing but honor. Even in death, its thoughts weren't for itself, for winning; they were for saving its fellows."

"But..." Joe interrupted, pausing to see if anyone was on the same thought path, "but it didn't."

"Didn't what?" Crash sniffed, wiping her dripping nose on the sleeve of her jacket.

Garen put a hand on Joe's shoulder, hoping that Joe would be smart enough not to complete his thought.

Joe just continued on. "It didn't save its friends. I mean, I'm new to all this giant-sized, fighting boat stuff, but you already told us how banged up your boat was when it came upon Franz and his bunch. I doubt that the dragon-riding bandits would have just let you go with you so close to defeat." He took a deep breath, not understanding the dismayed looks he was getting from the others, and plowed on. "So, clearly…" he was feeling a little proud of himself now that he had seen the point he was about to make and the others had not. "Clearly, you and your men must have killed all the other bandits and their beasts to get away. So, if you think about it, in the end, that dragon wasn't really so smart, right? By saving your ship, he doomed his dragon pals. So nothin' to feel bad about there, right?" Joe looked around triumphantly, waiting for some acknowledgment of his brilliant and empathetic observation.

Most were staring at him in some degree of disbelief. Tosh had his face buried in one hand, shaking his head as he tried to process his combined embarrassment and annoyance for Joe. Dicesh's appearance had softened, but she kept her gaze upon Crash as though she had not heard Joe speak. Crash was wide-eyed, staring at Joe, taking short breaths. She was trying to hold back the barrage of sobs trying to explode from her as though she were a capped volcano.

Franz gave a small chuckle. "Yup, like this lad a lot. One should never let good sense get in the way of the truth. The way I hears it, the Seraphene and her crew went an' hunted down the rest o' them riders' kin all through Westerlan in retaliation for the beating they took that day. Nearly killed off all five clans. Not but a few ugly old bastards from each clan left now, an' some o' them don't even have no dragon to ride no more."

Crash pulled herself together but had to look at the floor to continue. Her voice was small and tinged with the tiniest bit of frustrated anger. "Not with me at the helm, she didn't. That dragon was a noble, thoughtful beast of feeling, and I…I was just the heartless monster that had brought about its end." She looked up at Joe then, sniffing back her sadness into some manner of confidence again. "And the end of all of its fellows, that day." Wiping her tears away with the back of one hand while she reached with the other into the collar of her green and white leather top, she fished out a gold chain upon which a heart-shaped, smooth, aqua-colored gem hung. "I found this on the deck of the Seraphene just before I decided to spare Franz and his crew. It's one of the dragon's scales. It may be the only heart I have, but it's the one that spared this man." She turned directly to Dicesh then, the strength in her voice returned. "I didn't spare this man's life that day just to see him murdered now."

"You'll understand, girl, if my former ship's captain and his dead cook aren't so appreciative of your moment of reformation; nice a bauble as that is." Franz did little to mask the contempt in his voice despite his sickly, sweet smile.

Dicesh did not appreciate being challenged, whatever Crash's reasons, and a look of anger flared across her face again.

Franz interjected again just as Dicesh opened her mouth to speak. "In my own defense, Marm, Captain-sir, I never agreed with the actions or activities of any of the previous three captains of the Harmaton nor their crews. I simply go where the ship goes, regardless of who is at her wheel. My loyalty has always been to this ship what saved me and will remain so 'til my last breath."

"Fat lie, that is," Barry said flatly. "Where was your loyalty to the ship when we were trying to work her flight machinery?"

"A true gentleman keeps a lady's secrets, don't he? And a fine lady the Harmaton is if you take her good care." Franz laughed, "'Sides, I expected it wouldn't be too long before the Flying Fox showed you how to fly her."

"Sorry 'bout that," Crash sniffed, looking at Tosh and Barry, "should have helped out from the start. I'm afraid the celestialite gas vents are seized up now; probably melted shut. You might be able to put her down by filling the void head, but until you can vent the gas orb, it's probably better just to keep her in the air. She won't steer well 'cept in the air, for now, anyway."

"Keep me on as quartermaster, and I'll help you get this gal runnin' proper. Teach everyone on board how to fly her, too. Don't much care who's givin' the orders, just want t'keep this 'ol gal proper." Franz was still keeping a safe distance from the bars of his cell.

Captain Braxis turned to Franz, "Why such a loyalty to this ship?"

"The harpy," Franz said flatly. "One day, that bitch is going to wake up, and when she does, I'm going to be there to look her in the eye as I put this through her salted heart." He gave the talon in his ear a little flick.

"If that day comes," Dicesh said in a low, flat, menacing tone, "I'll hold her down myself, but understand this, you old fool, if we open this cage, your loyalty is to us alone and should I find you betraying that trust, with the slightest breath or twitch, I'll toss the harpy to the winds and nail your sorry carcass in her place."

"Seems fair enough," Franz said lightly, as though he had just made a trade of a basket of fish for a basket of apples.

"And you'll serve better as boatswain. I have a quartermaster," Captain Braxis put an arm around Dicesh. "You'll answer to her just as you answer to me."

"But you," Dicesh turned on Crash. "When we reach Cravenhuddle, you'll be leaving with the bladesman and his companions. This deceptive persona makes it clear that our trust in you was gravely misplaced."

Crash didn't answer, continuing to stare at the floor. She gave a small nod to show she understood and choked down another swell of emotions and tears.

Joe started to protest on Crash's behalf, feeling that they were being grossly unfair to the one person who had just kept them from falling out of the sky. Braxis calmly but firmly warned him that he had no say in the matter, and that was that. Dicesh unlocked the cell door, letting Franz out.

One by one, everyone made their way to the upper decks to get on with their day until there were only Joe and a very dejected-looking Crash left by the jail cell. They both stood in silence for a bit, Joe looking around for something to say or some means of a comfortable escape. Crash just kept staring at the floor.

"So you were some sort of captain then…" Joe started awkwardly but was interrupted by a frustrated, growling outburst from Crash, who stormed past him and up the ramp, a fresh bout of tears streaming more black streaks down the white makeup of her cheeks.

The rest of the day went by slowly for Crash. Joe, Ugor, Adriga, and even the twins continually tried to talk to her or cheer her up. Crash, really just wanted some time alone.

Runara, meanwhile, like Crash, had been keeping to herself as well. She had continued to use the guest quarters on her own without protest from anyone. The other brookshins had grown comfortable with their more social arrangements in the crew quarters, or perhaps they simply had some sense of chivalry, given her emotional state over Drix.

That night, having taken all she could of trying to dodge the others, Crash knocked on Runara's door, asking if she could hide in her room. Runara, reluctantly, let her in. Seeing the black streaks of makeup, she could hardly be so heartless as to turn away someone who had clearly been crying at least as much as she had been herself. Nothing more pathetic, she thought, than a crying clown.

Though neither had much to say at first, slowly, polite exchanges of words evolved into conversation. The topics were light at first, covering nothing much more profound than how beautiful the sunset was through the room's one multi-paned window. Within an hour, however, the two were baring the emotional demons that had been gnawing away at the spirits of each of them for some time. As the hours passed, their stories became full of tears and laughter, divulging their biggest hurts, greatest joys, fears, and dreams until their demons were tamed, if not exorcized. They each slept better that night than they had in days, curled up together like a couple of long-lost sisters in Runara's bed.

* * * * * * * * * * * * * * * * *

The following morning, Joe was up earlier than the others, just as he had been for most of the trip. He looked forward to watching the sunrise, finding it as mesmerizing as its setting every night. He greeted the helmsman of the night's skeleton crew as he made his way to a spot near the ship's stern. A couple days back, he had stacked two small crates in the spot to use as a seat, and the new crew had been considerate enough to leave them be. Joe sat himself down and marveled at the dazzling red and yellow display. The voice of a lone gull greeted the sun as it peeked over the watery horizon. It was all so magically serene, Joe thought.

The lone gull that Joe had heard distantly glided into view, rising up alongside the ship right in front of Joe. Pacing the flying vessel gave the illusion that it was hovering in one spot. Joe could nearly reach out and touch it, and he tried. The gull rose above Joe, trying to get a better look at what might be in his hand, but seeing that it was empty, gave a disappointed cry and soared on further up the ship's length. Another gull cry answered it, followed by another and another. The moment of serenity had certainly passed. The flock of seagulls concentrated near the ship's bow then, and Joe could see Ugor and Adriga standing at the heart of the gulls' interest.

As Joe made his way to the bow, he could see Ugor tossing bits of stale bread and leftovers from dinner the night before. Adriga, meanwhile, was bobbing his head with his arms spread, occasionally mimicking a seagull call. It looked quite ridiculous.

"What are you doing?" Joe asked, truly curious.

"Asking the seagulls if we're getting close to Cravenhuddle," Adriga responded as though it was pretty obvious.

"You're not-so-secretly a bird, right? Wouldn't it be easier to talk to them as a bird?"

"No," Adriga shrugged, "seagulls don't have much respect for parrots. They think we're a bunch of pompous, neurotic, know-it-alls."

"They aren't hardly wrong," Ugor added with a small laugh. Adriga shot him a small sneer.

Joe laughed, "So, what are they saying, then?"

"Mostly, they're just shouting 'over here,' trying to get some bread, but a few of them have said there is a town at the water's edge about an hour from here directly ahead. That ought to be Cravenhuddle."

As good news as that was, it turned out to be sooner than anyone had anticipated. Despite Franz's assistance, Tosh and Barry were not able to get the ship into a condition fit to set down in the water. Worse, Franz seemed certain that they wouldn't be finding the material and equipment needed to make the repairs in a small town like Cravenhuddle.

The only option they would have for dropping Joe and the others off was the ship's gossaphyr gun pod. The gun pod was designed to be a small cargo hoist as well. It could be disengaged from the bottom of the ship and lowered on a long, thick chain. It was meant to allow the Harmaton to pick up small supplies, like food or fresh water from lakes, but it had the capacity to transport, comfortably, up to four people. It would be a slow way for Joe and the rest to disembark, but it was certainly a better option than Garen had suggested. Garen had looked a little disappointed when they had told him that he would not be getting the chance to dive into the ocean and swim to shore.

As the next hour ticked away, the rest of the group slowly gathered on the deck, crowding onto the bow and waiting for the town to come into view. After half an hour, a range of mountains was visible. Twenty minutes later, the smoke and activity of the small town were evident. Small fishing boats could be seen in the water below, their tiny little occupants working their nets. Joe found seeing this familiar sight from such a perspective completely fascinating. He was leaning dangerously over the rail, trying to keep the little boats in his view.

Soon after that, the coast and Cravenhuddle came into view.

Franz sauntered up behind the others as they looked out at the speck of civilization. "Don't get too excited yet. We're a good half hour away, and that's if we keep the wind. By the look o' the smoke, there's a crosswind ahead. Could slow us a bit."

"Seagulls have a poor sense of time and distance," Adriga commented quietly to Joe as if he was concerned that one of the seagulls might overhear him.

The day crew was soon out, along with Captain Braxis and Dicesh. After some discussion among Braxis, Dicesh, and Franz, it was decided that they would bypass the town and take Joe and his group further in, directly to Nashtar's keep, since stopping over Cravenhuddle wasn't going to do them any good. With Franz's guidance, the crew managed to get the ship to drop down to just two hundred feet as they approached the seaside edge of Cravenhuddle. So it was, then, that everyone watched the sleepy little town drift by below.

A row of two and three-story stone buildings formed something of a wall between the town and the sea. The building looked like misshapen blocks, haphazardly stacked upon one another. Though apparently strong and solid, given their long-weathered appearance, their seemingly improvised architecture gave the impression that they might topple over should someone happen to lean on them in the wrong spot. The dark wooden buildings that made up the rest of the town were of similar crooked construction, leaning out at dangerous angles over the narrow streets paved in wooden slats.

A few children playing in one of the streets noticed the ship and excitedly began shouting and waving. To their delight, everyone looking over the rails waved back. The children chased after the ship to the short stone wall that marked the town's inland edge.

Nashtar's keep was clearly visible by then. Earlier, it had been masked by a dense layer of fog drifting down from the surrounding mountains. The fog had dissipated, but the keep was still in the dark shadow of a heavy cloud cover. It gave the uniquely constructed tower an even more foreboding appearance than the looming, ebony stone structure already conveyed. Though in some disrepair, the tower did not look to be the war-ravaged husk that Runara had described.

The keep, which had been built atop a fifty-foot tall butte on the edge of the river Katsfyr, sat upon four upside-down pyramids, the points of which each appeared to be buried in the tops of four pillar-like guard towers. Though it appeared so, the central tower did not truly sit upon the pyramids but continued down through the large square platform they formed. Its enormous, peaked entrance was nearly hidden among the four guard towers. Built upon the platform formed by the upturned pyramid bases surrounding the central tower was a series of nine smaller round towers. Similar in construction and appearance to the four guard towers at the base, they were more narrow, with large glassed-in ogival windows on each level. They stood nearly their own diameter out from the central tower. All but two of the towers, the seventh and ninth, looked to have been reconstructed in a loose masonry style compared to the smooth appearance of the central tower. The first tower was two stories tall, and each of the following towers was a story higher, save for the fourth and fifth towers, which were mostly hollowed-out half-shell rubbles. The ninth and tallest of these was topped entirely by a multifaceted atrium that spanned, with a decoratively sculpted arched base, across the gap into the central tower.

The ornate wrought iron architecture of the atrium was slightly mismatched with the rest of the keep. It was one of three significant modifications Nashtar had made to the keep since taking possession so long ago. The most apparent addition sat at the very top of the central tower. It was a domed observatory with an enormous brass telescope protruding from the dome's opening. A web of metal scaffolding supported the observatory above the third modification to the tower. A large, silver-looking sphere, nearly half the tower's diameter, sat upon a pedestal of gold. The central structure of the orb and the observatory was surrounded by three enormous black metallic fins. They were rooted to the stone disc platform that topped the tower, stretching up in sweeping arcs, coming to points just below the base of the observatory. It made the observatory look as though it was being held aloft by the talons of an enormous beast.

It was this clawed structure at the top of the tower that had caught the attention of both Crash and Franz as they watched the growing form of the tower from the bow of the Harmaton.

Joe, noticing the shocked look on Crash's face, was glad someone else was seeing what he was seeing. "Whole thing kinda looks like a giant zerd," he snickered like a young teenager.

"A what?" Adriga questioned from nearby.

"I think he means a phallus," clarified Drix, who was just walking up to join the group on the bow. He grabbed his crotch, giving it a little shake just for further clarity. "and it does, really."

Joe laughed, happy that someone else was seeing the joke.

"No, we have to turn," Crash said quietly, barely loud enough for anyone to hear, with more than a little trepidation in her voice.

Many of the others were laughing and making silly comments about the keep's phallic nature, but not Franz and he was now looking at Crash with some concern. He had heard her, and it confirmed his own worry.

"Shut it, you fool arses!" Franz shouted. Everyone went quiet then, shooting Franz quizzical or annoyed looks. "Is it what it looks like, lass?"

Joe snickered again.

"It is," Crash said emphatically, ignoring Joe as he failed at trying to stifle another burst of laughter. "We have to bring her about. Too much momentum!" She wasn't making sense to anyone but Franz. "Turn 'er about!" She shouted then.

"You heard her; turn this bitch starboard!" Franz shouted.

"Belay that!" Captain Braxis's voice boomed then before Franz's order could make its way down the ship to the wheel. He was at the base of the steps of the bow's forecastle. "You two had best remember whose ship this is, and I won't stand for any attempts to delay our time to the wizard's keep," he said sternly as he bounded up the steps. "I'm not keen to see you on your way, Grashon," Braxis's voice softened, "but I'd prefer spending as little time in the wizard's territory as possi—"

The ball below the observatory at the top of the tower was sparkling now with a blue light. Though Braxis had never seen an arc cannon in his long years, the mind of the original Morimar Braxis he had consumed certainly had.

"Blast my fool ass!" Captain Braxis exclaimed softly to himself.

"I believe that's the intention, sir," Franz said in a smug, sarcastic tone.

Braxis growled in frustration as he turned to shout out the order for the crewman at the wheel to turn the ship hard to the right. Though Franz had been giving them pointers and guiding them through the operations of flying the Harmaton more properly than they had been, the crew was unprepared for such a dramatic course change. More than a simple tack, shifting the booms was not enough; the wings needed to be adjusted to keep the ship stable. As the skyboat turned, more directly catching the wind, it began to lean steeply to the right. Everyone on the bow clung as hard as they could to the railing. Adriga, who had already been leaning dangerously far over the side, trying to see what all the fuss was about, fell overboard. Joe tried to grab Adriga's leg as he went over, but it happened too fast; the beast tamer was gone before Joe could get a grip.

There was, at first, a commotion of alarm from the group. A crewman up in the sails, clinging to the rigging with all his might, seeing Adriga fall, gave the cry of "Man overboard!"

"Whoohoo-oo-oo-oo!" Adriga called out as he fell. Then suddenly, his form shrank, and a parrot was in his place, flapping furiously to catch the wind. He was soon out of view somewhere below the sharply banking ship.

Crash, Braxis, and Franz hadn't taken their eyes off the tower. There was a blinding, bright blue flash from the sparkling orb at the top of Nashtar's tower. It was almost immediately followed by an ear-splitting boom and the awful cracking clap of the ship's left wing exploding into a cloud of splinters. The ship shook. The canvas of the left wing had incinerated, leaving nothing but a swarm of glowing embers that caught the wind and flitting about in an orange flurry across the deck. Black smoke billowed from the small stump of the wing's armature, trying to become a fire. A positive side effect of the wing loss was that the Harmaton was righting itself.

"We'll be out of range before it has another charge," Crash shouted. "But we need to drop all topsail and close up the starboard wing."

Braxis frowned at the overstep of the volume of her voice but knew she was right. He gave a nod to Franz, and soon, the two were barking orders to the crew to do just as Crash had suggested. The Harmaton limped safely away from the tower and its arc cannon.

Dicesh was at the bow then, checking first that Braxis was alright but then turning to Crash.

"You are still leaving this ship, Flying Fox." Her voice was cold, but her heart seemed less behind her words than before.

Several discussions broke out simultaneously among the group on the bow then. There were suggestions that Crash be allowed to stay aboard. Suggestions that Joe abandon his quest for home and Runara her quest for vengeance. But neither Joe nor Runara were willing. Joe brought up the possibility of still approaching the wizard's keep as a circus troop, which mostly went ignored. Concern was brought up then that any approach by ground or air would be met with a bolt of lightning from the tower. This seemed to be a problem the group had no solution for, and so the talk moved on to the matter of the state of the ship. Several in the group suggested going back to Cravenhuddle, at the very least, to make repairs if they could.

It was at this point in the discussion that Adriga came flapping up the length of the deck, landing on Braxis's shoulder. All conversation came to an immediate halt, replaced by joyful greetings to the bird from all on the bow, save Franz.

Adriga silently went through his post-flight preening as if the entire group was not there, silently staring at him with waiting smiles. He eventually looked up from his grooming, a little surprised to see everyone looking at him.

"Hello," he said, sounding like nothing more than a trained parrot. It was met with laughter from all. "The keep is empty," he said then, punctuating his statement by picking out a bit of feather fluff from under his left wing.

"What do you mean? They just fired upon us." Braxis cocked his head, trying to face the bird on his shoulder.

"No guards on the tower tops. No guards at the gate. Big monster at the end of the road."

"Monster? That's a little vague," Joe complained. "Anything we can sneak around?"

"No! Bad," Adriga flapped angrily. "BIG monster!"

"Okay, okay, big monster, we got it. So how are we going to get in there?"

"Through the top." Adriga squawked. "The dome is open."

"That's brilliant!" Crash said excitedly. "We were going to disembark using the gun pod anyway. We can just lower ourselves in."

Tosh interrupted her there. "Am I missing something? We'll be blasted to bits if we take the ship anywhere near that tower. We're lucky we didn't explode, going by your stories earlier."

"So we don't let ourselves be seen," Crash offered. "If Adriga is right about the castle being unguarded, then chances are the arc cannon is set for proximity fire. Anything larger than a bird coming in under a kraken's arm away is going to get it. Big objects, like rocs, dragons, or us, seem like we have a league and a half before we set it off. Pretty standard."

"Right," Tosh agreed, while the others looked a little confused, "that's what I just said. We can't go near it."

Crash gave Tosh's cheek a little pat and planted a little kiss on the tip of his bulbous nose. "Knowers," she said with a sarcastic snicker. "You're right; we can't get close, but the proximity detection of the arc cannon relies on us being visible. So, we skirt around her range 'til we reach that blanket of clouds coming off the mountains. We'll empty the ship's void head a little, get her up into the cloud cover, and then sail ourselves over and anchor this lady right on top of the wizard's big ol' zerd." She shot Joe a sideways glance and a small smile as she said it.

"Ha! Told you all," Joe said triumphantly. Drix let out a humored huff.

Some argument followed then, initially about the morally wrong approach of breaking into the wizard's home, but eventually just about how they would know when they were directly over Nashtar's tower if they could not see it. Despite Tosh and Garen's moral concerns, a plan was agreed upon.

Steering the Harmaton was more precarious, with one wing missing and the other retracted, but it took just five minutes to circle the ship around the tower and set her above the layer of cloud. Crash volunteered to strap herself into the gun pod, which was then lowered until she was just below the cloud layer. At the wheel, Braxis kept in communication with her through the pop-up console, steering the ship according to her course correction updates. It was agreed that at the slightest sparkle of light from the arc cannon, they would reel her in, but it was hoped that she would blend with the cloud enough to ride it out all the way to the tower. They were flying against the wind now, which would make the Harmaton's course a slow-going zigzag path, but that was better than approaching too fast. The wind also caused the dangling gun pod to swing quite dramatically. Though it would have made most of the others ill, for a seasoned aeronaut like Crash, it seemed like nothing more than a relaxing sit in a rocking chair.

Taking Crash's cues, Braxis serpentined the Harmaton directly toward the tower. A multi-arched stone ramp wound twice around the butte before reaching the tower's gate. As Crash approached the tower, she could see what must have been the enormous beast that Adriga had mentioned seeing. At this height, it was hard to make out its features or even judge its size, but it certainly seemed to be larger than King Kotep. Its skin was a mottled mash of pinks, reds, blues, blacks, and browns, with random patches of hair. It was lumbering up the ramp on its six thick legs, leaving a black trail behind it as it went. From what she could tell, the creature seemed to have two heads, one at either end of its body, but that may simply have been an illusion of its body shape. Crash didn't linger on looking at the creature too long, keeping herself focused on guiding the Harmaton to the tower. She was glad they were not taking Tosh's more civilized approach of simply walking up and knocking on the front door. Not only would it have been a much longer trip up the winding ramp, but avoiding whatever that beast turned out to be was probably best.

Just as Adriga had said, the tower seemed unguarded, abandoned even. The sliding closure to the opening of the observatory looked to be bent and rusted into an open position. Much more in keeping with Runara's description, at this proximity, it was clear that much of the entire tower's stonework was in disrepair. There were even large holes punched in portions of the lower guard towers, remnant scars of a long past battle, never repaired.

Perhaps Nashtar had died long ago as well, Crash thought.

She gave the call to slow to docking speed. The arc cannon showed no signs of having detected their approach, just as she had hoped. She hit the release lever for the anchor and called for it to be lowered seven aych (approximately forty feet). The three-pronged, hinged anchor scraped along the top of the dome as the Harmaton drifted perfectly on target over the tower. The anchor bounced off the edge of the dome's door, spinning and swinging out into the open air. There was nothing Crash could do to get the anchor back on target but watch helplessly as the anchor swung in an arc, skirting around the top of the dome. She didn't want to have to try this again.

"Weight of the chain!" She called into the communication horn. It was a call for the anchor to be allowed to fall free for the entire length of the chain.

The anchor dropped with a deep, echoing clang on the dome. Any stealth they may have had must undoubtedly have been lost, Crash thought. The chain continued clattering through the gun pod's central column at a near-deafening level. It hit the edge of the dome's opening close to the protruding telescope, making an awful racket. At first, the slack bit of chain followed the anchor as it began sliding down the dome, but the bulk of the rapidly falling chain tipped into the opening. Soon, the chain inside the dome was out-weighing the anchor. A moment later, the anchor scraped its way back up the dome but then caught one of its three flat arms on the edge of the door.

Back in her days as a pirate captain, she would have called it a successful drop. It would be enough to hold the Harmaton in place, but they needed to be able to pull the chain tight if they were going to be able to lower the group down in the pod. She would have to get down there and move the anchor, unhook it, and drop it down into the observatory. Getting herself down there was going to be a trick in itself, but once down there, she wouldn't be able to move the anchor herself.

Crash disengaged the ring lock on the gun pod. The outer ring of the console on the main deck lit up red, indicating that the pod was set to lower. A brief argument between Braxis and Crash ended with Crash turning off the communicator console and Braxis shouting for Joe and the others to be ready to disembark. Adriga was chortling in Braxis's ear then.

"Off with you then." Braxis's tone was full of frustration as he brushed the animal trainer off his shoulder, causing Adriga to fly off.

Below the ship, Crash flipped the lever that set the pod slowly crawling down the anchor chain. A flaw in the plan became quickly evident. The Harmaton had already drifted a little off-center, and as a result, the pod was lowering a little off-target. Were she not strapped in, the only other thing keeping the weighty glass pod from tipping over and dumping Crash to her death was that the chain still had plenty of slack, which also meant that the pod was dragging the chain back out of the observatory opening. She had just ten feet to go, but if she continued much further, she would be too low on the smooth dome to climb up and might pull too much chain out of the hole as well.

It was going to be a tricky jump. Crash wouldn't be able to roll out of it, but she would have to diffuse the impact somehow. She unstrapped herself and began rocking the pod. Her intention was not to swing the pod but to get it tipping up and down in the hope that its weight would more than compensate for the force of her jumping and propel her forward. It worked, but too well. She had been aiming for landing on the door by the anchor, but she shot just a little too far, landing on the very edge of the opening. With so much momentum, her instincts pushed her reflexively into a leaping forward summersault. The move diffused her momentum but landed her on the steeply angled brass telescope on all fours. Finding herself sliding down immediately, she pushed off with her hands, getting herself, briefly, to her feet, enough to make a desperate jump to the dangling loop of the anchor chain. The chain, already swaying from her jump and then tossed about by her impact, had been a little tricky to grab, but she managed, torturing her hands in the process as she slid two feet down the chain before establishing a grip. Painfully, she pulled herself up the chain. The dull ache in her hands was sapping her strength. She was able to reach the lip of the opening, but she wasn't going to be able to pull herself up.

Crash looked down into the dark depths of the observatory. It was hard to judge how far down it might be — too far, she knew, in any case — or what sort of surface or objects she would land on if she let herself drop. Whatever the scenario, it was going to be painful and likely somewhat fatal, at best.

"They don't call me Crash for nothin'," she muttered to herself with a nervous little laugh.

Just as she had mustered herself to let go, a hand reached over the edge of the opening, grabbing her by the forearm.

"Dicesh may have kicked you out of the circus, girl, but this won't be your last performance." Adriga greeted her with a broad smile as he helped Crash hoist herself out onto the top of the dome.

Together, the two of them quickly managed to drop the anchor down into the observatory. Crash gave her hands a stretch and a shake, getting ready to climb down the chain, but Adriga stopped her.

"Makes more sense for me to go down there and secure it. I should be able to manage one more change today and just fly back out." Without giving Crash the opportunity to argue, he shimmied down the chain. A few moments later, he shouted, his voice echoing in the hollow dome. "When I say so, pull. I need more slack."

At about that time, the pod began crawling back up the chain. Crash and Adriga pulled hard on the chain. Crash nearly pulled herself off the dome, losing her balance more than once. They managed, however, to get the few extra inches that Adriga needed to secure the anchor.

A few minutes later, the gun pod was coming back down with Drix at a less than ideally safe angle. It didn't bother Drix, who casually had hold of the gunner straps and was leaning precariously over the side.

"Host, I mean Morimar, thought you might need my help." He said to Crash in his usual detached, casual tone. Kicking the lever to stop the pod just before it contacted the top of the dome, he hopped out, keeping a firm grip on the chain. The dome rang a little as he landed on the door, as though it had been struck by an enormous hammer, and the door dented slightly where he landed. He gave the chain a mighty yank and let it go. "That should do it," he said, brushing his hands together. "What else you need?"

Crash and Drix watched as the chain slowly cut a self-healing path through the grey cloud above, indicating that the Harmaton was moving as a result of Drix's pull on the chain. The chain's progress slowed until it eventually came to a halt at a point where the pod was sitting exactly upright. Crash gave a little, girlish giggle, impressed by the precision of Drix's feat of strength.

"Probably gonna need you to stay down here to keep 'er straight until they all get down," she said to him.

"Got nothing else to do." He gave a little shrug. "So you were a pirate, huh?" There was no judgment in his voice, and he was still staring up at the cloud.

"Yup," Crash said flatly. "Nasty one too. Could have done with a big guy like you on my crew." She shot Drix a sideways glance and a smile. "But you're too nice."

"Ya, you've probably got that right," Drix said with a warm smile, turning to her. "Going to miss our crazy little clown girl."

"Gonna miss you too," she said with a sad smile and no hint of the manic clown character in her voice."

The gun pod started to ascend back up toward the cloud.

Drix sat on the edge of the opening, his legs dangling into the darkness. For a few moments, there was just the sound of the wind accompanying each of their nostalgic contemplations.

"What are you going to be now?" Drix broke the silence.

Crash sat down beside Drix, watching the gun pod as it disappeared into the cloud. "Not sure; something good, I hope."

Chapter 17

Disembarking had gone reasonably smoothly, given the circumstances. Heartfelt and tearful goodbyes had been said in the lower hold by those remaining on the ship to those departing. Dicesh made one final attempt to convince Kord to stay, but he explained his debt to Runara, which she understood and respected. Runara, meanwhile, could hardly pull herself away from the musicians who chose to remain with the circus, hoping to have far less adventure than Runara and Joe's quest had brought them in the past two weeks.

Adriga had stayed at the bottom of the telescope to catch the others as they slid down. Tosh had been the first to go down, sliding on his belly, feet first, laughing at the adventure of it all. Runara had considered just staying with the circus rather than sliding down the telescope, especially after being put into a state of shaking fear by the swaying pod ride down with Joe, Garen, and Tosh. This was despite her sliding into much better-lit conditions than the knower. Tosh had brought two lamps from the ship and had the observatory chamber illuminated before any of the others came down. With the help of both Crash and Drix, Runara straddled the telescope, screaming even before Drix let her go.

Garen had simply leaped onto the sky spying device unassisted, gracefully sliding down on one hip. At the bottom, he vaulted himself over Adriga, who stood on the viewing platform, and landed with a rolling summersault onto the metal floored chamber further below. Not wanting to be outdone, Joe jumped unassisted as well, but without much of a plan. He landed upright, riding down the steeply angled telescope, in a precarious squat, his arms flailing to maintain his balance. He crashed into Adriga at the bottom, his momentum nearly carrying him and Adriga over the railing of the viewing platform.

Runara's drama aside, the most traumatized among those leaving was Koobara. The day before, sad though it was for him, Adriga had already agreed that if Koobara wanted to go with Kord, that was simply the way it would have to be. Kord and Koobara had become inseparable, and when Kord squeezed himself into the gun pod to be lowered, Koobara quickly leaped in as well. Once the pod began descending, swinging freely on the chain, Koobara seemed to have second thoughts, at least about being in the precariously swaying pod. The cat's anguished howls were equally pathetic in their tone and frightening in their volume. Any remote chance that the group's entrance into the tower was still going unnoticed seemed unlikely. The pod was still well over ten feet above the dome when Koobara decided to risk jumping rather than spend another moment in the pod. The jungle cat landed gracefully on the telescope and was at the bottom of the chamber in two easy bounds. Landing near Garen, Koobara gave the monk a small growl, prompting Garen to step aside. Koobara slinked along the perimeter of the chamber as if on a hunt, eventually settling into an unlit portion of the chamber and began grooming itself as it tried to regain its composure.

In contrast to the dramatic slides and leaps the others had made going down the telescope, Kord's method was far less frantic but perhaps the most impressive. Waving Drix's assistance off, he picked up a rather startled and vehemently protesting Crash. He simply hopped onto the telescope before Drix or Crash could do anything about it and walked down the telescope as though gravity had simply shifted for him to the giant spyglass. Crash's protests, meanwhile, quickly shifted to delighted giggles. Reaching the bottom, Kord leaned down and gently handed Crash over to a much impressed and relieved Adriga, who had failed in recruiting both Tosh and Joe to help him catch Kord. The manhunter then leaped to the lower part of the chamber, landing surprisingly softly, and strode over to comfort Koobara.

"It is a shame that none of you can remain in our circus." Adriga had said then, trying to stifle the tears welling in his reddening eyes. He gave Crash a strong, lingering hug.

A thumping sound came from above. The group looked up to see Drix give them a wave from the already ascending gun pod. Adriga had Garen dislodge the Harmaton's anchor, and it quickly drifted up and out of the dome.

"Though I've known most of you only briefly, I will miss you all. May the world spirit guide your instincts, and may your instincts guide you to a destiny of joy." He spread his arms wide as if to pull them all into a collective hug. His entire body began to glow with a faint, sparkling red light. A moment later, he shrank down to his parrot form and loudly flapped his way out of the observatory opening, quickly disappearing into the cloud cover.

A few moments of silence followed. Crash was still staring up at the opening, though there was nothing to be seen now but the low, light grey cloud. Joe clapped his hands together loudly, breaking the silence. The jarring sound echoed off of the observatory's lofty dome, drawing the frowning or surprised faces of his companions immediately in his direction.

"So, who's ready to get us a powersword?" Joe grabbed one of the lamps and handed it to Tosh, giving him a hearty, encouraging slap on the chest. "Now, this should be a bit of an adventure."

His adventure stalled rather quickly. There did not appear to be any doors leading out of the observatory. The group looked around in all directions, seemingly hoping that a door would magically pop up. Soon, they started groping about at the walls and floor, hoping to discover some sort of secret hatch. It was Tosh who determined that a panel on one side of the giant telescope platform was actually a sliding door of sorts, opened by pushing a small, inconspicuous button next to it. When the door first slid open, most of the group dismissed the small room revealed as a closet or unused storage room of some variety.

It was Tosh again who determined that it was a lift, citing the lever within the door and the very narrow gap in the floor through which one could see the dome of the arc cannon below. Joe, Garen, and he went in first, closed the door, and dropped the lever. The walls stayed in place, but the floor and ceiling dropped, and the three men were taken with them. Clearing the walls, the three found themselves in a finely meshed cage descending through the arc cannon, which was not the sphere it had appeared to be from outside. In truth, it was a toroid, and the pedestal upon which it sat was a thickly walled, hollow tube. Electricity arced from the toroid as they passed through it, dispersing across the surface of the cage. The three men huddled closely in the center of the lift, trying to avoid being anywhere near the sides as they snapped and crackled with luminous energy.

As the lift cage reached the floor below, new walls slid into place, concealing the cage mesh again from the occupants. The door slid open, revealing a green-lit room full of buzzing and whirring machines. Some of these crackled with electricity arcing between their components. Others had panels of glowing crystal knobs and metal switches. Large metal tubes ran between the machines or from a machine to the ceiling or down into the floor. One pipe that ran up the stonework wall had a small valve that would hiss with a stream of steam at random intervals. As a result, the air in the room was rather thick and muggy. Some manner of moss, or perhaps a wildly out-of-control form of purple mold, covered many portions of the walls. A pipe, much thinner than the others, ran across the ceiling, disappearing into opposite walls. A thick blue fluid dripped from a small crack in the pipe. Each drop bubbled, hissed, and sizzled as it hit the stone floor, quickly evaporating. A small, smooth, bowl-shaped divot had formed on the floor where the fluid fell.

Garen remained in the lift, taking it back up to the observatory. Tosh excitedly pulled out his journal and began feverishly sketching down all he could. Joe wandered about the room, reaching a hand out now and then to touch a nob, switch, or lever, and every time, the action would be intercepted by an emphatic "Ah!"," Ah, ah!" or "Uh, uh, uh!" or a simple stern "No" from Tosh. Joe was undaunted, however, and the multitude of things to try to fiddle with was simply too tempting.

"Stop it!" Tosh finally shouted, growing frustrated as Joe again reached for another switch. "We do not know what any of this machinery does. Playing with it could be quite dangerous."

Joe snapped his hand back from the equipment, frowning silently back at Tosh. "I'm not the one that nearly broke the flying boat," he muttered defiantly to himself. If Tosh heard him, he made no indication of it.

Looking a little defeated, Joe proceeded to shuffle about listlessly, pouting like an admonished child. A few moments later, seeing that Tosh was again fully absorbed in his sketching, Joe, a small, spiteful smile creeping onto his face, shot a hand out, quickly flicking a random switch. This particular panel had what appeared to be a round window in it. The window would glow intermittently with blue light but ceased to do so the moment Joe hit the switch. A small shrill bell gave a short ring from elsewhere in the room.

Tosh whipped around, facing Joe, who had slapped on a ridiculously innocent face. "What did you do? What did you touch?" Tosh demanded.

Joe struck as casual a posture as he could muster, simply shaking his head negatively and shrugging his shoulders. Tosh was about to make more of it when the door on the lift compartment reopened, and Runara and Crash emerged. Garen remained inside yet again, taking the lift back up to fetch Kord and Koobara.

"What, exactly, is our plan?" Runara asked Joe as she stepped from the lift. "This place seems to be abandoned, and if it is, I have nothing to gain by coming here."

"It may not be entirely abandoned," Tosh offered. "Someone has been maintaining these devices." He sidestepped around the dripping blue fluid as he spoke. "Well, running if not maintaining. So, I suspect there may yet be a good chance of finding the wizard here. Whether he'll be willing to help you put together one of the power swords and one of the three forbidden swords, at that, is another matter. Stop that!" he shouted then, distracted by Crash, who had taken to the same switch-flipping exploration of the room that Joe had earlier.

"I honestly don't care about the sword," Runara said sharply. She looked at Joe then, realizing her harshness a little too late, "I mean, I want you to get home, but understand that the only reason I'm here is to ask for Nashtar's help in avenging our family."

"Right," Joe said, fiddling with the latch on a large, flat, green metal door that appeared to be the only door leading from the room. He frowned a little as the door seemed locked. "Kill the king," he continued, turning his attention fully to Runara. "That ought to make a good conversation starter with your grandpappy anyway; get him on our side. Then, when he's all swept up in the emotion of being reunited with his long lost kin and the chance to help you with your — what did big n' slimy call it?"

"Blood quest," Runara said with an annoyed huff, walking toward him and the door.

"Right, blood quest!" Joe repeated with dramatic enthusiasm. "We already know your grandpappy doesn't much care for kings, so with you and your blood quest, he ought to be in one heck of a good mood. Then I'll just casually slip in something like, 'Hey, you know what would make this moment even better; if you had a powersword that matched this crystal.' Before you know it, you'll be a queen, and I'll be home."

"I am not going to be queen," Runara growled through gritted teeth. "Is this the door out of here?" She reached around Joe, trying the latch on the green door. It was not locked. Joe found the door's sudden unlocked state a little puzzling but quickly shrugged it off.

"Wait, are you an heir to the throne?" Tosh asked then, "I had read accounts of the monarchy having possibly survived among the brookshins, but…" Tosh put a finger to his chin as he pondered for a moment.

"It's nonsense," Runara grunted as she hoisted open the heavy door. Its rusted hinges squealed loudly, causing Joe and Tosh to cover their ears.

There was a sudden, surprised squeal from Crash then. They all turned to see what the problem was.

"I saw a bug," she said sheepishly, realizing that the conversation had stopped and all eyes were upon her.

"Really?" Tosh scoffed, "The dreaded Flying Fox is afraid of a bug?"

Crash squinted daggers at the man. "It was a really big bug." She said quietly. The others snickered a little.

"Not sure, but this might be the most stealthy break-in I've ever been part of," Joe threw in sarcastically. Crash stuck her tongue out defiantly in response.

The lift door reopened at that moment. Koobara anxiously jumped out with a snarl, followed by Kord and Garen.

Taking a second stab at rallying the group for an adventure, Joe clapped his hands together, rubbing them with anticipation for whatever lay beyond the big green door. "Well, looks like we're all here again. What d'you say we go find us a wizard."

* * * * * * * * * * * * * * * * * *

The walls of the tower's corridors were not the stonework that might have been expected. They seemed to be made of blackened glass that had cooled while in a melting state. It looked as though large dripping globs had solidified in place. The walls did not meet the floor at right angles. Instead, they looked to have oozed partially across the floor, melting into the grout of the floor's deep, red, six-inch hexagonal stone tiles.

As they walked along, Tosh held his lamp close to one of the walls. He was surprised to find that the black-looking surface had a faint red translucence. Curious, he reached out to touch the wall to get a better sense of what material the glassy-looking surface had been crafted from. His fingertips fell a few hair widths short of touching the surface as Joe grabbed him by the wrist.

"You might rethink that," Joe said firmly, pointing at a bend in the hallway a short distance ahead. Just at the edge of Tosh's lamplight, a human arm stuck out of the wall. It was sunk into the wall halfway up its forearm. The arm's dried, tightly clinging, shriveled skin seemed to be all that now held the bones of the arm together. The hand was a claw of frozen desperation.

Cautiously, the group approached the arm. Around the corner, the corridor stretched off into the darkness beyond the light of Tosh's and Garen's lamps. Another passage branched to the right a short distance down.

Joe gave the arm a curious little poke with his finger. The skin felt like paper, dry and thin but surprisingly flexible. More surprising was that the hand twitched a little as Joe touched it. Joe, Garen, Tosh, and Runara had all jumped when it happened. Kord and Koobara had missed it. They were distracted by something else.

Down the continuing corridor, something, somewhere in the darkness, had Koobara's attention. The cat sniffed at the air. The barely perceptible seed of a growl was building in its throat.

"I sense it too," Kord whispered to the cat as he crouched down a little, giving the jungle beast a couple of pats on its left shoulder. "It's watching us. Trying to decide what we are; what to do with us." Following his companion's lead, he sniffed the air, hoping to further identify the spy in the dark. Whatever it was, its scent, Kord thought, was similar to the one now calling itself Captain Morimar Braxis. It smelled of many dead men and animals but of living blood, too.

Joe and the others were still occupied with the hand, despite Runara's suggestion to leave it be.

"Let's see your lamp," Joe said, grabbing Garen's lamp before he could say no. "I want to try something." He pushed the lamp's handle into the palm of the dried, dead hand. Its pointy, bony fingers immediately snapped down, closing on the handle. Again, Joe, Garen, Tosh, and Runara jumped back. The hand continued to clutch the lamp like a grim wall sconce.

Joe laughed and pointed. "That is so great! Bet your grandpappy has a bunch of these all through here."

"We'll be fortunate not to become one of them, I suspect," Garen said grimly. He reached out and gave the lamp a gentle tug. The near-skeletal hand refused to let go. "We best continue to avoid touching the walls." A look of annoyance washed over Garen's face as he tugged a little harder on the lamp without success.

Joe grabbed the arm just below the wrist and, with a sweeping slash from Death Seed, cleanly detached the arm, leaving what remained nearly flush with the wall. A muffled, whining moan followed from within the wall behind the stump. Joe handed the arm, still clutching the lamp, to Garen, who took it reluctantly.

"There you go," Joe said cheerfully. "Look, you can hold it higher now, out of your eyes." Garen, grudgingly, had to concede that it was actually an improvement.

"So we're going to pretend we didn't just hear that?" Runara asked of the group in a frantic whisper.

"Yes?" Garen half-heartedly offered in a hushed voice lest whatever was behind the wall might hear. "For the sake of our sanity, leastways, it would seem wise." He held the arm a little higher, more to put the arm out of his line of sight than to improve the lighting.

Tosh was mesmerized by the grim appendage in Garen's hand. He had nothing to add to the commentary of the others as he stared, trying to discern any clue as to the secret of the arm's post-mortem animation.

"Wasting your time trying to figure it out, pal," Joe said dismissively. "It's magic."

Tosh smiled at Joe's comment. "Magic is just a word for things we have yet to understand."

Joe's face puzzled, "Ya, that's what I just said."

Garen was about to interject something when a deep, loud moan echoed from further up the corridor.

"Go! Back into the room!" Kord grunted.

Out of the darkness, down the corridor, a hulking misshapen figure, nearly two feet taller than Kord and just as wide, lumbered into the edge of the group's lamplight. The creature was so oddly configured that it was difficult for Joe and the others to make out just what it was they were looking at. It took another step forward, further into the light, making another chilling, grunting moan as it did so. The top portion of its head was that of a large grey hare. Its lower jaw, that of an ogre with two large protruding tusks, had been broken, re-angled, and reset to accommodate being joined with the much smaller rabbit skull. Bare, glistening muscle formed the creature's thick neck, like a tangle of wet, red ropes. Thick blood oozed in multiple trails from the creature's neck down its torso, which was already caked in dried blood.

Its torso had been stitched together from the upper bodies of four separate humans, each split and splayed down the middle. The right arm of one of these bodies remained and sat roughly in the proper location on the patchwork creature. Just below this arm, a long, thin, green arm with long, knife-like claws had been attached. The left arm, the shoulder seams of which oozed a green and yellow puss, was massive; the former arm of an ogre or perhaps a troll. The dried, grey, cracked skin gave no clues to the arm's former appearance. Where a hand might have given some indication of the arm's origin, there was only a stump onto which had been grafted a large, curving animal tusk. The legs of the creature were huge as well. Its right leg seemed very human-like, save for its enormous size and the thick coating of brown fur. The left leg was a complete mismatch in all ways, save for size. It appeared to be the thick grey-skinned hind leg of a rhinoceros or a small elephant. The creature feebly tried to block the light of the group's two lamps with its thin, clawed, green hand.

"Yo nabeereyer!" The creature bellowed in a voice that sounded as distressed as it did angry. Thick saliva flew in all directions with every incomprehensible syllable.

"What?" Joe shouted back at the creature.

"Go, I said. Koobara and I will deal with this beast." Kord kept his eyes on the stitched-together behemoth.

The others were already heading back down the corridor toward the room, quickly leaving Joe, Kord, and Koobara in the dark.

"Hey!" Joe shouted after his companions, annoyed that they had fled so quickly. "Seriously though, what did it say?" Joe's tone was a little dejected, and he seemed to be speaking only to himself.

Torn between staying to assist Kord or following his fleeing friends, the choice was quickly made for him. Darkness began to overtake Kord and him as the light from the two lamps sped down the hall with his companions. He was going to be of no use to anyone in complete darkness. He looked over his shoulder as he ran to see, in the quickly diminishing light, the immense, horrible beast descending upon Kord. Koobara roared as the jungle cat and Kord stood their ground. Out of the group's sight, there was a horrendous bellow from the bizarre creature and then silence.

Joe assumed that Kord had made short work of the monstrosity but found it odd that there had been no sound of any sort of impact. Joe glanced back again, but there was nothing but blackness behind him. Looking forward again, the shadowy silhouette of Runara was rushing toward him.

"Go back!" She shouted, sounding on the edge of panic. Behind her, Garen and Tosh's lamps bobbed erratically as they ran.

Garen was looking over his shoulder, shouting, "Go! Go!"

Completely puzzled by the situation, Joe just stood there, trying to imagine what could possibly be coming from the completely empty room they had left just a few minutes ago. Runara ran into him, still urging him frantically to run.

"What is the…" Joe's question was answered before he could finish it. Inexplicably, the hallway's walls, floor, and ceiling were squeezing together like some sort of giant sphincter. It was closing so quickly that it had already blocked the way of Tosh and Garen. Garren had just barely managed to pull back his undead lamp-carrying hand from being caught as the hole closed. Runara screamed as she and Joe were left in complete darkness. Consumed with panic, she was crying and babbling, then about being trapped, about the monster, about Garen and Tosh being eaten by the hall.

Joe held Runara by her shoulders and gave her a little shake, telling her to calm down. "You have some sort of fire magic, right?" He spoke slowly, almost patronizingly, trying to settle her frayed nerves. "Conjure up a little light for us so we can see what we're dealing with."

For Joe, coming from an entirely underground world, although never desirable, being caught in completely dark, small spaces was just a natural hazard when venturing beyond the communities of Midgorn. If you didn't keep your head, you were more likely to gravely injure yourself, fumbling about in a panic long before falling victim to any of the monstrous creatures that inhabit the tunnels and caverns. Given that the present monstrosity in the corridor wasn't making any noise, Joe had already decided that it was no longer a problem; in fact, Kord and his new pet might be the scariest things presently lurking in the dark.

There was a faint red glow from the crystal nestled in Runara's bosom, and then, suddenly, a bright light danced off the glistening black-red walls of the corridor. A white flame flickered in Runara's left palm, producing an audible, angry, roaring sound. She was attempting to wipe tears away with her other hand, but they were quickly evaporating on their own; so intense was the heat coming off of the flame in her hand.

"Whoa!" Joe said, taking a couple steps back. "Good, good, but maybe pull that back a bit before it either cooks us or eats all of our air." Looking around, Joe realized that the former was likelier than the latter. Although the corridor was now completely closed, both in the direction of Kord and Kubara and in the direction of Garen and Tosh, a new corridor had opened in one of the side walls. Joe noticed something else then, or rather, noticed something he had not been noticing for some time now. "Was Crash with you?"

Runara looked surprised by the question, realizing just then that she, too, had not seen Crash since they had left the room below the arc cannon. They both looked about themselves as if it were possible that Crash might turn out to just be standing behind one of them.

Joe looked down the new corridor dimly lit by Runara's now far less luminous and far less hot, orange flame. The new hall was grey stonework, not the disturbing, organic composition of the shape-shifting corridor in which they presently stood.

"Maybe she went down that way," Joe said, nodding toward the new corridor. He knew it was not true even as he said it, but moving along made more sense than staying put.

"What about the others?"

"I'm sure they're fine; no worse than us anyway," Joe said, pulling Runara along by her non-flaming hand. He was pretty sure that this, too, was a lie. "So, doesn't that hurt?" He asked, looking back at her flaming hand. Clearly, it didn't, but he wanted to keep Runara distracted with conversation. It was also helping to keep his imagination off of what had possibly become of the others.

No sooner had they stepped into the new corridor than the wall behind them closed. Runara hadn't noticed, and Joe kept talking to keep it that way lest she lose her composure again.

The new corridor led to a steep, winding stone staircase. The inner wall of the stairs had thin window slits at regular intervals. From these, many strange sounds, growls, grunts, and howls echoed and overlapped from some dark, distant depth in the center of the tower. What sounded like a horse whinny was followed by the horrible guttural scream of a man and then what sounded like an angry pig. Joe looked back at Runara, who looked wide-eyed and near the edge of another panic attack.

"I'm sure that wasn't anyone we know," he said with an uneasy smile, trying to keep her calm.

"That really isn't helping." Her voice was choked, but she found that her annoyance with Joe was overriding her anxiety.

The staircase ended in another long hallway lined with four large wooden doors, two on each wall. At the end of the hall was a pair of polished brass doors flanked by tall, narrow windows of stained glass that depicted elaborate clusters of ferns, flowers, and thorned vines. A light from behind illuminated the stained glass and provided enough light to the hall that Runara could extinguish her flame.

The pace of their steps increased a little, drawn by the promise of light behind the metal doors, but Joe paused briefly at each wooden door along the way. He would listen at each door first before trying their handles. All of them had been quiet, and all had been locked. Runara followed each vain attempt to open a door by burning an arrow in the wooden surface of the door with the tip of her finger, pointing down the hall to the brass doors. If any of the others managed to find their way here, they would at least have some indication as to where she and Joe had gone.

Reaching the brass doors, Joe first tried to peer through the stained glass, but it was far too colored and murky to make out anything but unidentifiable shades of dark and light. At least none of the shapes seemed to be moving, so he decided they should be safe. With a lifetime of experience exploring dangerous caves and structures, Joe exercised a little extra caution, putting an ear to the metal doors as well before trying to open them. Surprisingly, as he leaned against one of the doors, the slight pressure of his head against it caused it to swing slowly open. Joe stumbled into the room, not expecting the lack of resistance from the door. Runara quickly followed, flames burning hotly in each hand, ready for any monstrosity waiting beyond the doors.

The room seemed void of monstrosities, however. It was quite the opposite, in fact. Before them appeared to be an entire forest, lush with green undergrowth. Fireflies winked in and out within the thick foliage while tiny bees buzzed, busily, among flowers of seemingly every possible hue that speckled the dark undergrowth like colorful stars. Great numbers of butterflies with iridescent wings of orange and gold fluttered above, clustering on the branches of various trees. So thick were the clusters of butterflies that some of the trees appeared to be covered in metallic orange leaves at first glance. There were small pine trees, tall oaks, countless other species of nut and fruit-bearing trees, and a wide variety of tall and low bushes.

Above the treetops, sunlight came in at an obtuse angle. The light glinted off a lattice of metal and glass that revealed the cloud cover above the tower. Close to where the lattice met the side of the building was the source of a small waterfall that poured down a very natural-looking rock face into a large pool, the edge of which was just to the left of the doorway. The mist drifting over from the falling water hissed and steamed off of Runara's flaming hands.

While Runara marveled at the unexpected beauty of the enclosed ecosystem, Joe was finding the ceilinged environment strangely comforting. It reminded him much of home. Even if he could see through the ceiling, the cloud cover helped the illusion of a solid torvug. It was, somehow, reassuring that something was holding the world together instead of a giant blue or black abyss above. Both Joe and Runara couldn't help but spin in place, trying to take in all they could of the wondrously constructed forest. It was a similar fascination to that which had grabbed Joe passing through Loncodi's monolithic entrance gate.

This atrium, jutting out from the side of the tower, seemed so much larger from the inside than it had appeared at a distance as they had approached aboard the Harmaton. He was not used to being able to see buildings or structures from such vast open distances and marveled now at the enormity of the tower in general from the inside.

Runara cleared her throat, subtly refocusing Joe's attention on the way forward.

A gravel and dirt pathway led through the undergrowth, and having no other option other than to go back the way they came, they followed it into the encapsulated forest. The path wound this way and that through the trees before opening to a grass-covered clearing. A small, plain, round, stone pedestal, no more than four feet tall, was in the middle of the clearing, and upon it sat a small, clear glass box. Somewhere above, a bird twittered as Joe and Runara entered the open grassy space. It was answered by several others.

"I can't help but feel like they're talking about us," Runara said. Joe nodded in agreement, a serious look on his face as he pulled out Death Seed. Runara laughed, "I was kidding, they're just birds."

Joe answered with a slight negative shake of his head and silently pointed at the pedestal. That's when Runara noticed the two sets of faintly glowing green eyes, seemingly floating in the air, midway down on either side of the pedestal.

"Who plays in the master's garden?" A hissing, scratchy voice came from one of the two pairs of glowing eyes.

Runara's hands were then fully engulfed in fire, ready for whatever malicious intent these mysterious creatures might have. "I am the wizard's…"

"None of your business who we are," Joe interrupted, trusting these creatures far less than Runara was willing. "Tell us where your master is." Joe pointed Death Seed at the invisible creatures as he took a cautious step closer.

"Ooh," came the hissing voice again, "Did the lumpy one just say it belonged to the master?"

"It did, it did!" A slightly higher pitched but otherwise identical voice came from the other pair of eyes.

"Lumpy?" Runara protested angrily.

"The one with the shiny stick is a thief. Stole her he must have, and come here to steal another of the master's pets. Do the master harm."

"Kill it, I say," hissed the other.

"Eat it. Eat them both. The master will never know."

"The lumpy one does look juicy."

Joe had heard enough. Before either of the conspiring, floating pair of eyes could react, he had let fly two of his knives. Each knife flew with deadly accuracy right between each set of eyes but continued harmlessly, sticking into the grass several feet behind the eerie floating orbs. Both sets of eyes were laughing then. Joe looked a little concerned.

"It tries to kill us."

"Try it will. Die it will."

The air directly behind the pillar began to shimmer.

Joe winced at the miss. "Damn, knew I should have tried directly for an eye."

"We should run." Runara pleaded to Joe.

"Run to where?" Joe edged toward the pedestal leading with Death Seed, another of his knives already in his other hand. "'Sides, how scary can a few little eyeballs be?"

The shimmering behind the pillar turned into ripples in the air, and then, as if thousands of tiny red eggs were flipping into existence, a singular body formed around the two sets of eyes. The red-scaled creature wasn't tall, but it was large. Its squat torso, if that is what it could be called, was, on its own, the size of a grizzly bear. The body looked like a collection of red-scaled balls, each about the size of a human head, held together by what looked like taut, sinuous, red, melted taffy. A thick tail arched over the body, segmented much like a scorpion tail, but ending in a wide, menacing, bony, jawed mouth full of a hundred sharp, silvery teeth. Hundreds of tiny black tentacles writhed around where otherwise lips might have been. The creature shuffled back and forth with anxious, murderous energy on four spindly legs ending in long black spikes as it sized up Joe and Runara. Two long, sinewy arms extended from the front of the creature, having an eerie human-like appearance. Where the hands should have been were instead two large orbs, and from each orb, two long tentacle-like stalks protruded. At the end of each tentacle were the creature's glowing green eyes. Between each eyestalk was a long muscular finger ending in a spike, much like the deadly-looking spikes at the end of the creature's legs. These fore-claws tore anxiously at the ground before the beast. Runara screamed at the frightening countenance of the monster and its sudden materialization. Joe took a few steps back. The look on his face was an odd mix of analytical surprise.

"Joe, please!" Runara pleaded again, her flaming hands extinguished, tugging then on Joe's sword arm, trying to coax him into running back through the atrium to the entrance.

"The lumpy one is right to fear the Grix." Hissed one of two vertical mouth slits nestled between the creature's arms at the very front of the beast's torso.

"Enough talk," said the higher-pitched voice from the other slit.

"Time to eat!" Both voices finished in unison as the large silver-toothed mouth snapped hungrily above, thick saliva dripping down onto its body below.

"Runara, I'm going to need your fire," Joe said anxiously, coaxing her to free her grip on him while keeping his attention fixed on the Grix. The creature stepped around the pedestal in a slow, predatory gait. "This thing is like a stalkren, back home, well, except this thing has eyes, which might complicate things,"

The Grix made a sudden lunge forward. Runara screamed again. Joe made a move to parry the slashing finger talons, hoping, truly, that Death Seed would simply lop them off. The reflexes of the Grix were swift, however, and it pulled the claws back out of the path of the sweeping blade. Quickly, it shuffled backward on its crab-like legs to reconsider its attack. Joe sent a knife flying. It sunk deep between the two vertical mouths. Both of its voices cried out in pain and rage.

A brightly colored, green bird flew by just then. In a silvery blur of movement, the large upper mouth snapped closed on the unfortunate little flyer, leaving nothing but a small cloud of green feathers fluttering downward. Joe was about to let a fourth knife fly when the Grix lurched forward again, narrowly missing Joe with its slashing fore-claws as he safely rolled out of the way.

Without warning, the distracted creature was engulfed in a blast of fire roaring from Runara's hands in a wide stream as though she had some enormous dragon secreted up one of her white, billowy, linen sleeves.

When the flames ceased, the creature was gone, seemingly entirely incinerated, but then Joe saw them, the four glowing eyes drifting to a spot just to his right. He let loose with two knives, taking out one pair of the eyes. The voices of the Grix burst with a flurry of cries of pain from one and curses from the other. Its egg-shaped scales flipped back into existence, giving the beast visible form again, but it was already charging. Joe had barely enough time to react to the giant mouth full of silver fangs crashing down upon him, flipping Death Seed up defensively.

At first, Joe had thought he had cleaved the beast in two with the momentum of its own attack, but the Grix was dissolving from the center out. The scales of its body flipped a path of non-existence for Joe to pass through, then winked back, pulling the two portions of its body back together behind Joe. Perplexing as the moment was, Joe didn't allow himself the luxury of pondering it. Spinning around, he screamed his pasta-based battle cry, catching the creature's left back leg with Death Seed. The leg flopped on the ground with a life of its own before quickly dissolving away like water sizzling into vapor on a hot griddle.

The Grix staggered as it tried to turn on Joe with its remaining three legs and struggled to use its fore-claws as additional legs for balance. At that moment, Runara assaulted the Grix with another deluge of flame, though not nearly so voluminous as her first salvo. Again, the creature defensively dissolved, its remaining two eyes darting back toward the pillar.

Joe was ready this time and quickly shot his remaining knife at the fleeing green orbs. It hit its mark. The creature lurched from the pain of losing another eye. Joe was already running up as the beast once again reconstituted its body.

The Grix lashed out at Joe with its fore-claws and snapped at him with its huge mouth, but now, with only one eye, its depth perception was dramatically flawed. Joe easily dodged the misguided attacks, coming out of a rolling somersault as he brought Death Seed down on the arm of the beast's remaining eye.

The Grix once again cried out in pain, dissolving into nothingness. The eye, still attached to the taloned finger of the amputated arm, looked to be trying to claw itself along the ground to some measure of safety. It was quickly consumed by a ball of fire from Runara. As the flames dispersed this time, the charred black husk of the amputated arm and eye remained. Joe stomped on it, grinding it down to ash.

For a minute or two, Joe and Runara stood with their backs to one another, expecting the blinded Grix to reappear. Birds that had gone silent around the moment of the untimely death of the little green bird began twittering again. Only then did Joe and Runara relax, accepting their unscathed success.

"What was that?" Runara still sounded wound up.

"Your world; you oughta know. Apparently, it's a grix," Joe shrugged. "So let's have a look at what the big nasty was protecting." Joe took a few steps over to the pedestal, peering into the square glass case on top of it.

"Just leave it be, Joe," Runara said anxiously. "Whatever it is, if it's in Nashtar's keep, it's likely something we don't want to mess with."

It was too late; Joe was already lifting the glass. A puzzled look swept across his face. "Nothing in here 'cept some sort of big yango."

"A what?" Runara now felt compelled to look out of curiosity. A snail with a large green shell was slithering, with as much haste as a snail can, to the pedestal's edge away from the two curious onlookers. It left a glistening, slimy trail as it made its way from the center of the pedestal where it had been resting before being disturbed.

"It's a snail," she said quietly, with a little question in her voice, doubting her own thoughts on what the little creature truly was.

"That's a snail?" Joe placed the glass cover back over the snail. "Didn't you say something about your grandpappy changing somebody into a snail?"

"Yes, the Duke of Estobrex, but that was so long ago and just a story. The truth is Nashtar probably just had the Duke poisoned. Even if it were true, it couldn't possibly be the same snail after all this time."

"So you might buy the idea that a man may have been turned into a little green-shelled yango but won't swallow the chance that he might be magically alive? What sort of witch are you?"

"I'm no witch; I mean, before this crystal of yours, I was never a real witch. A healer, yes, but no witch. Sometimes, I'd tell villagers their future for a coin or two. Just tricks."

"Nah, wizards always have little wizard babies," Joe scoffed. "Isn't a kid that comes out of Dreema that can't toss around a little magic."

"Dreema?"

"City full of magic folk back in my world. My guess is that crystal gives your magic an extra little kick in the ass. Go on, try changing him back." Joe pointed at the snail that had now crawled up the inside of the glass case closest to Runara.

"Magic isn't that easy. You need to learn specific spells. It can take years, decades sometimes, of apprenticeship, practice, and research."

"Like your fire," Joe said with a smirk.

Runara just glared at Joe, unable to counter his obvious observation.

Joe laughed triumphantly. "Oh, this is going to be so much fun!" He was rubbing his hands together in anxious anticipation.

Runara rolled her eyes, frustrated and embarrassed for a reason she couldn't quite place. "Let's just go find my grandfather. And the others, who knows what's happened to them, and you just want to play with snails." She tried walking around Joe but he grabbed her gently by the arm.

"Come on, just try it," Joe urged, a mischievous smile on his face. "Just like you do with your fire. Just wave your hands about at the thing and think really hard about it being a man." She tried, vainly, to pull away. "Just try it once, for me." He let go of her arm and struck an innocent, begging pose, one hand on his heart.

Runara glared at him momentarily, unsure if she wanted to scream or just cry. She opted to do just as he had suggested, more or less. With a half-hearted wave of her hands toward the glass case and speaking sarcastically, her words laced with a healthy dose of spite, "Hocum-Perocum, now you're a man."

"Aw, you're not even trying," Joe complained but then noticed the red crystal glowing between Runara's breasts. Smiling, he pointed at the crystal. Runara had an astonished look on her face. Unable to find words, she franticly waved her hand, trying to get Joe to turn around.

"Lad, when a woman has a pair of mountains like that, there's no trying," he cleared his throat slightly for dramatic effect. "She just wins."

The unexpected voice made Joe jump and spin around.

A tall but average-looking man, slightly overweight, with excessively thinning black hair, now stood where the pedestal and glass case had once been. He was dressed in the finery of a Senuvian noble. A thick green velvet overcoat, the trimming of which depicted a variety of sexual positions in obscenely detailed embroidery, covered his yellow silk doublet and matching yellow-on-black brocade pants. The pants were accented by a ridiculously large, black codpiece with an ornate gold vine pattern upon it. He put one black knee-booted foot forward in an exaggerated motion and a flourish of both arms, bowing deeply. "The Grand Duke of Estobrex at your service or, more accurately, ready to be serviced. Truly phenomenal set of prick-pillows, lass." His gaze returned directly to Runara's chest as he stood up straight again. "She yours, boy?"

"Seems you're not much of a duke of anything anymore," Joe said, striding up to the man, giving him a hearty slap on one shoulder, ignoring his lewd comment. He didn't wait for a response from the former Duke as he walked on, set on the task of looking about the clearing for his throwing knives. "Magic, magic, magic," Joe mumbled to himself, shaking his head as he set about his search.

Runara was trying to ignore the former Duke's comment. Her mind was still swimming with shock over the transformation. She absentmindedly fiddled with the red crystal pendant, pondering this new expansion to her magical repertoire. When she realized that this just seemed to be encouraging the former lord's inappropriate gawking, she let go of the crystal and cleared her throat loudly, hoping to draw his attention upward. It didn't work.

"You don't quite look the way I've been told," she said, keeping her distance from the man.

That drew his attention to her face. He then quickly looked down at himself and began patting himself down all over, trying to confirm that all of his parts were just where they ought to be and just the way he remembered. Everything seemed in order, and he was about to protest Runara's assertion when he noticed her looking at the top of his head. A quick hand to his scalp confirmed that his once glorious blonde mane was missing.

"Ahh, the hair. Didn't survive the sorcerer's spell, it seems. Worst sort of magician that one; sloppy work. Can't imagine why the King suffered his company. Not surprising, the only woman in the kingdom that would bed that little weasel was some farmer's whore of a daughter." He was still rubbing his head. "I must confess that it was always just a wig." He walked up to Runara as he straightened his posture and his garments. "So, Red, they talk about me, do they? Care to have a taste of what has me so missed in the King's court?"

Runara took a few steps back as he drew uncomfortably close. Impossibly, his breath wreaked of ale. She gritted her teeth as she tried to maintain a civil composure. "Sir, I'm not sure you're aware just how much time has passed since Lord Nashtar transformed you."

"Must be some time indeed if they're calling that officious little hex-flinging dilettante 'Lord.' Has the King made him the thane of some backwater? Ooh, the Aglog swamps, perhaps. Couldn't even pay a noble to minister that stench heap."

Joe walked by, slapping him on the shoulder yet again, as he made his way across the clearing to fetch another knife. "You might want to brace yourself for this one, and, uh, maybe watch the way you talk about her great-granfolk. She did change you back after all."

"Your, your great…" the ex-duke tried to process this for a moment.

Runara calmly nodded a yes. "And, he was made the Duke of Estobrex."

His eyes grew wide as his racing mind tried to reconcile the impossibility of it. "Your great-grandfather? But that's…" Anger was welling up inside the former Duke as the reality of his situation, of the time that had passed, grew clearer to him. "I'm the Duke of Estobrex… My father and his father and… It's our family name!" His face turned red as he spun around, realizing that the strangeness of his circumstances also included his present surroundings. "Where are we. This, this is no real forest." He was pointing at the glass ceiling.

Joe was digging around in some bushes on the edge of the clearing, only half paying attention. "Your old castle, isn't it?" He asked briefly, looking over his shoulder at Runara.

"Keep." Runara corrected.

"Nashtar!" the bewildered nobleman bellowed, fully enraged. He turned on Runara then, grabbing her by both shoulders. "How is this…more magic…His magic! Is your grandfather still alive?"

"Great-grandfather," she corrected in an overly calm demeanor, hoping it would help to calm the former Duke as well.

"Take my name? I'm going to kill him! I swear! Tell me where he is." He began to shake her.

"I…he's…" Runara was having difficulty getting a word out as he shook her more and more violently. She struggled in vain to break free of his grip.

"Tell me! I'm going to kill him! Tell me, you little slut!" He grabbed her by the throat with both hands.

Joe turned around, Death Seed drawn, and made to run to Runara's aid, but suddenly, her assailant was covered in white flames from head to toe.

Screaming, the flaming ex-duke let go of Runara, screaming and howling in pain. He flailed about, frantically spinning in circles, as though it might be possible to, somehow, shake the fire loose. Within only a few seconds, he collapsed, silent, to the ground, still in flames. A few seconds later, he was nothing more than a charred, smoldering, skeletal husk. The foliage, even the grass, around the smoking remains were untouched by Runara's enchanted fire.

Joe cautiously strode up to Runara's side, putting Death Seed back in its sheath. The red crystal pendant around her neck was glowing, pulsing with energy. Joe could feel a heat radiating from Runara's entire body. She was glaring with disgust at the blackened smoking form lying in the grass of the clearing. It was disgust for the way he had grabbed her, disgust for his words, his demeanor, disgust for what he had caused her to do, disgust for her own lack of regret.

"I did tell him to watch his tone with you." Joe shrugged. "Seems like an awfully long time to spend as a yango, just to get burnt to death, though." Joe's tone was filled with its usual flippancy. "Not that I'm judging."

Runara didn't look at Joe as she turned and headed for the continuing path on the far side of the clearing. "Time to find my great-grandfather," she said solemnly as she walked away. She didn't notice Joe kneel over the charred form on the grass and remove the blackened throwing knife from the back of the former Duke's neck.

* * * * * * * * * * * * * * * * *

The path through the atrium had led to an opening in the ground with a wide stone staircase leading down. Runara was already quite a distance down into the winding darkness by the time Joe reached the edge of the opening. Only the faint glow of the flame from her one palm could be seen, illuminating a small portion of the dark stone walls. Joe raced down the spiraling stairs, trying to catch up to her, but the faster he ran, the faster the light receded ahead of him. A scream from her echoed back to Joe then. He called out for her, nearly stumbling down the stairs as he increased his speed, trying to catch up with her.

"Joe, stop!"

Runara's warning had come out of the darkness just in time to prevent Joe from running off the end of the stairs into a dark abyss beyond. His momentum, however, had been enough to carry him skidding over the edge. Twisting as he fell, he barely managed to catch the edge of the last stone stair. It wasn't just the stairs that had come to a sudden end, but the walls, the ceiling, seemingly all of reality. Joe dangled over an empty, endless void. He hoisted himself up, his fingers straining painfully to maintain their tenuous grip on the smooth stone. Ignoring the pain and pulling himself high enough, Joe threw an elbow over and then, with some effort, a knee. Eventually, back on his feet, he turned to look out into the dark nothingness that extended before him. Runara looked to be about forty feet away, floating in the darkness, adrift on a small four-foot square island of stone flooring. It was one of the larger platforms of stone among a countless number that was inexplicably suspended in space, scattered throughout the void.

Large or small, each stone platform was drifting slowly in its own direction. Occasionally, two would collide and bounce off one another, moving off in new trajectories. Runara's island was drifting away from Joe, taking her dim firelight with it.

"How did you get out there?" Joe shouted to her.

"I don't know. Everything just flew apart. You need to get me ba—" Before Runara could finish her request, Joe leaped onto one of the smaller floating stone platforms.

Screamin' Joe Blade's Ten-Point Guide to Life:
Point #9: If you aren't moving toward the prize, the goal, the girl (especially the girl), you're doing it wrong.

"What are you doing?" Runara yelled, her dismay and frustration causing her voice to crack slightly.

Joe just barely managed to maintain his balance on the small platform. He had expected it to have some give when he landed, but it was rigidly maintaining the plane it was floating in as though it were connected to an invisible steel track.

"Way I figure it," he said, eyeballing the next jump. "Your granpappy has to be able to get around this place somehow, and it probably involves more magic than jumpin'."

"So that's why you are jumping then." Runara's voice was an odd mixture of sarcasm, anger, and concern. She was having a hard time with Joe's lack of both logic and common sense. She gasped then as Joe made the leap to the next platform, a narrow piece just one foot by two feet in dimension. Joe was far more sure-footed on this leap, however, and he flashed her a broad smile as he stood up straight.

"See, not so bad," Joe said confidently, "I'll be over there in no time at all, and then we can figure this out."

The tiny platform Joe was balancing on was drifting just slightly faster than Runara's wide chunk of misplaced stone flooring, and it was slowly closing the gap between the two. Joe seemed to be enjoying the ride, looking around the surrounding void. As he grew closer to Runara's light, he could make out more floating stone platforms above and below. He nearly lost his balance, ducking a small one traveling across his path at head height.

"All you're going to accomplish is getting yourself killed or getting both of us stranded."

"Although I'll give you that I might be in for a long fall, I can tell you from experience that death doesn't always come as part of the package. Anyway, I figure you're the one with a growing knack for all things magic, so better a jump or two to get to you and keep moving forward than trying to figure out a way to get you back there," he thumbed over his shoulder, "and not get anywhere."

"I still think you're insane. And I don't have a knack for all things magic."

"Seems like you have that fire magic down pretty good, and what do you call what you did changing that yango back into the Duke." Joe saw Runara's face drop and immediately regretted mentioning the smoldering nobleman. The platform Joe was riding had drifted close enough to Runara's platform by then to casually step over. "Sorry." He said quietly and earnestly.

Runara took a deep breath, reining in her emotions as best she could. "So now what?"

"Well," Joe said, rubbing his hands together, flashing her his ever-confident smile, "now we have a look around." Joe carefully pivoted about. Runara cautiously followed his example. Light was dimly apparent coming from the staircase from which they had arrived and was dishearteningly diminishing as their platform continued to drift away. All else was darkness. Runara's fire illuminated little around them. Stone blocks and platforms of all sizes drifted lazily in and out of view all around them, as well as above and below.

"I am not jumping off of this block," Runara said matter-of-factly into the void as she and Joe scanned the darkness.

"Not in that dress you're not," Joe added with a laugh, in agreement. "You might think about taking it off." He had tried and failed to muster as much innocence into the statement as he could. "To make it easier to jump," he added, responding to her unimpressed glare.

Just then, something caught both of their attention. It was a column of soft blue light, the invisible source of which seemed to be far away and far above. In the infinite black depth, it was hard to tell. The light column scanned back and forth, angling slightly up and down, occasionally lingering on any floating bit of stone that crossed its path. It was growing larger, or more accurately, drawing nearer. Joe and Runara watched the column of light, mesmerized. Occasionally, the light would wink out and seem as though it was simply gone, only to reappear much closer. Runara had doused her flame the first time the light had jumped closer. Soon, its long sweep was illuminating chunks of rock and floating stone pads just a few feet away from her and Joe. The ambient light from the column revealed far more floating rock objects nearby than Runara's light had reached. They were so numerous that in the column of blue light, the drifting stones and platforms looked much like stirred-up dust particles, lazily drifting within rays of sunlight pouring through a window into a darkened room.

"What do you think it is?" Joe asked Runara in a whisper.

"Quiet!" Runara whispered emphatically back at Joe, trying to stifle him, but it was too late.

The column of blue light immediately swung around in their direction, illuminating and blinding both of them, then winked out again, leaving bright spots dancing before Joe and Runara's traumatized retinas. Runara fumbled about in the dark with her right hand, finding one of Joe's hands and gripping it tightly. The spots were making Runara feel dizzy in the darkness. Holding on to Joe was helping her keep her balance, but it wasn't helping her fend off the increasing fear nearly as much as she would have liked. Joe was making strange clicking sounds with his mouth.

"Stop it!" Runara whispered anxiously, tugging on Joe's hand.

"Okay, okay," he whispered back, relenting. "It's just that, whatever it is, it's like…" Joe's words trailed off in contemplation.

Something made a whooshing sound in the darkness. They could hear it landing lightly on one stone, not far off, and then another, and another. It seemed to be circling them. Whatever the owner of the light beam was, it seemed to be able to navigate the darkness.

Runara could feel the panic rising within her. She fought against it and channeled it into thoughts of heat and fire. She shot her left hand high into the air, letting loose an immense ball of orange flame. It briefly illuminated twelve enormous blue-colored eyes that had formed a circle around them, and they were looking right at Runara and Joe.

"…like, there's more than one of them out there," Joe said, finishing his regrettably redundant deduction.

Runara's ball of flame diminished endlessly into the dark void above, taking its light with it. She immediately produced another large orange flame, keeping it in the palm of her left hand. She could not help but let out a startled gasp. Even Joe let out a little shout of surprise. In the brief moment between the fireball and the new flame, the eyes had all moved much closer. During the first brief glimpse, Joe had thought the eyes to be like the disembodied eyes of the Grix they had encountered in the atrium, potentially belonging to something much larger and more numerous. In the glow of Runara's new flame, it was clear that these eyes were something very different. Each eye was a separate creature. Aside from the five-foot diameter eyeball itself, there was not much to their form. They were covered in thick blue skin, much like the scaled texture of an alligator, that formed large blinking eyelids. Long, muscular but spindly arms ending in very human-like hands with exceptionally long fingers extended from the back end of the eyeball, which the creatures used to perch upon the drifting stone platforms like enormous round birds. Adding to their avian appearance were ethereal wings that looked to be made of nothing more than several impossibly suspended streams of smoke.

Joe drew out Death Seed. Immediately, the irises of the eyeball creatures began glowing. Several adjusted their positions, shuffling anxiously, giving the impression that they were ready to pounce. Runara let go of Joe's hand. Before he could protest her rash action, a small fireball was already blazing toward one of the creatures. It quickly leaped out of the fireball's path, floating to a great height above Runara and Joe on its misty wings. Without a further movement or sound as warning, the glowing irises of the creatures burst forth blinding columns of white-blue light. So intense were the spotlights produced by the beasts that Joe and Runara felt physically buffeted in all directions. Joe blindly swung Death Seed in a series of aimless arcs that caught nothing but air. Then, two massive hands were about him, clapping his arms to his sides and restraining him as the long fingers wrapped around his body like thick, binding ropes. The action had nearly caused Joe to cut his own leg with Death Seed. He could feel cool air pouring in through the fresh gash in his leather pants. Joe noted that the sensation of the air was actually quite refreshing and that he should consider leaving the hole, should he survive, to allow his 'boys' to breathe. Not letting the breeze be too much of a distraction, Joe realized that he really had to contemplate how he would be getting out of his current situation.

Judging his odds of survival was difficult. He had little to go on. His sight was nothing but blue dots as his eyes tried to recover from the intense blasts of light they had taken. Joe was being carried aloft by one of the eye creatures. By the sound of Runara's screams, which were an ear-splitting combination of fear, anger, and desperation, she was being carried nearby as well.

Joe began playing over in his mind different scenarios for how he would retaliate if the creature loosened its grip or even put him down somewhere. He had quickly decided the latter would be the likely eventuality, assuming that if the beast intended to rend him apart midair or drop him, it would have already done so. Indeed, the beast carrying Runara would have already dispatched her, Joe thought, just to end her noise. Then again, he had not noticed any ears on the creatures. Her seemingly endless screams had become so grating upon Joe's nerves that he started hoping that the beasts would opt for rending or dropping either one of them very soon.

Instead, Runara's screams soon came to a choked pause as Joe felt the stomach-churning sensation of dropping rapidly. The creatures were descending far into the void below. At first, the rapid descent reminded him of the terrifying drop down the Mouth of Kodin that had brought him to this odd world. There was a difference to this, though. There was almost something comforting, he found, in being so securely bound by the eyeball beast's grip that he suddenly felt the flight to be something very serene. The sensation of controlled, purposeful speed, the sound of the air rushing about him; it was a bit like being back on the deck of the Harmaton, but more exhilarating. A moment later, Runara caught her breath and resumed her screams, shattering the serenity of what had nearly been a profound moment for Joe.

It was then that Joe noticed one of the spots in his vision was no longer blue like the others. This new spot was a soft yellow and growing larger by the second. As he focused his attention on it – having nothing but the spots before his eyes to entertain himself with, other than imagining various ways that he might silence Runara – the spot resolved to the shape of a softly illuminated, open stone archway.

The speed at which they descended toward the impossibly suspended opening was a little concerning to Joe as he would be taking the brunt of any landing impact. His concern shifted to wonder very quickly. The peaked opening was much larger than it had looked at a distance in the void; large enough for five King Koteps to walk through side by side, stacked six Koteps tall. The stone blocks that made up the arch had been carved to look as though the arch had been fashioned from the bones of some giant beast, or perhaps the bones were real. It was hard to tell. They looked real enough. Joe found an even deeper appreciation for the grandeur of the ever-growing archway, as the spectacle of it had prompted a much-needed second pause in Runara's screams. As they neared the opening, a lengthy, well-lit corridor could be seen within.

The two flying eyeballs swept through the middle of the archway and down the corridor, side-by-side. Though brightly illuminated with what seemed to be sunlight, the source of the corridor's light was elusive. There were no windows, torches, or lamps; no visible source of any sort. The walls were lined with archways identical to the one that they had just flown through, but their openings were bricked in. Joe, craning his neck around to look back, could see that the massive arch they had flown through to enter this hall was, puzzlingly, similarly bricked over.

"No! Stop!" The distressed cry from Runara snapped Joe's attention back to her and then forward. Ahead, too, was a similarly bricked closed archway, and the eyeball creatures' speed gave no suggestion that they intended to stop. Joe closed his eyes, his body tensing instinctively as he braced for the imminent impact. Runara let out one final scream, which was quickly silenced.

A second or two more passed than Joe had expected without the bone-crushing impact he had anticipated. He popped open one eye as though looking with one eye might lessen the horror of whatever doom awaited him. To his surprise, the wall they had been hurtling toward was gone, and from what he could tell, neither he nor Runara were harmed, nor were the winged eyeballs. Runara, however, had fainted.

"About time it was someone else's turn," Joe mumbled to himself.

The bright light of the hall was gone as well. The torch-lit room they were in now was huge, with grand stone columns. It reminded Joe of the great church in the city of Orter dedicated to the Midgorn god Kodin Havwen, where hundreds of the faithful would gather in the month of Zulool for the two-day celebrations of Nin Zuset and Nawn Rathor. Much like his memories of the Midgorn circus, this made him nostalgic for the days when he and his sister would liberate the faithful from the oppressive weight of their would-be offerings to the eternally sleeping god. Joe could only assume that this was also some sort of church as it had a large altar on the far end of the room, set high upon a twelve-stepped semi-circular dais.

The altar had been sculpted to look like two wyverns locked in a deadly battle. Half-melted, lit candles adorned the steps of the dais and surrounded the altar as well. Some of the candles had even found convenient perches on parts of the eternally combative altar drakes. Curiously, another collection of candles drifted around, held aloft by some unseen force, as they slowly circled the ominous black marble altar.

The smoke from the multitude of candles and torches did not drift up to the far reaches of the vaulted ceiling but instead lingered in a flat, swirling plane somewhere in between.

Unlike the church of Joe's memories, where a massive idol would have stood beyond the altar, an immense throne was fashioned from the bones and skulls of innumerable people and creatures.

The eyeballs set Joe and Runara down gently just shy of halfway down the chamber, the disturbed plane of smoke swirling and mingling with the ephemeral wings of the creatures as they came to rest. Joe immediately leaped to his feet, drawing Death Seed and swiping wildly at the eye that had been carrying him. Its iris lit with a dull blue glow as it slid back and upward beyond the reach of Joe and his sword. The other eye followed its companion's example, floating upward until the two were an eerie pair of tiny glowing orbs staring down at Joe and Runara from the darkness of the room's lofty arched ceiling.

There was no sign of the entryway they had flown through, just a solid wall, barely visible from halfway down the chamber in the shadowy firelight. There seemed to be no exit of any sort as Joe looked about. He had hoped there would at least have been a window handy.

Not trusting the creatures that had borne them here, he shot a quick glance up and over his shoulder to make sure they had not moved. They had, and a quick scan of the room, found the two glowing blue eyes back at ground level, concealing their full forms in the shadows by the wall through which they had entered. Joe hoped they were in the process of leaving, but they just kept staring. It was a little unnerving. The smoke in the room now seemed drawn towards the glowing orbs, but something else was stranger. Joe had the sense that the eyes were growing closer, more into focus, perhaps, but they were not getting any larger with their approach. Maybe, he thought, blinking, the wall was sliding farther back? That did not appear to be the case either.

He was about to look away, convinced that he was simply spooking himself, when suddenly the smoke swirling about the eyes formed into the distinct shape of a face.

"Thieves!" the swirling face of smoke accused. Its eyes flashed an even brighter blue. The voice was deep and booming as it echoed off the distant arches of the ceiling, but it had the distinct wavering quality of a man well beyond his natural years.

"Are not!" Joe shouted back quickly, sounding a little childish. A moment later, after quickly reassessing his less-than-accurate assertion, he added, "Well, she's not." He motioned toward Runara, who had just then awakened.

The roiling edges of the smokey visage grew more defined as though contained within a clear, face-shaped jar. "You and your cohorts have come for the sword," the voice boomed again. With this accusation, the face suddenly snapped into starkly white solidity and, much to Joe's astonishment, was now less than a foot away from him. As Joe stumbled back in surprise, the view of the room, below the deeply wrinkled face, distorted and smeared, bleeding down as if it were all made of melting wax. The warping image of the grey stone and dark shadows of the room beyond swirled and churned, quickly forming a body cloaked in a heavy robe and a hood formed about the face. Tendrils of smoke strayed from the solid form of the face, taking on the appearance of a long, undulating, heavy, white beard and a thick mustache.

A pale white hand, nearly looking skeletal in its bony thinness, pointed at the pommel of Death Seed. "Fools, you came to steal my sword away, but to my delight, you have brought the shard here. I'll thank you to hand the shard to me, or would you rather that I rip it from the hand of your corpse."

"Is there a third option?" Joe asked, "Because right now I'm going to be a little busy using the sword it's attached to, carving up a creepy old man."

Runara's mind was still in a bit of a fog. "What — who?" A look of astonished realization swept across her face as she gazed upon the ethereal image of the elderly man with glowing blue eyes. "You're…"

"Nashtar? Of course I am, you stupid little witch," he said sharply. The bright red crystal dangling from Runara's neck as she struggled to stand up caught the old wizard's attention. "Can it be?" he said in half a whisper, sounding truly astonished; his blue eyes unnaturally wide and glowing so intensely that they were nearly white.

Before Joe or Runara had time to react, the wizard gave a flick of his right hand. The red crystal ripped itself violently free from Runara's leather necklace. Runara gasped in shock, nearly stumbling back to the ground from the force of the wizard's pull. The crystal flew into Nashtar's hand, but instead of stopping, it continued to a point directly in the middle of the wizard. The image of Nashtar swirled in upon itself in a mad vortex, as though Nashtar was made of nothing more than ink in a sink full of water, swirling down the drain. In an instant, he and the crystal were gone.

"So much more than I could have hoped for," came Nashtar's voice from the altar the very second he had disappeared. Joe and Runara both spun around in surprise. Nashtar was standing behind the altar, holding the red crystal before him in his right hand. As before, the surroundings seemed to be bleeding into the form of Nashtar, feeding his image. Even the flames of nearby drifting candles would momentarily be pulled in, creating luminous streaks across the wizard. He reached down onto the altar with his left hand, hoisting a bulky one-handed sword from its surface. The sword shimmered in the candlelight as though it were made of glass embedded with millions of tiny rubies.

"Hey, I think that just might be what we were looking for," Joe casually shouted to the wizard. The fingers on his left hand twitched a little with anticipation as he tried to determine if he could make the throw across the room with one of his knives.

"Come closer, young ones," Nashtar's voice echoed unnaturally among the twelve large, dark blue marble pillars that formed an aisle down the length of the room. His demeanor shifted abruptly to being far more welcoming. "You are about to witness the rebirth of a powersword. A rare moment to be sure."

Runara gave Joe a wary look, clearly hesitant to approach her great-grandfather. Joe just flashed her a confident smile and gave her what was meant to be a reassuring nod. With a casual swish of Death Seed, motioning for her to follow, Joe began confidently striding toward Nashtar and the altar.

"Glad we got past this whole misunderstanding about us being here to rob you. You can keep your sword. I just want to get home, and if the rock in this thing can help make that happen, I say let's turn that thing into a powersword." He flipped Death Seed over in his hand, looking at the pommel, squinting as he examined the metallic skeletal hand that clutched the roughly shaped, dark crystal.

"Yes, boy, bring me the shard." Though the wizard's tone was inviting, his face was expressionless.

"How do you think you get this thing out of here?" He gave the shard a few futile yanks as he made his way up the steps of the dais.

Runara was still many steps behind Joe. She didn't trust the old necromancer, kin or not, and was in no hurry to be anywhere near him. Her slow pace was also giving her some time to assess if she could still summon fire without Joe's red crystal. As she feared, the magical energies she had tapped into with the crystal simply were not there for her now. She would be lucky just to be able to make her hands mildly warmer.

"So, about the joining ritual," Joe started as he reached the top of the dais, ducking a candle as it floated by. "I'm not sure if you're familiar with it, but there's this whole nasty matter of old blood and new blood." There was a swagger in Joe's voice as though he knew what he was talking about.

"Yes, a piece of the puzzle you and your monk friend helped me with. It was my grotok that sat upon the monk's shoulder in the Loncodi library. Fortunately, through its eye, I was able to read all of the text before that little, bouncing, clown menace crushed my pet."

"Sorry about that," Joe said, making a wincing expression. "Did it have a name? I once had a pet dog. Got ate by a pack of vorv. I was pretty shook up. Could hardly pull off a smooth pick-pocket for days."

Nashtar paused for a moment, staring at Joe, before looking back to the altar. He placed the red crystal upright in a slot near the front of the altar that had clearly been designed specifically for the precious trinket. He ignored Joe's question. "With you and your lovely friend here assisting me, the ritual should not be a problem. Now, the shard?" Nashtar held out a hand as a pleasant smile broke across his otherwise stony face. His glowing eyes stared, unblinking and without emotion.

"You know, this isn't going anywhere near the way I expected." Joe gave Death Seed a casual twirl. "Your reputation as some sort of evil hard-ass seems off the mark. Sorry about busting in." Joe leaned on the altar, with one hand still twirling Death Seed. He looked over his shoulder at Runara, who was now nearly at the base of the dais.

"See, he's not such a big scary monster," Joe said to her, "I mean, ya a little creepy lookin', and this castle of yours, Nashy — not exactly inviting."

A look of frustration and impatience was beginning to wash across Nashtar's face with Joe's every word. It gave Runara more reason to pause, and she stopped on the first wide step of the dais and again futilely tried to summon some sort of magic. She didn't understand; before, the crystal had left a residual energy within her, but when Nashtar took it, it was as if he had pulled all of its magic out of her, too.

"So, do you have special jars of magic blood or something? You wizards and your jars, right? Always got all sorts of this and that." Joe chuckled a bit, but seeing the serious looks on Nashtar's and Runara's faces, he realized his audience wasn't in the same jovial mode. He straightened up then and cleared his throat. "No, seriously though, what's the plan?"

"This comes to mind," Nashtar said in a flat yet ominous tone, pointing the shimmering ultimorite sword at Runara.

Runara had enough time for nothing more than a shocked gasp in reaction to the sudden unseen pressure taking her breath away. In that same instant, she was flung forward through the air, up the steps, and onto Nashtar's waiting sword. It slid through her bodice, through her chest, and through her heart as though she was made of no more substance than the air around her.

"No!" Joe cried out, hardly believing his eyes. Despair and rage mingled in a confused explosion of emotion. For a moment, his normally lightning-like reflexes failed him. All of his senses felt numb, and time seemed to slow as he watched Nashtar guide her limp, seemingly weightless body to fall upon the dark altar, a look of terror and confusion still being expressed by her wide, staring, lifeless eyes.

Barely perceiving his own actions through the fog of his shock, functioning in some instinctive survival mode, Joe watched as his arm, seeming to function of its own accord, brought Death Seed down hard and fast upon the wizard.

The violent reverberating shockwave shooting down Joe's arm from Death Seed being blocked by Nashtar's ultimorite sword was enough to bring Joe back to his senses. It had also nearly caused him to drop Death Seed, and in the split second it took for him to reinforce his grip on the weapon, Nashtar was already making a counterstrike with the glittering red sword.

Joe parried the assault and came back with several quick strikes, but the old wizard moved with the agility of a man several lifetimes younger and easily deflected each of Joe's attacks.

Joe jumped back to give himself a chance to reassess his strategy, taking a few extra fleet-footed steps back as a further precaution. The wizard was a formidable swordsman.

"What is with everyone in this world being experts with a sword?" Joe's words came forced through his teeth, gritted in anger and frustration.

"Tired of the swordplay, thief?" Nashtar responded casually, clearly feeling no physical exertion from his rapid exchange of blades with Joe.

"Then let's try this." The wizard thrust out his free hand, issuing forth a torrent of green fire.

The blast was too wide and came too fast for Joe to evade; he was completely engulfed. The heat from the green flames was incredible, but to his own surprise, Joe found himself completely unharmed. Even his eyes, wide open as they were, did not feel the slightest burn. Joe took in the spectacle of the flames rushing about him with great wonder. It was beautiful, like falling through a chaotic, green kaleidoscope. Then it stopped, leaving Joe staring at Nashtar. Both men had a look of astonishment on their faces. Nashtar's gaze diverted to Death Seed then, and both men suddenly came to the same realization.

"The sword protects you from magic," Nashtar said, sounding genuinely impressed. "Even mine. Clever elves." At that moment, three throwing knives narrowly missed the wizard, turning, it seemed, of their own will, skirting around Nashtar before continuing on their original course. They clattered against stone somewhere in the darkness behind the old wizard.

"Please, you just insult me now," Nashtar said snidely. "Do you honestly think I would have lived as long as I have if some fool could simply finish me off by throwing some trinkets at me?"

"Everybody dies, old man, sooner or later." Joe charged toward Nashtar then, bellowing his battle cry. He leaped into the air at the last moment, putting all his weight behind the thrust. It was a bold but bullish maneuver, and the wizard easily swept Death Seed aside with the red sword, leaving Joe open and helpless to do anything but fall upon Nashtar's waiting point.

Joe could feel the cold metal of the sword run through his body. He felt the excruciating pain as it separated his ribs, slid through his right lung, and emerged from his back. His weight carried him to the hilt of Nashtar's sword, bringing him face to face with the sword-wielding conjuror. Nashtar, unmoved by the impact as if he existed in his own realm of gravity, smiled then, the ends of his mustache rippling in wispy triumphant curls.

"Now, thief, your story comes to an end." With that, the wizard pushed him off of the blade.

Joe staggered back but didn't fall. He was in a state of shock. It was wrong, he thought to himself, for him to die by some blade. He was the blade that others feared. Did anyone fear him? How long does it take to die? Was he dead yet? How would he know? Shouldn't he be coughing up blood? What comes next? Would he see Runara? Would he see his sister? What happened to the others? How did the wizard do that smoke thing with his mustache? All these questions flashed through his mind in a fraction of a second. It took Joe another moment to realize, not having had any prior experience with being run through entirely by a sword, that he felt perfectly fine. A quick hand to his chest added to the confusion of the moment; there was no blood, no wound, not even a small knick.

"And now, boy, I'll take that sword of yours." Nashtar reached for Death Seed.

Joe bolted upright, much to Nashtar's astonishment. "My thoughts exactly." Joe thrust Death Seed upward, deep into Nashtar's abdomen. Despite Nashtar's ethereal appearance, the sword met a very material body, and Joe plunged the sword, with more force than necessary, all the way to the feet of the naked elven women that made up Death Seed's guard.

Nashtar looked a little confused. There were a couple of things troubling the ancient wizard. The first perplexing matter was the sword piercing his belly. It was an event that just should not have been possible as he had not had a fully corporeal form for a little over a hundred years now. Only by his will could any object interact with him, and he certainly had not willed the possibility of being skewered by a sword. As disturbing as this lack of control over his form was, he found his body's solidity quite novel, noting a slight breeze in the throne room. He wondered where it was coming from since there were no doors or windows. This minor distraction, however puzzling, was not the second thing that had him truly perplexed. Being that he was now, quite evidently, solid and unable to revert back to his usual phantom-like cast, he was surprised to find himself experiencing the same unexpected lack of mortality that had spared Joe just a moment ago. Clever elves indeed, he thought.

"Seems we are at something of an impasse," Nashtar said contemptuously. His starkly white mustache and beard were now just hair, and his robes, though still a dark blue-grey, no longer took their form from the surroundings, and what had once been the streaks of stolen candle flame were now merely golden embroidered trimmings.

Joe's face betrayed his disappointment with the wizard's lack of dying, and he wiggled the sword a little. "You're sure you aren't feeling even a little faint?"

"Stop that!" Nashtar gave a wave of his free hand, sending Joe flying back with a powerful telekinetic push. Death Seed remained deeply embedded in Nashtar.

Joe tumbled across the dais, bumping his head slightly on the throne of bones.

"Ah, at last!" Nashtar pulled the sword from his body with wide-eyed reverence for the object and turned to the altar, holding both swords high before him.

Joe could only watch. It was too late to save Runara, and it would not serve him to stop the wizard from restoring the red powersword. He would work out his next move once Nashtar completed the weapon.

Upon the altar's surface, Runara's body continued to bleed. Her blood filled grooves that were carved into the table's surface in an ornate knotted pattern. The knotted grooves channeled the blood into a larger recess in the surface, near the back edge of the altar, shaped to receive the shimmering red ultimorite sword. The candlelight danced across the sword-shaped pool of blood unnaturally, nearly mimicking the shimmering nature of Nashtar's sword.

The wizard laid the large ultimorite sword, with ritualistic respect, into the pool of Runara's blood. With a few strange words and the wave of a hand over the bathing sword, the pool lit on fire the entire length of the sword. The flames were a vivid purple. A few moments passed as the fire continued to burn, making an angry rustling sound. Nashtar spoke another set of odd ancient words of magic. He repeated them several times, but with each repetition, the frustration became more evident in his voice.

"Something isn't right," Nashtar spat angrily. "The crystal should be glowing." He slid Death Seed into a slot close to him on the altar directly opposite the red crystal. It slid down to the guard, with the skeletal hand holding the crystal shard pointed toward the pool on the altar. Again, he spoke the ancient words, shouting them this time. "

"Pemboyaga ohm tel Godé wekafaehek; pusiris: Yavezdoz!"

Nothing happened. The purple flames diminished then and, with a slight popping sound, went out.

Joe had stood up and cautiously approached the wizard, who still had his back to Joe, looking down upon the altar with a look of anger and frustration.

"So, that seemed a little less spectacular than I had expected," Joe said, pulling a knife from his bandolier.

"I don't understand," Nashtar complained aloud, ignoring Joe. "The altar is a perfect replica." He slammed a fist down upon the dark altar.

"Replica?" Joe rhetorically questioned in a snide tone. "Don't know much about magic, but the way I've heard it told, substitutions in spell recipes never work out well. Serves you right, anyway, for killing your great-granddaughter, you crazy old freak." Joe lunged then at the wizard with his knife, hoping it would have more success in harming the sorcerer than Death Seed had, but all he struck was air. Nashtar had vanished.

"Greatgrand…" Nashtar's voice came from the throne, trailing off to an inaudible whisper.

Joe spun around in surprise and was even more surprised at not seeing the wizard there. Quickly scanning the dais but seeing nothing, Joe's attention was returned to the throne. Nashtar's glowing blue eyes appeared first, then the rest of him slowly materialized, sitting on the throne, a look of dismay on his face. He was staring at the form of Runara lying on the altar.

"I was told they were all dead; my children, dead. There had been rumors of some of the royal line living as brookshins, but I had no reason to believe that any of my own line had survived as well." He put his head in his hand, and it seemed as though he were about to cry. The moment was completely awkward for Joe. He wasn't sure if he should go over and try to console the shaken wizard or try to kill him again. He took a step toward Nashtar as he contemplated which course he was going to follow.

As Joe took that step, Nashtar leaped to his feet, clapping his hands in a jubilant manner. "Ha ha!" he cried out, his voice echoing throughout the pillars and off the grandly arched ceiling. The sudden movement and noise took Joe so by surprise that he stumbled back. The old wizard stroked his long white beard in contemplation as he walked back toward the altar. His pace across the dais was faster than his shuffling stride should have afforded, and his image winked in and out rapidly and randomly as though his entire existence was illuminated by some unseen strobing light.

Joe had knives in both hands then, "Stay away from her, old man; you've done her enough wrong."

Nashtar shot Joe a brief sideways glance as he reached the altar, "Put your dinnerware away, boy. I think we've already well established your inability to harm me. And if you're going to go about intimidating wizards and the like, you best have the protection of this sword of yours." He motioned then at Death Seed, but the focus of his gaze remained on Runara.

Joe approached cautiously, sheathing one of his knives. He reached past Nashtar, keeping an eye on the distracted wizard, as one might reach around a rearing snake, watching for any sudden moves as he pulled Death Seed from the altar.

Nashtar turned to him with a sly smile as Joe took a few quick steps back with the sword. "Although I'm sure we're both very aware that the sword is not truly yours. An elf by the name of Solvar had claim to it, if I'm not mistaken. One of Ethdab's lackeys, correct?"

Joe gave a hesitant nod.

Nashtar began sweeping his hands back and forth just above Runara's body. "One of the soldiers in the Loncodi market, yes?"

Joe gave another hesitant nod. "What are you doing?"

"Bringing her back, of course. What is the point of being a notorious necromancer if you can't even bring back your own mistakenly murdered great-grandchild? You'll want to step back now." Nashtar waved Joe back toward the throne as he pulled the ultimorite sword from the pool of Runara's blood. Both the sword and his hand came out completely clean. Unseen to Joe, distracted by the bloodless red sword, Nashtar dipped his other hand in the sword-shaped pool of his great-granddaughter's blood, collecting a sample of it in a vile he had secreted from his robes. With the same hand, he quickly and deftly stopped up and tucked the vile away. He then took several steps back from the altar, speaking ancient words that seemed to boom from the room's walls, pillars, and ceiling rather than from the wizard. "Awcksfaerise virosin kasmodin!"

The entire altar was suddenly engulfed in a vortex of green fire that exploded up from the dais. It extended up in a swirling funnel to the ceiling, illuminating ornately carved gargoyles and other strange beastly statues that had before been hidden in the shadows. The candles that had been lazily floating around the altar now orbited at a mad pace, their flames sputtering from the speed. It looked as though the candles were to be pulled into the fiery tornado, but just as suddenly as it had appeared, the vortex dispersed in a spectacular, dense burst of millions of tiny green embers that quickly faded.

To Joe's astonishment, Runara was now standing on the altar. Her hair, billowing about her head as though it were alive, looked more like a vibrant red fire than hair; it even gave off a subtle light of its own now, and small, pink, ember-like lights winked in and out amongst her luminous locks like tiny little fireflies. Her eyes glowed green and darted about as the bewildered witch tried to fathom what was happening or what had happened.

Nashtar leaned over slightly to Joe and, in a hushed tone, casually said, "When you bring someone back from the dead, there are always some side effects."

"Did I — you killed me!" Runara pointed a finger at Nashtar. A vivid green stream of fire shot out from it. The fire deflected around Nashtar, stopped by some unseen barrier. Runara gave a startled gasp, stopping the fiery burst, and she looked quizzically at her now smoking finger. Her other hand went absently to her cleavage, feeling about for the crystal that was no longer there.

"You won't be needing that any longer, granddaughter," Nashtar said with a broad smile. There seemed to be something softer, less sinister in his countenance. Nashtar held out a hand, and the red crystal, still in the slot in the altar, shot out between Runara's legs. It punched two holes in her dress as it went but seemed to have all the impact of a falling feather when it reached Nashtar's hand. He held it up momentarily for Runara to understand what he was talking about, then quickly tucked it away in some unseen location within his robes with a bit of prestidigitation.

"As wonderful as this little family reunion is," Joe said then, clearing his throat, "and as truly awesome as you raising Runara from the dead is…"

"Thanks," Runara interjected with sarcasm in Joe's direction as she walked down what seemed to be an invisible set of steps from the altar. Her hair still sparkled with a life of its own, and her eyes continued to glow vibrantly. She seemed to be unaware that there were not actually stairs beneath her.

"I mean, look at your hair; how are you going to comb that? Pretty, though. The eyes are a nice touch, too. I really see the whole family resemblance now."

Joe was whipping Death Seed back and forth between Nashtar and Runara, using it as a pointer as he spoke.

Runara ran a hand through her hair, trying to see what Joe was talking about. The action stirred up a flurry of pink embers that sparkled about her head, drifting in all directions. "Oh!" was all she could muster as she watched the display with fascination. Joe had gone silent, watching the odd spectacle as well.

"You were getting to a point, boy?" Nashtar queried, sounding a little impatient.

Joe shook his head, breaking the hypnotic hold of Runara's mesmerizing and now magically accentuated beauty. "Uh, ya, so, my point is…"

"Can you put the sword together and send Joe back to his world?" Runara interjected, helping Joe finish his thought.

The two men looked at each other, then at Runara, both trying to figure out the best way to explain the failed attempt. Nashtar was the one to speak up. He apologized to his great-granddaughter for his involvement in her death and went on to explain that he had clearly misinterpreted the poem that Joe and the others had found in the Loncodi library. He further explained that his reproduction of the altar may have also been a factor in the failed attempt to restore the red powersword.

Runara was the one to ask where the true altar was and why Nashtar had gone to the trouble to replicate it. He explained that long ago, during the height of the war with King Mazeze, he had spun some very dark spells to fuse his essence with that of the keep so as to better command the defenses both without and within. As successful as the spells had been, it had rendered him something of a phantom, and despite his attempts, he had never been able to reverse it. His enchanted link to the keep also made it impossible for him to leave. He relied on an army of grotoks, and other similar, conjured entities, wandering and lurking nearly everywhere, to be his links to the outside world. Through such creatures, he could see, hear, and sometimes even speak. It allowed him to interact with and explore the world, albeit in a limited capacity. It had been through one of these conjured beasts that he had found the true altar of the godés, but he would never be able to use such creatures to carry out the magic ritual of restoring the sword.

He then thanked Joe for breaking the enchantment by trying to kill him with Death Seed, for he would now be able to travel to the location of the actual altar. Once there, he assured the two he could restore the red powersword. Joe and Runara looked at each other with some concern, but before either could protest, Nashtar quickly asserted that her sacrifice would not be necessary if he was right about the poem's meaning this time. They seemed less than convinced, and just as Runara was about to express her reluctance to trust Nashtar, he vanished.

Joe looked at Runara, hoping she might have some insight into why and where the old wizard had vanished, but she simply shrugged, just as mystified as he. A few minutes passed as Runara and Joe looked around the room, finding no sign of Nashtar or that he might return. Runara pointed out to Joe, who had already noticed when they first arrived, that there did not seem to be an exit from the room. Joe put Death Seed back in its scabbard as he noted to himself that the wizard would have to return for the sword, or at least the shard in its hilt. It was then that Nashtar reappeared, his image flickering for a moment like a freshly lit candle flame.

"Bit out of practice doing that with a physical body," he said, giving his shoulders a shake and a shrug as though he had just relieved himself of some sort of heavy load. He was, in fact, somewhat more encumbered than when he had left them. A large, flapped, black leather satchel was slung across his chest, resting on his right hip. The ultimorite sword was now in a simple, deep scarlet leather scabbard hanging off of his left hip, and in his left hand, he held a tall, black staff, nearly a foot taller than himself, capped with a large, dark, red, egg-shaped crystal. Joe found it vaguely familiar, and Nashtar noticed his focus on it.

"You've seen the likes of this before, eh boy?"

Joe nodded. "Ya, it's like the sticks some metal fellas in the Loncodi library used to knock my friends and me senseless. Shot out some sort of light."

"Well, now, that is interesting," Nashtar said with a pondering look. "The things those knowers dabble in. The magic they call science will someday be this world's undoing, you know," he said, waving a declarative pointed finger in the air as he walked over to Runara in his blinking fashion. "I would know, I was once a member of the Mokaren knower's guild. Youngest member of any of the Senuvian city guilds, I was." Nashtar puffed his chest a little at this, and the beginnings of a proud smile crept into one of the corners of his mouth.

Nashtar fished around in his satchel with his free hand, producing the red crystal pendant. His look and demeanor became very serious once again. "Don't be deceived by the narrow-minded truths of science, girl." He waved the crystal in the air. "The energies that flow through this bauble will serve you far more than any understanding of its geometry." His form winked out, and suddenly, he was by the throne again, the crystal once again tucked out of sight. "Shall we go then?"

"I have some questions," Joe responded in an even tone as he turned casually, finding he was actually getting used to the wizard's teleporting ways.

"Yes, like, where are our friends?" Runara interjected before Joe could ask anything distractingly pointless.

"Of course, of course," Nashtar said, waving a dismissive hand. "After a hundred years or so without proper guests, one forgets the manners of court. They should still be all right, mostly." He uttered a variety of strange words then and motioned for Runara and Joe to look back to the shadowy pillared center of the chamber. Several of the candles floating about the altar rushed out to the center of the chamber, then, like scurrying servants, summoned to service. They hung low, illuminating a portion of the floor at the center of the room.

"The keep gets hungry, and it's been far too long since its last meal," Nashtar explained as the entire room quaked with a low, rumbling vibration. "Seems a shame to make it give up a meal, especially given the north exit's state of disrepair."

The shaking of the room became more violent. Runara grabbed hold of the altar for stability. Nashtar seemed unaffected by the room's motion, standing comfortably in place as though nothing was happening. Joe, however, was stumbling about, unable to catch his balance despite some very acrobatic effort. Runara held out a hand just as he was about to tumble down the stairs of the dais. Joe was pulled by an unseen force to Runara's side at the altar.

Then came a thunderous clap as the stones in the illuminated portion of the dark chamber floor split apart. Thick red fluid gushed from the large crack, like blood from a wound. The crack widened as more of the blood-like liquid poured out across the violently heaving floor. Cracked bits of masonry fell from the walls and ceiling. A blob of the bloody mess erupted from the floor like a horse-sized clot being purged from the veins of the keep.

Horrifyingly, the clot seemed to be alive, roiling and rolling about the blood-soaked floor. The candles followed its movements, casting flickering shadows that added the illusion of even more oozing movement from the thing. Behind the great, bloody creeping mass, the crack in the floor closed, and the blood that had covered the floor was disappearing, seemingly being soaked back into the stone flooring. A roar came from the shambling clot as it produced a set of talons and what appeared to be some sort of horn.

"We are not afraid of your beasts, wizard," Joe shouted back over his shoulder to Nashtar. "We'll end this… thing, like we did your garden monster."

Nashtar simply laughed and motioned for Joe to return his attention to the bloody monstrosity. Where the talons and horn had emerged, great rips and tears formed, and soon, it was clear that the twisting blob was no monstrosity but simply a bloody membrane containing some other monstrosity. The membrane burst apart then, sending bloody flaps of goo flying in all directions. Kord and Koobara stood among the bloody remnants of their shredded prison, both huffing as though they had nearly suffocated. Neither looked particularly happy.

"Now that you mention it, thank you for dispensing with the Grix. Independent-minded that one was. In hindsight, It's clear that summoning a celeston immune to magic and binding it to this keep as its container was not a particularly wise move on my part. Tremendously curious that your magic burned the beast; curious indeed." He gave Runara a smile. There was something sinister in his smile, pleasant though he tried to make it. "Oh look, here comes your little clown friend."

Joe and Runara spun around in time to see a large yellow and black striped beetle crawl onto the top of the altar. The candle lights glinted off of its highly polished body shell. It was about the size of a kitten but not nearly in the same universe of cuteness. Its six black legs were covered with sharp spines. Its antennae were twice the length of its body and flicked around chaotically, snapping like tiny, dangerous whips. A thick purple fluid oozed from its vertically aligned hard-shelled mouth. It had no protruding mandibles. Joe and Runara leaped back, startled by the enormous insect's arrival. Before Joe could draw a knife or Runara could summon a lick of flame, Nashtar spoke in the creature's defense, reassuring them that it would do them no harm. He explained that it was called a mincing bug. The bug was rare to Senuvia but common to the old temples of Kil'Velhara.

"I suspect the poor little thing was drawn here by the energies of my replica altar," Nashtar postulated. "Quite a compliment, really, given that it doesn't seem to work. In any case, she's made a remarkably affectionate pet and a welcome addition to the keep's security." He clapped his hands at the fidgeting insect. "Go on then, give the girl back to her friends."

The mincing bug turned to look at the wizard directly and rattled its thorax defiantly, which made what sounded like a couple of knives being quickly sharpened.

"Don't you start with me," Nashtar barked. "You'll not be making any eggs today. Now give her up." The mincing bug twitched its thorax slightly but made no sound, and its feverishly thrashing antennae came to rest. "Now!" Nashtar's voice boomed with the same menace it had earlier upon meeting Joe.

The mincing bug immediately opened its mouth. It continued to open, impossibly, beyond the size of its head until it no longer resembled the creature's mouth but looked to be a fathomless, dark slice in the fabric of existence as tall as Joe.

A sick, wet, sucking sound issued from the void, followed by the ejection of a large human-sized, purple, slime-covered mass that shot over Runara's head, causing her to duck and scream. Suddenly, Kord was at her side. Koobara pounced onto the altar with a roar. The mincing bug's mouth collapsed instantly to normality, and the insect quickly scurried away from the jungle cat, its antennae snapping loudly as it fled into the surrounding darkness of the room.

"Quite the dramatic lot, aren't you?" Nashtar sneered with an amused smile as he took a few steps over to the purple slime-covered form of Crash lying on the dais floor. "Nothing to worry about, just a little paralytic intestinal muck. Nothing we all haven't experienced before in one form or another, right?" Runara, Kord, and Joe all nodded in conceding agreement.

Nashtar made a little circle in the air with his staff above Crash. The slime covering her evaporated into a hissing cloud of steam, leaving the distinct smell of raspberries in the air. Crash gasped and bolted up into a sitting position. She looked around frantically, clearly bewildered.

"There, see, not so bad." Nashtar offered Crash a hand, bracing himself on his staff as he helped her to her feet. She looked a little different now. The clown make-up was gone, making her look younger and certainly prettier, Joe thought, and her green hair was no longer the myriad of tiny ponytails but lying flat and slicked back. Crash's senses quickly returned, and she gave her friends a happy little wave as she got to her feet. Her demeanor was as though her means of arrival had been perfectly normal. She hopped over to Joe and Runara, giving them each warm hugs.

As Crash pulled back from her hug with Runara, she paused, holding her by both shoulders. Her eyes lit up as she took in the dance of embers in Runara's fiery locks. "Love what you've done with your hair," she said with a broad smile, her expression full of wonder.

Runara giggled slightly putting a self-conscious hand to her hair, stirring up a small cloud of twinkling embers. "Died; I mean, I died, and then…this."

Crash nodded as if she thoroughly understood. After watching the pink embers with fascination for a few moments more, she managed to pull herself away, motioning a hug towards Kord, who only frowned and grunted in return.

"Later then," Crash said with a little pout, eliciting another stoic grunt from Kord.

Koobara was slightly warmer, coming up to Crash and nuzzling her hip, allowing Crash to give the large cat a couple pats on the shoulder. It quickly slinked away, however, before things could get any more affectionate.

"Where are Garen and Tosh?" Crash asked, looking around. "And you, you're…" she started to say as she spun around to face the wizard.

"Yes, I am her great-grandfather, the man whose home you and your air pirates broke into, your host, and soon to be your guide." Nashtar gave Crash a slight bow. "As for the monk and your knower, getting them back will be a little trickier. They have been trapped within a complex mathematical equation. It will take me some time to calculate them back into a product of this dimension. I should have them out along the way."

"Along the way to wh—" Before Crash could finish her question, a bright, blinding, green light erupted from Nashtar's staff. The entire group, including Nashtar, vanished. Crash's interrupted question echoed in the empty altar room as the mincing bug skittered across the dais, trying to find an exit.

Chapter 18

Mickalbane and Broyer watched from atop a large elephant-shaped rocky outcrop as an old man led a motley group of six others and what may have been a large black dog to a long, wooden landing. Being quite a distance down the beach, the two men had gone completely unnoticed as the group made their way to the end of the decrepit dock.

There was little of the ancient marine platform left. Much of its structure had long since rotted away, and portions of what remained were partially submerged. Despite this, the group managed to navigate to a reasonably stable part near its end, far out over the water.

It may have been a trick of the fog, but it had appeared to the two men, observing from the rock, that the old man and the others had simply materialized on the beach when they arrived. Few sorcerers would have the ability to teleport so many at once, forcing the two observers to conclude, as unlikely as it seemed, that it was the reclusive necromancer, Nashtar, who led the group. It was quite a rare moment to note, as nobody had seen the wizard in decades. Only one other in the group looked even remotely familiar to the two men. Even at this distance, Mickalbane and Broyer recognized Joe as the man they had found over a week ago, washed up on the shore near the King's castle. Presently, under the command of Baron Solvar, they had been tasked with finding Joe, or more precisely, the sword he had stolen from the Baron.

After the sword thief had evaded capture in Loncodi, Solvar had dispatched Mickalbane and Broyer on their marhorses to this distant northern coast. Solvar had been confident that should he not manage to catch the thief pursuing him aboard the Roc's Tooth, Joe was likely to show up at precisely this location.

The waters in this area were permanently shrouded in fog, making it far too treacherous for many ocean travelers. It was not an area frequented by travelers or even merchants. It was also very close to the border of the elven land of Gizesh. The elves were not fond of the conquering human King and would be less than pleased to find two of his guardsmen so close to their border. It made both men extremely uncomfortable as they waited for days without a sign of any ship approaching the area, let alone the Harmaton. It seemed unlikely they would see anyone coming to this remote area by land or sea, but the two men would have to wait for further orders to arrive before they could even think about leaving. It was proposed on several occasions, while they waited, by one or the other, that a wager be placed on whether the sword thief would actually show. However, a bet was never struck between the two as neither wanted to risk their scant wages by taking the stance that the thief would turn up.

Solvar, it turned out, had been right though. The group's sudden appearance on the beach had made their arrival even more of a surprise. It was Mickalbane who had suggested that the group had likely come ashore further up the coast, and their seemingly sudden appearance was just a trick of the fog. Broyer was more inclined to believe his eyes and was pretty sure that there was magic involved. Regardless of how the group arrived, their presence meant the end of him and his partner being stationed there.

At this distance, it was hard to tell if either of the swords worn by Joe or the wizard was the sword they were looking for, but Solvar would be pleased enough that Joe and his accomplices had arrived just as he had predicted.

Broyer had already sent a messenger bat to Baron Solvar, informing him of their sighting. The bat had returned in less than an hour. It was unexpectedly quick. It had ignited a heated argument between the two marhorsemen regarding the correct deployment procedures for a messenger bat, which somehow evolved into a debate over the gender of the bat and its possible state of pregnancy. Unable to reach an agreement on any portion of the matter, Mickalbane, hoping to make the best of the bat's premature return, asked to see the message again. He had been uncomfortable with the grammatical structure of his partner's original note to the Baron and felt this was an opportunity to make a better impression on their commander. However, opening the small brass canister on the bat's chest harness did not reveal the note they had sent to Solvar, but surprisingly, a response from their commander. He commended the two men for a job well done and informed them that the Roc's Tooth was docked on the other side of the peninsula, resupplying at the town of Markam. They would be departing soon and could be expected by sundown. The note went on to urgently instruct them to send out another bat to inform the King of their location and to be sure to indicate the possibility that the thief was in the company of Nashtar.

As Mickalbane continued to keep an eye on the group, his polarized crystal visor cutting through the surrounding fog, Broyer had ridden off to a location further up the coast. Mickalbane had assured him, after much discussion, that this location would be more appropriate for deploying a westbound messenger bat, especially if it were potentially pregnant. Broyer eventually conceded to Mickalbane's insistence on the deployment location, if only for the reason that it would not draw any undue attention from the group on the dock. It would also afford him the freedom of writing out the message to the King without Mickalbane correcting every other word.

As Broyer wrote the note, trying not to make too much of a mess with the tiny portable but awkward quill and ink, the three messenger bats in their small wire mesh cages behind his saddle suddenly began screeching and flapping. They were clearly disturbed by something. He had barely turned to see what was troubling the bats when his dark grey marhorse began stomping its front hooves anxiously, the spines of its fin mane fully splayed, and it was snorting fiercely. Soon, the marhorse was tossing its head in complete agitation, prompting Broyer to look out across the water in the direction that seemed to have his marhorse so disturbed.

Buried deep in the thick fog across the water but fairly visible through Broyer's visor, a dark shrouded figure guided a large, shallow ferry made of black, twisting, driftwood timbers. Broyer recognized the figure instantly. Though he had never seen him before, he knew the ominous figure had to be the ferryman of the Isle of Graa. Some believed the ferryman to be one of the four embodiments of Death and the Isle of Graa, the gateway to the land of the dead. If legend was to be believed, the only way to reach the mysterious island was by taking the ferry, and nobody ever made a return trip.

Broyer modified the note to the King, happy that Mickalbane was not over his shoulder to see him scratching out words. If the thief was indeed traveling with the necromancer, Nashtar, it seemed likely that the old wizard had somehow summoned the ferryman, and the King would need to know they were headed to Graa. With any luck, the King would recognize the hopelessness of pursuing the thief to the island, sending Broyer and his partner back to their far less adventurous beach patrol back at the castle.

Rolling the note into a tight scroll – a true task with his thick, fumbling fingers – he quickly pushed a hand into the one-way hinged side of one of the small meshed baskets, seizing the messenger bat trained to seek out the King. He slid the note into the squirming little creature's canister and set it free. It screeched loudly, flying inland away from the ferryman. It was exactly the opposite direction Broyer had expected the bat to fly if it were going to seek out the King, and his hopes of a quick release from his assignment flittered away on the wings of the fearful little creature.

* * * * * * * * * * * * * * * * * * * *

They had been on the ferry for an hour with no way of telling if they were anywhere near their destination. Despite several attempts by Joe to start a conversation of some sort, the group had traveled almost entirely in silence to that point. The problem was that Crash, Runara, Tosh, and Garen all had a foreboding sense that they were being ferried to their doom. Each had been told the same tales, as children, about Death ferrying the bad little boys and girls to the gates of the underworld city of the damned on the Isle of Graa, never to be seen again. Even Kord and Koobara seemed uneasy, neither taking their eyes off the enormous, mysteriously cloaked ferry driver.

The driver's tattered, sea salt-encrusted, black robes covered every aspect of his towering twelve-foot countenance. Only a single curving ram-like horn on the right side of the driver's head poked through a tear in the driver's hood, giving a glimpse of a glistening, white, bony skull beneath. Even the giant's hands remained covered, grabbing the ferry's massive oar through the weathered cloth of the sleeves, giving only the hint of the large but thin, bony hands beneath.

It had been an argument to get all but Joe onto the boat and was only resolved by Nashtar teleporting the rest onboard. Heated words and even some threats followed, coming to a quick, silent end when Joe pointed out they had already pulled away from the dock. In fact, the dock's location was already lost in the surrounding fog. Tosh had tried to jump out of the ferry, only to find that an invisible force prevented any such attempt. He accused Nashtar of conjuring the invisible cage, but Nashtar assured him that he had nothing to do with it.

The ferry driver spoke then in a deep, hollow voice that seemed to be echoing up from the bottom of a deep well. "All will stay within until the boat has come to rest."

Another argument amongst the group and Nashtar erupted about the nature of the Isle of Graa. The group continued to bicker about their plight until Joe piped up, observing that it would not make sense for Nashtar to have got in the boat as well if he thought he was sending them all to their doom. It was at that point that all further vocal interaction of any sort had come to an end, much to Joe's torture. Having had no success starting any conversation with his friends, he fell to recanting tales of his adventures among the islands and water hills of Beedo back in Midgorn. He felt they seemed to vaguely relate to their water travel now.

"You seldom shut up, do you lad?" Nashtar interrupted what was Joe's third tale of having inadvertently instigated a barroom brawl in yet another in a string of fishing villages.

Joe laughed. "Well, it's always been my experience that a quiet man is up to something."

"And the one talking is usually trying to distract you from that 'something,'" Nashtar added with a knowing smile.

"Fair enough," Joe said with a broad smile, happy to finally have someone engaged. "I know I'm certainly not up to anything sly, so what are you up to then? Why take us on a boat ride when you could have just blinked us to the island? I mean, if I were a wizard, I'd never get off of my arse again. I'd just find me a big comfy chair and blink myself wherever I need to be, chair and all."

Nashtar frowned a little, still not used to the workings of Joe's mind. "Simply because I couldn't. The island is protected by an old magic; the oldest, in fact. It keeps anyone from reaching the island or even being able to find the island except by this ferry."

"Well, that hardly seems like any kind of foolproof security," Joe smirked. "If anyone can just hop on the boat, why hide the island at all?"

"Did you see me call for the ferry, boy? Do you think we just happened to be here in time for its regular stop? You saw the state of that dock, lad; no one goes there expecting to catch a ride. One has to have the right credentials."

"Credentials?"

"Yes." Nashtar patted the hilt of his ultimorite sword. "I suspect the shard in your sword and perhaps even the red crystal helped us as well. Likely why the boat showed up as quickly as it did."

"But if the only way onto the island is by this ferry," Joe pondered aloud, "how did your spy critter, whatever it was, get there to see your table thing?"

"The altar," Nashtar corrected Joe. "Well, now, that involves the story of an unfortunate fellow whose reputation for bringing unintended destruction with him wherever he went brought him to be known as The Hand of Death."

"Oh, that sounds like a good story. Go on then, let's hear it." Joe leaned forward with an anxious, child-like smile as he anticipated the coming tale.

"No, no, far too grand a story, and I certainly do not have all the details. Much of what is told is simply rumor, I'm sure. I can only tell you with certainty the part of the man's tale that I, or rather, my garatok, was part of.

Joe and Nashtar's conversation caught the attention of Tosh, who pulled out his journal, ready to record any interesting bits of the story.

Garen's interest had been captured as well, and he nimbly skipped over the twelve bench seats from where he had been sitting near the front, softly landing in the seat beside Joe. "Did you say The Hand of Death?

There was an illustration of a man, supposedly with the black powersword, in that book in the library." Garen was speaking to Joe more than Nashtar.

"So there was." Nashtar smiled. "A fairly accurate likeness, too, from what my grotok saw."

Now Crash shuffled into the seat behind Joe. "Whose head did that grotok come out of anyway?"

"A pirate foolish enough to try to enter my home uninvited," Nashtar replied, giving her a grave look. Crash frowned but sat silent, unsure if the wizard was actually aware of her past. Nashtar turned back to Joe and Garen with an artificially bright smile then. "But we stray from the tale, and, as I said, it was one of my garatoks, not a grotok, that traveled for a short time with the bearer of the forbidden black blade."

"What's a garatok?" Crash interrupted. The smile instantly dropped from Nashtar's face as his glare was once again drawn in her direction.

It was Tosh who quickly responded with the answer. "It's a sort of golem, fashioned from the bones of two creatures, usually a blackbird and a rat, held together with thin, silver wire. A clay, mixed with the sorcerer's own blood and some of the organs of the two animals, is molded around the skeleton to form the body of the garatok. We're not sure how the figure is animated, however."

"Magic," Nashtar said flatly, clearly trying to restrain a growing frustration with the group.

"Of course," Tosh responded politely, but there was the slightest hint of a patronizing tone in the two words.

Nashtar straightened himself then into a more assertive posture. All in the group, save for Kord and Runara, who were busy now with a conversation of their own, sat back slightly in response, even Tosh. It made the wizard smile. It was good for them to fear him, he thought, at least a little.

"There is more to this universe than the knowers of this or any of the other worlds will ever allow themselves to comprehend." He looked directly at Tosh then, "Only a novice uses silver; gold conducts much better and makes for more fluid movement. And rats and blackbirds are for magic-fumbling apprentices trying to seem darker and more mysterious than they truly are. I prefer squirrels and parrots; the garatoks come out far more clever."

Tosh madly scribbled away in his journal with Nashtar's every word. It brought a legitimate humored chuff from the old wizard. Nashtar cleared his throat. "But we continue to stray from the story." The wizard touched the center of his forehead with his left hand while he repeatedly made a circle in the air before him with his right. "I've never been one for painting images with words," he said, still making circles in the air. He looked directly at Tosh then. "I find that a little magic helps."

The air within the invisibly defined circle rippled. From the perspective of the others, it looked, at first, as though Nashtar had transformed from the shoulders up into a different man.

The man's hair was black, long, and greasy, yet well combed. His face was younger than Nashtar's by far, with an uneven scruff rather than a beard and mustache, but the features of his face were a complex contradiction of age. There was none of the jowls or sagging of age, but his features were sunken with dark, nearly black circles around his eyes. His skin was pale and smooth, as though it had never seen the sun, yet had a weathered and leathery stiffness. He did not have the multitude of wrinkles and creases that the old wizard's face had, but there were deep lines in his face, particularly around his mouth and brow, that seemed far beyond the years of the rest of his face. He puffed on a shallow pipe, the bowl of which had been carved into the shape of a sorrowful skull. Smoke curled out of the nostrils of the man's long, pointed nose.

Upon his shoulder sat a purple-grey gargoyle-like creature. It greedily sniffed in the wisps of smoke that drifted by its upturned piggish nose. The creature's head was misshapen, having one pointed ear larger than the other, while the empty sockets that were its eyes were mismatched in size but opposite to the size differences of the ears. Three bony horns, each of a slightly different size than the next, curled from its forehead. A sharply hooked, suspiciously parrot-like beak formed its mouth. It clung to the dark canvas garment of the man, with curiously human-like hands but with long, sharp talons. A swishing tentacle of a tail flicked into view from behind the man's shoulder from time to time, and if the man moved too suddenly, the little creature flapped out leathery, grey feather-backed wings to keep its balance.

The group was mesmerized. Even Runara and Kord were distracted from their private discussion, taking in the curious sight.

"The Hand of Death," came Nashtar's voice from behind the image of the man who continued to puff upon his pipe. Crash leaned forward and to the side to see around the image floating before Nashtar, just to confirm that he hadn't, in fact, transformed. Nashtar gave her a wink. She giggled like a little girl and sat back.

"Are we looking through time?" Garen questioned.

"In a sense. What you see is a visually approximated, perspective-shifted, ocular remembrance. It is based on the experiences of my garatok, the little fellow on the man's shoulder."

"It sorta looks like a monkey." Crash asserted.

"Yes, quite; if a monkey had a beak, no eyes, horns, and could fly, then yes, the resemblance would be striking." Sarcasm dripped from Nashtar's words, causing Crash to once again sit back with a pout on her face.

Joe was scrutinizing the image, leaning in closer for a better look. "It looks like he's on this same ferry." From Joe's close perspective, it was as though he were looking through a window, with more of the scene visible if he looked up, down, or to the sides. It was not a flat image limited to the borders of the floating circle. The pipe-smoking Hand of Death did, indeed, seem to be sitting exactly where Nashtar now sat, the ominous figure of the ferry driver looming behind him, moving in perfect sync with the one in the present.

"Cursed, as I mentioned, by the black powersword, to bring destruction with him everywhere he went, this poor soul sought out the isle of Graa. He had learned from the King of Azizoo that on the island, he might find the means of dispensing with the sword that he was otherwise unable to rid himself of."

"Azizoo? Where's that?" Crash piped up again.

"It's nonsense, Miss Crash," Tosh answered back as he continued to write down Nashtar's narrative. "Barry would speak of it often. He believes it to be a kingdom found on the moon Zeebo."

"Not nonsense at all," Nashtar said, shuffling himself to one side to better see the rest of the group beyond the floating vision. "But, again, a part of this man's tale to which I am not entirely privy." He waved his hand at the floating vision, and the image changed. Now the man was standing on a rocky shore, among the rubble of a great ruin."

"Why is he all wet?" Joe questioned. "What did we miss."

"Nothing at all," Nashtar said, waving his hand at the scene again. "Just a little trouble involving getting off the ferry before he ought to have." The image changed again.

Tosh frowned at this, wondering how it was possible for the Hand of Death to have jumped overboard but not for him. He stopped himself from asking, however, certain that Nashtar's response would simply be "magic."

The man known as the Hand of Death stood before an altar in a ruined, overgrown temple open to the sky. Nashtar's garatok skittered about the altar, scrutinizing its entire surface. Fog or perhaps smoke swirled about the scene. The man looked completely frantic. His hair was entirely gone; not even eyebrows or eyelashes remained. The hair was not the only notable absence. He was naked now as well. All that remained was the sword in his hand, and this he placed upon the altar. He opened his hand with a look of trepidation on his face that quickly gave way to a look of surprise and then tearful elation. The man jumped back from the altar, shouting and leaping about with a primal joy.

"What happened to his hair?" Crash asked, leaning over Joe's shoulder to get a closer look, nearly knocking Joe over and into the image in the process.

"Fire trap," Nashtar said flatly.

"Seems an improvement," Garen said with a bit of sarcasm, rubbing a hand across his own bald head.

"I'd say it's an improvement." There was a little too much enthusiasm in Crash's voice, and her gaze was clearly at a much lower angle than the man's head.

Joe coughed slightly in surprise as he followed Crash's gaze into the floating scene. "Looks more like they should have called him Two and a Half Hands of Death. How is it he isn't burned?" he asked, happy to turn his head in Nashtar's direction. "The sword, right?"

Nashtar simply nodded affirmatively in response and pointed for Joe to continue to pay attention to the vision.

The garatok, which was now looking over the sword with the same scrutiny it had given the altar, had its attention suddenly pulled in another direction. It began screeching and pointing, trying to get the man's attention. It wasn't necessary; the man already had a look of terror washing over his face as he, too, looked upon whatever horror approached outside of the view of Nashtar's memory window. Then, the unseen could be heard stomping closer and closer. It sounded massive, whatever it was.

"But, but you were dead! I killed you!" the hairless man screamed, his wavering voice an exasperated blend of his present terror and an anger born of decades of frustration.

"Mortal fool," rumbled back a voice like rolling thunder.

The man's horror seemed to build, and his eyes darted to the sword lying just a few feet away on the altar. Letting out a horrendous bellowing scream, he made a sudden move to reach for the blade that he had sought so long to be rid of. In that same instance, an enormous set of jaws that looked to be made of white diamond, lined with a hundred long spiked crystalline teeth, descended from somewhere above and bit the man in two. The garatok screeched and started to fly away, and then the image faded.

The group sat silent, still staring at the space in the air where Nashtar's vision had been floating.

It was Joe who finally broke the silence. "Well, what in Kodin's ass was that?" He asked in a distressed, raised tone.

Crash answered before the wizard could. "A dragon," her voice was low and gravely serious. "But not any sort I have ever seen before. It's much larger, and…" She searched for words.

"Made of crystal?" Joe offered with questioning doubt, "What sort of dragon is made of crystal? How is that even possible? How does it move?"

"And it spoke!" Tosh added. Unlike the others, his voice was full of excitement. "The real question is, what manner of dragon speaks? It would be fascinating to see the whole beast!" The others looked at Tosh then as though he had gone slightly mad. "From a safe distance, of course," he amended.

"The 'beast' is known as Oxidisis, the guardian of Graa," Nashtar said. "Whether he is a dragon or not is debatable. What I can tell you is, The

Hand of Death was fortunate enough to encounter the beast asleep and had dealt it what should have been a killing blow before the beast had a chance to awake."

"Fortunate?" Joe scoffed.

"If one of these powerswords cannot kill it, then what hope have we against this guardian?" Garen's voice was calm and emotionless. "We do not even possess a complete powersword."

"Yet," Nasthar corrected. "And you will have me. I'm confident that I can restrain the creature."

"If it lives, it can die." Kord's unexpected interjection drifted from the front of the boat, pausing the conversation momentarily.

"But dragons are resistant to magic." The sincere concern in Crash's voice was unsettling to Joe.

"Most magic." Nashtar glared back at Crash. "We will avoid going to the trouble of destroying the monster, if we can."

"Okay, look, as much as I appreciate the size of your magic-blasting balls, I've said it before," Joe stood up, turning about to address everyone in the group. "I don't do dragons. Maybe we find me another way home. What d'you say?"

Crash quickly responded with a small, sad smile and an agreeing nod.

"There will be no turning back now, boy." There was a restrained anger building in Nashtar's tone despite his attempt to make the words sound cordial through a forced smile.

"There is trouble ahead," the haunting voice of the ferry driver interrupted then, one of his long arms outstretched, looming above their heads, pointing a cloaked, bony finger forward.

The group turned to look out across the front of the ferry. An enormous ball of flame erupted somewhere in the mist, briefly illuminating a large portion of the fog ahead. The heat from it washed over the group. Then, as if in response, lightning, far above, lit up the entire surroundings in a brilliant flash with an immediate, thunderous boom. Joe was so startled by it all that he nearly stumbled over the side of the ferry. Garen grabbed him by his bandolier and pulled him back down onto his seat. The water all around the ferry began to churn, heaving the ferry in every direction.

"You will pay me now." The ferry driver's hollow, emotionless voice echoed. Lightning, thunder, and another burst of flame followed the ferryman's words as if on cue.

"You heard the man; let's pay him and get ourselves outa' here before that island-guarding dragon figures out where we are." Joe was patting himself down, looking for any spare coins, ignoring the gems from the Loncodi market in his pocket. Runara, Tosh, and Garen, too, began digging into their coin purses.

"Yes, yes, pay the man." Tosh's voice was frantic. "What do we owe?" Another burst of lightning flashed and boomed at a deafening volume.

"We'll do no such thing," Nashtar roared, grabbing his staff. "And I'll not stand for your tricks, ferryman." He thumped his staff down hard on the floor of the boat. A spherical wave of green energy burst from the head of the staff, spreading out across the water and into the fog. The sea calmed, and the flame and lightning bursts ceased. "You will be paid once we reach our destination and not before, but not a single coin should any of us fail to reach Graa's shore.

The ferry driver said nothing but gave Nashtar a subtle, solemn bow, and the ferry glided on deeper into the endless fog.

* * * * * * * * * * * * * * * * * *

Seeing the Roc's Tooth approach through the fog, Mickalbane set out upon his marhorse to meet the ship. The marhorse, its belly barely submerged, cut through the water with the speed of fifty oarsmen. Its broad tail, looking like an opalescent combination of a tattered, ribbed fish's tail with the rigid thickness of a dolphin's, splashed on the surface each time Mickalbane spurred the beast ahead. As they drew near the massive ship's larboard side, Mickalbane lit a lamp and waved it emphatically to ensure it would be seen. A shout came up from the ship to turn about, and it began to steer in Micalbane's direction. He turned his marhorse around then, his lamp held high, guiding the ship through the fog, into the small bay. Just as Baron Solvar had anticipated in his note, the Roc's Tooth had arrived and threw down its anchor just as the sun was setting.

Solvar and a group of six royal soldiers set ashore in one of the Roc Tooth's skiffs, rowed at great speed by a member of the ship's ogre crew. The sailor made three more trips, bringing twenty-one of the King's men ashore, counting Solvar, along with a large number of supplies in crates. Much to Mickalbane and Broyer's surprise, the Roc's Tooth departed the moment the skiff returned to the ship after its last delivery.

Mickalbane was certain that they were simply repositioning the ship for the night so as to be less affected by the currents so close to shore.

"Wonder if they've found any calm water yet," Broyer said snidely, taking some delight in his partner clearly being wrong as the ship shrank from view. Still, it was a little puzzling why Solvar would be bringing men to shore and not using the Roc's Tooth to further pursue the sword thief.

Seeing the puzzlement and concern on the two men's faces as he approached them on the beach, he guessed their minds. He explained that following Screamin' Joe and the others into the fog would not have been possible. The only way to the Isle of Graa was by the ferry, and it would be by the ferry that Solvar and his men would be departing shortly. Mickalbane and Broyer were to remain onshore and maintain the camp that the other men were already assembling and wait for the King's arrival.

"The King?" Broyer said, surprised. "He's coming here?"

"That is what I just said, fool. Yes, and he will be expecting a hot meal upon his arrival before following the men and me. He has sent word that he will be here tonight, but I expect that I and the men will have already left for the island, perhaps even reached it, before he arrives. With a test of fate in our favor, we may even have the two swords in our possession before the King catches up to us on the island. It would be better for all of us if the King doesn't have to get his hands dirty in this matter."

"But how will you summon the ferry, sir?" Mickalbane queried. "From what we have observed these past days, it does not arrive on any sort of schedule. In fact," he said, leaning in and lowering his voice as though sharing some sensitive information, "it did not turn up at all until the thief and his friends arrived. I believe it requires some sort of magic, sir."

"But the wizard did nothing that we could see to summon the boatman," added Broyer, contradicting his partner. "I expect it was some sort of fluke of timing. Perhaps if you blew a horn of some sort," Broyer offered, "the ferryman might at least know that you are here."

Solvar's eyes went wide, darting back and forth between the two men who he had thought to be simpletons. His already stern countenance was now tinged with an astonished anger.

Mickalbane, seeing that his partner's unsolicited suggestion was angering their commander, quickly turned on Broyer. "Idiot, as if such a thing would work. Do you come every time some random fool blows on a horn?" He turned back to Solvar then, "I apologize for my —" Mickalbane found himself with the point of Solvar's arm blade at his throat.

"Did you just call me a fool?" Solvar was seething.

Mickalbane could manage no more than an incoherent, flustered stammer.

"How do you imbeciles know about the horn?" Solvar growled. "I only just acquired it this morning in Markam. It has taken me months to have it tracked down. Men have died to bring it here in secrecy, and then that screaming dolt steals my sword. I was lucky the King left me with my head. Weren't you the two that brought the thief to the castle?"

"We just found him on the beach. Brought him in like we're supposed to," Broyer quickly responded, concerned for his partner, still at sword-point. "Sir!" he added emphatically as Solvar's glare fell upon him.

"Yes, so you say, but now you mention the horn, having no way of knowing about it. Who have you spoken to?" He nudged the tip of his blade slightly, drawing a trickle of blood, to prompt a response from Mickalbane. Mickalbane had already broken into a profuse sweat and was still struggling to find his voice.

Broyer found himself in an unusually torn state. He was reveling in the moment of his garrulous partner's rare tongue-tied state and yet found himself fearing that Solvar may actually kill Mickalbane. "Only a suggestion, sir," he quickly blurted, "Nothing more. I certainly didn't know of your horn or a horn, if there is a horn, that is, and it's rare for my comrade to know much of anything."

Now, Mickalbane found himself in multiple states of emotion and shot Broyer an annoyed sideways glance.

Solvar stood in silence a few moments more, looking both men over, probing for any hint of deception. Finding none, he retracted his arm blade. Both men snapped to attention. Solvar stared at the two of them for a very uncomfortable minute. "No matter, in any case, but should I find either of you simple-minded grunts meddling in matters beyond your station, I'll have you both gutted, tanned, stuffed with pig dung, and used for target practice." He dismissed the two men to their camp preparation duties then. With overly stiff salutes, neither of the two marhorsemen hesitated to remove themselves from the situation.

Within an hour, Solvar gathered the other men on the beach by the decrepit ferry dock. One of the soldiers approached him with a wooden chest cradled in both arms. Its entire surface was carved in the runes of a language long forgotten, forming intertwining circles and knots of unknowable phrases. Its corner flashings and hinges looked to be made of gold and were shaped like a variety of flowers. Solvar opened the chest, removing a gold-gilded, curved, ivory horn.

The instrument, which Solvar had set many a bounty hunter scouring the entire world for, was fashioned from the coiling horn of an extinct beast, as the story went. The last of its kind, the great winged creature known as Hermerkyar, had served as the messenger to the godés of Graa before meeting its end in a confrontation with Nolis, father of dragons. When the flames of the battle subsided, all that remained of the golden messenger was the horn that Solvar now held in his hand. According to the legend, Death itself had been so devastated by the magnificent creature's passing that it vowed to answer the horn's call, continuing the beast's work as messenger ferrying the callers to and from the island.

With the horn firmly in one hand and a lamp in the other, Solvar carefully made his way to the end of the precarious, rotting dock. The fog was so thick now that the light from his men's torches at the other end of the dock was barely visible. He looked out into the dark, murky oblivion of the bay and pondered momentarily upon the wisdom of potentially summoning Death. He took a deep breath and blew the horn.

Unlike earlier, when the ferry arrived for Joe and the others, the ferry and its driver had seemed to materialize just a few short feet from the end of the dock. Mickalbane decided it was simply an illusion of the fog and the dark, as his and Broyer's crystal visors had difficulty cutting through the dense fog in the darkness of the night. Whatever the case, the towering figure of the ferry driver was ominous as he slowly waved a beckoning arm to Solvar and the other men to board the ferry. When the last man had sat aboard the ferry, the driver looked up onto the shore and waved for the marhorsemen to join the others. Not questioning how the ferryman could even see them through the fog, each man had felt, at that moment, that the shadowy, hooded figure had looked directly at him in particular. They argued for some time afterward as to just which one Death had beckoned.

Seeing that neither of the men was going to be coming aboard, the ferryman pushed away from the dock, and the ferry slipped silently into the foggy darkness of the bay. It was only a few seconds before the light of the torches carried by Solvar's company winked out of view.

With the other soldiers gone, the evening continued to pass in relative silence, with little more noise than the waves lapping up on the beach or a splashing hoof from one of the men's marhorses catching crabs in the retreating waves. Mickalbane and Broyer stripped off their visors and scarves, returning to their duties, now focused on readying the King's tent for his arrival. This included preparing a feast, to the best of their limited culinary skill, fit for his majesty. King Goms had a notoriously large appetite. It was not unusual for him to consume an entire turkey or similarly sized beast during a single sitting, in addition to any accompanying fruits, vegetables, dessert, and at least three bottles of wine from the Mandifarian valley of South Eastworld. Tonight, the beast on the menu was a small young beach hog brought by Solvar's men from Markam. It had been roasting for nearly four hours by the time Broyer brought it to the table. Mickalbane was about to admonish his associate for bringing the cooked pig out so soon — concerned about the meal being cold for the King's arrival — when an unmistakable rushing crack of thunder heralded the King's arrival outside.

The two men scrambled out of the tent, immediately straightening to attention on either side of the entrance. King Goms, astride his chrome-skinned steed, Tyrant, was just outside the tent. The gold leaves of his armor seemed to glow with their polished brilliance in the firelight of the camp torches. He was looking out to sea and remained in this thoughtful pose for a few more awkward moments while Mickalbane and Broyer stood patiently, shooting each other looks, trying to goad the other into speaking. It was Tyrant, watching the two marhorsemen with one of his glowing red eyes, who finally brought the King's attention back inland, stamping a heavy metal hoof and snorting out a hot cloud of steam. Like his armor, the King's bone-white, scowling face had a reflective luminescence. It was in stark contrast to the murky night behind him, adding to his ominous countenance as he looked down at the two men.

"Is my dinner ready?" the King asked gruffly.

Both men bowed deeply, pulling back the flaps of the King's deep green tent, revealing the inviting, warm firelight inside.

"Ready, m'lord," Mickalbane said with as much reverence as he could muster, bowing his head even further as he spoke.

"The roast pig was just taken off the spit and is already on the table, Your Majesty," Broyer added, shooting Mickalbane a look. "Hot," he emphasized for Mickalbane's benefit.

"And ready to eat," Mickalbane responded with a squinting disapproval.

"Excellent," the King said without the enthusiasm that should have accompanied the word. He smoothly dismounted, giving Tyrant a pat on the shoulder as he did. The King's gauntlet clattered against the horse's metal skin. "Go on, I know you are anxious to get at those two mermaids," he said, pointing at Mickalbane and Broyer's marhorses down by the water's edge. Tyrant gave another steam-filled snort and trotted off across the sand to the two fish-tailed horses. Mickalbane and Broyer shared looks of concern with one another but straightened to attention as the King turned back to face them.

"Join me inside, gentleman," Goms said sternly as he walked between the two men and entered the tent.

Neither man hesitated, nearly colliding with one another in the entrance. Once inside, Mickalbane and Broyer reassumed their positions on either side of the exit, snapping back to rigid attention.

"Ah, well done!" Goms said with legitimate appreciation as he walked around the wide makeshift table of bound wooden slats set atop a set of crates. There was a lavish amount of food that the two men had managed to arrange in three bands of color, red, green, and white, about the steaming form of the perfectly roasted young beach hog. The cooked beast's juices dripped from the cracks in its deliciously caramelized skin. A large bottle of Mandefarian wine sat open, breathing, next to the King's table setting, with three other bottles waiting, corked, behind it.

Three tin mugs had been used to hold a collection of thin bread rolls. The

King removed his gauntlets and immediately dumped out the contents of two of the mugs onto the table. He filled them both with wine before filling the finely crafted goblet, decorated with an ornate leaf pattern and jewels that had been set for him. Sitting down, he took a closer look at the jeweled goblet, turning it about with a great deal of contemplation as he did.

"I suppose Solvar is responsible for picking out this ridiculous, girly thing," the King grumbled. "Elves," he huffed further with mild exasperation. Goms reached over to the third bread-filled mug, dumped out the rolls, replaced its contents with the wine from the goblet, and then topped the mug off with a bit of extra wine from the bottle. He grabbed handfuls of food from the serving platters and slapped them hastily onto his plate. Seizing the heavy carving knife beside the hog, he started slicing into the beast but stopped, looking up at the two marhorsemen still standing rigidly and silently at attention. "I've already poured your mugs; don't expect me to serve your food, too," he barked.

Mickalbane and Broyer gave each other slightly confused and concerned looks. Neither were entirely sure they had heard the King correctly, and neither wanted to be the first to be so presumptuous as to move from their station.

The King let the slightest smile creep onto his stony white, scowling countenance. "A man should never drink without the company of fools." His smile faded then. "Now sit."

Both men scrambled from their stations at the exit, taking seats at the table before each mug.

"I understand that you two were the men responsible for notifying Solvar and me of the movement of the one who calls himself Screaming Joe Blade?"

Both men nodded.

"If you mean the sword thief, sire," Mickalbane added. "We were not aware of the man's name. Is he known for screaming? I only ask as he was quite silent the times we…saw him." Mickalbane's voice trailed off uncomfortably, noticing the King's glare, realizing that the nod alone would have been enough of a response.

The King let a moment more pass, glaring at Mickalbane and making sure that the man was done. He took a bite of meat straight from the tip of the carving knife. "And you," he waved the knife at the two men, "were also the men who found the 'sword thief' on the beach, yes?"

Again, both men nodded. Mickalbane again opened his mouth to add something further, but a wide-eyed look of warning from his partner quickly stifled him.

Stabbing the carving knife into the hog and leaving it there, the King continued with his meal, leaving the other two men in awkward silence. Neither of the marhorsemen touched their drinks nor helped themselves to any of the food, still not entirely sure they were free to do so despite the King's invitation to the table.

The King looked up from his meal to see the two men trying to silently communicate with one another through a series of subtle but increasingly absurd facial expressions and head movements. Unaware of the King's attention, the men continued. However, by that moment, their communication had broken down. Mickalbane had tried to get Broyer to break the silence with a toast to the King, but he was sure that Broyer had responded that there was some sort of bug in one of their drinks. Broyer, meanwhile, was trying to figure out why Mickalbane had suggested that he was about to throw his drink at the King and was desperately trying to talk his partner out of the suicidal act.

The King cleared his throat, getting their attention back. Both men snapped to attention in their seats, shooting frowns at one another.

"Eat," the King commanded.

Both men dutifully began serving themselves from the various selections on the table, despite neither having a plate to place the food upon.

The King raised his glass as the two men scrambled to dine as instructed. "The two of you are to be commended. Your diligence and dutiful action have set in motion events that shall make it possible to bring the harmony and peace we know in this land to all the world. I drink to you both, Torga!" Goms waited then, his drink held aloft, as it took the two soldiers a moment to realize that he was waiting for them to join his toast. It was not until both men had raised their mugs, shouted Torga, and drank from their cups that Goms took a long drink from his cup as well.

"I have a further task for you, but we'll discuss that when I return from the island."

"Of course, sir," said Broyer with a mouth full of food.

"Whatever you wish, m'lord." Mickalbane followed with as much polite reverence as he could muster.

King Goms stood up from his meal, stepped over to Broyer, and wiped his hands and face on Broyer's black cloak. Broyer could only respond with a humiliated grimace to Mickalbane's smug smile across the table.

"There will be a little matter of a promotion to get out of the way then as well." Goms casually put his gauntlets back on, apparently done with his meal already. It was unexpected and unusual for the King to have finished with a meal so soon and having consumed so little.

"Thank you, Your Highness," the two men chimed in happy unison as the King walked around the table to the tent's exit. Both men were in a state of confusion and delighted surprise over the King's early exit and good news. They raised their mugs again, giving one another congratulatory nods.

Goms paused as he pulled back the tent flap, turning back to the men with his ever-present scowl. "I believe you may have misunderstood me. Only one of you is to be promoted. As much as Blade's presence may be a boon to the future of my empire, his presence has also been a costly disruption. There have been a great number of lives lost since his arrival. Too many of my subjects are needlessly without their husbands, fathers, brothers, or sons. Someone needs to be answerable for bringing such disorder into our midst. I expect one of you to be dead when I return. I'll let the two of you work that out amongst yourselves. Whatever you decide, it has been an honor to have shared a small portion of your last meal with you and your comrade-in-arms. You have both served your land well. I am confident that whichever of you remains will be up to the coming mission. Goodnight, gentleman." With that, the King departed, leaving the two men staring at each other in troubled silence.

* * * * * * * * * * * * * * * * * * * *

"You will pay me now." The ferryman's hollow voice echoed out across the turbulent waters.

This must be Nashtar's doing, Solvar thought as he looked out into the fog that flashed and boomed with fire and lightning. "I'll pay you double your fee; just get us to the island," he shouted back to the ferry driver from his position at the bow.

350

"You will pay me now," the ferryman repeated.

"Curse you, driver!" Lightning flashed just as Solvar spoke, taking him by surprise and causing him to instinctively duck. Had all his men not been distracted doing much the same, it would have caused him some embarrassment. "What is your fee, damn you?"

"One gold coin for every soul. "The ferry driver's voice seemed to supersede the volume of the tumult of the surrounding storm. "Now, two gold coins," the ferryman amended, making a slight bow.

"Of course, whatever. Give the man his money," Solvar shouted to one of the men near the back of the boat.

The soldier fished about transferring gold coins from a larger sac to a small coin pouch. As the man began to get up and turn around to pay the driver, he was immediately met by the ferryman's long-reaching, outstretched, cloaked, bony hand. The driver snatched the coin purse from the soldier, who quickly sat back down, happy not to have had to stand fully with how the boat was rocking.

"Thank you," the driver said, pulling his oar from the water. "The island is that way." He pointed in a direction just slightly starboard. At that moment, the ferry quickly began to sink, water gushing in from the bottom and sides of the boat as if the whole vessel had suddenly become a large sieve.

Within four short seconds, the entire well-armored company of men was in the water and sinking. Most could not swim, and these men were already beneath the turbulent waters. The rest were scrambling to remove their armor as they desperately tried to keep from going under.

"Driver!" Solvar shouted in a rage as he struggled to keep his head above the churning water.

The hooded form of the ferryman towered above Solvar, laughing, looking momentarily as though he were standing upon the water's surface. A streak of lightning flashed behind the ominous, dark giant, and then he too quickly sunk straight down beneath the waves, his hollow echoing laughter mingling with the thunder.

* * * * * * * * * * * * * * * * * *

Though the Isle of Graa was surrounded by fog, there was no fog on the island itself. The sky above was clear, a dazzling spectacle of stars.

Runara noticed Joe staring up at the majestic cosmic display, and it made her smile to think that he still found them so fascinating. How sad, she thought, to spend one's entire life underground.

Joe's gaze drifted down from the twinkling stars to the sparkling, glowing radiance of Runara and her hair. It made his already broad smile all the wider. She was embarrassed to find that the way he was looking at her was causing her to blush slightly. The firelight glow of her hair, though, illuminating her face, made it impossible to tell that she was blushing.

"Well then," Joe said with loud enthusiasm as he pointed at her hair, "we won't be sneaking up on anyone, will we."

"Not with you blabbering like that, we won't." Crash said sternly in a hushed tone, stepping between Joe and Runara. "So much for slipping past the sleeping dragon. I'm surprised it hasn't already come over here and bit off your stupid face."

"Hey, what's your problem." Joe tried to keep his voice more of a whisper.

"She's right," came Kord's low, gravelly voice behind Joe. "We need to be quiet."

"Hey now, wait," Joe was starting to feel a little ganged up on, and his voice took a slightly defensive tone then. "If anything was going to wake that dragon up, it would have been that horn that blasted just as we got off the boat."

"Yes," came Tosh's voice softly as he stepped into the light of Runara's hair. "What was that?"

"Company, I expect." Only Nashtar's glowing blue eyes could be seen in the darkness, a short distance away. "The King, or his men at least. I can't imagine anyone else with a reason or the resources to summon the ferry."

"Yes," Kord agreed. "There were two men in black armor on the large rock when we arrived at the dock on the other side."

"You're just telling us this now?" Tosh asked in annoyed astonishment. He started looking around nervously, squinting into the darkness as though they might already be surrounded by some unseen enemy.

"What men? What large rock? How could you see anything in that fog?" By Joe's tone, he was less than convinced. Kord just stared at Joe, providing no answer. Joe quickly felt that a fog would have to be ten times thicker than himself to stop Kord from seeing straight through. "Whatever," he said dismissively, giving his head a little shake, trying to shed the creepy feeling that had just washed over him. "We should probably keep moving before whoever shows up." He turned to the glowing blue eyes several feet away in the darkness. "Where to, Gramps?"

"Into the temple, of course," Nashtar replied.

The temple loomed behind them in the darkness. The entire island, formed by a dead volcano, had been carved out and reworked into a massive, towering, multi-storied, stepped pyramid temple. Thousands of years of thick plant growth and trees masked most of the stonework now, making the island look quite natural. It had once truly been the home of the godés. Their faithful followers, who revered the godés as gods, would come here to pray for the assistance of the powerful beings. Depending on the issue, the pilgrim would come seeking help from the particular talents of a specific godé. The devout would seek out that godés home — a temple within the temple — and there they would leave their offerings or sacrifices. They would declare their devotion, hoping for the godé to emerge and hear their plea. That age had long passed, however, and the godés and their followers had long since abandoned the temple. The reason for their leaving became as lost to time and legend as the island's true nature, replaced with myths about Death and the gateway to the underworld.

"Koobara and I will stay." Kord's voice rumbled low. He turned to Garen then. "You will keep her safe," he said, referring to Runara. It was more of an order than a request, and Garen gave only a slight polite bow in response.

"Very well," Nashtar asserted, stepping into the light of Runara's hair. "The rest of us should continue on immediately. If it is the King or the elf who follows, we do not want to linger any further. I was hoping to simply teleport to the altar, but my magic is being suppressed by the temple in some way. I may not be able to use it at all once we are inside. We will have to follow, on foot, the same path as the Hand of Death. It is not an easy walk, and we'll need more light than Runara's hair."

Runara held out her hand, producing a small but bright flame.

Nashtar gently touched his great-granddaughter's shoulder. "That's well and good out here, young one, but once inside, we may not be able to rely on our magic. And, to be honest, we'll need more light than that out here."

Runara's flame and luminous hair illuminated little beyond the immediate area around her.

"I have this," Tosh said, unfolding a compact lamp and lighting it with a small, mechanical sparking device that he pulled from one of his robe's many pockets. He angled the reflector and adjusted the focal lens until the lamp cast a broad, far-reaching light ahead. It illuminated the stonework facade of the temple entrance. Runara smiled at Tosh as she closed her hand, putting out the flame in her palm.

Two statues of beautiful, naked women, each thirty feet tall at their heads, stood on either side of the opening. The arch of the opening was overgrown with vines save for the capstone, which sat approximately at the height of the statues' breasts. On the capstone was carved, in relief, a large eye encased in a triangle and further enclosed in a circle. The eye seemed quite realistic, its lids organically emerging from the stone. Its iris glittered as if alive as the light reflected off the facets of thousands of tiny, cut, green gems embedded in its surface.

The statues appeared nearly identical in form; both were depicted with long, flowing hair. Their poses were slightly different, however. One held her face in her hand in a sorrowful posture. The other had her face turned away, in, toward the temple and the center of the island. One of this figure's hands was held down by her side, half closed, as though it had been crafted to hold something that had long since gone missing. Between the two women, held high above them with their other hands, was a large stone sphere, roughly the size of either of the figures' heads.

"My kind of place!" Joe said with enthusiasm. "Naked lady cults always have the best treasure, and even if they don't, who cares." Joe was laughing at his own comment. "Am I right?" He was met with silence from the rest of the group, bringing his own laughter to an unceremonious halt. "You people really need to raid more ancient temples."

"Focus, thief. We're not here for treasure; we're here to get you home," Nashtar reminded Joe.

"And to put your sword together to do it, which is essentially treasure, right?" Joe argued. "And you can't tell me we won't be grabbing a bobble or two along the way. You might be right, though. The place looks like it's already been picked over." He pointed at the left figure's clenched but empty hand.

Tosh spoke, his voice full of reverence and wonder as he held the lamp high and approached the entrance for a closer look. "I've seen this before or something similar. They had clothes, though." He wheeled around facing the others, causing them all to shield their eyes from the blinding brilliance of the lamplight. "It was a drawing in that book, the one that mentions you," he said excitedly to Joe. "But it wasn't this. It was something smaller; some sort of source of power for a…" he searched for a sensible, singular word but failed, "for a magical fortress. And this one's hand was clutching at a necklace, if I recall. Her arm wasn't down like this." He wheeled back around, illuminating the entrance once again.

"Fascinating, an interesting coincidence, to be sure. You will have to show me this book one day, knower," Nashtar said with sincere interest but slight impatience in his voice. "But we need to proceed, and with caution. The temple's corridors are full of traps."

"Hold up. I might have been wrong about this place being picked over." Joe said just as Nashtar moved toward the entrance. "I kinda have a knack for this stuff, and I have a hunch about these fine ladies. This one in particular," he said, pointing at the one holding her clenched hand at her side. "I think you were on to something with the other version you saw holding a necklace." Joe patted Tosh on the shoulder as he stepped forward and positioned himself just below the statue's clenched hand. "Garen, hoist me up onto your shoulders."

Garen was reluctant but complied, walking over and cupping his hands. Joe squinted a little at Garen, giving him a big smile.

"I see you've done this before," Joe slapped Garen on the shoulder. "Never would have pegged you for a second story sort." Joe used Garen's hands like a stirrup, swinging himself up to sit on Garen's shoulders.

Garen rolled his eyes. "Although I was introduced to all of you from a rooftop, I can assure you my days of burglary have not yet begun."

"'Not yet,' I like the attitude!" Joe teased. "Nope, no good, not high enough, maybe if I…" Joe didn't get to complete his thought before Crash climbed up the two men as if they were some sort of tree. Rather than straddling Joe's neck as Joe had done with Garen, Crash stood herself up, a foot on each of Joe's shoulders.

"Now what?" she asked with a slight giggle, warning both men below her not to squirm too much.

"Well, the way I figure it," Joe said with a little grunt as he grabbed Crash by her legs to help keep her stable. "The godés probably locked the place up before they left, as one does, or in this case, since there's clearly no door, activated the traps. Nashy, you got that red crystal handy."

"Yes, but we need it for the bonding ritual." Nashtar's tone was skeptical. "We're wasting time, thief."

"I expect to save us time, wizard," Joe said snidely. "Anyway, if the crystal is needed for both things, then I'm sure the nice, naked, giant rock lady will give it right back."

Nashtar handed the crystal to Garen, who passed it on to Joe. Joe held his arm up to pass it to Crash, but she told him to toss it up to her, which he did, his smile broadening.

"I think I'm going to have to keep you lot," Joe said with a chuckle.

"It's glowing!" Crash exclaimed then. A bright red glow from her hands illuminated Crash's face. "There's a little cross inside!"

"Great," Joe shouted up, not really sure what to make of that bit of information. "What about the hand? Does it look like there's a place for the crystal to fit? There might even be a similar mark up there."

Crash held the crystal up to illuminate the top of the statue's slightly down-angled hand. She was just high enough to peek at it. "Yes, there's a little cross etched in here too!"

"Great, good, put it in already; you're getting heavy!" Joe grunted, trying to hold her still.

"Hey!" Crash shouted back, a little perturbed. She reached up to try fitting the crystal into the statue's hand. The opening of the hand had been carved to fit the crystal precisely, and it slid in easily.

A crack like thunder sounded then, and a low rumbling sound briefly came from deep within the temple, followed by the distant roar of a freshly woken dragon. The stone sphere between the two statues started to glow with a dull orange light, growing brighter by the second.

"Pull it out!" Joe shouted up to Crash. She did; it came out as easily as it had gone in. Doing a backflip to the ground, she landed in a defensive position, readying herself for whatever trap they may have just set off.

Joe jumped off Garen and looked up at the sphere, trying to assess what they had triggered. Continuing to grow brighter in intensity, the sphere was also now generating a high-pitched squeal. The others were all backing away, but Joe remained at the entrance. The squealing ceased, and in that same instant, a bright beam of white-blue light shot up from the sphere into the night sky.

"On the upside," Joe commented over his shoulder to the others, "we aren't going to have to worry about Runara's hair giving us away to the dragon."

Just then, a loud clap came from within the temple, like an enormous door being slammed shut, drawing the group's attention back down to the entrance. The corridor within illuminated as torches and marble brazier bowls burst into life with flame.

Tosh extinguished his lamp and hooked it back on his belt. "Still, better than us fumbling about in the dark. Good job!"

Joe took a deep bow and stepped aside. "Lead the way, Gramps."

"There's no guarantee that the traps are disabled, so do only as I do, step only where I step."

The group followed single file behind Nashtar, with Joe waiting to go last. Nashtar ceased to wink in and out in his usual eerie, strobing manner as he stepped into the temple. Crash handed Joe the red crystal as she walked by him, and he quickly tucked it away. Joe turned to say goodbye to Kord, but Kord and Koobara had long since vanished into the surrounding undergrowth and shadows. He peered into the darkness, giving a little wave, knowing that the two hunters would be watching, and then scrambled to catch up with the others.

"Hey," Joe shouted to the others, "did I ever tell you about the time I was hired by a memory seeker from Orter to steal a crystal orb from a dragon."

"Please don't," came Nashtar's voice from the front of the line.

"You'll need a silencing spell," Runara sneered jokingly as she carefully stepped just as Nashtar did ahead of her.

"What is a memory seeker?" asked Garen, who was just ahead of Joe.

"They collect old stuff and stash it in museums." Joe was happy to have fished in an audience of some sort. "Kinda like your library, Tosher, but with more bits of junk and treasure and far fewer books."

Tosh was carefully following Crash's every step. "I thought you didn't do dragons."

"Well, that job is why. I mean, the traps in that place were intense too; nothing for me, of course, but we lost three of our group before we even reached the dragon, and those guys were our guides." Joe haphazardly strolled along behind the others.

"This story sounds familiar," Tosh said as he thought about it a bit. "Seems to me I recall a similar tale in the Midgorn journal. A memory keeper named Booleer, I think, hired the journal writer and his companions to retrieve the orb after his first failed attempt. There was even an illustration of the dragon. I assume you were part of the original unsuccessful venture."

"Ya!" Joe exclaimed, sounding just a little too exuberant. "Booleer! That's the guy!" Wow, he went back? Crazy."

"Why, what happened when you got to the dragon?" Crash asked as she concentrated on stepping on the same stone tiles as Runara.

"Oh ya, well, that's just it; nothing happened. Everybody just died. Burnt to crisps the moment we set foot in her nest." Joe's tone was casual as he strolled behind the rest of the group, completely ignoring the path of stone tiles that his companions were carefully following. His eyes were drawn this way and that by the beauty and potential riches that made up the corridor.

The stonework hallway was full of statues of various creatures in life-like detail, most of which Joe could not identify. Several of the more human-shaped beings had large gems in their eyes, and Joe made note of them. Should things not work out with the powersword getting him home, they would make a decent consolation prize on the way back out. The floor upon which the rest of the party was so transfixed was a complex assemblage of differently shaped stones, each roughly a square foot in size. Some were square, many triangular, and a few were hexagonal. It was the hexagonal stones that Nashtar and the others were being careful not to stray from.

"Everybody died but you." Garen corrected Joe.

"Ya, well, ya." Joe's words stumbled over his thoughts. "And Booleer, the memory seeker. Last I saw, he was still alive anyway, hiding behind a boulder. Never saw him again, though. I had assumed he got roasted, too. He was pretty determined to get that crystal ball. Nice to hear that he might have survived for another try."

"So, how exactly did you survive?" Tosh queried. "Any insights from your encounter may help us form a strategy of our own against the dragon here."

"He ran." Garen guessed.

"Hey!" Joe said, feeling a little hurt. "I successfully executed what we in the business prefer to call a 'sustained dodge.'"

"So you ran then," Runara smirked.

"Oh ya, the moment I saw the thing. It was ridiculously huge!" Joe confessed as he looked around, distracted by the multiple holes he was just now noticing worked into the ornately carved stone walls. Pretty obvious dart or spear traps, he thought, and either they had already been set off or just were not working. Joe concluded that these godés were clearly amateurs in temple trap construction.

Nashtar was shouting then. "Quickly, quickly, all of you close to me!"

The others looked up to find that Nashtar had led them down a dead-end, causing all but Joe to be a little alarmed.

"You know," Joe said, pointing over his shoulder as the others huddled together. "There was a hallway back there to the right that looked pretty safe. Also, I kinda gotta drain my own dragon, if you get what I mean, so…"

Before Joe could finish, a large stone slab dropped from the ceiling, an inch behind him, with a cacophonous boom, cutting off the corridor entirely. The entire group was trapped in the small dead-end space.

"That wasn't me," Joe casually asserted before anyone could throw more than an accusing look.

* * * * * * * * * * * * * * * * * * *

Baron Solvar had barely made it to the shore. His new mechanical arm had been a considerable hindrance. Not only had it weighed him down significantly, it did not function well in the water. As Solvar clawed his way up the beach with his good arm, pulling himself out of the water, he made a mental note to gut the knower that had crafted the mechanical one and perhaps the man's family, too. His metal arm twitched, dragging along by his side, trying to flex, as he crawled further up the beach. Feeling sufficiently clear of the wash of the waves, he flipped over onto his back, exhausted.

He had been lucky to find the island. Solvar wasn't sure if the ferryman had been lying when he had pointed out the direction to the island or if they had simply veered off course while swimming. Between scrambling to release the fittings on his armor before his arm had seized up and then trying to swim with one arm, he may have just lost the way, but the reality was probably a combination of both. Had he not noticed the great beam of light cutting through the fog to his left, he and his men surely would have swum off to nowhere until they drowned. The outcome wasn't all that much better, however.

Three of his men had managed to make it ashore with him, minus their armor and weapons. Most of the rest had, in fact, drowned shortly after the ferry had sunk, while four others were the victims of some sort of large water serpent. It might have been a nogodar — a dragon pup — Solvar had thought when he briefly saw the creature's scales in the starlight just before it pulled one of the men down. Fortunately, such young beasts do not travel in groups, and this one was likely to have had its fill with the four men it had already pulled beneath the waves. Luckier still, perhaps, as nogodars were very territorial, there would be few other predators, if any, between the mainland and the island. Whatever the monster had been, it had left the rest of them alone to flounder their way to the island.

Water gushed then sputtered from the muzzle in the palm of Solvar's mechanical hand as gears further up the arm whirred and clacked back to functionality. Solvar rolled back over and pushed himself to his feet. "Up, gentlemen," he said breathlessly to the three other men lying on the beach. "We can't risk letting them complete the ritual." In truth, Solvar already feared that it may be too late. He thought that the great beam of light that had guided them to the island might have resulted from the magic called forth to join the pieces of the red powersword. It appeared now that the light was coming from the base of the ominous dark temple that loomed above them, which was of some encouragement. Undoubtedly, the ritual would have to be performed within, he thought. With any luck, the sword thief and his companions had fallen victim to some ancient trap.

Having come ashore quite some distance from the source of the light, it was going to take some time to reach it. It was hard to judge in the darkness, but it looked to be a half-hour's walk away. A setback, to be sure, but less of a time loss than the unexpected swim had been. Solvar's main concern now was that they might not be at the temple's entrance before the King arrived. He could only hope that the beam of light was not misleading them.

He looked down at his mechanical arm. The metal fingers clacked as he flexed them one at a time. The whole arm seemed to be working much better with each passing moment. With a slight move, his arm blade shot out to its full length. The sharp, metallic, grinding sound of the blade shooting through the self-sharpening mechanisms as it emerged pierced the silence of the night. The deadly sound caused Solvar's men to pause their plodding up the beach and turn around, concerned that their commander had sensed some sort of danger.

His men might not be armed, he thought, but at least they were still sharp. "Don't stand there staring, you lugs. We have a sword thief to catch."

* * * * * * * * * * * * * * * * * * *

The King had not had the sort of trouble with the ferryman the others had encountered. Mounted upon Tyrant, Goms made his way to the end of the ancient dock. The rotting timbers of the decrepit pier creaked, cracked, and moaned beneath the extreme weight of the chrome-skinned steed and its massive rider. Looking out into the endless fog, Goms brought forth the green powersword. Almost immediately, the ferry rose from beneath the water right next to the dock in a roiling torrent of bubbles and steam. Without any visible prompt from Goms, Tyrant strode confidently onto the age-worn craft. Like the pier, the wood of the old vessel complained loudly beneath the beast's massive hooves. The ferryman gave Goms a deep bow as they came aboard, saying to the King that it pleased him that the old ones were returning. Completely covered in the tangled vine armor of the green powersword, Goms let the ferry driver think what he might and kept the sword drawn for the entire uneventful trip across the misty channel.

The driver bowed low again as the ferry came to rest alongside the long stone pier of the island. Goms leaned back in his war saddle as Tyrant stepped onto the pier, trying to take in the looming enormity of the temple. Despite his many readings on the subject of the powerswords, he had not expected the temple to take up so much of the island, nor had he expected the entrance to the temple, visible in the distance up the hill, to be fully illuminated. It was concerning, as it suggested that the old wizard knew the ways of the temple and, perhaps then, the procedure for binding the crystal shard to its sword. It may already be too late. He could only hope that Solvar had managed to catch up to them to slow or stop them. Goms could not afford to have anyone in his lands, especially someone like Nashtar, acquiring a powersword.

Tyrant's heavy metallic hooves clopped down the pier to the shore as Goms scanned their surroundings. A stone path, well maintained, it appeared, led up from the pier through the thick undergrowth and trees in the direction of the temple entrance. The dense plant growth surrounding and engulfing the temple made Goms wary. Too much could be hiding within the dark tangles of brush, leaf, and vines; any number of enemies, known or new, could be waiting in ambush behind, or up, every tree. As if thinking the very same thoughts as his master, Tyrant came to a halt mid-step as he reached the end of the pier where the stone path began.

At that moment, out of the corner of his eye, Goms saw a shadowy form scrambling in the darkness along the beach at the water's edge. Tyrant shuffled nervously.

"Steady, old man," Goms said loudly enough for any nearby hostiles to hear. "Whatever it is, it's no bigger than a man. Nothing but a snack for you." He slapped the chrome-skinned horse affectionately on the neck and then pointed the glowing green blade in his right hand at the shambling shadow. "Declare yourself or taste oblivion." The shadow immediately stopped in its tracks.

"It's me, sire!" came the desperate voice of a man from the shadowy form. "I mean, grolon Ribes, your majesty. I arrived with Commander Solvar and the others."

Goms looked beyond the man but saw only darkness. "Ribes, you say? Approach," Goms commanded. Tyrant was still shuffling and snorting nervously, prompting Goms to tell the beast to hold steady several more times, losing some patience with his steed's unusual behavior.

Grolon Ribes scrambled up the slope from the beach to the path, entering the green glow of the King's sword. He was covered in patches of sand, wearing only a shirt and badly torn leggings.

"You are a grolon of my guard? Why are you out of uniform? Where are your arms?"

"My arms?" The soldier looked side to side, happy to see in the dim green light that both of his arms were still there, realizing too late what his King had meant.

"Your weapons, your armor!" Goms shouted angrily, losing patience.

"Lost, Sire, when the ferry sank. Most of the men drowned," came Baron Solvar's voice from the beach. He and the other two men stepped into the King's light then. "We managed to swim to shore but had to abandon our arms and armor. These three are all that is left."

"Wonderful," said Goms with a sarcasm filled with simmering anger. "When we catch up to the sword thief, you other three can try slapping him into submission."

"Two," came Kord's low, menacing voice from seemingly everywhere. The word was immediately followed by the thudding sound of a large metal bolt hitting grolon Ribes in the back. The tip of the deadly bolt's sharp, metal blade protruded from the center of the soldier's chest. The young grolon had a shocked look frozen on his face as a dark stain of blood, looking black in the green light of the sword, quickly expanded on his shirt around the bolt. He crumpled to the ground, dead.

Tyrant took a defensive step back, letting out his ear-splitting whinny as Goms commanded him again to steady himself. It took a moment for the King and his men to fully comprehend what had just happened. By that time, three more bolts had come flying out of the darkness from somewhere just off the path ahead, leading to the temple. The first two fatally struck the remaining soldiers. The third shot was just as deadly in aim, sinking into the King's chest. Goms slumped forward in his saddle, his sword arm swinging limply at his side, causing the glowing blade of his powersword to knick Tyrant's front haunch. Tyrant bellowed in pain and then almost seemed to vanish in a blur of movement as it fled with its master down along the beach until beyond view.

Solvar spun around, instinctively determining the direction the shots had come from. He held up his living arm and a flurry of brightly glowing red orbs shot from his palm. The orbs spiraled off in slightly varying directions, striking the ground in several locations along the path, bursting in violent explosions of light. Foliage and dirt flew into the air. The explosions were bright enough to illuminate the hulking shadow of Kord, who now was nowhere near the location of the explosions but, disturbingly, barreling down the path directly toward Solvar. As Kord launched himself into the air to pounce upon the magic-wielding elf, Solvar had just enough time to volley one more spell. A large blue disc of light shot out from his hand, enveloping Kord like an expanding cast net. Kord's whole body flashed with a brilliant burst of white light, and then he was gone.

Solvar scanned the darkness, his arm blade ready. "Where are you, sword thief?" He muttered through clenched teeth.

There was a rush of air behind him then.

"I've faced that menace before, and it's the second time he's got the better of me."

Solvar spun around, startled by the voice of the King. Goms seemed to have recovered entirely from his grievously injured state just moments before. Tyrant, however, was oozing molten metal from the wound where the King's sword had accidentally cut him.

"Did you incinerate or teleport the creature? If you have the power to teleport, Baron, you could have saved us all a journey, wielding that level of magic. I'm torn between taking another limb for keeping such zeshian secrets and thanking you."

"Neither would seem appropriate just yet, Sire," Solvar boldly corrected the King with a slight bow. "It was nothing so grand as a teleport spell, and I'll not have any further magic at my disposal until I can get some sleep. I've only made the monster disappear, and there's no telling for how long. It will be back; it could be minutes, could be hours. Either way, we should head into the temple before it's back, Your Majesty. Is Tyrant okay? I've never seen him injured.

"He's fine. He'll heal."

A burst of firelight came from the top of the temple, followed a few moments later by a distant roar. It nearly looked as though the volcano had reawakened.

"They've roused the guardian." Goms's voice was low, talking to himself more than Solvar. "They've reached the altar!"

Solvar turned to the King. "We'll never get through the temple in time to stop them now, Sire."

A burst of brightly colored lights came from the temple's peak, drawing both men's attention back.

"We're not going into the temple. The altar is at the top." The King held out his free hand, hoisting Solvar up onto Tyrant. "I suggest you grab some of the vines of my armor and hold on very tightly.

With a clap of thunder, they were gone. A flurry of foliage and two glowing streaks of green and orange traced their zigzagging path up the side of the enormous multi-terraced temple.

Chapter 19

"I told you to do exactly as I!" Nashtar growled.

Joe tried to adjust his leg to see Nashtar better but found he couldn't do so without his foot slipping. "Ya, but y'know, we did the thing with the statue's hand and the crystal. I mean, the torches lit up. All that was missing was a sign saying, come on in, it's all safe. Who knew these godé folk were so paranoid?"

"He did!" Garen retorted with an uncharacteristic anger in his voice. He was straining to keep hold of Nashtar, who, despite his own anger, was trying to move as little as possible lest Garen lose his grip.

Below Nashtar was a deep well of darkness save for a sinister-looking, tightly woven, orange, glowing grid several feet below. When the group first got tnto their present situation, Nashtar had dropped his satchel and staff. Rather than hitting a solid surface, the satchel had passed right through the grid, being rendered instantly, along with its entire contents, into a hundred or so tiny pieces. The staff suffered the same end but with a slight burst of electricity that skittered across the entire surface of the grid. The tiny pieces then quickly burned away to even tinier embers that fluttered down, disappearing into the darkness below.

"All I did was touch that squiggly thing," Joe offered in further defense of his innocence in their circumstance.

"Stop moving!" Runara scolded from Joe's chest. "You are going to make us fall!" She very much wanted to move as well. The way they had fallen, her face was uncomfortably wedged between Joe's chest and one of Garen's legs. Her breasts were nearly strangling Joe. Naturally, Joe didn't seem to mind much. There were certainly worse ways to be asphyxiated. To add to her humiliation, based on the breeze she was feeling, her dress had certainly fallen about her waist, leaving her lower half exposed. Indeed, Tosh and Crash were getting quite a show. Curiously, she wasn't feeling the expected rush of blood to her head in this upside-down position.

"It is an octopus, and you were trying to take the jewels out of its eyes." Tosh was clinging to his lamp, one arm wrapped around its small canopy. He had been lucky enough to grab it as he fell and luckier still that its handle had happened to hook itself on the blunt tusk of a carved depiction of an ogre's head. Tosh and Nasthar were the only two in the group not wedged together in the narrow shaft, but he was having difficulty maintaining a hold of the lamp. Even if he did manage to hold on, the lamp's heavy wire handle was slowly giving out from the strain of the weight. One way or the other, he would be falling onto his companions below. Crash, meanwhile, was doing the best she could to delay that inevitability by stretching one arm up, putting her hand out as a foothold for Tosh. She was not sure how much of a role her other hand, against one of the walls, was contributing to keeping the group from sliding down the shaft, and she really did not want to test it.

The journey through the temple had been going well up until this moment, despite Joe's disregard for following the complex steps and body movements that Nashtar had the others executing. The dead-end hallway had turned out to be some sort of a lift. It had transported them several stories up inside the temple. It opened to an elaborate indoor garden plaza that looked freshly groomed and tended to. It was well-lit, as was the entire temple, it seemed. Life-like statues of exceedingly muscular, giant men and women, scattered seemingly at random, served as support columns. They were all posed as though they each strained to support their portion of the ceiling.

Beyond the garden, they passed through several passages and up various staircases. Along the way, Nasthar would point out dart holes in the walls or spouts near the ceiling that he claimed would pour acid or burning oil should anyone misstep. At one point, they had come upon three skeletons pierced by a multitude of spikes sticking out of the ten-foot ceiling of a narrow hallway. The skeletons were being held in place by the thin vines that grew across the ceiling, but there was no indication of just how the bodies had gotten up there. Until then, the group had been skeptical of Nashtar's claims of the place being trapped, but they all now followed Nashtar's every move with even more care, except, of course, Joe.

They passed through a cavernous hall containing various small buildings; they were the home shrines of some of the former resident godés. It was the one area Nashtar assured the group that they need not tread so carefully through. They had been traveling through the temple for nearly an hour by then, and Nashtar suggested they take some time in this relatively safe area to rest for a bit. It was then that Joe asked how it was that Nashtar even knew what moves to make to avoid the potential traps or how he even knew if they were in danger or safe.

"You witnessed some of it on the boat," Nashtar replied as he sat himself down on a stone bench. He went on to explain that the Hand of Death had spent nearly five years slowly working his way through the temple and, in that time, fell victim to nearly every trap. Each time, he would suffer the devastating effects of the traps but be kept alive by the black powersword. Once recovered or free, he would eventually work out the safe way past or through every trap. "The Hand of Death was a bored, lonely man. Figuring this temple out was the most fun the poor fellow ever had, I expect. Made for quite entertaining viewing through my garatok. I almost didn't know how to spend my time when he finally met his end."

The group rested for nearly two hours, admiring the magnificent, angular architecture and beautiful sculptures. They passed much of the time, though, sharing stories and eating a surprisingly tasty set of spongy orange wafers that Nashtar had brought along. When Runara asked what the odd two-inch wide discs were, Nashtar assured them all that it was simply better if they didn't know. Joe and Crash both shrugged and helped themselves to a few more, but it put the others off from having any more.

Half an hour after moving on, the group found themselves in another narrow hall. Much like the entry hall, its walls were covered in carved reliefs of various creatures and beasts, and just like the entry hall, it came to a dead-end. As the group huddled together, knowing what to expect from the lift this time, a carving of an octopus caught Joe's eye. Its tentacles curled in artful waves around its bulbous head, forming a shape that resembled a clamshell. More than the craftsmanship, Joe's attention had been drawn by the carving's eyes. They were made of dazzling, multifaceted gemstones as blue as the daylight sky. As the stone door closed them into the lift, Joe pulled out one of his knives and, with its tip, tested the edge of one of the gems.

A loud thump sound came then, like a huge weight falling somewhere behind the wall with the octopus. The lift door began sliding inward, making the space they were in increasingly smaller. More troubling was that the floor beneath them moved with the door, sliding under the opposite wall. It forced the group to shuffle along to keep themselves off the wall and off each other. Really, however, they had nowhere to go and quickly found themselves huddled together.

Among the accusations and alarms being expressed by the others, Tosh shouted out that they needed to try pushing on some of the other carved icons as one of them was likely an emergency off switch. He was almost right, but before Nashtar could explain that the icons needed to be pushed in a particular sequence, it was too late. One of the group had pushed on an icon that did stop the tiny room from getting any smaller, but a second later, the floor quickly slid out from under them, sending the group tumbling into the deep, narrow shaft below. They had not fallen far before Joe, Crash, and Garen had instinctively spread themselves out, each having some prior experience with falling in a cramped space. The result was the group becoming quickly and precariously wedged together. Should any of the three move a foot or a hand, they would certainly all fall.

Despite her embarrassing and physically awkward upside-down state, Runara was uniquely free to move her limbs without changing the dynamic of their situation. She was using that freedom, however, to do the only thing she really could; cling to Joe. As she futilely attempted to adjust her grip onto something more stable than Joe's shirt, her hand fumbled upon the red crystal in a hidden pocket on the inside of Joe's jacket.

"While you're gropin' around," Joe started with his usual obnoxious swagger.

There was a surge of energy through Runara's whole body, just as she had felt back in the caravan when she had first picked up the crystal.

"I," Runara's mind was racing in a mix of panic and directionless hope. "I think I have magic!"

"Impossible." Nashtar scoffed from below.

"No, I'm touching the crystal. I can feel the energy building inside of me." The panic in her started to win. "I can't control it. It feels like... like I'm going to explode!" She was unable to let go of the crystal, and the energy was pulsing through her then in increasingly intense waves, just as it had in the forest when the Kingsmen had massacred her family.

"It's the crystal, girl." It is trying to save itself, and it's using you to do it. Calm your mind and the crystal will show you what to do; show you how to save us all."

"Um, you're getting a little warm," Joe said with more than a little concern in his voice. Runara's body was casting so much heat that Joe was pretty sure that there would be an impression of her burnt into his face, neck, and chest. Whether they fell or not, they would soon be burned to death, he was sure. Garen and Crash were feeling it, too, and each was desperately trying to ignore the growing heat to maintain their grips.

"Clear your thoughts, child; let the energy merge with your mind; let it become your thoughts."

"I can't! It's too…"

"Quiet girl!" Nashtar scolded. "Of course you can! You are my kin; there is no magic that you can not bend to your will."

Runara closed her eyes, clenching her teeth as she tried to hold back the energy that now felt like thousands of snakes winding about every bit of her body. To her surprise, a vision, as clear as though she looked upon it with open eyes, dominated her mind, and she found that she could look about as though she were truly within the scene. She could see a vast multi-terraced courtyard with high walls, overgrown with a multitude of large, broken statues strewn about. An enormous stone archway framed a dais and apse at one end of the courtyard, decorated with thirteen massive stone swords. Each sword was easily the height of two average-sized people. It seemed to Runara that every sword's pointed tip seemed to nearly touch one of thirteen particularly bright stars forming a celestial arch in the night sky beyond. On the dais below was a large dark altar that looked identical to the altar upon which she had been sacrificed in Nashtar's tower.

This was it, she thought, the top of the temple. If only they could have made it here, she wished. With that thought, she heard a cry of surprise come from all the others and the brief sense of both freedom from being wedged between her companions and the startling sensation of falling upwards. Her eyes shot open, but she found the scene in her vision unchanged. She was standing upright, firmly on the stone floor of the temple's rooftop courtyard. She spun around to find the others standing behind her. Each of them looked just as confused and surprised as she imagined herself to look at that moment, save for Nashtar, whose face was beaming with an uncharacteristic amount of emotion that was unmistakably pride.

"Remarkable," he said loudly, nearly shouting with excitement. "Unprecedented!"

"Well, that's not entirely accurate, given her history, as I understand it, with that crystal over the past days." Tosh pointed to the red crystal clutched tightly in Runara's left hand, glowing brightly, drawing her attention to it. She had almost forgotten that she was still holding the crystal. As she looked down, the crystal's glow quickly diminished and went out.

"Oh, do shut up!" Nashtar snarled at Tosh.

"I think you both need to shut it," Joe said, pointing behind them. Runara looked up past Nashtar, Tosh, and the others. She gasped.

"So pretty," Crash gushed.

At the far end of the courtyard, an immense shimmering form loomed. The light of the field of stars behind it warped and flickered as it moved, and the ground trembled as it took a step toward them. It was the immense, crystalline dragon whose terrifying snout they had seen in Nashtar's vision on the ferry. The vision, however, had not prepared them for the beast's frightening countenance.

It was, at least, the size of ten elephants, maybe even ten King Koteps, and despite its fluid movement, seemed to be made entirely of clear crystal. It was wingless but otherwise had the features of any other classic dragon. It walked on all fours. Two long, thin, twisting horns sprung from its crystalline scaled head, and long claws, like icy swords, clacked deafeningly on the stone floor with each step. Icicle-like barbs stuck out from its long tapering tail that coiled and whipped like a giant snake, almost with a life of its own. Only its eyes had any color, and they glowed and sparkled like windows onto an immense illuminated treasure of gold coins. They were mesmerizing, and so the group stood, each in their own degree of terror and awe, staring at the glittering orbs floating among the distorting field of stars above their heads.

"Nahin mashru herati tel pashpilua ohm tel Godé? Aedinyd kufusku ilki warsyan." The voice of the crystalline beast was like the roar of a thousand lions.

"What what what, now?" Joe questioned as he and the others backed away from the slowly advancing monster.

"Anwa Oxidisis, wataki ohm tel pashpilua. Majha anwa alanye ex negamut ilki keftu tahima."

"He's Oxidisis, guardian of the forge. He means to kill us!" Runara shouted as she tugged on Joe's arm. "We need to run."

"Ya, run. Right." Joe said, still staring at the dragon's hypnotic eyes. He shook his head then, looking at Runara. "Wait, do you understand that thing?"

Nashtar snatched the crystal from Runara's hand. "Yes, she can, and you do need to run," he said with an urgent calm. Runara ran immediately then. Joe half followed, turning back slightly, torn between fleeing and staying with the others who continued to face the beast, awestruck.

"I think they're right. We sh-should r-r," Tosh stammered, terror-struck, staring at the crystal dragon whose pace was increasing.

"I said run! Run to the altar!" Nashtar shouted, snapping the other three out of their stupors.

Crash immediately turned and bolted, quickly catching up to Joe, who took her by the hand. They continued in a sprint down the courtyard toward the altar. Tosh made to run but caught his foot on his robe and stumbled to the ground. Garen, who was just slowly backing away, still awestruck by the sight of the dragon, stopped to help Tosh back to his feet.

Nashtar stood his ground, muttering dark, arcane words, trying to tap into the energy of the red crystal as Runara had done so naturally.

"Shouldn't we be helping them?" Joe asked, looking over his shoulder as they ran.

"Time for a sustained dodge!" Crash huffed, tugging him along. "He's a wizard, he's got this."

They bounded up the dais and ducked behind the large black altar. The dragons depicted on it seemed to have more significance now. Runara was already crouched behind the altar, her eyes wide with frantic fear.

"Alsapram!" the dragon's voice boomed as it approached the middle of the courtyard, and a glowing stream of numerous green bolts of light erupted from the creature's chest in rapid succession.

Garen pulled Tosh out of the path of two of the glowing bolts, sending both men rolling to the ground. The bolts exploded in brilliant, multicolored bursts against a distant outer wall of the courtyard. Nashtar quickly held a hand out, producing an invisible barrier before him, upon which five more bolts exploded. The wizard's shoulders slumped as he let out a slight sigh, relieved that he had actually managed to produce the spell. He could feel the energy of the red crystal surging through him, but he could also feel the crystal trying to pull that energy back. Fighting with the crystal for its magical fuel was going to be a distraction.

"Stelactora," Nashtar said, scowling as he concentrated, pointing a finger at the dragon.

The dragon immediately stopped, now just twenty feet from Nashtar. It opened its mouth wide as if to roar, but nothing came out. The beast's clear form began to turn cloudy, almost as if a frost were forming from within, and in another few moments, the entire dragon's body had transformed to stone. It now looked to be nothing more than an elaborate, colossal, white marble statue.

Garen and Tosh were on their feet then.

"Remarkable!" Tosh said, amazed, stumbling a bit as he made his way over to Nashtar. "What – how?" He struggled to form a proper question. Nashtar only scowled at the knower.

Joe, Runara, and Crash peaked their heads over the edge of the altar.

"Well, that went much better than I expected," Joe quipped, giving Crash cause to utter a slightly nervous but happy laugh and giving Joe a tight hug of relief.

Runara and Garen both noticed the cracks appearing on the dragon's stone form, each shouting "Look!" simultaneously.

As the others looked back at the dragon, the stone form exploded, sending large pieces of stone flying in every direction. One large stone fragment caught Tosh full in the chest, sending the knower flying back several feet. Garen had managed to flip out of the way of another such fragment, and Nashtar had managed to shield himself again just in time. Runara, Joe, and Crash ducked back down behind the altar, protecting themselves from the small stones that shot by at this distance.

Oxidisis, once again his crystalline self, gave his whole body an earth-trembling shake, like a dog shedding water, sending the last few remnants of the stone shell flying in every direction. It bellowed angrily, causing leaves to fall from the surrounding overgrowth. Garen started to rush over to check on Tosh's unmoving form. The sudden movement caught the attention of the angered dragon.

"Aigahro," the dragon guardian roared, and a large blue disc of light shot from its mouth as it did. The disc wrapped around Garen, enveloping the monk in brilliant light, and then he was gone.

"No!" Nashtar shouted back, then "Destrokar!" A series of ten brilliant red orbs rocketed forth from the crystal in his hand. They smashed against the dragon with explosive force, sending shards of shattered crystal scales flying through the air.

Despite the protests of Crash and Runara, Joe poked his head back up to peek over the altar to see what was happening.

Oxidisis stepped back into a defensive stance, the wizard's attack clearly catching his respect. Its long neck stretched to the sky as its glowing golden eyes glowered down at the old wizard. "The magic of mortals has grown powerful indeed with the passing millennia to work here." The dragon's words came out in its ancient tongue but echoed off the courtyard walls in a voice that all of the temple raiders understood clearly. "But that crystal you hold serves my masters, serves me, and now, sorcerer, you shall perish."

Nashtar's mind raced, preparing to shield himself yet again and searching the library of his mind for the spell that might defeat this ancient guardian.

An orange ball of light formed within the chest of the mighty beast and quickly grew in intensity, illuminating the entire courtyard.

Joe quickly ducked back down. "This is it, ladies; here comes the fire."

No sooner had he uttered the words than they were awash on all sides by a torrent of flame. The dragon's thunderous roar was nearly drowned out by the rushing roar of the fire that burst from its widely opened maw. Joe, Crash, and Runara all screamed, holding each other tightly as the flames licked close to them around the edges of the altar. The heat was intense, so intense that Joe and Crash both felt that they might spontaneously burst into flame at any moment. Runara, however, felt only a tingle, an almost pleasant sensation, like the energy she had felt from the red crystal.

As the flames subsided, Joe and Crash edged away from Runara. Her skin was glowing slightly, fading as the heat of the fire faded.

"Uh, you okay?" Joe asked, realizing as he asked it that it seemed a silly question, in some way, to a woman who was recently murdered, raised from the dead, and whose hair now had a fiery life of its own.

Runara had been staring at her hands, watching the glow diminish but feeling the energy remain. She looked up at Joe, a strange, steely confidence in her face. She said nothing but stood up and walked out from the altar, heading toward Oxidisis. Joe and Crash poked their heads up yet again, watching Runara descend the steps of the dais and step out into the courtyard.

Smoke and steam curled up from the stone floor. Fires continued to burn all around among the overgrown foliage. Nashtar was on his knees, clearly physically tired. There were two eight-foot circles of unscorched stone floor. One was beneath Nashtar, the other beneath the body of Tosh, where the wizard's shielding domes of magic had protected each of them.

"No, Runara. Go back," Nashtar warned. "I haven't the magic left to protect us all!"

Another storm of fire swirled, building within Oxidisis's clear, crystal chest. The dragon's gaze turned then to the defiantly approaching Runara.

"You will not harm my friends," she shouted. "You will not harm my family."

Oxidisis said nothing. His head shot forward slightly from the force of the flames that erupted up his clear throat, turning it into a pillar of fire. It shot from his open maw with another volcanic roar, and the entire courtyard was again a sea of raging flame.

The torrent of fire rushed around Runara like a blinding river of luminescent water, but it left her unharmed. Not even her clothing felt the heat of the dragon's flames. She held her arms out, continuing to stride forward, bathing in the primal energy of the firestorm as it whipped through her hair. As the exhilaration of the energy surged within her, she could not contain an ecstatic laugh. She felt herself pass through another, weaker flow of energy. It was a bubble of magic shielding that Nashtar had tried to protect her with. She could sense the red crystal's magic even through the fire. Nashtar had tried to shield Tosh as well, but the bubble was failing, and he would have to pull the magic back to maintain his own shield. Runara's mind reached out to both men, and the flames did her bidding, bending a large path around each of them.

The fiery assault ceased, and Oxidisis surveyed the smoldering scene. He was instantly confused by the unharmed appearance of the two men and even more baffled by the defiant woman still advancing upon him.

"Impossible!" the dragon growled in astonishment.

"I've been excelling at that sort of thing lately." Runara shot her hands forward, palms out. A concentrated beam of intense white light burst from her hands, striking the dragon in the chest.

The light refracted in a dazzling spectral display, illuminating the dragon's whole body and casting a multitude of tiny spectrums into every dark corner of the courtyard. Oxidisis roared and tried to walk against the physical force of Runara's beam. He managed, nearly, to get within reach of her, swiping, vainly, with one of his massive, clawed forepaws but fell just inches short of shredding the fire witch. Popping sounds started coming from the dragon as deep white cracks formed violently over its entire body. A moment later, the dragon burst into millions of rough, tiny crystal blocks. The crystal shards rained down in an enormous tinkling heap. Only one of Oxidisis's hind legs remained in any recognizable shape.

"Ya!" Joe exclaimed triumphantly as he ran to Runara's side. "Take that, you fire-breathing guard dog!" He made a lewd hand gesture in the shattered monster's direction. Rolling her eyes, Runara asked him to help her as she hurried over to Nashtar. The two of them assisted the ancient wizard to his feet. Nashtar was beaming with pride despite his exhausted state.

"Quickly, you two, back to the altar with us." Nashtar steadied himself, looping his arm around one of Runara's.

Crash, meanwhile, had run over to check on Tosh's condition. He was alive but unconscious. Aside from a cut bleeding slightly on the back of his head, it was hard to tell if he was otherwise injured. She gently attempted to rouse him but, failing that, tried to make Tosh as comfortable as possible. He had a pulse, and for now, that was enough.

As Nashtar, Joe, and Runara reached the altar, Nashtar's eyes lit up, literally. They were glowing an intense blue. Joe and Runara now noticed, too, what they had missed in their run for cover earlier. In the sword-shaped impression sculpted into the altar's surface lay a sword nearly identical to the ultimorite sword Nashtar carried. Unlike Nashtar's sword, the hilt was wrapped in a tattered, worn, black leather, and this sword already bore a dark crystal shard in its half-spherical base. The dark crystal was much like the shard held in the skeletal hand of Death Seed's hilt.

"Hey, this looks like the sword that poor dodger left here in that magic window thing of yours," Joe said excitedly as he went to pick the sword up.

"Do not touch it!" Nashtar shouted, sounding more wrathful than a simple warning.

Joe instantly snapped his hand back as though he had nearly risked burning himself. "What in Kodin's arse is the problem?"

"Nashtar shooed Joe aside. "Do you pay attention to nothing, boy?"

"I wouldn't say nothing." Joe gave Runara a sly look, causing her to roll her eyes, as she had grown used to doing around Joe.

"Careful lad, I've still enough magic to turn you into a snail." Nashtar pointed the red crystal at Joe.

Joe raised his hands in compliance and slowly backed away, grumbling like a reprimanded child. "Hardly seems right to threaten a man with his own crystal."

Nashtar began waving his arms above the sword, chanting some strange words.

Joe leaned sideways, getting himself within whispering distance of Runara's ear. "What's he doing?"

"I think he is trying to remove a curse from the sword," she whispered back.

A concussive wave burst from Nashtar, washing lightly over the others. "There, that should do it," Nashtar said loudly then. He reached down and picked the sword up in his left hand, holding it aloft, turning it this way and that, admiring it. The expression on his face was like that of a young boy discovering a wonderful new toy.

Runara cleared her throat, snapping Nashtar out of his seemingly mesmerized state.

"Yes, well, that's out of the way," Nashtar said, shrugging off the distraction from his mind. He reached across the altar, placing the red crystal in the slot near the front edge. "Now let's get you home, lad." Unlike Nashtar's replica, various swirling lines in the intricately sculpted altar lit up with a deep pulsing red light. "Ah, always what is hidden inside, Nashtar said, taking a few steps back to take in the altar's display. "Seems we're getting this one right." He pulled out the red sword with his right hand and placed it on the altar where the black sword had been. "Now, your sword, lad."

Joe stepped confidently forward, feeling far more comfortable around the gruff wizard with the red crystal safely on the altar. He slid Death Seed into its slot near the sword impression on the altar.

"I'm not dying this time," Runara said in a warning tone, a grim, defiant look on her face. She was holding a hand up that was already producing a sizable blue flame.

"No, no. Calm yourself, child," Nashtar half chuckled as he made to reach into his satchel for the vile of her blood that he had collected before their departure. His eyes went wide as his hand found nothing at his hip. His thoughts flashed to the image of the satchel and its contents being incinerated just minutes before in the temple trap. It was an unfortunate situation, he thought, but it seemed unlikely that such a small amount of Runara's blood would have been enough anyway. He would have to be delicate about requesting her death a second time. With his magic blocked, there would be no guarantee of being able to rouse her with the energies of the red crystal. Even if he could, second resurrections rarely had favorable results.

Before anyone could say anything further on the matter, a thunderous boom shook the temple top. Tyrant, having leaped from terraced level to terraced level of the temple until reaching the top, now stood in the middle of the courtyard, the King and Baron Solvar still clinging to his back. The vines that had grown around Tyrant's torso and the Baron, holding them both in place, diminished back into the tangle of the King's armor. Solvar immediately jumped down from the metal steed.

"I've got the sword thief, sire," Solvar growled with a deep, vengeful malice in his voice, his remaining eye fixed on Joe.

The King dismounted without a word. Noticing that Nashtar held an ultimorite sword in his hand, he was emboldened. He mistook it for the red powersword but concluded rightly, just the same, that they had not managed to complete the bonding ritual.

"Oh crap!" Joe pointed in the direction of the new arrivals to the courtyard.

"You're right to fear me, sword thief," Solvar sneered as he strode toward the dais, extending his arm blade. "I'll bleed you out proper this time."

"Not you, you kruptan moker; that!" Joe pointed again with exaggerated emphasis. Runara gasped; she saw it now, too, growing in the darkness behind Tyrant. Everyone looked in unison to where Joe was pointing just in time to see the monstrous crystalline body of Oxidisis finish reforming. It had apparently regrown from the leg that had remained intact. Its body was longer and more slender now, rather than tall. Wings, icicle-like extensions of its ribs, with nearly invisible crystal membranes stretched between them, now protruded from its sides. The beast glittered in the dim surrounding firelight of the burning vines and bushes.

Tyrant bellowed a terrifying whinny and charged Oxidisis in a blur of movement. He crashed into the temple guardian, head down, producing a surface crack that spread out in all directions across Oxidisis's chest like a grim, misshapen spiderweb. Oxidisis staggered back two steps, so great had the ground-shaking impact been. Tyrant's glowing red eyes flared as he shook his head, snorting a cloud of steam, and stomped a threatening heavy hoof, letting the guardian know he was in for a fight.

Solvar turned back to Joe, confident that the King and his steed had the temple guardian well dealt with. "I'll be taking back my sword now, thief," he shouted as he charged forward.

Joe let loose with four knives, knowing full well that the danuwan was likely to knock the flying blades aside, which Solvar did with ease. It had not slowed Solvar's charge, and he was now at the top of the dais.

"No!" Runara shouted, holding out a hand. A red ball of energy shot from her hand toward Solvar but dissipated with a loud booming clap that came from Solvar's own raised mechanical hand. He had managed to fire his arm gun just in time to intercept the spell. Runara had a stunned look on her face. A small red dot had appeared in the center of her head. She moved to feel her forehead, having an abstract sense that something was wrong, as a thin line of blood trickled down from the hole. She collapsed, dead.

The moment had given just enough pause to the Baron's attack to allow Joe time to roll onto the altar, grabbing Death Seed as he did.

"Gw-a-a-rav-a-a-a-tra-a-ar!" Joe screamed as he vaulted off the altar toward Solvar, his battle cry echoing forth like the voice of a god, amplified by the temple apse.

Solvar reacted just in time to parry the bulk of Joe's aerial assault, but Joe managed to catch Solvar in the shoulder of his remaining real arm. Solvar shouted with pain as he grabbed at the wound with his mechanical hand. Joe rolled off to the side, managing to stop himself before tumbling down the dais steps.

Nashtar rushed over to Runara. She was gone, and he dared not use any more of the red crystal's magic on a second resurrection that may not bring her back properly. He looked past Joe and Solvar as they clashed their swords repeatedly in a frantic battle. Somewhere midway between the dais and the King, Nashtar saw Crash cradling Tosh's limp form behind the ruined torso of a godé statue that had long since been toppled over by weather and time. It was impossible to read her face at this distance. She and Tosh were barely visible in the shadows. He didn't want her acting rashly, however, and put a finger to his lips, trying to tell the girl to stay quiet and hidden.

Beyond Crash, Oxidisis's voice boomed, addressing the King, its words cloaked in its ancient language. Tyrant cautiously stepped back, readying itself for another charge, steam trailing from its snout.

"Your words have no meaning to me, creature," Goms shouted at the dragon. "Meet your doom, monster!"

"Imposter! Murderer! Thief! Trespasser!" The dragon's voice thundered, the translation echoing off the courtyard walls this time. Oxidisis reared its head back, preparing for a fiery assault. The fireball in its chest quickly grew. The light refracted in all directions through the cracks in his scales where Tyrant had hit him.

Tyrant saw his moment and was a silvery streak in an instant, once again crashing into the dragon's chest. The temple top shook from the loud collision, and the cracks in Oxidisis's scales lengthened in all directions, wrapping around his front haunches slightly. This time, however, Oxidisis was ready, quickly smashing the metallic horse down to the ground with one of its massive foreclaws. Tyrant struggled against the weight of the gigantic crystalline guardian but to no avail.

"Tyrant!" Goms shouted with genuine concern as he ran to his steed's aid.

Oxidisis brought his massive jaws down hard on Tyrant's head, but his deadly collection of enormous, clear, stalactite-like teeth could not penetrate the chrome steed's thick, polished, metal skin. The teeth squealed, vainly scraping against Tyrant's iron-strong neck. Goms was quickly closing on the guardian, swinging the glowing blade of the green powersword well back, mustering the strength to take the dragon's enormous head off if he could. Suddenly, the fire building within Oxidisis exploded from his mouth. The blast sent Goms flying back. The vines of his armor blackened and burst into flames, but they were regrowing as quickly as they were burning, and the flames were out by the time Goms leaped back to his feet. A storm of roaring fire surrounded Oxidisis, not quite drowning out the horrendous bellows of Tyrant. The fire ceased abruptly. Oxidisis pulled his head back violently to its full height, leaving a glowing trail of molten globs arcing out through the air. What remained of Tyrant's glowing head melted through the guardian's menacing teeth, falling in heavy, luminous orange clumps to the temple floor.

A terrifying cry of anger came from Goms then, as he reached Oxidisis, too late to save his steed. He had the powersword pointed out before him. There was no technique, style, or strategy to his attack, just blind rage over the killing of his longtime companion. He crashed into Oxidisis before the guardian could react, his powersword sinking deeply and easily into the dragon's chest where Tyrant had cracked it moments before.

Oxidisis roared with pain as the spider web of cracks radiated out, illuminated in the green light of Goms's powersword. The temple guardian's entire body was now covered in a complex net of cracks, looking as though it could crumble again at any moment. He thrashed from side to side, raising up on his hind legs. The violent action dislodged the green powersword and threw Goms back through the air thirty feet. The King landed hard, skidding and then tumbling across the temple floor more than another fifteen feet beyond. Oxidisis's whole body lit up with a bright blue light as it spread its wings. Electricity arced all about it as the guardian swiftly rose high into the night sky without a single flap of its wings.

"I have failed you, my brothers and sisters!" Oxidisis's roaring words echoed off the courtyard walls as he continued to rise. His form quickly faded into the distance until he appeared to be nothing more than a twinkling blue star in the sky, and then, just as quickly, he was beyond view entirely.

"Pity about your horse." Nashtar's voice came from just behind Goms, who was still lying on the stone floor where he had been tossed. The King immediately sprung to his feet, swinging the deadly green blade in the direction of the wizard's voice, but found Nashtar to already be several steps back from where he had been a split second before.

The wizard leaned on the black powersword as if it were a cane. Compared to the hulking form of the King, he almost appeared to be a dwarf. Goms laughed as he looked upon the frail old man. Looking past Nashtar, he could see the ongoing sword battle between Joe and Solvar. Joe had several bleeding slashes in a variety of locations and looked to be tiring. Solvar still only had the initial slash to his shoulder, and his maniacal grin gave the impression that he was toying with Joe to some degree. Indeed, he seemed to be making no attempt to attack, simply parrying Joe's increasingly desperate swipes. He was wearing Joe down. Beyond them, Goms could see the dead form of Runara.

"Pity about the fire witch," Goms said sarcastically. "Pupil of yours?"

"You could say," Nashtar responded flatly, giving away no emotion.

Goms began to circle the old wizard, like a wolf looking for its opportunity to attack. He wanted to keep the man off balance, but Nashtar was not playing along. Instead of turning to stay facing Goms, he merely turned his head to track the King's movement.

"I'm aware that this temple restricts your magic, necromancer, and you are all the more fool to face me with an incomplete powersword." Goms continued to circle beyond Nashtar's field of view, and still, the wizard made no attempt to face the King.

"Sure about all of that, are you?" Nashtar's back was now completely to the King, and Goms took his opportunity to strike.

At the last possible moment, Nashtar began to turn. He was slow and only managed to get halfway around, but he got his sword up just in time. The impact of Goms's swing was immense, and for a moment, Nashtar had thought it may have broken his arm. Indeed, for the smallest fraction of a fraction of a second, the mighty blow had not only broken Nashtar's left arm but had also dislocated his shoulder and fractured a rib on that side. However, the arcane magic of the black powersword healed them all immediately. As the swords clashed, the glowing energy of Goms's phantom weapon began being drawn into the black sword. The green sword flickered between its ethereal state and its solid metallic form.

"Not possible! You have no magic here!" Goms fumed. Three more disturbing things were taking place as well, the first being that Goms found he could not pull the green sword away from Nashtar's weapon. The second, perhaps even more distracting, occurrence was that Nashtar appeared to be growing rapidly younger, his whole body glowing with the green energy his sword was absorbing. Lastly, and the most disturbing of the three, as quickly as Nashtar grew more youthful, the living tangle of vines that made up the armor granted by the green powersword was diminishing. Already, the King's marble white head, one arm, and half of his back and chest were exposed, revealing his gold, scaled armor beneath.

"More than possible," came back the strong, confident voice of a now twenty-something Nashtar by appearance. His hair and beard had transformed from grey to glistening black, glinting blood red wherever they caught the light. "Just one of the powers of the black sword, and you may not realize it yet, but you are quite likely dead already." Nashtar, though still very gaunt, now had the vigor of youth and had grown somewhat in height. With a great heave, he pushed Goms back. "Some form of plague is usually the way. For the sake of your empire, you'll want to avoid company, I think." Nashtar's body had stopped glowing, but a green glow briefly lingered in his eyes before returning to his usual icy blue. They continued to glow blue with no sign now of diminishing.

In Goms's hand, the green powersword had fully reverted to its ultimorite state, a form Goms had not seen for several hundred years since the moment he had first picked the sword up. The nearly identical appearance of the sword in his hand to the sword in Nashtar's made it hard to refute Nashtar's claim that it was indeed the black powersword he possessed. The only difference between the two swords was the stone held in the semi-spherical receptacles of the pommels and the color of the wrapping of the grips. Suitably, the stone in the green sword was a finely crafted, multifaceted, round gemstone of deep forest green. A faint light glowed within. Likewise, the wrapping on the grip was a deep green.

"Black sword or not, wizard, you are no match for me," Goms barked. His vine armor continued to recede, exposing the gold armor of his left leg and most of his torso. He moved to lunge at Nashtar when a great cry came up from behind him. The deadly scream was immediately followed by the impact of something large on his back, two legs wrapped around his waist, and what felt like two large fangs sunk deep at the base of his neck, just above the edge of his gold armor. He howled with the pain of it. His left hand went back instinctively, grabbing Crash, who still clung to the two throwing knives she had sunk into Goms's back. He ripped her free of his back as though she was little more than an angry house cat and threw her across the temple floor. Nashtar attempted to use the King's distraction to take a swipe at his neck, but without even looking at Nashtar, Goms had the green sword up, blocking the black. Both swords rang from the impact.

Crash tumbled in a half-controlled summersault through a field of small, blunt, crystal shards that had been Oxidisis's first shattered body. She struck her head on a much larger piece and fell unconscious.

Goms pushed Nashtar off of him, nearly knocking the wizard off his feet. He went to take advantage of the off-balance wizard, now wide open to one quick thrust, but he was suddenly seized by a fit of deep coughs. Thick globs of blood spattered from Goms's mouth onto the temple floor.

Nashtar took the King's weakened moment to try a spell, as he could feel the magical energy stolen from the green sword surging within him. However, the temple was still blocking his magic, leaving him pointlessly holding his hand out in the King's direction. Goms noticed Nashtar's futile attempt out of the corner of his eye as he recovered from his coughing fit. He started to laugh, but it sent him into another fit of blood-spewing coughs.

Past Goms, Nashtar could see that things did not seem to be going well for Screamin' Joe, and he debated leaving Goms to a slow, coughing death and helping the young bladesman. He also considered just leaving the temple. Now that he had the powersword that he had truly come for, there was no reason to linger. Still, he could not risk the red sword falling into the hands of the King, the Baron, or any of these children, for that matter. His ruse of helping Joe had worked quite well, but now that he was here, he should, at least, try to assemble the red powersword. At the very least, he ought to secret the red sword away, back to his tower, whatever its state. He looked about as the King continued to cough and swords continued to clash in the distance.

The clown girl was unconscious, possibly dead. Either way, she would not be a problem. The same could be said for the knower. Nashtar's great-granddaughter was dead again, too, which was good. He really would not have felt right about having to kill her a second time for her blood. The King would be dead soon enough. All that remained was Joe and Solvar. If he helped Joe end the elf, he could put the red sword together. He could then send the dimwitted bladesman happily off to oblivion and leave the temple without a further fight with not one but three complete powerswords. For a brief moment, he wondered if it was even possible for someone to possess more than one at a time. He would soon find out, he thought with a sly smile across his now youthful face.

No sooner had Nashtar made up his mind than the loose substructure of his grand plans for triple sword possession crumbled apart like a temple guardian facing a semi-undead fire witch. As he looked upon the battle between a very tired-looking Joe and the far more energetic Baron, Joe made a lunging attack. Solvar, in a masterful spinning display of swordsmanship, parried Death Seed aside, grabbed Joe by the neck with his free hand, and thrust his arm-blade deep into Joe's belly and out his back.

Joe, at that moment, found himself in another one of those strange instances where time seemed to have all but stopped. His mind raced over a multitude of subjects all at once; thoughts of the sensibly roofed homeworld he would never see again, a strangely attractive set of petite, red-headed trall twins he had encountered in the Midgorn city Kursik, which also brought to mind a raid of an ancient trall mine, or was it a tomb, that had certainly gone much more positively than this apparent muck-up. His mind went to each of his fallen friends. He wondered where Crash had got to. He had glimpsed her a moment ago, running off toward the King. And poor Runara, he thought. She was way too hot to be dead again. Hot; that's funny because she's a fire witch, he mused. He supposed that he, too, was technically "dead again" since Nashtar had run him through earlier. It was upon this thought that time came rushing back to its normal tumultuous pace as Joe realized this was exactly like the moment with Nashtar. He wasn't dead or dying at all, but he was coming to the solid opinion now that he really did not like the sensation of steel being run through his innards. He pushed the smugly grinning Solvar off of him with all of the strength he could muster, causing Solvar to stagger back, slamming the elf against the altar.

Solvar laughed. "Such fight in you yet, but you are done," he said, giving his arm blade a defensive swirl before him lest Joe attempt anything rash. "Just be a man about it. Hand me the sword, and find some quiet little corner where you can bleed out with a bit of dignity."

"Nah," Joe said, giving Death Seed a casual, sweeping flip, end over end, his free hand probing at the smooth spot on his belly where the fatal sword wound should have been. "Thanks, but I've got other plans for the rest of the night." He glanced over at Runara's still corpse. "Well, minus one, that is."

The look on Solvar's face was a tortured mix of astonishment and indignation. "Let's see if you survive me taking your head!" He pushed himself off of the altar, hurling himself at Joe, his arm blade arcing in a deadly, offensive convolution.

Joe was exhausted, but the adrenaline rush of nearly dying was providing him more than a second wind. He parried Solvar's rush, ducking and dodging Solvar's two following counterstrikes in a manner of twisting agility that even Joe found surprisingly impressive. Joe tried to quickly take note of just what action had followed what for use in the next barroom brawl that he would inevitably find himself in. The moves left Solvar lunging forward and off balance, giving Joe a rare moment of vulnerability to take advantage of. In a single swift maneuver, Joe brought Death Seed down on Solvar's mechanical arm, severing it at the elbow, grabbed him by his remaining arm, and, leaning in, flipped Solvar over his shoulder, slamming the elf hard onto the altar.

Solvar made a move to right himself, but Joe met him with a punch to the face, breaking the elf's nose. It knocked the Baron back down, hard, against the altar. Before Solvar could attempt anything further, Joe sunk Death Seed into the elf's abdomen, just below his right rib cage. To Joe's surprise, the sword did not seem to impact the altar and plunged all the way to the hilt. The pointed toes of the two female figures making up the sword's crossguard pierced into Solvar from the forceful weight of Joe's thrust. By chance, Joe had managed to stab Solvar directly above the slot in the altar meant for Death Seed. The Baron was pinned to the altar.

"Fool," Solvar sputtered, half choking on the blood gushing down his throat from his smashed nose. "I'm a child of Danuwan; Death Seed can never bring my death, thief."

"I'm beginning to think this thing needs a new name. Now these," Joe began to say as he reached to his bandolier for a knife. He quickly discovered that he had none. In the next instant, he instinctually leaped back from the altar, just in time to avoid a deadly slash from Solvar. The Baron had managed to secret away Joe's last two knives when Joe slammed him onto the altar.

Solvar fumbled at Death Seed's hilt while trying to hold on to the two knives. He tried to budge the sword, but it wasn't moving. Joe took a step toward him but halted when Solvar quickly snapped the knives out in Joe's direction, waving them in a warning fashion.

"Back, thief! You've lost. Just leave while you can." Solvar tried to sit himself up but found the sword made it impossible.

"Are you kidding me right now?" Joe scoffed. "Everyone who isn't pinned to a table by a magical sword, raise a mechanical hand." Joe scooped the Baron's mechanical arm from the ground, giving Solvar a high little wave with the Baron's own hand.

The sound of swords clashing down in the courtyard made both men look. Goms, bent over in some state of anguish, had renewed his assault on Nashtar. Despite his condition, his superior, battle-honed skill was forcing Nashtar to be on the defensive, constantly backing across the courtyard.

Solvar laughed, wincing as he did. The movement caused Death Seed to slice repeatedly into his quickly healing flesh, muscle, and organs. He turned back to Joe.

"You are weaponless. The King will soon dispatch that mad old necromancer," The Baron's voice was full of manic malice, foaming, bloody spittle flying with every other word. "And all of your friends are dead. You… have…lost!" With that last word, he pushed himself, hard, with the stump of his mechanical arm, away from Death Seed. The sword sliced through his side while the crossguard tore deep bloody gouges in his flesh. The Baron bellowed through gritted teeth from the pain as he kept the knives pointed at Joe. He glared at Joe, a frightening one-eyed mess of sweat and blood. Joe just watched, cautiously weighing his offensive options but mostly just fascinated by the grim spectacle of determination. Solvar used Death Seed to pull himself upright and waited for the muscles and flesh of his side to magically knit back together.

The Baron hoped Joe would be sensible enough to run then, but Joe just stood there smiling at Solvar, a sly twinkle in his eye.

"Did you not hear me, fool? Your friends are dead!" Solvar spat.

"Ya," said Joe in a long, slow drawl, crossing his arms casually. "But I've got more friends."

In a fragmented flash of a moment, expressions of amusement, confusion, and grim realization mingled simultaneously on Baron Solvar's face. He started to turn around, but it was too late. Koobara's fangs sank deep into the elf's neck, severing his spine, while the jungle cat's full weight crashed down upon him, further breaking his back. Joe's knives rattled to the ground from Solvar's lifeless hand.

Joe cautiously approached the giant black cat. "Good work, buddy!"

Koobara growled back, Solvar still firmly clamped in its jaws. It made a quick chomp to adjust its grip on the elf's corpse, stopping Joe in his tracks as it stared at Joe with its wild yellow eyes.

"Whoa! Easy big guy, he's all yours. I just wanted to maybe…" He put a hand out slowly, trying to reach for Death Seed. Kubara roared then, swatting at the air in front of Joe. "Nope, nope." Joe stammered as he jumped well back. "That's yours now, too. Got it. Thing never worked anyway," he grumbled to himself.

Joe looked past Koobara to see how the confrontation between Nashtar and the King was going. He was surprised to find that neither of them was in the courtyard. With a quick scan, he found them again. Somehow, their battle had taken them to the top of one of the outer walls. Goms was holding Nashtar by his robes, easily blocking the wizard's futile sword flails. The King's sword was glowing green again, and the vine armor was slowly regrowing, having already crept up most of his sword arm.

Joe whipped around the altar, giving enough space to keep Koobara from getting anxious. He scooped up the two knives Solvar had just dropped. As Joe launched the two knives, Goms lifted Nashtar off his feet, winding back with his sword to run the wizard through. The first of Joe's knives glanced off the King's scaled armor, but the second knife, just a fraction of a second behind the other, found a gap created by the individual scale impacted by the first knife, bouncing up. The knife sunk deep into the King's back.

Goms paused, looking over his shoulder at Joe, Nashtar flailing above him, then toppled over the side of the temple, taking Nashtar with him. Joe stared for a few moments at the empty space on the wall where the two men had just been.

"Well," Joe muttered to himself, feeling a little defeated. "That could have gone better."

"What could have gone better?"

Joe spun around, not believing the voice he was hearing. Standing next to the altar, petting Koobara, pink embers winking in and out among her eerily animated, vibrant red locks, was Runara. She gave the jungle cat a little pat, and Koobara hopped down from the altar, slinking off into the shadows of the courtyard.

Joe shouted with jubilant enthusiasm as he rushed over to her, picking her up and spinning her around. The two laughed together, but then Runara started looking around.

"Where are all the others?" She stepped away from Joe and walked to the edge of the dais. "Where are Nashtar and the King?"

"About that," Joe started hesitantly. Before he could say another word, there was a bright flash of white light and a loud popping sound that reverberated in the courtyard.

Garen came somersaulting out of, seemingly, nowhere, landing in a controlled defensive stance and looking more than a little confused.

Crash came walking up behind him just then, rubbing her head. "What's all the noise? What did I miss?" Garen could only shake his head, having no answers for her. She took Garen by the arm, and they began walking over to Joe and Runara. Crash looked over her shoulder and back into the courtyard as they made their way up the steps of the dais. She spotted Tosh still lying where she had left him. Koobara was curled up next to him like a giant sleeping house cat. "What happened with Nashtar and the King?" she asked, with a fair amount of confusion in her voice as she hugged Runara. "You seem…better," she added, assessing Runara at arm's length.

"So, what happened was," Joe started again.

Garen interrupted him with a sudden outburst. "Solvar!" Crash, too, had a shocked look on her face at that moment.

Joe and Runara spun around to see what had both Garen and Crash agape.

Solvar's broken, bloody body was glowing with a purple, almost pink light and floating approximately three feet above the altar. Blood continued to pour from his wounds, filling the glowing red patterns etched into the altar's surface, bathing the red powersword in a deep pool of his life fluid. The red crystal glowed brightly and pulsed at irregular intervals.

The sight of Solvar not simply lying on the altar had so startled Runara that she defensively let out a tremendous stream of flame that burst forth from her entire body. It made the others jump back as they watched the flaming deluge envelop both Solvar and the altar. By the time she brought the flames under control, Solvar's body had been reduced to embers. What remained of his mechanical arm tumbled down, bouncing off the edge of the altar, an unrecognizable clump of twisted glowing metal.

The designs on the altar glowed a brighter red now, no longer full of Solvar's blood, while the red powersword, no longer in a pool of blood, was now covered in a thick black crust. The eyes of the dragons on the front of the altar were glowing red as well, and smoke curled in puffing wisps from their nostrils. A red line of focused light shot from the red crystal across to the dark crystal shard held in Death Seed's cold, metal, skeletal hand. The roughly shaped shard lit up brighter and brighter until it no longer looked black but a deep, blood red.

The group stared at the illuminated spectacle, not sure if the altar had anything more that it might do. Garen spoke up as a realization of what was happening took hold. "I believe we've somehow initiated the joining ritual for the red powersword."

Joe took several steps closer to the altar to get a better look. "What, how? I thought we needed Runara's blood and nobody has even said any magic words." He turned to the others. "Nashtar said some sort of crazy words when he tried back at the tower."

Garen stepped closer, too, then walked around the altar to examine Death Seed and the encrusted powersword. "I think the Baron's blood was the key. Yes, yes! That's it! Runara may be the descendant of one of Modnar's oldest wizards, but any elf is a child of a legacy of magic that predates written history." Garen's eyes lit up as he came to understand the poem from the book in the Loncodi library. His eyes darted to the still-unconscious form of Tosh. "He's going to be so annoyed that he missed this. He is okay, right?"

"I think so." Crash offered, sounding less than confident.

Garen motioned for the others to join him on the back side of the altar.

"Come, come, listen. 'With the last breath of Nolis,'" He began reciting the poem. "It's not saying dragon's fire, just fire. Legend has it that Nolis's last breath was what gave the early people of Modnar Fire. Runara's fire woke up the crystal." He pointed at the red crystal. "'The wand of the triputhon glows.'"

"That's a tripa-thingy? I thought it was a crystal," Joe interjected.

Garen ignored him and continued. "'As the child of old magic dies, as the blood of Kronus flows;' has to have been the Baron. Perhaps Kronus was an ancient elf, maybe the father of all elves. Doesn't matter." He paused to look around to see if the other three were still listening; they were. Intently, they waited for him to go on.

He rattled through the next verses, feeling they had covered everything there. "'In conjured flame and ichor, the forlorn blade bathes so silent, dreams to rend the infinite, raging, it craves the violent.' I think it is just talking about reigniting the sword's magic. It might be talking about Death Seed, too, but that brings us to the important part. 'New magic's progeny speaks, initiates the tine shapers, waking the ancient metal, making all to it like vapors.'" He turned to Joe then. "The magic words. Runara needs to speak them. She is the progeny of new magic, human magic, Nashtar's kin. The words at the bottom of the poem had to be the words of the spell!"

"Well, great," Joe said, throwing up his hands. "You said you couldn't read it."

"I know." Garen's enthusiasm diminished slightly. "But you heard Nashtar say the words. Can you remember what he said?"

Joe took a few steps back. "Okay, okay, let me think." He closed his eyes and put his hands to his head as if he were trying to prevent his memories from escaping. "All right, okay, it was something like…" He spun in place, bent over, stood up again, and then, finally, throwing up his hands dramatically, blurted, "Pompom of God, whack a ho, festive puss!"

Garen frowned and was about to say something when Runara suddenly spoke up. "No, I know the words. Somehow, I know. It's like they are part of me."

She turned back to the altar, muttering quietly to herself. She paused and stepped back, her arms outstretched, pushing Garen and Crash back with her. As she pondered the words, solidifying them to perfect clarity in her mind, her hair began to lift and billow as though blown from a strong wind coming from beneath her. Crash and Garen both backed away from her. The pink embers from her hair were flying everywhere, filling the air. The spectacle made Crash giggle and clap, thoroughly entertained.

With the words now as clear to her as if they floated in the air before her, Runara blurted out in a voice that filled the temple courtyard beyond, "Pemboyaga ohm tel Godé wekafaehek; pusiris: Yavezdoz!"

The entire top surface of the altar lit up, sending a column of bright white light out into the night sky. A shockwave of hot air buffeted the group. As the light diminished, they could see the beam of red light between the red crystal and Death Seed's crystal shard had split at each crystal. The two new beams formed a triangle, meeting at the base of the red powersword. As the group drew closer to see what was happening, Death Seed's skeletal hand began to open. The movement took them all by surprise, causing all of them to jump slightly. The crystal shard, free of Death Seed's grasp, suddenly vaporized, leaving a small cloud of red sparkling particles that quickly faded into nothing. The beams of light disappeared in that same instant, and the red crystal's glow promptly diminished. Only the red glow of the patterns on the altar remained. Joe, Runara, Crash, and Garen began to draw closer to the altar to see what had happened, but suddenly, the altar erupted in another column of light, bright red this time. Scarlet balls of fire, to the left and right, shot out of the mouths of the snarling dragon sculptures on the front of the altar. All but Garen had taken several steps back and remained at that distance, not being confident that the altar's volcanic activity had subsided.

The altar went dark then. Only a faint red light came from the hilt of the red powersword. No longer encrusted, the sword looked as if it had been freshly polished. In its hilt, embedded within the semi-spherical base, was the rough crystal shard formerly held by Death Seed. More than merely set within the base, it looked as though the crystal had somehow melded with the metal of the sword hilt. The source of the remaining faint red light, the crystal glowed from somewhere deep within.

Without thinking, Garen grabbed the sword to show the others. He spun around, holding the sword before him in his left hand. A bolt of energy shot up his arm from the sword to the base of his skull. It caused his whole head to tingle. At that exact moment, the sword grew translucent and then quickly faded from his hand entirely before he could put it back down. It was simply gone.

"Well done." Joe grumped while Runara and Crash stood agape. "Where in Kodin's arse did it go? What did you do? How am I getting home now?" He was now right up in Garen's face.

Garen pushed Joe back with his right hand, a look of confusion and astonishment on his face. He made it clear that he needed some space. He brought his right hand up to his head, putting his fingers lightly to his temple. "Wait, Joe. Quiet. It is like the sword is in my head. I can see it, hear it, taste it even. It is hard to explain."

"What?"

"I said, quiet." Garen held out his left hand in a fist.

"Whoa, buddy, calm down," Joe backed away from Garen, "I'm disappointed about you losing the sword, but I don't want to fight you."

Runara was about to step in to keep the peace when suddenly a long, red, glowing translucent sword burst from Garen's fist. Wisps of luminous red energy flitted from the entire length of the blade. Garen looked surprised and slightly concerned as he quickly glanced at his three companions, holding his right hand up, warning them to stay back. A glowing red hexagon mesh seemed to explode from his sword hand, enveloping his entire body within a second. Instead of seeing Garen through the holes of the mesh, there now seemed to be nothing but a dark void within the Garen-shaped, glowing mesh shell.

Garen took a step toward them. "This is incredible! I can sense..." He paused momentarily, searching for the right way to express it, but his mind felt like it was spinning. "Everywhere. It is overwhelming! I feel dizzy. Hard to stay focused; to remember who, what I..." He began to babble then, mumbling a random assortment of words.

Runara touched his arm in concern. The red mesh armor would have burned anyone else's hand, but instead, her body reacted to the magical assault with its own magical defense, lighting her up head to toe in purple and pink flame. Garen looked at her, his focus returning to his surroundings. Runara's fire was being drawn toward Garen's armor, flowing down her arm and into his. The mesh of Garen's armor grew brighter and brighter.

Her magic was clearing his mind somehow, but it felt as though the skin on every inch of his body was being pulled into the mesh armor surrounding it.

It wasn't painful, but it was unpleasant and more than just a little disconcerting.

"I, I can, I am seeing other worlds, I think." Garen stammered toward Joe."

"My world, Midgorn, do you see my world?" Joe asked anxiously.

Images of different landscapes pulsed through Garen's mind like waves washing in on a beach. He tried to focus on the word 'Midgorn.' One particular image became fixed in his mind's eye. He saw a city. Its high surrounding outer wall formed an enormous pentagon. Farmland stretched off into the distance all around it. High above was a glowing ceiling of luminous rock. He described it to Joe.

Without hesitation, Joe shouted out, "Cur!" He laughed with joy. "That's not just Midgorn; that's the city I was born in! Can you get me there? How does this work?"

It was as if something in the sword, not quite like a voice, was communicating with Garen's mind, guiding his actions. "I think I can…" His voice trailed off as his movements slipped into a sort of automated instinct. He pulled away from Runara and slashed violently in Joe's direction. Joe had barely managed to leap back out of the blade's reach and was about to protest but then slipped into a reverent silence at what he now saw before him.

The red powersword had slashed a long gash in the fabric of reality. The fissure had split wide open, and through it, Joe could see the outer fields of the city of Cur. More than that, the earthy smells of the fields and farms and the fires, food, and filth of the city beyond washed over Joe on a gentle breeze that blew through the ragged portal. Joe could hardly believe it. Garen was using all the strength he could muster, holding the tear open with the sword at the bottom edge. He could feel the edge of the image pushing back, trying to close.

Joe, Runara, and Crash all walked around Garen and the floating portal, mesmerized by the spectacle. Much like the moving picture Nashtar had conjured on the ferry, it seemed to be a three-dimensional image but flat, fully visible from where Joe had been standing or from where Garen stood but disappearing entirely if viewed along its sides. More intriguing was that the perspective from Garen's position was completely in the opposite direction from the side Joe had been on. From Garren's side, they could see the city wall, one of the five city gates, and Arlosvol Road. It was a road Joe knew well as a highwayman, and even now, it was bustling, busy with merchants, farmers, and travelers, coming and going in their carts. It was home!

Crash was right next to Joe as the joy of the vision overtook him. He swept her up, twirling her around in an impromptu dance.

"Home, home, I'm going home." Joe twirled her out and away with a grand flourish as she laughed and chanted along with him, spinning away past the altar. Joe turned in place, coming face to face with Runara. It brought his dance to an immediate halt. Runara was smiling, but her face was full of bitter-sweet sorrow.

"It's wonderful, Joe. You did it. You found your way home. It's funny, but a part of me always thought, hoped really, that you were slightly mad. The whole other world thing, who could possibly believe…" She choked on her words, and her eyes welled up, not quite forming tears.

Joe took her by the hands. "You could come with me. I mean," he looked around at the three of them, a little self-consciously, adding, "you all could."

Garen answered first. "My path ends here, bladesman. I have responsibilities long neglected in Loncodi." His voice got quite anxious then. "I have no idea how long I can keep this open, though, Joe. I don't even know how I found it." Garen's glowing mesh armor flickered, and the image of Midgorn flickered with it. "This might be your only chance, Joe. If you're going to go, you've got to do it now."

"What about the big guy?" Joe asked, looking around. "Kord! Where are ya pal? Time to go!" He shouted out into the courtyard. "Come on out. Your invisibility isn't fooling anyone."

"Joe," Runara put a hand on his shoulder, "Stop. I don't think he made it. Think about it. The King and the Baron got past him, and Koobara is here. Those two are inseparable now – were inseparable."

"Honestly, I don't think I can hold this but a few more moments," Garen said in a weak voice, his whole body starting to shake.

"So?" Joe asked of Runara. "What d'you say?"

Runara looked down, shaking her head no, releasing a flurry of pink embers. "This is my home. My destiny is here. I can feel it." she added quietly.

Joe straightened himself. "Sure, of course. I get it." He cleared his throat, trying not to let himself get emotional. "Say bye and thanks to the little guy for me," he said, pointing at Tosh. It was mostly a ploy to distract the others from the tears now welling up in his reddening eyes. "Been there more than my fair share," he said, referring to the knower's unconscious state. His voice was low and just a little nostalgic. "Right, alone then."

"Not alone," Crash said, taking his hand and flashing the brightest of smiles. "And you ought to take a souvenir. She put Death Seed into his other hand. It brought him right back, and he flashed her a smile almost as broad as hers.

"You sure?" He said with his familiar sly swagger. She nodded.

"Now, Joe!" Garen's voice was desperate.

Crash stepped through the dimensional tear with an excited giggle, still holding Joe's hand. Joe paused at the last moment, turning back to Runara. "Oh ya, you should know that I may or may not be partially responsible for your great-grandpappy potentially falling to his death."

"What?" Runara frowned.

"The good news is, you're probably the Queen now. So have fun oppressing the masses or whatever it is Queens do here. "

"Joe!" Garen shouted, his voice cracking slightly. The tear was growing smaller very quickly. Joe ducked in, blew Runara a kiss, and forced out the biggest smile he could just as Garen let go, and the portal snapped closed.

Epilogue

Joe sloshed back a giant gulp of ale, spilling nearly as much down his cheeks as he managed to drink from the large, dented copper mug. The Glithian Inn's ale was just mildly distinguishable from kruptan urine, but the heavy dose of nostalgia that came with it made it seem like the sweetest nectar to Joe. It had been far too long since he had been back to his old hometown watering hole. Even before his detour through Modnar, it had been months since his last visit to Cur or the Glithian. He leaned back in his chair, gargling the ale as he searched his memory.

The last time he had been there, he had instigated what turned into a full barroom brawl. He had smashed a stool over the head of a rather extra-ugly wolgar who had been picking on a scrawny little human iconic priest. Watching the scrawny fellow get tossed around had been entertaining at first, but then it started to look like the little guy was about to cry, and Joe just couldn't stand to see a grown man suffer that sort of unprovoked indignity. After hitting the wolgar with the chair, which, incidentally, had little effect on the brute, the rest of the bar immediately split into a humans versus non-humans free-for-all.

The Glithian, many decades long past, had once been a beautiful, lavish inn. Evidence of this existed in the form of elaborate decorative wooden carvings worked into the bar, tables, wall panels, and the various core-cave beast trophy heads that hung on the wall. It was hard to see in the lofty, dark reaches of the ceiling, but there were even the remnants of large, square, wooden chandeliers. Time and a near ceaseless string of brawls, similar to the one Joe had started, had not been kind, however, and the inn had fallen into a state of disrepair and filth. This was masked somewhat by the subdued lighting and lack of windows. As the city of Cur became a hub of criminal activity in Midgorn, the Glithian had become the common watering hole for thugs, thieves, and smugglers of every race in Midgorn. Joe could not remember a time when the place had not been full of rowdy scum looking to spend their spoils on whores, booze, and bad food. Such great times, Joe thought. This day, the inn was uncharacteristically quiet and empty save for the portly, unkempt innkeeper casually picking his nose behind the bar.

"Single-handedly, an entire troop of danuwan soldiers?" The perfectly feminine voice interrupted Joe's nostalgic daydream.

Joe let his chair drop back onto its front legs with a loud, hard thud. "Ya, that's right, just like I said." He couldn't read the faces of the two shadowy figures across the table from him. They had bought the ale, so it didn't matter much if they believed his tale or not, but any free drink deserved at least one story. "It's like number four in my ten point guide to —"

"Hardly single-handedly," interrupted Crash's voice from behind. "I helped — a lot. Well, me and Death Seed," she amended.

"Ah, yes, well, I was about to explain…" Joe turned in his seat and was immediately dumbstruck by the vision before him. Instead of the green-haired, grimy girl that Joe had expected to introduce to his new table companions there was a beautiful, red-haired woman dressed in black leathers similar to Joe's. He was particularly distracted by the deep purple shirt the woman wore, or rather the flesh provocatively visible through the loose black lacing that ran down to her navel.

"Eyes up here, sailor," she said with a smile, pulling his chin up with a finger until his gaze met her rich, golden brown eyes. Parted in the middle, the curls of her bobbed red hair framed her smiling, clean, lightly freckled face. She had painted small black circles around her eyes. It was the only remnant hinting at her previous makeup and the only real clue Joe could discern that this stunning beauty was indeed his Crash.

"But…" Joe stammered, at a loss for words.

Crash took a seat beside Joe, stealing a healthy swig from his mug before addressing the other two across the table. "Grashon Bondas; pleased to meet you, I'm sure, and you are?"

The figure on the left, directly across from Grashon, leaned forward into the light of the table's single candle. Her long blonde hair caught the light like spun gold, and in the shadows of her brow-length, golden bangs, the candlelight danced upon her eyes in flashes of silver and yellow. It gave the illusion that her eyes were two small kaleidoscopes. Her face was flawlessly symmetrical and without the slightest blemish. Even in the hard shadows of the candlelight, it was evident that she was inhumanly attractive. She flashed them both a wide smile full of mischief.

"I'm Ojinks, Ojinks La, and the quiet one here is my bodyguard, Pilex." She casually swept her hair back with one hand, tucking it behind her pointed left ear. "Tell me about this 'Death Seed' of yours."

Glossary

Advan
The second largest of the major human communities of Midgorn, Advan is known for its vast fertile farmlands, fine dining, and opulent architecture. It is Midgorn's cultural hub and home to many of Midgorn's wealthiest citizens, best cooks, and most renowned authors and artists.

Aglog
Aglog is a district in Senuvia (North Eastworld) primarily consisting of swampland. Dukes appointed to the region tend to have notoriously short lives. This may have something to do with the area being a haven for pirates.

Balconsul
The Balconsul is a board of twelve elected officials that form the governing body of Midgorn. Ten members each represent one of the ten major communities of Midgorn. The eleventh member represents the interests of the minor or outlying communities, while the twelfth member represents the trall clans governing the tunnels and the city of Kursik.

Battapod
This is the mander word for a fruit in Midgorn, similar to the coconut of Modnar and Earth. The only notable difference of the Midgorn variety is that rather than the white flesh of the coconut, the flesh and juice of a battapod is blue. Manders often fill emptied battapod shells with sand, using them as the weighted ends of bola weapons.

Beedo

Beedo is the largest and most complex of Midgorn's community caves. Comprised primarily of a vast sea, the human community of Beedo is located on a large island. Being of a more tropical clime than the rest of Midgorn, Beedo is a vacation destination for many. The island's inhabitants are known for their "pleasure" skills, introducing visitors to the delights of exotic foods, dance, music, massage, and more. Smaller fishing communities exist in an area adjacent to the main island, which is spotted with numerous small islands known as the water hills. Beyond the water hills are the shallow marshlands, which are home to the non-human, mander people. The larger area of Beedo is also where the Mouth of Kodin, an enormous circular waterfall of unknown depth, can be found.

Boggorat

The boggorat is a horse-sized rodent popular throughout Modnar for the large meat sacs that grow on the rear haunches of the females. The meat sacs detach quite easily and without harm to the female. A defensive mechanism, the meat sacs grow back in about a month. A common herd, referred to as a "nest," consists of six females and one male. Males are very aggressive and breathe out streaming blasts of flaming gelatinous fluid. The skin and fur of a boggorat are prized for their flame-resistant properties.

Boxwater

Boxwater is a small town found deep in the swamps of Aglog. There are no roads that lead to Boxwater. For this reason, it became a popular hideout for criminals. In time, the entire town fell under the control of thieves and pirates.

Broon

A unique male warrior caste of the manders, broon are noted for being born with three horns on their head and changing from male to female approximately midway through their lifespan. Many also lose their horns during the change. Broon manders grow to be significantly larger than regular manders and, for this reason, are trained to be warriors, given the responsibility of guarding the mander city. Once changed, a broon often produces a single, asexually fertilized egg. It will be the only offspring they produce. The hatchlings of such eggs are never born broon, but their offspring, especially that of the males, often include at least one broon. A broon's offspring are often larger framed than the average mander, but subsequent generations tend to be of normal size. It is also notable that broon prefer only the company of whatever same sex they happen to be at the time. It is not only for this reason that they are shunned by most other mander. As guardians of the city, they are not permitted the distraction of hunting. To the mander, however, nothing is more important than one's skill as a hunter. Not hunting, whether by choice or by station, makes one less worthy of respect within the mander culture. Paradoxically, broon are appreciated by the Mander society as a whole for their service as protectors and provided a comfortable life. However, individually, most manders will avoid interaction with them if possible. It is even considered unlucky to come into physical contact with a broon, whether by intention or chance.

Celeston

Celestons are beings from a neighboring dimension in Modnar that come in a nearly endless variety of shapes with an equally varying set of supernatural abilities and traits. They often emerge from randomly appearing warpholes. Although known for their deadly hostility, they are occasionally sought by those with knowledge of how to contain them. Celestons, due to their multidimensional nature, can be trapped within containers much smaller than themselves. For this reason, small bottles or similar containers that can easily be kept, carried, or hidden are often used. Once contained, a celeston's essence becomes bound to the container, and they will do the bidding of the possessor of the container. Given the chance, however, they will do what they can to kill the one enslaving them and free themselves of the container.

Chackler(s)

Wandering lawmen of special privilege in Midgorn, chacklers are part bounty hunter, part judge. They are often highly skilled fighters and have full authority to jail or carry out whatever punishment they deem fit for the criminals that they are charged to track down. Chacklers are appointed by members of the Balconsul, with each of the twelve members appointing no more than one chackler at any given time. Therefore, there are never more than twelve active chacklers roaming Midgorn.

Convenor

A convenor is an officer of a municipal government responsible for granting or denying permits for various activities within the boundaries of their community in Modnar. Examples of such permits include the right to sell goods for local or nomadic merchants, construction permits, or performance permits for street entertainers. In some Modnarian cities where laws are much more oppressive, convenors are sought for permits to own books or practice magic within municipal borders.

Cur

One of the major communities in Midgorn, Cur, is Joe's hometown. It is notorious as a haven for criminals and the only community to border the Sky Caves of Midgorn's elves. This is primarily why the elves have such a poor opinion of the humans. Cur is also the heart of the Iconist cult. Iconists believe that a world called Earth exists somewhere beyond the infinite rock of Midgorn, and the cult's priests often claim to be from that mystical world. A large rock in Cur's market square serves as the gateway to the home of another reclusive race known as the Indazerk. From time to time, a new human iconist priest emerges from the metal iris on the surface of this large rock mound, often to set off on a quest for a fabled gateway to Earth. Each such human has a crystal pendant given to them by the Indazerk. These crystals light up with a glowing icon when near the market square's iris, other similar irises throughout Midgorn, or other mystical "keyholes" or gateways.

Damina kazo

Known to be the second oldest martial art form in Modnar, damina kazo is said to have been taught to the original followers of the ancient god, Zanx, by the third face of Zanx, herself. Practiced exclusively by Zanxian monks and nuns, it is one of the most respected and feared fighting styles in Modnar. Confrontations with Zanxian nuns, in particular, are avoided by most, as they practice an even more dangerous form of the art than the monks that incorporates magical elements. Fortunately for everyone, the followers of Zanx lead a life of peace, helping those in need whenever possible.

Danuwan

The Danuwan is the race name by which the elves of Midgorn refer to themselves. In fact, it is the common reference in Midgorn for the pointy-eared race, who live separated and secluded from the other races of Midgorn. Only Iconists or outerworlders refer to the Danuwan as elves. A more archaic Midgorn word for a Danuwan is froyk, but this is generally considered a racist term.

Dreema

One of the major communities of Midgorn, Dreema, is primarily populated by practitioners of magic and science. Legend has it that a woman, claiming to have traveled back in time from Midgorn's distant future, founded the community when she was unable to return to her own time. Previously, Dreema had been a sparsely populated farming community. An inventive genius herself but unfamiliar with the technology that sent her through time, she gathered the greatest minds of Midgorn to Dreema, hoping that together, they might find a way back to her own time.

Frimble

Frimble is the brookshin word for panic but usually more in reference to needless worry.

Gatal

The smallest of Modnar's three moons, some believe the moon to be tied to the random appearance of warpholes on Modnar. It is nearly identical in appearance to Earth's moon (at least on the side always facing the planet).

Glackfish

The glackfish is a round, flat fish found in the shallow waters of Midgorn's water hills. On average, an adult glackfish grows to be twenty inches in diameter. Their backs are dotted with hundreds of tiny spikes. Although the spikes are not poisonous, stepping on a glackfish will often result in severe infections picked up from the bacteria-laden waters that the glackfish prefer.

Godé

This is the name ancient Modnarians in upper Senuvia gave to a race of powerful beings that they worshipped as gods. The godé were responsible for creating the thirteen powerswords, which were wielded by their thirteen leaders. After a great war that resulted in the death of all thirteen leaders and the scattering of the thirteen swords across Modnar, the remaining godé abandoned their temple home on the Isle of Graa. Most of the godé were never seen again, but some are still worshipped as gods in obscure regions of Modnar.

Godling

Godlings are beings of energy that emerged during the early formation of the planet Modnar. Some influenced the actual formation of the planet, some manifested as aspects of the planet, while others gave rise to some of the living beings. In some cases, the energy flowing through those structures and beings can be called upon and communicated with. Some godlings are thought to be the conduits through which avatars for the true gods are formed on Modnar. Still other godlings took on shapes of their own, channeling the energies of their surrounding counterparts in the environment, becoming the first and most ancient of Modnar's gods.

Gorleander (pup)

The gorleander is a creature of indescribable horror encountered in the Core Cave of Midgorn. Those encountering a gorleander have often died of fright, while those surviving an encounter, if they actually looked upon the beast, have been left in a vegetative state. No one who has encountered a gorleander has ever been able to describe it because they were fortunate enough to have avoided seeing anything beyond an immense shadowy form. In contrast, the pups of a gorleander are adorable, little brown or black balls of fur, with large dark eyes, a pair of prominent primary antennae, and six spindly, jointed, secondary antennae trailing three each down their sides. However, anyone who has tried to take a pup from its nest has died, quickly hunted down by the pup's parent.

Garatok

An amalgam of various dead creatures brought to life through sorcery and alchemy. The creatures are often imbued with magical abilities and are frequently used as visual and audio conduits for their creators. They are similar in function but usually significantly larger and more independently intelligent than grotoks. The creatures used in their construction determine their shapes, sizes, and abilities. Smaller creatures such as rats or squirrels are often used, however, as the use of larger creatures requires significantly more magical energy and skill to imbue with life. The smaller creatures also serve the more clandestine purposes of the beasts.

Grolon

A grolon is a mid-ranking officer in the Eastworld royal military.

Grotok

A small magical servant used as its creator's remote eye and ear. Grotoks are generated by a traumatic head wound combined with a spell. The victim often dies as the Grotok emerges days later from the victim's head. One of the victim's eyes becomes the creature's head. Advanced forms of Grotoks can have wings and the ability to fly, but most have either four or six legs and long whip-like tails. Their size and appearance are much like that of a small red combination of lizard and salamander.

Hellgoat

Commonly found in the volcanic deserts of Modnar, hellgoats are comparable in size to horses and have the general appearance of a wooly goat. Both males and females have long, curled, black, iron horns that constantly glow with an inner heat. They are carnivores, hunting either alone or in mated pairs. The wool of a hellgoat can be woven into a fire-resistant cloth, while the outer hide has an acidic property, burning any substance coming in contact with it, save for ultimorite and hellgoat wool. When alihellgoat'sllgoat's wool has the same acidic properties. The wool can only be collected with ultimorite shears and must be left to cure in the sun for one week before it can be handled and spun safely. The hide loses its acidic property after one week, reverting to a normal leather that offers some protection from both acid and fire. Handlers of the wool or hides will wear entire suits made of the cured hide.

Keelbare

Keelbare is an aeronautical term used on elven sky vessels to descrcraft's craft's airborne state. The vessels are capable of both air and sea travel.

Klopam

Klopams are enormous beasts residing in hollows behind the large waterfall in Midgorn known as the Mouth of Kodin. Klopams use their long, sticky tongues to snatch falling fish and other edibles from the falling water. They reduce their catches to an absorbable goo in tethered, digestive pouches that they expel through a rear orifice.

Kodin / Kodin Havwen

The multifaceted god commonly believed in and worshipped in Midgorn, Kodin is thought to be the great creator of the endless world of rock, while Havwen is said to be the manifestation of the now perpetually sKodin's Kodin's thoughts, dreams, and nightmares. One of the many forms of Havwen, referred to as the Forger, is believed to have created the people of Midgorn. True zealots believe the other races, such as the danuwan and trall, were early attempts by the Forger before creating the balanced perfection of the humans. It is believed that Havwen waits in a paradise, far above the realms of the danuwan, for the worthy dead, the only ones capable of passing through the fiery barKodin's, Kodin's blood, that protects the sanctuary.

Koli

This is the midgin(human) word for a fruit in Midgorn, similar to the coconut of Modnar and Earth. The only notable difference of the Midgorn variety is that rather than the white flesh of the coconut, the flesh of a koli is blue. They only grow on palm trees found in the Midgorn area called Beedo.

Leviathan

The leviathan is an enormous fish found throughout Modnar's oceans. They are capable of swallowing entire ships whole. Their digestive juices are very weak. Therefore, it is not uncommon for the crews of such swallowed vessels to find other vessels still reasonably intact with their crews still sheltered and alive inside, despite having been swallowed weeks or even months before.

Loncodi

The only city on the east coast of North Eastworld, it is the primary trading hub for the northern communities. As the only major port on the country's eastern coast, it is also the busiest shipping port in all of North Eastworld, receiving boats from the countries of Westerlan to the west and Oddesia to the east. In the days of King Repsum (great-grandfather to King Mazeze), the city had been much smaller and truly more of a fortress, where experiments with ancient, magical devices were often conducted. The city is divided into four distinct quarters. The southern quarter is actually the original old fortress city and the location of the second-largest library in all of Eastworld. The northern quarter is the theatre district, known for some of the most elaborate and impressive productions in all of Modnar. Actors from all over the world come to Loncodi hoping to reach the pinnacle of their craft. The west quarter is the arts district, where some of the most skilled artisans of every imaginable skill set can be found. The eastern quarter is the industrial district, comprised primarily of warehouses, banks, and businesses of a questionable moral foundation. Loncodi is also notable as one of the most heavily defended cities in Eastworld. When Goms Ethdab's forces swept across what was then Senuvia, they were unable to take the city. The four families controlling the city quickly realized that there was nothing to be won by resisting. They negotiated a truce, the terms of which, among other liberties not found throughout the rest of Eastworld, was a limited royal military presence and a lack of taxes paid to the crown by business owners. Consequently, nearly everyone living in Loncodi is registered as operating some sort of business.

Mander

Manders are a large amphibious race native to the swamps and water hills region of Beedo in Midgorn.

Manrian

This is, simply, the word for a citizen of the community of Manri in Midgorn. Manri is a sparsely populated area in Midgorn, consisting of only a few buildings at its core. Much of the area is barren rock. It is a common gathering place for mercenaries and assassins and is generally considered an unsafe area for a common person to go to. Once a year, however, many citizens from Midgorn's communities gather in Manri for the Grand Fain festival, turning Manri into an enormous city of tents. The Grand Fain is a multi-day festival focused on a variety of physical challenges. The festival culminates in the competition that gives it its name inside a massive stadium dug into the rock floor at the center of Manri. Top competitors from the previous days' challenges negotiate their way through elaborate obstacles, trying to gather flags. Fearsome beasts often roam some areas of the stadium, and deadly force among the competitors is also allowed. The surviving competitor with the most flags within the time limit wins. Winners of the Grand Fain are awarded an identifying ring, a money prize, free accommodations in many Midgorn communities for the following year, and notoriety that allows them to charge a top price for their mercenary services.

Marhorse

The marhorse is an amphibious beast that looks very similar to a horse. The primary differences from a normal horse are the wide three-toed webbed and clawed feet, the long snaking tail, the tip of which fans out, fish-like (though not as frail and far more rigid when fanned out) when in the water, and a spiked fin in place of a mane. Tendrils, looking much like a trail of matted hair, skirt their rear jaw, which functions as a form of gills when the creature is underwater. Marhorses come in a variety of shades, from black to white. Some prize breeds have vivid, near-neon colors on their gills, fins, and tail fans. Marhorses are found in lakes, oceans, rivers, and swamps in Modnar. In the wild, they travel in herds, feeding on both water and land plants. Their top speed is comparable to a dolphin.

Marhorsemen
Members of King Ethdab's royal guard, marhorsemen, are specially trained to ride marhorses. They wear special head wraps that allow them to breathe underwater and visors that enable them to see underwater. The visors also give them the ability to see in a broader spectrum than normal, affording them enhanced vision in low light and hazy conditions. They are generally used for coastal patrols, but more notably for special stealth strike missions against enemy ships, drilling or exploding holes in enemy vessels below the waterline.

Markam
Markam is the northernmost town in North Eastworld. A port town, it is notable for being the only community within the fog shroud surrounding the elven land of Gizesh and, therefore, also notable for having the largest lighthouse in all of North Eastworld. The small town is continually covered in a thick fog and, for this reason, has become a common meeting location for anyone needing to make clandestine transactions. It is the only human town in Eastworld that is regularly visited by elves.

Memory keeper
Memory Keeper is the title for museum curators in Midgorn.

Memory seeker
Memory seeker is the job title given to, often adventurous, individuals who search for ancient artifacts of interest to the specific museum that employs them. Quite often, they, in turn, employ mercenaries and other adventurers-for-hire to assist them on their quests.

Midgin

The language spoken by most humans in the world of Midgorn is Midgin. Though the ancient form of the language hardly resembled English, the modern form is almost identical to Earth English of the late twentieth and early twenty-first century. The change occurred abruptly during the rule of the Mad Wizard King (the last of the human monarchs in Midgorn and a fanatical Iconist), who made it law to speak his Earth-like English when he came to power. The word midgin is also used to refer to the humans of Midgorn or things made/used by them (i.e., midgin clothing vs. danuwan clothing).

Midgorn

Midgorn is a world entirely encased in rock, populated by a wide variety of races. Most inhabitants believe their rock universe extends infinitely. It should be noted that one race, the danuwan, sometimes referred to as elves, do not consider their realm to be part of Midgorn and hold the belief that there was once a surface world that is now both lifeless and inaccessible.

Modnar

Modnar is a planet much like Earth but dominated by magic and magical creatures. It is thought by some that Modnar might actually be the Earth, though where it falls in Earth's history or future has proven elusive if such is even the case. Much like Earth, it is the third planet from its yellow sun, a sun identical to Earth's. However, there are twelve planets in its system, and there is no asteroid belt.

Moiler(s)

Moiler is another term in Modnar for slave.

Moker

Moker is a profane midgin word generally used in the context of implying that someone is prone to performing perverse sexual acts.

Moshan

Moshan is the word for a chef in Midgorn, primarily referring to a culinary expert from the city of Advan.

Nawn
Nawn is the first day of a Midgorn week.

Nin
Nin is the last day of a Midgorn week.

Rathor
Rathor is the third week of any month in the Midgorn calendar.

Rock Toad
The rock toad is an enormous toad found in the water hills of Beedo. An adult rock toad can grow to the size of a medium-sized dog. Adult toads have four horns on their heads, one above each eye and two above their snout. These horns are poisonous, fed by a venom sac within the toad's skull. The venom is highly sought by ambitious musicians, as a single drop under the tongue is said to inspire wondrous musical compositions. It is extremely dangerous trying to catch the toads, however. The slightest prick from one of the horns will render a victim into a vegetative state within minutes. The same will result from taking more than a drop under the tongue. Some musicians who dose regularly have also fallen into similar vegetative states. However, it is uncertain in these cases if they have accidentally overdosed or if it is simply the result of repetitive use. Anything more than a slight prick or scratch from one of the horns will almost always result in an immediate death.

Shrok
Shrok is a general use Midgin word of profanity, which is also a synonym for fornication.

Soke
Modnarian word generally used to describe a person who is a victim of unfortunate circumstances. It can also be used as a synonym for fool.

Spordikan

The spordikan is a creature that roams Modnar's forests and jungles. Its body consists of from fifty to several hundred tiny, flying furry balls, depending on age and health. The balls can fly as far as fifty feet from any of the other balls of its body without losing psychic contact. A ball losing psychic contact will begin flying in an expanding spiral pattern and emitting a shrill squeal until contact is re-established. If contact is not established within three minutes, the separated ball will die. Any ball or group of balls need to be directly or indirectly in contact with no less than half of the other balls that make up the creature, or they will go into this same separation panic mode. They come in a nearly endless variety and combination of colors. It is rare to find a spordikan made of balls of a single color. Most spordikan hunt smaller forest animals, but larger, older spordikan are known to attack larger animals and people. One cult in Modnar believes that the world will one day end, consumed by one enormous spordikan. Everyone in Modnar thinks these particular cultists are extremely silly.

Torvug

This is the midgin word for the ceiling of a large cave area, especially the immense domes over the major communities, which are embedded with a multitude of crystals that generate a sun-like light for twelve hours each day. Some such torvugs also consist of a scattering of crystals that absorb the light of daylight crystals, glowing dimly for most of the night. The colors of these night illuminations can vary between white, orange, yellow, or green.

Trall

The Trall are a Midgorn race commonly referred to as dwarves by outerworlders or Iconists due to their striking similarity to the dwarves of legend on Earth and the race known as dwarves on Modnar. Though commonly more diminutive than average humans, Trall have been known to be as tall as five feet, four inches. The common height for a Trall is approximately four feet. In Midgorn, the Trall control much of the territory between human communities, maintaining well-crafted tunnels between those communities. Different clans control different areas and sometimes charge a toll for the use of the tunnels passing through their territory.

Vericberry

The vericberry is a bright green berry commonly grown in South Eastworld, looking similar to a raspberry but about twice the average size. The berry is very sour if eaten fresh. It is common practice to sun-dry the fruit, which then becomes a tangy, sweet flavor. Fully dried versions are often ground into a powder used for making tea. Such tea is said to have healing qualities, especially as a hangover remedy. Ironically, the berry is also used to make one of Modnar's most powerful liqueurs. A few sips of the potent alcoholic concoction is thought to give one visions through time. People have claimed to have had a glimpse into the future or the past. Mostly, it just makes one very, very intoxicated.

Warphole

A tear in the fabric of reality, a warphole appears as a dark void surrounded by a glowing blue, sparkling ring of light. They appear, briefly, in random locations throughout Modnar. The cause of these temporary tears is unknown, though some suspect it has something to do with the Modnar's smallest moon, Gatal. Those unfortunate or foolish enough to enter one and fortunate enough to return (usually to a distant location elsewhere on Modnar) speak of having traveled to other worlds. Celestons and other strange beings sometimes emerge from the warpholes, giving credence to the tales of otherworldly lands. The red powersword can generate temporary warpholes leading directly to other worlds or other locations on Modnar.

Water hills

The water hills is an area adjacent to the island community of Beedo in Midgorn, consisting of hundreds of small islands divided by relatively shallow waters and muddy, swampy areas. The water hills closest to Beedo are dotted with tiny fishing communities. Few inhabitants venture deep into the water hills as the hills are host to many dangerous creatures and the hunting grounds of a race known as the Mander.

Westerlan

The second largest continent on Modnar, Westerlan is a far less civilized place than Eastworld, being divided up into many feuding territories. There are few cities, and most towns are directly surrounded by the fortifications of the local king or warlord. The elves of Westerlan live on gravity-defying floating islands and are famous for the might of their fleet of flying ships. Westerlan also has the largest concentrated population of ogres on Modnar, which is divided into two factions; the dragon-riding marauders in the east, which are divided into a variety of gangs or clans, and the organized crime mob, the Westerlan Trading Company (WTC) in the west. The WTC controls nearly all shipping to and from Westerlan. The WTC often clashes with the dragon riders, who tend to raid their cargo caravans on land, air, or sea. Textile production is nearly nonexistent in northern Westerlan. For this reason, the humans of the north tend to wear leather almost exclusively. The craftsmanship of Westerlan leather garments is highly sought after on other continents.

Xenomod

Xenomods are an ancient race of powerful beings in upper Senuvia, called godé by the Modnarians, who worshiped them as gods.

Zanx

Zanx is one of the most ancient gods of Modnar, worshipped by a small order of monks and nuns in Modnar who are notable for their mastery of the martial art form, damina kazo. It is unknown whether Zanx was/ is an avatar for one or more of the so-called "true" gods of Modnar (as the followers believe), a godling (most theological scholars assume this to be so), some other sort of powerful being such as a Xenomod, or Celeston or simply a myth.

According to ancient Zanxian texts, Zanx is said to have five faces. Each face represents a particular discipline of teachings. Followers of Zanx try to perfect themselves in at least three of the five disciplines. The few who display mastery of all five are raised to the title of "paladin" and often become the founders of Zanxian orders of their own. Two of Zanx's faces are male. They represent the disciplines of knowledge and art. The other three faces are female. They represent the disciplines of will, wisdom, and charity. There are multiple layers to each discipline area, and few master all of the teachings of each of the faces of Zanx.

According to ancient tablets kept in the Loncodi monastery, Zanx, the avatar of creation, appeared during a great war among other beings claiming to be gods. The five faces of Zanx looked down upon the evil and chaos that the races of Modnar and their false gods had fallen into. All the faces wept and looked away with despair, save for the third. She looked upon the world, once beautiful and full of magic, now ravaged and twisted by war and darkness, and she resolved to show the false gods what war, what true wrath, looked like. With a single scream that tore apart the very seams of reality, she vaporized every living being that was not pure of heart. To her disappointment, not one of her favorite beings, the humans, remained. It was then that the fifth face looked upon the cleansed world and pleaded with the other four to give the humans a second chance. The other four agreed that if any souls worth a chance at redemption could be found, they would be granted a second creation. This task fell to the fourth face of Zanx. Only three humans were remade of the human race, two men and a woman. Zanx gave the three humans five crystal balls, each filled with the teachings of Zanx's faces.

Zanx then left the humans, ascending into the blue sky, promising to return one day. They would know that the five-faced god's return was near when a red, winged orb appeared in the sky for all to see. Zanx warned, however, that should the five faces find the world at war, in the hands of false gods again, and the humans not living in harmony with the other races, Modnar's destruction would be final. Most Zaxian followers are thoroughly convinced that Modnar is doomed but do what they can to make the world a better place.

Zeebo
The second largest of Modnar's three moons, Zeebo normally appears

as a sparkling, twinkling blue sphere or crescent, though from time to time, depending on the phases of the other two moons, Gatal and Kolo Supo, Zeebo can appear green. Some knowers believe Zeebo is inhabited, perhaps even rich with life, like Modnar. The lizardmen of Modnar believe their kind came from Zeebo and await the day when the mighty lizard king of the fabled moon city of Azizoo will return for them. The elves of Gizesh, too, have myths about a magic-wielding warrior race that once protected "the Great Garden," that were all but completely destroyed while fending off the mother of dragons. They believe the last of this great race of guardians still lives on Zeebo and await their return.

Zeshian

A Zeshian is an elf from the land of Gizesh. Zesh is the elven word for "elf." "Gizesh" translates to Elf Garden. Gizesh is not technically part of North Eastworld as it has not been conquered by King Ethdab's forces. It is rumored that King Ethdab will not move against the elves out of respect for his deceased wife, as her grandfather was said to be an elf.

Zulool

Zulool is the seventh month of the Midgorn calendar.

Zuset

Zuset is the name of the second week of any month in the Midgorn calendar.

Screamin' Joe Blade's Ten-Point Guide to Life:

Point #10: Always leave them…

A very special thank you goes out to...you!

You are one of the godlings helping to hold together the fabric of reality for Joe and all of the inhabitants of Midgorn and Modnar. Your support is deeply appreciated.

About the Author

Originally from Canada, Linton Valdock has called the United States home for two decades. Previously residing in Los Angeles, Linton and his wife moved to Maine in 2021. If he isn't generating worlds with words, he can be found doing something similar through his digital art or designing RPG's or board games.